READERS' GUIDES TO ESSENTIAL CRITICISM

CONSULTANT EDITOR: NICOLAS TREDELL

Published

Series Standing Order ISBN: 1–4039–0108–2

Palgrave Readers' Guides to Essential Criticism
Series Standing Order
ISBN 1–4390–0108–2
(outside North America only)

You can receive future titles in this series as they are published by placing a
standing order. Please contact your bookseller or, in the case of difficulty, write to
us at the address below with your name and address, the title of the series and the
ISBN quoted above.

Customer Services Department, Palgrave Macmillan Ltd
Houndmills, Basingstoke, Hampshire RG21 6XS, England

The Novels of Jeanette Winterson

MERJA MAKINEN

Consultant editor: Nicolas Tredell

First published in 2005 by
PALGRAVE MACMILLAN
Houndmills, Basingstoke, Hampshire RG21 6XS and
175 Fifth Avenue, New York, N.Y. 10010
Companies and representatives throughout the world.

PALGRAVE MACMILLAN is the global academic imprint of the Palgrave
Macmillan division of St. Martin's Press, LLC and of Palgrave Macmillan Ltd.
Macmillan® is a registered trademark in the United States, United Kingdom
and other countries. Palgrave is a registered trademark in the European
Union and other countries.

ISBN-13: 978–1–4039–4098–8 hardback
ISBN-10: 1–4039–4098–3 hardback
ISBN-13: 978–1–4039–4099–5 paperback
ISBN-10: 1–4039–4099–1 paperback

This book is printed on paper suitable for recycling and made from fully
managed and sustained forest sources.

A catalogue record for this book is available from the British Library.

Library of Congress Cataloging-in-Publication Data

Makinen, Merja.
    The novels of Jeanette Winterson / Merja Makinen ; consultant editor,
Nicolas Tredell.
        p. cm. — (Readers' guides to essential criticism)
    Includes bibliographical references and index.
    ISBN-13: 978–1–4039–4098–8
    ISBN-10: 1–4039–4098–3
    ISBN-13: 978–1–4039–4099–5 (pbk.)
    ISBN-10: 1–4039–4099–1 (pbk.)
        1. Winterson, Jeanette, 1959 – Criticism and interpretation. 2. Women
and literature – England – History – 20th century. I. Tredell, Nicolas.
II. Title. III. Series.

PR6073.I558Z77 2005
823'.914—dc22   2004065798

10 9 8 7 6 5 4 3 2 1
14 13 12 11 10 09 08 07 06 05

Printed and bound in China.

For Joanne, as a reminder of share-teaching practically all of these texts once upon a time and, of course, for Gill and Lyra

CONTENTS

A brief introduction to Jeanette Winterson and her novels to *The PowerBook* and an opening discussion of the two main aspects of the criticism, as a lesbian and a postmodern writer, using Lynne Pearce on the lesbian stance and Lyn Pykett on her postmodernism.

CHAPTER ONE

Oranges Are Not the Only Fruit (1985) as a Lesbian Text

Starting with a comparison of the reviews of Roz Kaveney and Ursula Hegi, the chapter looks at Gabrielle Griffin's view of the novel as portraying defiant lesbianism, Laura Doan's analysis of the binary switch of gender and sexual stereotypes, and Isabel Gamallo's view of the text's placing lesbianism as central to the narrative. Patricia Duncker, explaining the difference between lesbian feminism and queer theory, argues the text is not politically lesbian, while Lauren Rusk explores the text's refusal to 'other' lesbianism and Jago Morrison extends this to the way the novel 'others' heterosexuality and religious celibacy instead. In the second half of the chapter, the reception of the television production is examined, using Rebecca O'Rourke addressing a small lesbian audience, Hilary Hinds's analysis of the surprisingly positive press reception, Marilyn Brooks's comparison of the adaptation to the novel, and its watering down of the lesbianism, and Julia Hallam and Margaret Marshment's comparison of the different reactions of lesbian and heterosexual audiences, and the enjoyment of the mother's portrayal. For these two, the adaptation was a positive lesbian presence.

Oranges Are Not the Only Fruit (1985) as a Postmodern Text

Continuing the discussion of the first novel, chapter two looks at the criticism of it as a postmodern text. Paulina Palmer posits the way identity is constructed through narrative, looking at Jeanette's use of fantasy and fairy tale to develop an alternate sense of self, while Laura Doan examines the marmalade metaphor in the epigraph, as setting up a lesbian postmodernism. Laurel Bollinger discusses the intertextual reference to the biblical Book of Ruth as celebrating feminine loyalty, while Susana Onega looks at the deconstruction of history and the setting up of the multiple possibilities within the multi-layered narrative. Brinks and Talley argue for a more positive, revelatory use of the Bible than Onega and Palmer, while Tess Cosslett compares the intertextual references to the Bible, King Arthur and *Jane Eyre* in equal measure, and questions Bollinger's reading of the use of the Bible, since she sees all three intertexts stressing the isolation of Jeanette. Isabel Gamallo looks at the fairy tales as an alternative narrative for a specifically feminine voice and self, while Jan Rosemergy examines the intertextual presentation of Jeanette's individuation from her mother as she negotiates the search for self. Kim Middleton Meyer concludes the chapter by examining how the various narratives disrupt and dislocate the linear progress of the novel.

CHAPTER THREE 53

Boating for Beginners (1985) and *The Passion* (1987)

This chapter opens with a consideration of the reviews of *Boating for Beginners* by Emma Fisher and David Lodge, followed by Mark Wormald's reading of biblical fundamentalism's deconstruction through the postmodern narrative, and Jan Rosemergy's discussion of the mother–daughter relationship between Gloria and Mrs Munde. The chapter then moves to *The Passion*, considering Ann Duchêne's and David Lodge's reviews and the response of a range of critics. Lynne Pearce's argument that *The Passion* was not an effectively lesbian text, because it universalised same-sex desire, has proved controversial. Laura Doan sees Villanelle's cross-dressing as underlining the performativity of gender, while Lisa Moore regards her as positing a feminist lesbian erotics within a lesbian narrative that despite its postmodern slipperiness still advocates the Romantic importance of love. Cath Stowers examines the travel narratives and argues for a fluidity that links them to femininity, particularly in the representation of Venice. She also considers the femininity of Henri's character as a disruption of masculine stereotypes. Bényei Tamás explores the gambling motif as a way of living and loving. Judith Seaboyer and Manfred Pfister both examine the representation of Venice further. Seaboyer analyses the differentiation between the nationalist death drive of Napoleon's soldiers and the Venetians' erotic drive for pleasure. Pfister analyses the

English stereotypes of Venice, which he sees Winterson as reproducing. Scott Wilson gives a postmodern reading of the representation of history, while Paulina Palmer argues for Henri and Villanelle producing a politically effective lesbian narrative and, in a later essay, examines Villanelle as a queer theory representation of the lesbian as grotesque character. Jan Rosemergy continues her investigation of the search for the inner self, while Kim Middleton Meyer looks at the dual narratives of history and fantasy as a narrative grotesque. Jago Morrison concludes the chapter with his examination of the counter-narratives of history and fantasy and their dual focus on Venice's fluidity.

CHAPTER FOUR   82

Sexing the Cherry (1989)

Winterson's growing status is signalled by the wider reviewing of her third novel, and the chapter compares the assessments of Shena MacKay, David Holloway, Lorna Sage, Kenneth McLeish, Michiko Kakutani and Michael Gorra. Paulina Palmer begins the criticism with a consideration of the dual narrative and the lesbian strategy of the novel, a view that Lynne Pearce contests, as she looks at the use of fantasy. Alison Lee examines the dual time frames in relation to the new physics, while Laura Doan analyses the deconstruction of binaries that make the novel a successful lesbian postmodern text. Lisa Moore develops the postmodern representation of the fluidity of time, space and consciousness in relation to the new physics. Maria Lozano examines the central metaphor of grafting and Marilyn Farwell ties the postmodern deconstruction of gender binaries to a more political feminist agenda. Elizabeth Langland asserts an intertextual reference to Andrew Marvell, as she analyses the subversive portrayal of the Dog Woman. Sarah Martin contends that the Dog Woman is a conservative, tame characterisation. Rosemergy sees her as a liberating mother, the first in Winterson's work, and examines the plural narratives of fairy tale and myth. Kim Middleton Meyer distinguishes the elements of the grotesque and of multiplicity to posit a fluid subjectivity, while Jago Morrison discusses the fluidity of time and relativity, as well as the use of fairy tale.

CHAPTER FIVE   110

Written on the Body (1992)

The chapter opens with the reviews by Laura Cumming, Valerie Miner, Nicoletta Jones and Jim Shepherd. Lisa Moore starts the criticism with an analysis of the genderless narrator and the usage of new physics, and Christy Burns discusses the lack of gender and examines the poetic, Romantic depiction of the body. Marilyn Farwell also considers the loved one's body and examines the mutuality of a lesbian erotics. Heather Nunn gives a psychoanalytic reading, while Lisa Haines-Wright and Tracy Kyle examine the fluidity of the genderless narrator. Lynne Pearce suggests the book commodifies the female body and glamorises suffering. Ute Kauer examines the language and the challenge to the romantic discourse, while Patricia Duncker sees the lesbian aesthetic as allowing space for the male reader. Cath Stowers gives a different lesbian reading of the narrative, while Kim Middleton Meyer concentrates on the deconstruction of self and other in the fluid gender identities. Jago Morrison rounds off the narrative analysis by discussing the use of the medical and new physics's discourses.

The chapter compares the reviews by Lorna Sage, Michèle Roberts, Philip Hensler, William Pritchard, Peter Kemp and Rachel Cusk. Cusk's illuminating examination of the attack on contemporary culture is explored, before moving to the two critics. Christy Burns's two essays develop the theme of language within a postmodern culture, and the feminist politics of the novel. Patricia Duncker agrees about its effective politics and suggests a queer reading of the novel.

A comparison of the reviews of *Gut Symmetries* by Adam Mars-Jones, Philip Hensler, Hugo Barnacle, James Wood, Katy Emck, Michèle Roberts and Bruce Bawer begins this chapter. Helena Grice and Tim Woods examine the new physics discourse, while Kim Middleton Meyer analyses the fluid subjectivity of the characterisation. The very mixed response to *The PowerBook* includes reviews by Phil Baker, Kasia Boddy, Elaine Showalter, E. Jane Dickson and Kate Kellaway.

The conclusion briefly summarises the critical reception of Winterson's fiction and her view of the novels up to and including *The PowerBook* as a cycle that constitutes one emotional journey, and discusses the initial reviews of the latest novel, *Lighthousekeeping* (2004).

ACKNOWLEDGEMENTS

First acknowledgements must go to all the reviewers and literary critics of Jeanette Winterson, without whom this textbook would not exist. The next thank you goes to the staff of the British Library, both the Humanities Department at King's Cross and the Newspaper Library at Colindale, and the staff at Middlesex University library on the Tottenham campus. Anna Troberg's 'Jeanette Winterson Reader's Site' on the web has proved invaluable in chasing the critical material. As always, my thanks go to my son Nicholas, for his amiable fortitude in putting up with my neglect, and to the friends who helped take over the childcare to allow me time at my computer: to Julie, Liz, Tina, Simone and, of course, Anneli Makinen. Finally I would like to acknowledge Anna Sandeman for having the foresight to commission the subject, Kate Wallis and Felicity Noble for seeing the project through, and Nicolas Tredell for coping with my, at times, wayward style.

M. M.

Introduction

Jeanette Winterson was born in 1959 in Manchester, and adopted by a couple from Accrington, Constance and John Winterson, who both belonged to the Pentecostal Evangelical church. Her father worked in a factory and Jeanette attended Accrington Girls' Grammar School. From a child, she attended the Pentecostal church, wrote her first sermon at the age of eight, and preached there as part of her parents' plan for her to be a missionary. This plan foundered when the church was unable to accept her first lesbian love affair, at the age of 15. Jeanette Winterson left home and supported herself through Accrington Further Education College, by working in an ice-cream van, a funeral parlour and later in a mental institution. After her A levels, she went up to Oxford, to St Catherine's College, where she took her BA in English in 1981. On graduating, she moved to London, finding work at the Roundhouse theatre and arts complex and then at Pandora Press, who published her first novel, *Oranges Are Not the Only Fruit* in 1985.

Oranges Are Not the Only Fruit was a success, winning the Whitbread Best First Novel award of that year, and being adapted for television in a three-parter in 1990, with Winterson writing the screenplay. The quality, prime-time BBC production was also received with enthusiasm. As can be seen by the two chapters devoted to it in this study, *Oranges Are Not the Only Fruit* has remained the most popular and most written-on of Winterson's novels. Later the same year, she published *Boating for Beginners*, a comic novel that has received little critical attention, though to the few that do analyse it, it is often one of their favourites. Like *Oranges Are Not the Only Fruit*, it involves an intertextual rewriting of the Bible, though this time focusing on Noah and the Flood. Winterson published *The Passion* in 1987, winning the John Llewellyn Rhys literary prize, and became a full-time writer. *The Passion*, along with *Sexing the Cherry* (1989), takes place within an historical setting, the eighteenth and seventeenth centuries respectively, to question the nature of history and the relation of fact to fiction. Both sport dual narrators, a 'feminine' male narrator alongside a woman narrator singled out by her fantastic or grotesque features (Villanelle has webbed feet, the Dog Woman is a giant), to deconstruct the concepts of gender identity and the fluidity of sexual desire. These two novels have proved the most favoured by the critics after *Oranges Are Not the Only Fruit*. *Written on the Body* (1992), with its playfully ungendered narrator, was initially less well received, though the critical reception picked up during the later half of the 1990s. It introduced the theme of the sexual triangle of two women and one man that many reviewers noticed had become a new focus, and began the intertextual rewriting of one of the sciences, in its case the medical discourse of anatomy. *Art and Lies*, with its three narrators, two women and one man, including the famous lesbian writer Sappho, confused many and the critical reception of this and the next two novels, *Gut Symmetries* which continues the sexual triangle and *The PowerBook* (2000) where the married woman's husband does not appear, have still to establish a critical presence. *Art and Lies* and *Gut Symmetries* have shifted the intertextuality to a different scientific discourse, the new physics, looking at the relativity and simultaneity of matter, post-Einstein. *The PowerBook* engages with the technology of computers and the telling of stories in cyberspace, in a virtual reality. By the twenty-first century, Winterson's standing as an important and challenging novelist has become assured, and critical books striving to survey the second half of the twentieth century invariably contain a discussion of her and usually dedicate a whole chapter to her oeuvre.[1]

The main focus of the reception of Winterson's novels has been twofold: the discussion in relation to her as a lesbian writer and in relation to her as a postmodern writer. Other aspects have of course been analysed in the various novels, but these two debates have ranged across all her novels, and recur continuously. Winterson herself has helped fuel the debate as to whether her texts are successful lesbian texts, given her statement, in an interview in 1992, that while she herself was a lesbian feminist, her work should not be seen under that definition. The range of critical arguments on the texts run from their being effective as a lesbian deconstruction of gender identities and the fluidity of gender performances, but not politically lesbian; to those that argue they are effectively politically lesbian texts for their uncovering of the oppression and damage done to lesbian women within a heterosexualist culture; to those who argue that she is disappointing in attempting to universalise and hence normalise lesbianism out of existence. Lynne Pearce has been one of the most vocal on the final of these positions, and gives a clear explanation of the position, in an article that surveys the first three novels,[2] when she explains that the popularity of Winterson's novels is linked to how the novels could be read as universalising lesbian love:

■ This is an ambivalence that centres on the tension between the perception of romantic love as a non-gendered, a-historic, 'cultural universal', and as an 'ideology' which the specificities of gender and sexual orientation constantly challenge and undermine. By attending to the 'universalising' discourses in Winterson's work the (heterosexual) 'general reader' can, of course, see the texts as transcending the particulars of sexual orientation; regard the fact that s/he is reading about lovers of the same sex as incidental and, consequently, a-political. Indeed, the fact that in her later fiction Winterson has shown many different combinations of love-relationship (homosexual and heterosexual) has, perhaps, contributed to the reader's impression of (great) 'Love' as being transcendent of history, culture, and gender.[3] □

Implicit in the debates as to whether Winterson's novels are effective lesbian texts is the way in which lesbian literary criticism has changed in the last three decades. Initially, critics looked for positive representations of lesbian characters, as Gabrielle Griffin did in *Oranges Are Not the Only Fruit*,[4] and acclaimed the depictions. Or they looked for the ways in which the fluidity of characters challenged gender expectations and sexual desire, such as Villanelle in *The Passion*, as Laura Doan[5] and Lisa Moore[6] argue. Later critics have focused on the shift from a lesbian feminist challenge to patriarchal and heterosexual oppression, to a queer theory strategy of differentiating lesbians from heterosexual women, as an assertion of lesbian presence, and these have pointed to the more grotesque images, again Villanelle, for her webbed feet, and the Dog Woman in particular, as argued by Paulina Palmer,[7] Lisa Moore and Kim Middleton Meyer.[8] The refusal to name a gender in *Written on the Body* and the heterosexual relationships in *Gut Symmetries* have also raised questions as to Winterson's refusal to name or to focus primarily on lesbian desire and have allowed Pearce to argue she is disappointing lesbian readers.

The analysis of Winterson as a postmodern writer, given her meta-narrative, self-reflexive texts that deconstruct the divisions between fact and fiction, reality and fantasy, and masculinity and femininity, and rewrite intertextual references from the Bible to fairy tales, has been less a debate than a consensus. While a number of the critics have noted influences from modernist writers, they tend not to allow this to challenge their overall view of her as a postmodernist writer. Susana Onega comes the nearest to doing so, when she argues that the subjective solipsism advocated as the only truth available to history, in *Oranges Are Not the Only Fruit*, is not a postmodern but a modernist strategy borrowed from T. S. Eliot (poet, 1888–1965) and Marcel Proust (French novelist, 1871–1922).[9] Lisa Haines-Wright and Tracy Lynn Kyle's insistence on an intertextual conversation between Virginia Woolf's (novelist, 1882–1941) *Orlando* (1928) and *Written on the Body* holds similarities with Jago Morrison's view that the poems in *Art and Lies* share the same rapturous textuality as Woolf's novel *The Waves* (1931).[10] Ute Kauer allies the attempt to rewrite passion in *Written on the Body* to the same attempt during the modernist period by D. H. Lawrence (novelist and poet, 1885–1930)[11] and Kasia Boddy's review of *The PowerBook* suggests that Winterson's repetition of the same themes and the structure of the love triangle can be explained as Gertrude Stein's (novelist and poet, 1874–1946) practice of 'insistence', a repetition with a difference.[12]

Few have treated Winterson's own claims to be a modernist and the heir to Virginia Woolf, on her own terms.[13] Lyn Pykett's article, 'A New Way with Words? Jeanette Winterson's Post-Modernism',[14] does, however, take Winterson's thesis seriously and, while she acknowledges the novels as open to a postmodern reading, she suggests they may also be equally open to a dialogue with modernism, a continuation of certain modernist projects and hence postmodernist, in the sense of coming after modernism. Indeed, she suggests that *Art Objects* may well be Winterson's own attempt to reconfigure her oeuvre in retrospect, to rewrite the novels as part of a later modernist project. Pykett reads Winterson as deconstructing the binaries – fact and fiction; history and story – not to play one narrative mode off against the other in an endless postmodern deferral of meaning, but rather to assert the importance of one over the other, inserting a differing hierarchy of value, placing story and imagination, art in fact, over history. This reassertion of value, for story, for art and for love (a romantic undertaking that both Lisa Moore and Jago Morrison note) is a modernist project that Pykett allies to D. H. Lawrence's aesthetic. Winterson's assertion of her chosen, specified universals that transcend the self, sits uncomfortably within a postmodernist practice, with its distrust of grand universal truths or master narratives. In *Art Objects*, Winterson challenges the idea that modernism wrote itself into an esoteric silence, a backwater, which postmodernism fruitfully challenges, and argues instead for its continuing revolution of language, a revitalising and renewing of language through poetic intensity. The reification of the word, therefore, which many critics have linked to her Pentecostal upbringing, Winterson explains through a modernist identification with T. S. Eliot's aesthetic, and a deliberately self-reflexive attempt to write a 'new way with words'.[15] Winterson's work could thus be read as continuing the trajectory of modernism, but Pykett concludes that while Winterson's construction of High Modernism is one that critics often find problematic, they are happy to ally her playful and challenging 'writerly' texts to the earlier 'postmodern' writer, Angela Carter (1940–92). Pykett thus resists Winterson's own construction, or reconstruction of her oeuvre, while raising the critical issue of how much postmodernism is a reaction to modernism, and how much a continuation of modernist practices within a contemporary context.

One thing at least is certain, Jeanette Winterson's novels will continue to be read, enjoyed and criticised in a fruitful debate, whether seen as lesbian, modern or postmodern.

CHAPTER ONE

Oranges Are Not the Only Fruit (1985) as a Lesbian Text

J eanette Winterson's first published novel, *Oranges Are Not the Only Fruit*, has proved one of her most long-standing achievements and, as the York Notes (2001)[1] edition illustrates, has made its way onto the secondary school syllabus, a cultural accolade of acceptance and of literary value. Yet understandably the reviews of the novel were minimal. At the time of its publication, few knew the unknown writer would be a success or win a prestigious literary prize – the Whitbread prize for the best first novel of that year – and indeed the reputation of *Oranges Are Not the Only Fruit* initially grew mainly by word of mouth. Roz Kaveney, in the *Times Literary Supplement* in March 1985, was one of the few to note its publication and deem it excellent, focusing on the question of its autobiographical possibilities. Calling it a novel 'rich in malicious strategy',[2] where Winterson vengefully satirises her detractors, she concludes that actually it is immaterial whether its blatant realism is in fact autobiographical or imagination; what is clear is that the writer is juxtaposing a textual aggression alongside its humour. Having outlined the plot, Kaveney sketches in the novel's strategy in relation to its representation of a lesbian coming of age. The success of the novel is that it has us laughing about things that we realise should make us weep, as the character is forced, in order to preserve her integrity, to mock the sacred. From its publication, some critics have seen the narrative strategy of *Oranges Are Not the Only Fruit* as one of including the reader within its lesbian viewpoint, and have seen the humour as one of its most effective ways of achieving this. In the USA, the book was reviewed in the *New York Times Book Review* 'In Short' section, among a number of other fiction and non-fiction entries, by Ursula Hegi who described it as the tale of an adolescent's rejection of the religious fundamentalism of her upbringing on discovering her lesbian sexuality. Noting the mixture of generic styles, the stories, tales and essays that constitute the 'slight' narrative, she argues that Winterson 'glosses over the core of the novel',[3] which she sees as being Jeanette's acceptance of her lesbianism and her rejection of both community and religion in defence of this. For Hegi, the postmodern narration with its multiple narratives prevents the drama of the realist sections from becoming the all-important central focus.

Gabrielle Griffin's 'Acts of Defiance: Celebrating Lesbians' (1994) contrasts contemporary 1980s representations of lesbianism in Winterson's *Oranges Are Not the Only Fruit, Rubyfruit Jungle* (1983) by Rita Mae Brown (born 1944) and *The Color Purple* (1982) by Alice Walker (born 1944) with the depictions of Radclyffe Hall (1886–1943) at the beginning of the twentieth century, in the infamous *The Well of Loneliness* (1928), the lesser-known *The Unlit Lamp* (1924) and the title story from *Miss Ogilvy Finds Herself* (1934). Where Hall was prosecuted for obscenity for *The Well of Loneliness*, and her lesbian protagonists are presented as deviant individuals, '*afflicted* by a sense of difference which translates itself into a feeling of perpetual conflict as they strive for the "normalcy" denied them by an identity they cannot fully come to terms with',[4] the contemporary lesbian protagonists unapologetically assert their right to be different and in so doing, surprisingly find popularity with wide and diverse audiences. Seeing the three 1980s novels as narratives of feminine self-discovery, Griffin equates them all with a stance that refuses to figure the lesbian as a tragic character. Like Hall's earlier characters, they do all present themselves as separate from the rest of their community, as estranged from the male-defined society, but where nineteenth-century novels would have had the woman learning to integrate herself into the phallocentric ethos, the contemporary lesbian novel 'rather translates itself into a counter narrative of men as insignificant and/or grotesque. Jeanette's adoptive father in *Oranges* is described as "never quite good enough" and she is haunted by the story of the woman who "told us all she had married a pig". The notion of men as animals and as physically grotesque',[5] therefore, runs counter to the usual heterosexual romance script where the male body is what the woman covets. Where earlier heterosexual romances might have a woman try a lesbian experience before returning to her rightful place with her man, these lesbian scripts reject the idea that a woman's 'true' place is with the male. Jeanette is not interested in men, never has a sexual experience with one of them, and asserts her own sexual agency in making her own choices. The sexuality of lesbianism is an important element in these late twentieth-century representations, Griffin suggests, because they are challenging the thesis of Adrienne Rich (born 1929), in 'Compulsory Heterosexuality and Lesbian Existence' (1980), that *all* women who have emotionally significant friendships with other women are part of a 'lesbian continuum'.[6] Rejecting this silencing of the erotic difference between lesbian and heterosexual women, these lesbian texts dwell on specifically woman-focused desire in order to assert the view of the lesbian as a woman who sexually desires other women. The reasons the text offers for why Jeanette is a lesbian are, however, ambiguously twofold:

■ Both essentialist views (you are born one) and social constructionist views (you are made one) on lesbianism are offered. On the latter front, one of the most obvious potential contributing factors in Jeanette's lesbianism might be that her community is composed of strong women who offer models of independence and nurturance while men do not feature or are cast in a negative light. Marriages are not represented as fulfilling for women. ... On the essentialist front, ... Jeanette never shows any interest in men.[7] □

In suggesting both explanations, *Oranges Are Not the Only Fruit* does not decide between the essentialist or the constructionist versions as the other two novels seek to do, but where all three texts are in agreement in their representation of lesbianism, is in the important depiction of their protagonists' unequivocal acceptance of their sexuality, whatever its origin.

■ None of the protagonists of the texts discussed here feel guilty about their lesbianism. This is not the same as saying that attempts are not made to make them feel guilty. On the contrary. But all three refuse that guilt. To Molly [Brown's protagonist] and Jeanette their sexual experiences with other women, because they are so satisfying, seem 'natural'. Celie [Walker's protagonist] never questions her sexual preferences. Molly, Jeanette and Celie project an almost 'instinctive' affirmation of lesbianism; not they, but those around them, agonise about their lesbian experiences. Unlike Hall's lesbian characters, these protagonists are no longer presented as suffering from guilt or conceiving of their lesbianism as either a problem, a disease, or a sin. These views are held by their communities but not by them and in rejecting their communities' positions they reject negative stereotypes of lesbians.[8] □

The lesbian protagonists have no difficulty with their sexuality, accepting it as unproblematic, and this construction argues for an equivalent value with heterosexuality, indeed an open celebration of lesbianism. It is the community that objects, allowing the novels to examine issues of homophobia and the compulsory ways in which heterosexuality polices itself as the 'norm'.

Griffin devotes the second half of her examination of the texts to a reading of the communities' oppression of the protagonists. The reaction of the community, to the lesbian's openness about her relationships, is the other side of the coin when the protagonist refuses to remain secretive and in the closet. Jeanette's mother denounces her to the church congregation and the church seeks to expel her 'wickedness'.

> ■ However, in both Jeanette's and Molly's case, finding themselves castigated by their communities does not lead them to repress or sublimate their sexual desire. Both articulate their refusal to be subordinated to others' views as a necessary aspect of their sense of themselves. Thus Jeanette's sense of (sexual) self is shaped through a dialogue with an imaginary other, the orange demon, who appears to help her decide on how to handle the community's accusation of sinning and their demand for repentance. The demon identifies itself as 'different and difficult' rather than 'evil' and … suggests to Jeanette that the way to keep her integrity is by keeping the demon. Jeanette is thus split into an inner and an outer self; to the congregation she lies about repenting her lesbian experiences in order to be able to remain part of her community.[9] □

This pretence at conformity, though, is only a transitional period in the protagonist's journey of self-discovery, and is used by Winterson to highlight the oppression and the injustice meted out by those policing normality. In the case of *Oranges Are Not the Only Fruit* the oppressors are the evangelical sect and, by implication, the whole institution of Religion.

> ■ Both Molly and Jeanette manage to 'play the system' but eventually are forced into a situation where they have to choose between belonging to the community and exercising self-denial, or remaining 'true' to their lesbian selves and leaving. Both choose the latter. Indeed, *Rubyfruit Jungle*, *Oranges* and *The Color Purple* all construct lesbianism as a one-way choice the protagonist in the course of her development decides in favour of. It is not, these texts argue, possible to be a lesbian *and* to remain in the community in which you grew up. You have to put a space – literally – between you and it. Separation is thus acted out geographically; the defiant lesbian hero is an itinerant figure, catapulted into movement through her affirmative choice of living a lesbian lifestyle.[10] □

Griffin examines the communities in detail and argues for their being politically conservative, ruled by an obedience to hierarchical authority which is clearly phallocentric. The women within the communities divide into those who support the protagonist and those 'who act as gatekeepers to patriarchal regulatory prohibitions',[11] such as Jeanette's mother. In *Oranges Are Not the Only Fruit*, the mainly female community contains a number of lesbians, such as Elsie, Miss Jewsbury and the women who own the paper shop, amongst the heterosexual women. The heterosexuals are predominantly seen as the gatekeepers and the lesbians the support system, so that the protagonist's defiance is directed against the gatekeepers, who reinforce the hierarchical obedience to the authority of the church, ruled by Pastor Spratt. The wide popularity of *Oranges Are Not the Only Fruit*, Griffin therefore suggests, was because it fits into a narrative of escape from spiritual narrowness which allows it to speak to an audience beyond the lesbian ghetto. The 'particular environment depicted makes it very easy for *any* but the most zealously religious to appreciate why Jeanette might want to leave this community behind. Winterson in this text ... uses humour to create a distance between the persons represented and the audience; to the extent that as we, as readers, laugh about the foibles of the community we can dissociate ourselves from it which, in turn, helps us to accept Jeanette's need to dissociate herself from it.'[12] As readers, therefore, we find ourselves laughing on the side of the lesbian and hence included within the lesbian viewpoint. The novels of the early 1980s present the lesbian character as an attractive and widely accepted figure because of her defiance of oppressive systems and her rejection of any guilt about sexual preference. In the same year, Lynne Pearce, in a discussion of *Sexing the Cherry*, approved *Oranges Are Not the Only Fruit*, unlike Winterson's later works, as 'a "classifiable" ' lesbian[13] text that promotes lesbian representation, though she did not go into explanatory detail.

Where Griffin's essay focuses on a positive reading of the presentation of the lesbian protagonist and the acceptance of her relationship by her community, Laura Doan in the same year unpacks the dualistic binaries, or oppositions, used in the representation of both the mother's religion and Jeanette's lesbianism, in 'Jeanette Winterson's Sexing the Postmodern'. Pointing out how the opening of the novel switches the traditional gender divisions, making the father passive and inconsequential and the mother domineering and active, instead of the man as active and the woman passive, the essay looks closely at how the mother divides the world into enemies and friends, noting that only Jeanette crosses this neat segregation:

■ This maternal version of the 'natural order' is one permeated with oppositions reminiscent of Genesis, the title of the novel's first section: light/dark, good/evil, believer/heathen, order/disorder, lost/found, saved/fallen. Jeanette learns at an early age that such oppositions provide the faithful and vigilant with the strategies and the weapons necessary to wage battle; thus slug pellets destroy slugs and the dog attacks Next door. The devil and sex are singled out as especially pernicious for either can appear in 'many forms'. While God promises to be a powerful force for the righteous, a monolithic construct available to repel the devil's onslaught, nothing in this scheme offers protection from what is most dangerous and wicked: sex, which is only feebly and inadequately countered in the list by familial support (Aunt Madge, a character who appears rarely) and Brontë novels that valorize romance and passion.[14] □

The mother has a celibate marriage, rewrites *Jane Eyre* (1847, by Charlotte Brontë, 1816–55) so that it concludes in a celibate marriage between Jane and St John Rivers, and counsels Jeanette never to let anyone touch her intimately. The mother's dogmatic binary oppositions, linked to the biblical precepts, provide Jeanette with a framework of understanding the world which will finally lead her to indict the ecclesiastic homophobia. She has been taught that the natural world presents the battle between the forces of good and those of evil, and the confined binarism of this world view does not allow for any subtlety in her conception of desire; since it feels too natural to be evil, it must by definition be good. This goodness is reinforced by the fact that Melanie and Katie both attend her church and pray with her before making love. 'She perceives no discrepancy, moral or otherwise, between her sexual preference (natural and essential) and the prescriptions of the church (cultural and social) because she believes like Winterson, that love shouldn't be "gender-bound".'[15] This is not the view of the church, however, which defines everything by the heterosexual matrix, and when Jeanette is asked whether she loves Melanie 'with a love reserved for a man and wife', she answers both no and yes. 'Thus she simultaneously refuses patriarchal insistence to read her relationship as a pale imitation of heterosexuality and affirms that it is something other than, perhaps even more. … However, because she is caught up in the binary logic of her mother's (and the church's) version of the natural order, Jeanette never fully comprehends the political threat embedded in her actions; she can challenge those who question her right to love Melanie, but she cannot break out of the binarism – she is, after all, her mother's daughter.'[16]

While Winterson's representation of the lesbian seems extremely radical on the surface, since she has turned the tables and presents lesbianism as natural, and repressive heterosexualism as perverse and unnatural, it is still locked within a binarism that can only prove to be a strait-jacket. Though Winterson can be seen as political and potentially radical because she reverses which is natural and which is unnatural, she does not in this first novel embrace a truly postmodern position by questioning the very categories themselves. 'In *Oranges* binaries are revealed at every turn, though never erased or eliminated. For the lesbian writer, the task, the political agenda if you will, is to displace and explode the binary.'[17] For Laura Doan, the straightforward representation of the lesbian in *Oranges Are Not the Only Fruit* is disappointing as a lesbian strategy and partially ineffective as a challenge to heterosexualism, a judgement that will change when she looks at the portrayal of the lesbian Villanelle in Winterson's third book, *The Passion*. But where the depiction of the character Jeanette is lacking, Doan gives a personal reading of one of the alternate narratives that points the way towards the possibility of displacing binarism, with the metaphor of the orange, particularly when it is turned into marmalade. Where the orange as a fruit still links through its metaphorical employment to a binary, that of inner/outer or self/world, marmalade, she argues, combines rind and segments, inner and outer, in a much more complex confection. 'Marmalade embodies the orange's essence and at the same time, no longer resembles an orange per se.'[18] Doan, in contrast to Griffin and Pearce, is looking for a more postmodern deconstruction of gender and sexual preference in the presentation of the protagonist and so finds the figure of the lesbian less effective, for all that she acknowledges that it is political in its figuring of the lesbian as natural and heterosexuality as unnatural.

Isabel C. Anievas Gamallo's 'Subversive Storytelling: the Construction of Lesbian Girlhood through Fantasy and Fairy Tale in Jeanette Winterson's *Oranges Are Not the Only Fruit*' (1998)[19] looks at Winterson's revision of the genre of the *Bildungsroman*[20] in its adaptation into the 'Coming out'[21] novel, and argues the novel's effectiveness in subverting patriarchal heterosexualism. Contradicting readings that sideline the lesbianism in favour of a universalist reading of the novel, Gamallo contends that the lesbianism is the central concern of the text: 'lesbianism is not a mere accident in Winterson's construction of girlhood. On the contrary, the search for a sexual identity shapes and orients her literary project'.[22] She notes that lesbianism is introduced by the gypsy prophesying Jeanette will never marry and develops with the two women in the sweet shop. 'From here on, lesbianism will be an issue throughout the narration that is increasingly marked with the confusion and curiosity of a young girl's slow process of "finding out" about lesbian relationships, first through others (May and Ida) and eventually her own experience.'[23] The central chapters focus on the construction of her sexual identity, reinforcing the theme's centrality to the novel. Her dreams of marriage betray her fear of heterosexuality, and this is reinforced by the concept that men are beasts, and the repulsion she feels towards Uncle Bill. These carefully selected autobiographical moments establish the appalling prospects of marriage and men and allude to the existence of an alternative sexuality and its social stigma:

■ After having been so carefully and strategically announced, the actual representation of lesbian sexuality and eroticism in *Oranges* will probably take few readers by surprise. In any case, and by means of her lyrical and suggestive decoding of sexual practices that are generally silenced by dominant literary and cultural discourses, Winterson undoubtedly succeeds in subverting heterosexual constructions of sex and gender. From this point in the narration, lesbianism emerges as a growing awareness of the sensual power of the female body, and Jeannette's active, intense, and nonapologetic sexual desire becomes integrated as an irrenunciable part of her identity.[24] □

The oppressive reaction of the community and her mother creates her emotional and ideological separation from the mother, an individuation that is signalled textually by her questioning why grapes and bananas are not 'fruit' as well as oranges. This begins the 'complex process of "shedding" and "unlearning" necessarily involved in lesbian education'.[25] Like many lesbian novels within the tradition of the 'Coming Out' genre, *Oranges Are Not the Only Fruit* employs humour to convey its subversive point of view and to deal with painful and unresolved material. This tradition of lesbian humour 'remains a politically subversive weapon that challenges conventional standards of perceiving and writing the world'.[26]

Patricia Duncker places Winterson's novel within the context of feminism and its aftermath, pointing to how postmodernism in the 1990s has separated lesbian theory from feminist politics into the more recent queer theory instead. She argues a very different evaluation of Jeanette's mother than the usual reading. In 'Jeanette Winterson and the Aftermath of Feminism',[27] Duncker cites the moment when the mother shows Jeanette the world, from a hill, and declares that it is both full of sin, and transformable. Defending oversimplified slogans as an effective way of articulating political certainties, whether Marxist, anti-racist or pro-lesbian, Duncker explains that these provocative certainties are necessary for a belief in the possibility of changing things for the better, a utopian belief that fires political action. These heady days of 1970s and 1980s feminism which challenged the strait-jackets of men, femininity and heterosexuality, are a far cry from the sceptical deconstruction of 1990s queer theory, she argues, where certainties are rejected as erroneous, false knowledge. The mother's sloganeering and stubborn certainty that she knows best and can change her world, are therefore re-evaluated as a form of radical utopianism. However, for Duncker, Winterson's books have never been about changing the world; the view of most of her heroines is that 'if the world is full of sin then so be it'.[28] Her texts are too playful and oblique for politics. Nevertheless, growing up as a writer during the time of feminism, she is clearly influenced by its debates. The key central relationship of *Oranges Are Not the Only Fruit*, Jeanette's relationship with her mother, reflects one of the major concerns of feminism: the relationships between mothers and daughters. The mother is always the originating love object for the baby girl and whatever the dynamics that ensue between them, the girl can never outgrow that relationship; it is, as the novel describes, a thread around the button, a symbol of the umbilical cord's connection. Feminist theory reinstated the daughter's relationship with the mother, omitted from traditional psychoanalysis, and argued for the complex experience of overpowering love, powerlessness and aggression, present even when the girl child is loved. For the young lesbian girl, her first socialisation situates her as heterosexual, even while her first love is for another woman. In lesbian development, then, the love for another woman echoes the first desire of the baby girl. It is the mother who teaches her how to fabricate for social acceptance, to fit the culturally negated gender stereotypes of femininity in being 'a woman', and hence lies to her daughter and teaches her how to dissemble. Winterson's *Oranges Are Not the Only Fruit*'s relationship between Jeanette and her mother articulates exactly this complex relationship of desire and oppression that feminism was concerned with, within an Evangelical context, and accurately mirrors lesbian feminism's exploration of the childhood development of the young lesbian. So, despite a lack of direct feminist politics, the focus of the novel is indebted to feminist concerns.

Lauren Rusk, in 2002,[29] looked at the 'life writing' of a number of gay and lesbian writers and argued that *Oranges Are Not the Only Fruit* has a protagonist who resists being 'othered' (i.e. constructed in a negative opposition to the 'norm') and insists instead on an inclusiveness with the rest of humanity. 'I believe that *Oranges*, with its allegorical content, is a didactic narrative, though its lessons are not clearly served up. It teaches, for one thing, that we must work to achieve clarity … Jeanette, as she grows, disputes other people's assumptions and resists fitting into pigeon-holes: missionary, heterosexual, virgin, demon. Accordingly, her narrative also defies categorization.'[30] In this, Winterson's text shares similarities with other lesbian writers: 'the creation of hybrid forms to enact transgressive female experience'.[31] However, Rusk relates the interweaving of narratives as the protagonist's way of using the power of the imagination to cope with the oppression of both family and religious community. She thereby embraces a reading of psychological realism rather than postmodern multiplicity:

■ Since their many intertextual references keep pace with the protagonist's reading level, the fantasies seem *like* stories she might tell herself, polished up by the narrator, who interpolates them without comment. These allegorical sections correspond to adjacent events in the narrative, figuratively expanding on the psychological implications of those happenings. The early chapters each include one fairy tale, but after Jeanette is outed, the fantasies increase, which suggests that she must use all her imaginative resources to interpret and cope with the social repercussions of her private life.[32] □

Once Jeanette matures and has broken with her family and community, the imaginative resources develop into more complex alter egos, Sir Perceval and Winnet. 'These figures emerge when Jeanette can take a more active role in her self-construction, and when she most needs company.'[33]

Rusk continues to read the fairy tales and the Arthurian legend in terms of life writing when she sees the final chapter interweaving 'both these stories with Jeanette's own, giving a sense that she lived much of her new life inwardly and that this life requires a mighty exercise of her imagination to shape it'.[34] This mighty exercise is necessary because the novel shows no community or collectivity of lesbianism. For all that there is a mention of at least eight lesbians in her town, they never meet as a group and this leads to an isolation in the girl's development and the lack of any significant banding together to resist heterosexual homophobia. 'These alienated beginnings go a long way toward explaining the melancholic tone of Jeanette's escape into a more liberated life. ... An early lack of empathy and acceptance – in anyone's life – isn't easily compensated later on.'[35] In contrast, Rusk develops a more positive metaphor for lesbianism in an extended analysis of the image of the secret garden on the banks of the Euphrates, that comes just before Jeanette and Katy's first night together.

■ It is crucial for one thing, because it resides 'at the heart' of Jeanette's story, when she is about to decide for certain that lesbianism is not a spiritual 'illness' – as she was temporarily persuaded – but her heartfelt way of life. The imagery of circular forms and innermost parts suggests both this centrality, when viewed abstractly, and female eroticism, when viewed concretely. The passage announced its importance in several other ways as well. It speaks of deepest longings, danger, and banishment; it invokes the central religious ideas of Eden and the Eucharist; and it centers around the oranges of the title which often appear at emotionally laden moments in Jeanette's life.[36] □

The chapter develops the oranges motif, arguing that a distinction is made which serves to partially explain the metaphor's apparent ambiguity. Rusk distinguishes between the 'split' fruit which bleeds and links to the 'torn bonds of communal and familial love' when given by the mother or Melanie, which turns out to be 'sanctioned but insufficient fare'; and the 'halved' fruit that she shares with Elsie or is associated with the orange demon, which is linked to an 'equal sharing of lovers or close friends' and so proves to be much more nourishing. The oranges from Jeanette's rewritten tree of knowledge, therefore, show both the potential of love and its possible failures.

Strategically, the protagonist's rejection of the pastor's pronouncement of lesbianism as an unnatural passion, and her insistence on its naturalness and purity is read as both an overturning of the categories of natural and unnatural, as earlier critics have discussed, and as a refusal to accept the construction of otherness. This is developed in Jeanette's discussions with the orange demon, and its refusal to be located by sex. 'It may at first seem contradictory that the ally who promotes Jeanette's same-sex desire insists on remaining sexually indefinite. But ... the identification carries with it all sorts of culturally constructed norms and taboos, ... conventions that the demon reminds Jeanette she does not want to live by.'[37] Rusk sees this refusal to fix definitions as the reason for the novel never using the actual word 'lesbian' within its pages and as yet another rejection of otherness. This strategy allows readers to engage with the text without being alienated or deflected from reading it, whatever their sexual preferences:

■ Winterson's decision about what to call lesbian sexuality has a strategic and a conceptual dimension. Strategically, a writer who eschews the emptiness of labels has good reason not to invoke one that tends to rivet people's attention on sex to the exclusion of all other complexity. As it is, interviewers have infuriated Winterson by focusing on her sexuality rather than her work ... Winterson embraces [the theme of homosexuality] ... but avoids the hotbutton word that narrows many readers' attention before they have a chance to experience the fullness of the text.[38] □

Disagreeing with Doan's view of Jeanette as stuck in the same binary vision as her dogmatic mother, Rusk states: 'To the contrary. I find that, as she grows, Jeanette engages in an ongoing struggle with such dualistic thinking and more often than not subverts it.'[39] Instead the novel '[r]epeatedly ... constructs binary oppositions and then denies the choice between them, "othering" neither'.[40] Overall, however, she finds the novel flawed in its strategy of denying the categorisation of lesbian as other, because of how it depicts men. The representation of the male characters shows an inconsistency that questions the whole strategy: 'Winterson's book participates in the kind of othering it generally opposes, tainting for me the purity of vision that the author's namesake claims when she shouts at the pastor, "It's you not us".'[41] Rusk also sees a taint of implicit anti-Semitism in the novel, which she locates in the naming of Miss Jewsbury and her description. So, where Rusk sees *Oranges Are Not the Only Fruit* as eminently successful in its rejection of binary distinctions, she feels that it nevertheless falls into a similar bigotry in its own treatment of men.

Jago Morrison's exploration of Winterson's rewriting of the feminine body in four of her novels a year later, in his chapter 'Jeanette Winterson: Remembering the Body',[42] allies her to Judith Butler[43] (born 1956) and Luce Irigaray[44] (born 1932) in challenging the traditional inscriptions of both femininity and the female body. In *Oranges Are Not the Only Fruit* he looks at the representation of Jeanette's first lesbian love, Melanie, which he sees as a fascinating transition from her as attractive object of lesbian desire, to undesirable, rejected heterosexual body. 'Using a technique that becomes more important in her later fiction, Winterson writes this transition on Melanie's body itself, which quite abruptly changes from that of a compelling and beautiful young woman to a passive and sexless figure of "bovine" plumpness.'[45] Melanie's unattractiveness continues the text's 'presentation of the dysfunctionality of all the straight relationships' throughout all the variant narratives, realistic and fantastic, as the text 'consistently and comprehensively' marginalises heterosexuality as a critical strategy. A grasp of Evangelism is essential to comprehend the lesbian strategy of the text, since for Morrison it is the religious perspective that is the novel's main focus of attack. He explains St Paul's endorsement of celibacy as religion's real ideal, with sex within marriage only grudgingly accepted as a second best for the more fallible, whose flesh is weak. Within Jeanette's Pentecostal sect the policing of desire does not really accept even heterosexual desire, seeing that as suspect, and holds up celibacy, a complete absence of sex, as the best option. 'The church's prohibition on all non-heterosexual sex as "unnatural passion", and on non-procreative heterosexual sex as "fornication", forms part of a disciplinary framework in which *all* manifestations of the sexual body are more or less illicit.'[46] Jeanette's desire for Melanie brings down the whole force of the community's sanctions upon her head. The incarceration and the starvation, Morrison argues, are less difficult for her to handle than the fact that she may be excluded from the sect's communal certainty of being part of the saved, and the loss of her exceptional worth as a preacher. In his reading, the orange demon is Jeanette's acceptance and internalisation of lesbian sexuality as evil and deviant, and hence part of why she initially reverts to a masquerade of normalcy. Morrison's examination of the critique of Evangelism also stretches to the novel's treatment of the Christian notion of time:

■ Human history, from the Creation to the Last Judgement, is knowable and finite, and there is little time remaining before history comes to its ultimate end. At the same time, the meaning of life for the individual is defined in an intimate relation to a divine plan. Even one's moment-to-moment progress through a lifetime is filled with a definite structure of prohibitions and obligations, by the constant expectation of judgement. The surveillance of an omniscient God is total, and there is no place for secrecy, no sinful act, no impure thought or illicit desire for which one will not ultimately be called to account.[47] □

Such a conception of time and history not only has a profound impact on the notion of identity but also on that of desire as well. Within secular history, the conception of the individual's place within a society or the world is relatively minor, change will occur without the individual's say-so, and their power to intervene is negligible. Within the Evangelical conception of the subject in relation to time, however, the opposite construction occurs. The individual subject's role is magnified, and it is only by one's own actions that one can receive redemption. Evangelical history thus stands in complete opposition to Darwinian history. The opposition continues in relation to sex as well as identity. Religion limits sexual desire as something to be fought and negated, while evolution sees heterosexual sex and consequent procreation as the main function of women. This rift between the two conceptions of history is thus read as part of the novel's comedic challenge to compulsory heterosexuality. The episode of the mother's relationship with Pierre parodies popular romance's narrative of falling in love. Mother's experience of 'fizzing' and 'giddiness' which she assumes is the bodily manifestation of love, proves to be a stomach ulcer and so her body has betrayed her. Mother thereby unpacks maternity and bodily procreation from marriage in adopting the child she needs, instead. *Oranges Are Not the Only Fruit* critiques both heterosexual love and maternity, and this is a female *Bildungsroman* that deliberately does not end in the conventional closure of marriage. Rather, in circling around the mother and her relationship with Jeanette, the text rejects a linearity that would have constructed love and marriage as structurally inevitable, and instead in its variant narratives argues for a more multiple potential for the feminine subject. Morrison invokes Bakhtin's 'chronotope', a term Bakhtin coins for discussing literary space/time constructions within the text, which he points out can be multiple and even contradictory.[48] Carnival embodies this chronotopic potential of subversion of the normal cultural rules and prescriptions, and is traditionally linked to bodily excess and licentiousness. Winterson's multiple narratives in *Oranges Are Not the Only Fruit*, *The Passion*, and in *Sexing the Cherry*, can be seen as imaginative chronotopes that allow for the carnivalesque inclusion of the subversive and the unruly as a strategy of lesbian resistance.

The transmission of the television adaptation of the novel by the BBC in 1990[49] allowed a new debate on the lesbianism of the text to arise from a cultural studies consideration of the audiences' reactions to the programmes rather than from a literary reading of the text itself, the words on the page. The programmes were initially shown in January, repeated in the same summer and gained audience figures of nearly six million each time.[50] Rebecca O'Rourke's 'Fingers in the Fruit Basket'[51] concentrated on the written text, but looked at the reception of the novel within a specifically lesbian audience. She discussed the novel initially in 1985 with lesbian friends, and they identified both strengths and problems within it:

■ We found it exhilarating to read a book with a lesbian heroine, which had a strong plot, rooted in something other than the discovery or coming to terms with lesbianism. ... Although we liked this, it bothered us that most of our straight friends discussed the book with barely a reference to lesbianism. We talked, too, about the uneasy feelings that lesbianism was once again being identified with oddness and that the book might suggest that Jeanette's lesbianism was caused by her peculiar upbringing.[52] □

O'Rourke and her friends identify Jeanette's struggle with religion as the main plot of the novel, since they do not see it focusing on her discovery of her love for women. The idiosyncrasies of the Evangelical sect paradoxically are also seen as a negative element of the depiction, since it allies the lesbian to the odd. (Their view is borne out by the mainstream reception, as documented by Hilary Hinds a year later.) Professionally, O'Rourke chooses *Oranges Are Not the Only Fruit* as one of four texts to examine in a WEA[53] class, 'Lesbian lives and writing'. All the students were identified lesbians, and the focus of the course was on autobiographical writing. A debate ensued as to whether *Oranges Are Not the Only Fruit* was a lesbian novel, and the question of what defines such an epithet, the writer's position or the audience addressed by the text's stance. The majority of O'Rourke's group held the simple essentialist position that the writer's sexuality defines the text. They concurred that the second reading found the novel less funny, noting how the comedy masked many of the painful scenes. They appreciated the range of other characters involved in the depiction and felt an unease about their one-dimensionality in contrast to the more complex protagonist with her 'superior distance from the rest of the world'.[54] 'Going behind the main character and into the world of the novel is to find yourself in a distortedly huge landscape in which all the figures are nothing but painted cloth.'[55] They discussed the recent television adaptation and voiced their surprise at how uncontroversial the lesbian sex scenes had been. And they noted Jeanette Winterson's 'conciliatory attitude towards her family, as she spoke about how they had read the novel ... and been hurt by it, although that was not her intention. The adaptation was a much gentler affair altogether, and the characterisation of the mother by Geraldine McEwan gave her a dignified strength that was quite different from the maniacal zeal of the novel'.[56] Focused on issues of lesbian autobiography, O'Rourke's students were concerned with the fairness of the depictions and what they saw as the overbalanced and overweening authority of the narrator.

A year later, Hilary Hinds's '*Oranges Are Not the Only Fruit*: Reaching Audiences Other Lesbian Texts Cannot Reach'[57] asks much more complex and sophisticated questions about the reception of the television series, examining primarily the responses in the press:

■ This essay examines the meanings of the ambiguous cultural status of *Oranges*, a text which cut across the high/popular culture divide with its success as a BBC2 'quality' drama, and its acclaim from the popular press, lesbian audiences and serious critics alike. Through an analysis of its reception, I shall examine what it meant for an avowedly lesbian novel to be feted by the mainstream media and press as well as being so successful within a subcultural context. Did the reviewers in the lesbian, feminist and radical press read it differently from those in the mainstream? Was the text's 'literariness', its high-cultural status, apparent from the outset, and how important was this to the acceptability of its unambiguous reaffirmation of lesbianism?[58] □

The original reviews, both mainstream and from the feminist and left-wing presses, welcomed the novel in very positive terms, and this, Hinds argues, is partly to do with how it is categorised as literature rather than popular reading, and extends even further once the novel has won the Whitbread Prize for the best first novel. 'This initial acclamation of *Oranges* as a "literary" text by the radical press was later taken up by the mainstream reviewers, particularly once the novel had won the Whitbread Prize. The prize became an increasingly important part of Winterson's pedigree, particularly once she adapted the novel for television. This combined with the notion of *Oranges* as a "quality" text, and both became central to how the television adaptation was previewed and reviewed.'[59] The mainstream critics constructed the novel as dealing with an individual young girl from Lancashire, growing up within a lunatic religious fringe. The analysis of the text concentrated on the theme of individualism and on the novel's literary quality. One had to look to the alternative press for any sense of a political dimension, such as the feminist account of women within the institutional power of a religious and familial patriarchy. While most of the reviews acknowledged the novel had a lesbian character, their treatment of the lesbianism was less clear-cut, seeing it as just another part of the novel's quirky humour. 'Lesbianism was thus constructed as one more comic device, useful in moving on the action.'[60] For some, it was a narrative way of marking Jeanette's movement away from her family within the *Bildungsroman*, while for others its seriousness marred the comedy of the novel.

■ By the mainstream press particularly, then, *Oranges* was not seen principally as a lesbian text: Jeanette's lesbianism was seen merely as a suitable foil to her mother's Evangelism, its significance assessed in terms of humour, narrative and 'Character'. Far from confirming Winterson's own assertion that lesbianism is at the centre of the story, on the basis of the reviews one would think it were, as one reviewer put it, one of 'countless novels on the stands about families, separation, and the emotional spaces people create or don't create for one another'.[61] By suggesting that Jeanette is a character with whom we can all sympathise, because lesbianism is just another human experience, these critics aspire to a universal reading. Whilst this liberal humanist reading has the advantage of being accepted and inclusive of lesbian experience, it does deny all sense of the novel having any *specificity*, whether to lesbian experience or to Northern working-class experience. Lesbian oppression, whether in the form of violence, repression, stereotyping or denial, has no part in such a depoliticised reading, and thus remains unacknowledged.[62] □

Hinds clearly articulates the questions in play about the representation of lesbianism in *Oranges Are Not the Only Fruit*. In a feminist analysis, the inclusivity is its strength, but from a queer politics perspective, the specific differences of lesbians from heterosexual women are being glossed over and silenced. Having summed up the reception of the novel, Hinds goes on to analyse the reception of the television adaptation. The end of December 1989 saw both the television and the newspapers heralding the forthcoming event, with the focus of the tabloids in particular on the explicit nudity of the lesbian sex scenes. 'Its lesbianism was seen to be the text's defining characteristic, and was the prime focus of the pre-broadcast press excitement.'[63] However, as O'Rourke's students had observed, the expected furore and controversy was marked only by its absence. Instead of outrage, the BBC programmes were met by praise from both the broadsheets and the tabloids. In order to explain why the adaptation of *Oranges Are Not the Only Fruit* was accepted so effusively, Hinds places it within the context of its historical moment. Two years before, the Conservative Government had passed the highly contested Section 28 of the Local Government Act (banning the promotion of homosexuality) and so for the left-of-centre press, gays and lesbians had become the overtly oppressed minority. In 1989, death threats against Salman Rushdie (born 1947) had been issued by an Islamic minority, because of the blasphemy within his *Satanic Verses* (1989). This meant, Hinds suggests, that within the liberal arts establishment, the issue of freedom of speech was paramount and this had a direct impact on the reception of the TV version of *Oranges Are Not the Only Fruit*. 'Thus *Oranges* was read in a cultural context where high-cultural "art" had been established as having a meaning separable from questions of politics, sexual or otherwise.'[64] The fact that the Western press was almost unanimous in its condemnation of religious fundamentalism, in the case of Salman Rushdie, influenced the response to the adaptation. The extremism of the mother's Evangelical sect became consciously or unconsciously linked to the extremism of Ayatollah Khomeini's[65] followers, predisposing the press to react favourably to the mocking of a fundamentalism that seeks to silence the voice of the artist/Jeanette, whatever she sought to express: 'Thus, it appears that the yoking of the lesbianism with the fundamentalism was itself crucial for the favourable mainstream liberal response: lesbianism became an otherness preferable to the unacceptable otherness of fundamentalism.'[66] The lesbian expression, linked to high art through the 'quality' literary adaptation by the BBC (and European 'art' cinema's favourable depictions of lesbian encounters), within a context of antagonism to Section 28, meant that lesbianism, too, could be regarded in a positive light. This historical context, Hinds believes, partially explains why the lesbian television series confounded expectations and was received with applause by the newspapers.

Her second reason for the favourable reception is a more familiar one in relation to Winterson's text; the critics succeeded in decentring the lesbianism. The 'adaptation's success rested on the critics' ability to read it as being *really* about something other than lesbianism. ... As with the novel, the lesbianism is de-centred and the critics present us with a drama "about" all sorts of things'.[67] The humanist perspective adopted by the television reviewers ensures that they interpret the protagonist's desire for other women in a number of different ways, in an almost identical move to the novel's reviewers: 'the de-centring of the lesbianism does not involve denial: in most accounts of the story-line it is mentioned, but nearly always in relation to something else, generally the ensuing rejection and exorcism of Jess by members of the evangelical group. ... Lesbianism, then, is always seen in relation to other issues, be they religion, family, or simply "growing up".'[68] This misrepresentation was particularly acute when it came to discussing the lesbian sex scenes. Hinds explains how the director and the producer were categoric in their wish to give a straightforwardly explicit rendition of what women do in bed with other women, in contrast to what they perceived as an earlier idealised rendition (the television adaptation in 1989 of D. H. Lawrence's *The Rainbow*, 1915). Despite this intention, the mainstream press was almost unanimous in insisting on a portrayal that was anchored on its youth and innocence.

> ■ There is scant evidence, then, that these reviewers were shocked by this representation of lesbianism. Not only did the manifest youth of Jess and Melanie allow them to define and praise the relationship in terms of its tenderness and innocence, it also implicitly allowed the lesbianism to be understood as an adolescent phase, a naïve exploration that would be outgrown. Moreover, the fact that the critics ignored any other scenes that might modify or even contradict this reading of tenderness and inno-cence meant that this characterisation of the sex scene alone was allowed to represent the text's 'lesbianism', avoiding any broader or more challenging meaning of this concept.[69] □

Even the tabloids were not outraged, rejecting the sex scenes as untitillat-ing for heterosexual viewers (suggesting instead the use of 'page 3 models' and retitling it 'Melons are not the only fruit'). Only the gay and lesbian press saw the scenes as erotic and radical in their representations and 'situated the text firmly within the discourse of desire. Not only was "innocence" countered in these reviews, but also ... there was an emphasis on the subtlety of the sexual references employed'.[70] Where the heterosexual reviewers eschewed the eroticism, the gay and lesbian press feted it, clearly reading the scenes in very different ways.

Hinds concludes with a discussion of the lesbian politics of *Oranges Are Not the Only Fruit*. That it had a political significance for its lesbian viewers, she sees as undeniable. 'Lesbian viewers seemed to agree that *Oranges* was a milestone, staying home in droves on Wednesday nights to watch it. This enthusiasm was in part, no doubt, because it made lesbianism a visible presence on television where ... it was usually invisible. Moreover, it became visible in a mainstream slot, rather than in the furtive late-night positions of most representations of lesbian and gay issues on television.'[71] Not only was the lesbian protagonist a heroine, rather than a victim or a villain, but she was greeted with unambiguous praise by the mainstream reviewer. 'From many perspectives, then, *Oranges* signified something pleasurable and exceptional for lesbian viewers.'[72] The political impact of the adaptation, Hinds concludes, was an important intervention into the mainstream, whatever the complexities and the ambiguities of its reception. 'Although it may be true to say that the lesbianism is defused by the text's associations with high culture and its consequent openness to a liberal interpretation, it is also true that *Oranges* has retained, and increased, its lesbian audience and its sub-cultural consumption, and has also been praised in the tabloid press usually hostile to lesbian and gay issues.'[73] For Hilary Hinds, despite the liberal humanist misrepresentation of both the novel and the television adaptation in the mainstream reviews, the articulation of a lesbian viewpoint within a prime-time, quality, serious programme was a successful political act. Hinds never questions the text's representation of lesbianism, but looks solely at how the text is received, and it is the reception of the texts that she critiques.

In 1994, Marilyn Brooks[74] considered the television adaptation of *Oranges Are Not the Only Fruit* alongside two adaptations of the feminist writer Fay Weldon (born 1933); *The Life and Loves of a She-Devil*, 1986, and *The Cloning of Joanna May*, 1992. Looking at the issue of how to screen the openness and the ambivalence of feminist women's writing within what she deems the more fixed and closed-minded medium of the small screen, she asserts, 'Although discussion of adaptations tends to accommodate the idea that something has to be "left out", in the case of minority writings, what is left out is exactly relevant within the context of deliberate evasion or silencing. It suggests subverting the subversive in order to turn it into the televisual experience called popular entertainment.'[75] Where Hinds looks to the reception's distortion of the depiction of lesbianism, Brooks suggests that it is the adaptation itself that waters down the novel's complex representation. Similarly, where Hinds saw the prime-time showing as a successful political act, Brooks argues that prime time militates against the novel's subversive quality, creating 'a clear danger that the alternative strategies involved in the act of making marginal texts "popular" for screening will *necessarily* defuse the meaning which makes them perceived as marginal to begin with. Offering these texts prime-time viewing is insisting on compromise. Popular TV tends to be just that, and consequently, challenging and radical positions have to be accommodated within the parameters existing. There is a potential danger that raising these issues and then containing them visually, simultaneously contains the issues themselves'.[76] Brooks's view of the adaptation as making the religious bigotry so bizarre that Jess's lesbianism seems a highly understandable rebellion, and as portraying the lesbianism as sexually innocent so that it becomes even more palatable, accords with Hinds's reading of the critical response and so raises the question of whose the distortion is: the adaptation itself or the reception of it? Brooks suggests that the narrowing down of the plot-line and the visualising of scenes such as the exorcism (a few lines in the novel) particularises the oppression of Jess, making it specific to one religious sect rather than indicative of wider religious and familial institutions, and so defusing the novel's representation of society's homophobia. She further decries the loss of the quest to find an identity, which in the novel includes the various narratives of Winnet, Sir Perceval and the wise woman, because she views this as speaking to a more general female audience than just a lesbian one. This more complex feminist stance, 'Jeanette is everywoman, rather than lesbian woman',[77] becomes lost in the adaptation. Though perhaps a valid reading for many heterosexual women who enjoy the book, it is one that Hinds and Doan would disagree with in terms of queer theory.

Julia Hallam and Margaret Marshment's 'Framing Experience: Case Studies in the Reception of *Oranges Are Not the Only Fruit*' (1995)[78] agrees with Hinds that the television drama's prime-time slot, its categorisation as 'quality' drama and its 'high production values', were all important in creating its success. Hallam and Marshment concur to some extent with Brooks's analysis in believing that the television version adopted a reading of the novel that ridiculed religious fundamentalism as a way of playing 'off the representation of one unpopular minority position (religious fundamentalism) against another (lesbianism)'; by this means, 'they aimed to secure a reading in sympathy with the protagonist Jess', though for Hallam and Marshment this was subversive because the viewers were therefore 'accepting a definition of lesbianism directly counter to dominant ideological positions concerning "normal" sexuality'.[79] For them, this naturalising of the lesbian was in fact a positive strategy.

Having analysed the drama, Hallam and Marshment then conducted a series of eight in-depth interviews with women who had seen the three episodes to decide whether the screening did 'constitute a significant feminist, anti-homophobic intervention in popular culture'. Though their sample was small, the range of positions across age, occupations, ethnicity and religion was extensive. The born-again Christian saw most clearly the rhetorical aspect of the episodes, 'of how the text was constructed to persuade her that lesbianism was acceptable. She cited the sympathetic portrayal of Jess and the unsympathetic portrayal of the church members, especially the Pastor ("a sod"), as being designed to "manipulate me into accepting her point of view".'[80] Though she saw through the strategy, it did not prevent her enjoyment. Instead, it pushed her to question her beliefs in relation to the drama's thesis. None of the eight case studies challenged the text's placing viewpoint, and many identified similar experiences of church or family in their own lives. The young heterosexual viewers glossed over the issue of lesbianism, while the two lesbian viewers welcomed the positive depiction of a lesbian protagonist and the sharing of an overtly lesbian narrative perspective. 'Both likened their own experiences to those of Jess, expressing no sense that these were untypical of lesbians in general: "They still treat us like that", said one, and for the other the text revived painful memories of a similar teenage experience.' None of the respondents felt the church was the main focus of attack, seeing it rather as simply one example of repressive authority. Their recognition of the realities of religious dogma, relating it to their own childhood experiences, meant they did not construct the evangelical sect as 'other', and therefore resisted the drama's narrative strategy and were not inclined to view the sect as some form of 'lunatic fringe'. For one-third of the group, the main concern of the drama was familial, in the relationship between Jess and her mother. The group's responses to the mother were complex. Their disapproval of her narrow-minded bigotry was tempered with an appreciation of her love and affection for her daughter, particularly when Jess is young and first going to school, and a recognition of her power. 'She was described as committed, competent, energetic: it was clear that viewers enjoyed her strength in these respects, even as they rejected the particular values she espoused. In some contexts they also enjoyed her (over-)confidence and dominance of all around her. This was evident in the laughter at, for example, her "one-liners" which, far from being at her expense, came increasingly to be in sympathy with her irrepressible ability to impose her view upon the world.' This ambivalent enjoyment of the mother's power and the unambiguous espousal of Jess's strength in choosing her own way in the world, lead the authors to assert that the dramatic adaptation of *Oranges Are Not the Only Fruit* was 'clearly consonant with a western feminist view of women's autonomy' and so had a feminist impact even though it did not espouse any overtly feminist agenda. They conclude that the audience reception of the film, though generally favourable, was also varied and diverse:

■ We feel that on the basis of the responses we received, the 'naturalizing' of lesbianism that we identified as the text's strategy was largely successful. We also feel that in general, and despite differences of emphasis, all agreed that what the text 'was about' was 'female identity'. The pleasures we all derived from the text had a great deal in common, and were aesthetic as well as thematic. The high production values were enjoyed both for themselves and because they signalled that the (female) concerns of the text were being taken seriously. It seems that the 'quality' aspect of the production need not be seen only in terms of 'silencing the prudes'.

There were, of course, differences but they were not greater between researchers and respondents than between respondents themselves. Nor did they correlate neatly with socially defined identities: there were tendencies towards certain interpretations and/or pleasures according to age, sexuality and motherhood, but not such as to amount to a 'lesbian' reading versus a 'heterosexual' one, or an 'older' reading versus a 'younger' one. There was certainly not a 'black' reading versus a 'white' one; not even in the reading of Katy, Jess's second lover, who is black. We would say that overall the diversity remained within a recognizable 'we' of common experiences and common pleasures which seemed to owe much to our common positions as women.[81] □

For Hallam and Marshment, the television adaptation of *Oranges Are Not the Only Fruit* was a successfully feminist production because it silently engaged with feminist issues of women's power and women's identity, and naturalised lesbianism in a way that challenged homophobic attitudes. The pleasures of the female audience, both heterosexual and lesbian, were important as cultural statements about a prime-time showing, and the lesbian identification with the credibility of the oppression and abuse was important for the lesbian respondents.

Even though the novel was published in 1985, and the television adaptation was transmitted five years later in 1990, the majority of the literary analysis comes after the cultural studies discussion of the television serial and the audience reception of it, between 1991 and 1995 (the criticism of the novel considered runs from 1994 to 2003). This means that the analysis of the novel benefits from the earlier discussion that raises and questions what constitutes effectiveness in the representation of lesbians. O'Rourke initially queries what makes a lesbian text, whether it involves having an avowedly lesbian author, having a lesbian protagonist, or whether it is more the textual agenda of the narrative itself – a question that has haunted Winterson criticism, implicitly if not overtly, throughout her career so far, particularly in relation to the ungendered narrator of *Written on the Body* (1992). Most of the analysis of the BBC serial examines whether, in focusing on the Pentecostal religion and Jeanette's fight in relation to the church, it ended up sidelining lesbianism. O'Rourke wondered if it enabled heterosexual audiences to ignore the lesbian element altogether, a clear problem for a lesbian text, but welcomed the fact that a lesbian programme did not make lesbianism itself the problem and focus of the narrative. Hinds agreed that the reception was ambiguous and that the adaptation had both benefits and defaults in its treatment. She felt more strongly that it depoliticised the lesbianism, but also saw strengths in the fact that a programme with a lesbian content was given prime-time airing and succeeded in gaining both tabloid and broadsheet acceptance. In asserting a lesbian presence in mainstream television and in defusing the usually homophobic tabloid press coverage, *Oranges Are Not the Only Fruit* was effective programming. Hallam and Marshment largely concurred with Hinds, and welcomed the quality production and prime-time slot as endorsing female concerns as important. While they agreed that the adaptation universalised the lesbian issues into a broader attack on attempts of repressive authority in general to restrict young women's development, they saw this espousal of Jeanette's right to choose her own lifestyle as a focus on feminist autonomy and thus as having a strong feminist impact. In relation to the feminist effectiveness of the adaptation, their sample audience also enjoyed Geraldine McEwan's portrayal of the mother, which downplayed her intolerance and highlighted her strength, competence and commitment. As a television representation of strong women it was to be welcomed, and the 'naturalising' of lesbianism, for all that it glossed sexual differences, resulted in the audiences accepting the positive depiction and so effec-tively countered homophobia. Marilyn Brooks disagrees, seeing the prime-time slot as preventing any subversive message, watering down the lesbianism to a point where its presence and its political impact was ineffective. The focus on Pentecostal oddness figures lesbianism as simply a natural rebellion against bigotry, and ignores the fact that it is the whole of society, not just a small religious sect, which is antagonistic to lesbianism. Leaving out the alternative narratives of Winnet and Sir Perceval, the adaptation also ignores the quest for an identity and thus, for Brooks, loses its appeal to a wider feminine audience. For some critics, the fact that the religion was targeted as the oppressive system was a further problematic issue. For Hinds, this was because of its timing, during the *fatwah* levelled against Salman Rushdie, and the way that fundamentalist bigotry became an easy enemy. Hallam and Marshment worried that it effectively played one 'odd', unpopular minority off against the other, leaving the dominant mainstream complacently outside the target. All the critics, however, voiced their surprise at the lack of furore from either the press or the audiences in response to the depiction of lesbianism, and sexually explicit lesbianism at that, on television. Most pointed to the 'innocence' of the depiction, despite the production team's decision to make what women do together explicit, and Hinds raised the interesting point that while the heterosexual press constructed the scenes as innocent, the gay and lesbian press saw them as erotic, and so viewed them through different eyes and a different sexual perspective.

The literary criticism of the novel's lesbian representation seems to come in waves, with two in 1994, two in 1998, and another two in 2002 or 2003. Griffin, Gamallo and Morrison all see the lesbian depiction as both effective and political. Griffin welcomes the novel's celebration of same-sex desire, and its defiant refusal to see it as a problem for the lesbian; its turning the tables on phallocentric literature in marginalising the male characters and interests; and its feminist analysis of the oppressive institutions of power, and of how women often internalise these and themselves become the 'gatekeepers' of patriarchy. Like Brooks, she sees the novel's strategy, to construct Jeanette's quest as an escape from spiritual narrowness of any kind, as an effective way of including all women readers in its celebration of lesbianism, perhaps almost in spite of their preconceptions. Gamallo argues that the book makes lesbianism the central concern and the dominant viewpoint from its opening, not seeing religion as important. By making the representation of lesbian sex unremarkable and unsurprising, the novel effectively subverts homophobic constructions of same-sex practices as monstrous. Morrison argues further that the novel does not just marginalise men, but the whole of heterosexuality, since all the heterosexual relationships shown are dysfunctional. It therefore effectively invalidates the compulsory heterosexualism that it shows oppressing Jeanette. He sees the political power of the text arising from its analysis of the institution of religion and of how, stemming from St Paul's Epistle to the Corinthians, all sex and not just lesbianism is rejected in favour of the ideal of celibacy. He demonstrates how the novel parodies religion by contrasting its view of time with evolutionary history, and contrasts religion's distaste for sex with woman's relationship to sexual intimacy, in order to highlight the novel's view of religion's 'unnatural' opinion of passion.

Doan, Duncker and Rusk, for differing reasons, see the representation and advocacy of lesbianism as less effective. Doan acknowledges that the novel does switch gender stereotypes, portraying the men as passive and the women as active and domineering, and presenting lesbian desire as natural and heterosexual desire as unnatural and perverse, but argues that this is only a superficial attack. The text still endorses the binary division of gay and straight, natural and unnatural, for all that it has reversed the evaluations; to be really politically subversive it would have needed to deconstruct and untether the concepts of gender and sexuality to allow for a whole plurality of possibilities. Doan sees Winterson's first novel failing in its political agenda because it is not postmodern enough, a failing that her later novels transcend. For Duncker, in contrast, it is too postmodern, since the narrative style's playful lack of engagement denies any political quality. In the perspective of postmodern deconstruction and queer theory's assertion of difference and separateness from heterosexuality, the novel loses the certainty and engaged commitment that feminist lesbianism used to celebrate. Holding up dogmatic utopianism as the source of political engagement, Duncker argues for a position close to the mother's in her insistence to the young Jeanette that one can change the world. It is a position that Hallam and Marshment's audience recognised, in their enjoyment of Geraldine McEwan's forthright television portrayal of the mother. Rusk contradicts Duncker's argument that the novel takes a queer theory position, in giving a reading that Jeanette refuses to be 'othered' in the narrative and insists on being included within the rest of heterosexual humanity. Rusk calls the novel didactic but not openly political and links her description to the fact that it never once uses the term lesbian within its pages. Such a strategy is a way of refusing to be fixed within prevailing cultural terms and definitions. Rusk thus implicitly disagrees with Doan's view that the novel does not escape the binary construc- tions of phallocentricism. For Rusk, it is, overall, an effective escape from binary structures, and on the way to deconstructing them, but falls foul of its own critique in its portrayal of the 'enemy', men. The novel ends up 'othering' men in the way it represents them, and so negating its own didactic strategy.

Duncker notes that feminist topics are a major part of the novel, despite its lack of political strategy, and gives the focus on the complex mother–daughter bond as an example of this. Gammallo and Rusk agree that a main focus of the novel is the young Jeanette's individuation from the mother and the maturation of the feminine self. And the majority of the critics of the novel (Griffin, Doan, Gamallo, Rusk and Morrison) concentrate upon the importance of the sexual experiences within the novel as asserting lesbian specificity and difference from heterosexual women and hence a fundamental part of the lesbian portrayal. Interestingly, approval or disapproval of the lesbian effective- ness of the novel is not context-led; it does not stem from specific debates within gay and lesbian criticism during particular periods, since the critics of the novel divide neatly in the times of their publication, approval coming in 1994, 1998 and 2002, disappointment in 1994, 1998 and 2003. Most of the disagreement within the criticism of *Oranges Are Not the Only Fruit* as a lesbian text comes from the questioning of postmodern deconstruction's effectiveness as a political strategy and from the related issue of whether or not the text is a postmodern novel. This topic is explored in much more depth in the following chapter.

CHAPTER TWO

Oranges Are Not the Only Fruit (1985) as a Postmodern Text

O*ranges Are Not the Only Fruit* is clearly more than just a realist autobiographical text. Its fragmented and multiple narratives, which echo and pastiche a variety of different narrative styles from the Bible to fairy tales, along with its fantasy use of the orange demon, constitute a complex postmodern text. The number of critics that have focused on its writer's promotion of lesbianism is equalled by those who have concentrated their analysis on its narrative form. The examination of the Bible has been especially well represented. Some critics, like Laura Doan, have investigated the lesbian representation in relation to the postmodern narrativity.

Paulina Palmer, looking in 1993 at contemporary lesbian writing, deems *Oranges Are Not the Only Fruit* a mix of the *Bildungsroman* and the lesbian 'Coming Out' novel but focuses her analysis on the examination of narrativity, which she sees as an essential part of the novel's meaning and not the superfluous addendum that some early critics decreed.[1] 'The fantasy episodes of *Oranges*, however, far from being superfluous, are an integral part of the novel and perform a number of important functions. The interplay of narratives which they create highlights the part which fantasy plays in the construction of the adolescent psyche and gives a more complex and multifaceted representation of subjectivity than is usually found in the Coming Out novel.'[2] Indeed, for Palmer, the way we understand our sense of self is through telling ourselves stories that attempt to create a coherent identity, while postmodern concepts of subjectivity argue that we are in fact not singular but rather a series of sliding selves. Palmer suggests that the strength of the novel is that it highlights just this notion of multiple identity through its various narrative modes, showing Jeanette creating a sense of her differing identities in relation to realism, fantasy and myth, at times inhabiting a fairy tale princess and at others, Sir Perceval.

■ *Oranges Are Not the Only Fruit*, while rejecting a unitary model of subjectivity in favour of a delineation of fantasy identities and multiple

30

selves, also, in true postmodern spirit, envisages and depicts subjectivity itself in terms of narrativity. Jeanette, instead of uncovering a single, static identity, constructs for herself a series of shifting, fluid selves by means of the acts of storytelling and fabulation in which she engages. Storytelling enables her to acknowledge, in the words of Cixous, the existence of her 'monsters ... jackals ... fellow-creatures ... fears'.[3] ☐

Palmer examines the persona of Sir Perceval, which Jeannette adopts at certain points, and indicates how Winterson, rather than linking the persona to the heroic chivalry of the Knights of the Round Table, instead focuses 'on the disintegration of the company of the Round Table and the feelings of disillusion in which it results'.[4] Similarly, the Winnet narratives invoke 'an idiosyncratic version of the tale of the Sorcerer's Apprentice' as a way of exploring her notion of Jeanette's relationship with her domineering mother, transposing

■ into a fairy tale form the power-struggles and conflicts which it involves and the painful shift in which it culminates. The representation of the bond between mother and daughter in terms of the attachment between a sorcerer and his apprentice emphasizes its irrational aspect, acknowledging the 'magical' power which it wields. The fact that a gender displacement occurs and the figure of the mother is represented not by the witch but by a male wizard, universalizes the theme of power relations between parent and child and illustrates Winterson's refusal to be tied to biologistic assumptions. In the 'theatres of the mind' gender differences are subverted and our desires and anxieties and fears acted out by a myriad different figures, both male and female.[5] ☐

The transposition of genders is an important element in the alternative narratives and Palmer sees it as a feminist strategy of rejecting phallocentric constructions of the genders as diametrically different and arguing instead for more similarities. The representation could also be linked to Gabrielle Griffin's thesis that the mother is a 'gatekeeper' of patriarchy and so, in a sense, masculine in outlook despite her female sex.

Palmer develops the use of fairy tales and myths further, arguing that while they do serve the purpose of representing the young girl's changing identities and the fantasies she experiences, they also carry a literary import as well. Through the intertextual use of a variety of texts the novel develops the postmodern thesis that no text is completely original, but always develops out of earlier, culturally known narratives. Winterson's mixing of the fairy tales with other literary genres not only raises issues of literary originality and of transgressing generic boundaries but is also a feminist rewriting of the underlying ideology. 'Images of femininity constructed by a male-dominated culture are interrogated and problematized. In the tale of the princess who was so sensitive that she wept for the death of a moth ... the stereotypically feminine attributes of narcissism and sentimentality are confronted and rejected, while the story of the prince's search for a flawless woman examines male ideas of femininity and exposes their oppressive effect on flesh-and-blood women.'[6] She examines what she terms 'the Little Red Riding Hood intertext' as conveying the young Jeanette's worry about traditional heterosexual relationships and the untrustworthiness of male desire. *Oranges Are Not the Only Fruit* is placed alongside other postmodern novels written by women which all focus on how telling stories is a political act of asserting one ideological point of view over another.

The main ideological text the novel questions and subverts, though, is 'the Old Testament, the master text of Western civilisation'. Winterson challenges the authority of the Bible in the way she deploys biblical references, choosing to use them in deliberately unfitting or incongruous ways or in completely rewritten forms. Thus the books of the Old Testament become titles in a lesbian coming-out novel, structuring its tale of subversive sexuality. The portentous pronouncement of summer being ended but sinners not saved, reproduces itself in a young child's sampler, picked out in coloured wool, and Elsie recreates the prophets in the fiery furnace using real, live mice. 'Even bearing in mind the various weird and wonderful materials which postmodern artists employ, this must surely rank as a first.'[7] Even the representation of lesbianism she sees as intertextual in its engagement with Adrienne Rich's thesis of a lesbian continuum (see Chapter 1, note 6) in relation to the supportive network of women in the Pentecostal community. However, Palmer argues that Winterson's novel does not idealise this network, showing women to be weak and tyrannical as well as loving and loyal; moreover, in asserting the sexual component of lesbianism the representation challenges Rich's view that all women are in some ways lesbian if they have emotional relationships with other women. She concludes that the novel is influenced most profoundly by the Romantic poet William Blake (1757–1827) and his 'radical concept of morality'[8] which condemns all forms of sexual repression.

Where Laura Doan (1994) finds the realistic depiction of the lesbian ineffective (see the previous chapter), the multiple narratives proved, for her, a more promising development of Winterson's political aesthetics. In discussing the metaphor of marmalade, which challenges the overall binarism of Jeanette's viewpoint, in relation to Oranges/Not Oranges, Doan looks at the epigraphs as being an alternative narrative that sits alongside the biographical verisimilitude:

■ Thus the opening epigraph, a literary device predictably announcing the theme to follow, collapses inner and outer. The epigraph, taken from Mrs Beeton's cookbook, describes the process of making marmalade and states that 'when thick rinds are used the top must be thoroughly skimmed, or a scum will form marring the final appearance'. The thick rinds, evoking as they do the image of a thick skin, bring with them the danger of 'scum' rising to the surface: an image that can only be seen as a kind of self-contained morality tale. But as Jeanette herself admits, while gazing at some oranges in a moment of crisis, 'They were pretty, but not much help. I was going to need more than an icon to get me through this one.' Winterson's use of the fruit metaphor is more, much more, than an icon; it is her first tentative mechanism for imagining the fruition of a postmodern lesbian existence.[9] □

Doan sees the later novels as offering more effective lesbian aesthetics, due to their postmodernism, but clearly positions the beginning of the narrative experimentation with *Oranges Are Not the Only Fruit.*

In the USA, in the same year, Laurel Bollinger looked at 'Models of Female Loyalty: The Biblical Ruth in Jeanette Winterson's *Oranges Are Not the Only Fruit'.*[10] Bollinger claims that the *Bildungsroman* form, the narrative of coming-of-age, has traditionally been a masculine story and is inappropriate for women. Using the theory of gender construction developed by the feminist psychologist Carol Gilligan (born 1936),[11] she explains that where the men move away from the mother and home and out into the world as a necessary part of their maturation, women tend to stay within the family and voice their dissatisfaction with the status quo, while striving to preserve the relationships. Therefore, 'stories of maturation, with their emphasis on an "exit" solution, cannot speak to the need for connection within feminine development, nor can they provide a literary model for its occurrence in fiction'.[12] If the *Bildungsroman* is unavailable for women, the traditional fairy tale with its passive heroine, competitively related to the mother or stepmother, is even less available for appropriation, particularly if the writer wishes to portray the strong mother–daughter relationships usual within lesbian maturation. Few models are therefore available for Winterson to employ effectively, in the relationship between Jeannette and the bigoted mother but, Bollinger notes approvingly, *Oranges Are Not the Only Fruit* does conclude with Jeanette's returning to her home and continuing the relationship with the mother, a sign for her of a proper female maturity. Where the *Bildungsroman* and the fairy tale prove poor paradigms, the biblical Book of Ruth, the essay argues, is much more useful and textually appropriate, given Jeanette's family involvement with the Pentecostal Evangelists. The Book of Ruth centres on the relationship between Ruth and her mother-in-law Naomi, on female loyalty as important for female development, and proves an effective model for Winterson's representation of both Jeanette's realisation of her lesbianism and her relationship with her mother.

Bollinger is concerned with a variety of uses of the Bible, and notes how they connect with the postmodern questioning of the common-sense distinctions between fiction and fact:

■ In blending Biblical references with Jeanette's story, Winterson deliberately challenges the distinction between fact and fiction as well as between the novel she is writing and the Biblical texts she uses for her parody. These Biblical texts are already problematic; not quite history and not quite story-telling, their position on any kind of fact–fiction continuum changes with the point of view of the observer. In the self-reflexive chapter 'Deuteronomy', Winterson suggests that the distinction between fact and fiction arises from self-delusion; history and story are not in opposition but are, like 'knots' in a game of 'cat's cradle', so hopelessly tangled that we must learn to take pleasure in the blend. She plays out this concern through a narrative technique that juxtaposes autobiographical units with relatively strong truth claims (at least at the level of plausibility) next to fairy-tale units whose truth claims rest on psychological verity alone. This juxtaposition mirrors the actual narrative structure of her Biblical source texts, which contain materials purporting to be myth, poetry, or history in an often indecipherable blur.[13] □

Bollinger views Winterson's biblical framing of the chapter titles, employing the first eight books of the Bible, as 'reductionist' since she relies on only the simplest grasp of each of the chapters' meanings, and parodies one main concept alone. For example, in using 'Genesis' for the chapter developing the protagonist's adoption and infanthood, Winterson's omission of the Old Testament's disordered mix of stories for the more defined New Testament narrative of origin (the virgin birth) is seen as a lack, but her omission of the significant men from the creation is applauded, with the mother usurping the power of creation. 'Exodus' has Jeanette escaping to school, but unable to comprehend the 'pillar of cloud' the escaping Israelites had to navigate *their* way in an alien world. 'Leviticus', taking its title from one of the law-giving books of the Bible, deals with the mother's initiation of Jeanette into her role as an evangelist, and 'Numbers', the other prescriptive chapter, includes the fairy tale of the prince searching for the perfect woman, an allusion apparently to the 'Holiness Code' designed to perfect the Hebrews as the chosen race. In the Bible, the Book of Numbers presents the wandering of the Israelites, and in *Oranges are Not the Only Fruit*, the chapter details Jeanette's wandering from the evangelical strictures and her discovery of her lesbian desire:

■ 'Deuteronomy' ... mirrors its Biblical text in being a non-narrative chapter devoted to establishing rules for human behaviour. Like its Biblical namesake, this chapter includes dietary prescriptions: 'If you want to keep your own teeth, make your own sandwiches.' However, Winterson uses the rule to suggest the necessity of confirming facts for oneself; she terms secondhand information 'refined food' that contains insufficient 'roughage' to prevent intellectual 'constipation'. The dietary law serves as a metaphor for intellectual integrity.[14] □

'Joshua' refers to Jeanette 'blowing her own trumpet' in her public disagreements with her mother, and 'Judges' refers to the sect's judgement that she has usurped the male as they strip her of her ministry. Having elucidated the overt, parodic and, for her, simplistic uses of the Bible in the novel's choice of chapter headings, Bollinger goes on to develop the more complex usage of the Ruth story:

■ Instead of being limited purely to the 'Ruth' chapter, the Ruth material defines the nature of the novel as a whole by indicating the larger issues of mother/daughter relations and female loyalty that face Jeanette. If, as I am suggesting, the whole novel is in some respects a parodic retelling of the Ruth story, then the interaction between the two versions reveals the points of tension between Jeanette and the Biblical tradition: Jeanette's refusal of the tradition and her self-fashioning through it.[15] □

Winterson's final chapter, 'Ruth', uses a less overtly simplistic biblical parody. Ruth's choice to abandon her people and remain with her mother-in-law, after the husband's death, and to support her until an appropriate (and elderly) second husband and protector for them both can be found from within Naomi's blood-line, is termed 'one of the unusual instances where the Bible depicts profound female solidarity'.[16] Feminist Bible scholars have read Ruth's choice as a significant attack on patriarchal culture's use of women as an exchange value between men, and a re-evaluation of women's relationships with other women. Bollinger suggests that Naomi's conversion of Ruth parallels Jeanette's evangelising of Melanie and Katie and that perhaps she searches for a similar faithfulness in her own relationships to that which Ruth showed to Naomi. Jeanette's desire for an exceptional lover whose passion is fierce and devoted until death echoes Ruth's famous, 'Whither thou goest, I will go ... [till] death part thee and me'.[17] 'Because Jeanette finds such romantic love all but unattainable, her quest leads her back to the Ruth text more directly: she too concentrates on her relation to a maternal figure. At the conclusion of the novel, she chooses to return to her mother despite their conflicts. Jeanette's action thus reproduces the theology of the Ruth text; she opts to express to her mother the same *hesed* [loyalty/devotion] Ruth showed Naomi.'[18] Jeanette thus returns to the mother who betrayed her, demonstrating an exceptional female loyalty.

Bollinger looks at the scholarship that constructs the Book of Ruth as a form of folk tale (Winterson's 'Ruth' chapter contains two fairytale stories, that of Winnet Stonejar and that of Perceval) but then values it over traditional fairy tales in that the Book of Ruth does not set women in competition with each other and, moreover, Ruth is active in seeking a second husband, rather than passively waiting for her prince to come. In concentrating on the first chapter of Ruth, the devotion of the younger woman to the older, Winterson ignores the heterosexual marriage of the biblical conclusion. Fairy tales as models of feminine maturation, Bollinger suggests, defuse the psychic threat of challenging the maternal, by having a witch or a wicked stepmother as opponent; she notes how both the Book of Ruth and *Oranges Are Not the Only Fruit* use a similar trope in having a mother who is not the biological mother. Ruth remaining devotedly with her own mother would figure a story of female immaturity but in staying with her mother-in-law, it can be a narrative of female maturation alongside female solidarity. In choosing to have Jeanette return, at the end of the *Bildungsroman*, to her adoptive mother, Winterson turns away from the masculinist form that rejects the mother for independence and adulthood, and adopts the Ruth paradigm that acknowledges the bonds, and so 'Winterson's novel moves toward a space where subjectivity can be constructed out of female connection rather than exclusively through separation and silencing.'[19]

Such intertextual use of the Bible, Bollinger argues, forms a postmodern parody, a way of repeating this master text while contesting its values and ideology and thereby reclaiming it for the oppressed and marginalised lesbian position. While acknowledging that Winterson uses an array of intertextual references, she suggests that the biblical allusions are the most important, because they structure the novel; they are used in a complex way, involving both parody and pastiche. The

■ contrast between the Biblical material and the character's lived experience places Jeanette against the tradition that she narrates, but the occurrence of this narration within chapters named for Biblical books reiterates the significance the Bible has had for her within that contrast. The presence of Biblical material, then, constitutes not so much a mockery, which has often been associated with parody, as it does a pastiche, an unsatirical blend of history and story within the problematic realms of autobiography, fairy tale, and Biblical narrative – genres that typify the 'cat's cradle' approach Winterson describes.[20] □

Bollinger sees Winterson's distance from her biblical material as an appropriately 'postmodern ambivalence'.[21] The first seven books of the Bible are explored to demonstrate the lack of an available space for

Jeanette within this canonical text, and the final chapter finds an echo, in Ruth, of a narrative that allows bonds between women as part of the maturing feminine subject, though in this Winterson rejects the original's denouement of heterosexual marriage for a more open-ended conclusion. Through the novel's disparate narratives, Winterson fractures tradition and finally makes a space available for the protagonist in the final chapter, 'Ruth'. Bollinger's knowledgeable reading of *Oranges Are Not the Only Fruit*, helpfully elucidates the use of the Bible and demonstrates the postmodern parody and the pastiche that Winterson employs in her critique of the heterosexual master narrative.

Susana Onega, a year later, puts forward a different reading of why the novel might be seen as postmodern, though one that also looks at the inclusion of the fairy tale. In ' "I'm Telling You Stories. Trust Me": History/Story-Telling in Jeanette Winterson's *Oranges Are Not the Only Fruit*', Onega examines the meta-fictional aspects of the experimental and non-linear narrative to show that the novel is anything but the usual form of realist autobiography. Like Bollinger, she sees the 'Deuteronomy' chapter as central to the novel, both intellectually and formally (being the middle chapter); it is a 'two page-long reflexive commentary in which we hear the voice of the adult narrator theorizing on the true nature of reality, of story-telling and of history'.[22] The narrator's collapsing of the distinction between story and history, in which the former is purported to be subjective and incoherent and the latter objective and coherent, allies Winterson with the critical school of the New Historicists who reject the concept of progressive 'world history' developed by the German philosopher G. W. F. Hegel (1770–1831). Like them, the narrator recognises that Western history is actually an imperial statement, a way of silencing or denying alternative views, and moreover a way of embedding the dominant ideologies of those who are in the positions of power to write it. Onega links the New Historicist position to that of the postmodern theorist Jean-François Lyotard (1924–98)[23] in the 1970s: 'Lyotard saw the unchallenged position of the patriarchal system and its "myths of totality" suddenly being challenged by a wide spectrum of competing "ideologies of fracture", whether sexual, political, ethnical or religious.'[24] History thus becomes simply another subjective and relative, if not biased, account of the past and loses its claim to have a universal truth value.

In 'Deuteronomy', Winterson seems to be arguing that history is just a series of individualistic memories but Onega sees this as pushing her towards a solipsistic position that is problematic. Where male critics can embrace the postmodern undermining of the 'concept of the "bourgeois individual subject", which is denounced as one of the most widespread artificial constructions of the patriarchal system',[25] women have a different experience, since patriarchy has marginalised and fractured them already. For women writers, the importance of being heard as a feminine voice/self and of challenging their allotted role as 'other' to the dominant masculine culture, prevents them embracing the 'death of the self' so enthusiastically. To collapse the term 'woman' in a postmodern flux would create the problem of how to argue for change and legislation from the position of a woman. For Onega, Winterson's answer is that history is simply a series of individual recordings of the past, and this does at least allow for the writing of a feminine subjectivity if the narrator is a woman, a her-story. Onega argues that Winterson's focus on individual memory as a basis for history points less to postmodernism than to modernism, since it was a strategy of writers such as the poet T. S. Eliot and the French novelist Marcel Proust in *Remembrance of Things Past* (1913–27), but their strategy leads to a dead end in solipsism, the theory that nothing exists except oneself and one's mental states. The way in which *Oranges Are Not the Only Fruit* manages to transcend the solipsism and find a space for the feminine voice is by incorporating and rewriting myth and fairy tales, both wider cultural narrative forms that escape the purely personal.

Winterson's *Bildungsroman* of 'coming out' is written in a parody of the Bible, 'the most totalitarian, patriarchal but also most unquestionable history of all: sacred history, written, according to Jewish and Christian doctrines, by God himself and containing both history and revelation, the recording of the past and God's plans for the fututre'.[26] However, in having the chapters go from 'Genesis' to 'Ruth' the novel rearranges history, as Winterson's 'Deuteronomy' advocates, as 'the story moves, interestingly enough, from the "monologic and totalising" history of the creation of the world by God to the "individual" story of the redemption of a woman enduring threefold marginalization, as a woman, as a poor widow and as a stranger'.[27] The narrative's linearity is further compromised by the insertion of the fairy tales and allegorical passages that recall the miracles of the Bible. For Onega, the resulting postmodern narrative 'juxtaposes history with story-telling, Jeanette's "real" life-story with fantasy'.[28] The fantastic and meaningful additions to the story give a differing, perhaps 'truer' viewpoint to the autobiographical since, for Winterson, fiction can convey more emotional truth than fact. Using Rosemary Jackson's *Fantasy: The Literature of Subversion* (1981), Onega argues that fantasy, 'the uncanny hesitation between the mimetic and the marvellous, creates a space of epistemological uncertainty where the real and the unreal coexist',[29] a space where the woman, and particularly the marginalised lesbian woman, can find a voice. In traditional realist fiction women, frustrated within the patriarchal system, indulge in day-dreams of power and adventure to escape their constrictions and voice their desires, but repress these in their day-to-day lives as escapist nonsense. *Oranges Are Not the Only Fruit* allows both the fantasies and the day-to-day to coexist equally within the narrative, 'levelling reality and unreality to the same category and so creating a space of epistemological no-woman's land where her lesbian heroine can truly fulfil her innermost desires and bring about her process of maturation'.[30]

Onega elucidates the fairy tales, 'The beautiful princess turned magician' and 'Winnet Stonejar and the Wizard', to show how the two tales comment on the realist story:

■ It is easy to see that the tale 'The beautiful princess turned magician', sandwiched as it is between Jeanette's mother's stories of conversion and her dream of Jeanette's future as a missionary, is an overtly fantastic version of the same story. Indeed, the equation: 'missionary/magician', or rather, 'prophet/magician' runs through the whole novel, reaching its climax in the last chapter, 'Ruth', which opens with the story of 'Winnet Stonejar and the Wizard', itself a version of 'the magician's apprentice' topos ... in it, Winnet – whose name interestingly echoes that of Winterson herself, rather than her character – achieves perfect mastery of the magic after having become the sorcerer's adopted daughter. Jeanette, who has also been adopted, is likewise trained by her mother, not only to use her religious knowledge as a missionary to convert the heathen but also as a prophet to 'interpret the signs and wonders that the unbelievers might never understand'. Like Jeannette, Winnet uses her occult knowledge to teach the villagers and, like her, leads a happy life with her adoptive parent until she falls in love with the wrong person, causing the wizard's apocalyptic rage and her expulsion from the paradisal *hortus conclusus* [enclosed garden] where they lived. Yet again, as with Jeanette after her estrangement from the parental home, parent and daughter continue to be inextricably tied by an invisible magic thread.[31] □

The reality/fantasy, history/story-telling narratives coexist and allow the novel to give a more complex account of the protagonist's life which is able to incorporate both the day-to-day and the fantasies learnt from her mother or from her dreams. Telling stories helps her, and the reader, to comprehend the world in its complexity and fluidity and to reject the 'totalizing and absolutist categories of truth and falsehood, of good and evil'.[32] This is elucidated at the close, with Jeanette's story linked to both the Winnet Stonejar fairy tale and the Holy Grail myth of Sir Perceval. Perceval, Winnet and Jeanette all feel the pull of returning to a single-minded reality, the pull of the invisible thread of cotton, but in Onega's reading of the novel, in direct contrast to Bollinger's view, all three of them resist 'the temptation to go back'.[33] Jeanette discovers the multi-layered, inconsistent nature of reality. 'Jeanette's reflexion leaves her, like many an existentialist hero, caught in the present moment and doubtfully pondering on the next step to take. However, the parallel between her heroine's quest for maturation and Sir Perceval's quest, that is, between Jeannette's history and myth, works in the opposite direction, adding to Winterson's rational awareness of solipsistic closure, her paradoxical faith in transcendental openness.'[34] For Susan Onega, the multiple narratives of *Oranges Are Not the Only Fruit* point to a complex, postmodern distrust of grand narratives such as history, and a championing of fantasy as an equally important way of perceiving and understanding the many-layered nature of the world and its values, thus allowing a valid space for the lesbian woman's voice to be heard.

Ellen Brinks and Lee Talley see the inclusion of the Bible, and particularly the mother's use of the Bible, as being less dogmatically prescriptive and more subversive than the earlier critics saw it. In 'Unfamiliar Ties'[35] an essay looking at how lesbians are traditionally refused the rights of family and home, they suggest that these aspects are constructed with a visible difference in lesbian texts such as Winterson's *Oranges Are Not the Only Fruit*. Where Onega sees the Bible used as an oppressive, phallocentric master narrative, Brinks and Talley see it informing Winterson's 'understanding of language's generative power to testify to family and literary forms' mutual flexibility and transformative potential'.[36] Where Onega reads the Bible as standing for dogmatic laws, Brinks and Talley see the Bible as illustrating the word as revelation. Though they both agree on the Bible being challenged through postmodern intertextuality, revelation allows the lesbian quasi-biblical writer to transform the originary family. Winterson, therefore, deconstructs biblical Genesis where God creates man and chooses one tribe, one family, then finally one patriarch, Abraham. *Oranges* makes biblical origins about women's matriarchal history, since father and son do not exist in this world.[37] They argue, similarly to Onega, that the 'narrative collage' of the novel illustrates the impossibility of encompassing an identity within any single genre or text, and suggest that such a mix of fairy tale, myth and autobiography rejects the binary opposites initially set up by the mother. In contrast to Doan, they do not see the novel as reinforcing binary thinking, arguing that Jeanette's narrative is far more diverse and that even the binary opposites are not, when examined closely, opposites. 'The dog' is not a traditional binary opposite to 'next door', nor is 'Brontë' a binary opposition for 'sex (in its many forms)'. The mother's teachings are therefore seen as informing and allowing a space for Jeanette's mixed feelings and her non-binary thought. The role of the missionary allows for an exhilarating epistemological flux, as she learns the powers of language and of story-telling. Elsie thus 'becomes a feminist Moses of sorts'[38] in reading her *Goblin Market* (1862) by Christina Rossetti (1830–94), with its oral eroticism between two sisters, demonstrating the power of creativity and its endless potential for rethinking traditional concepts such as the family. Charlotte Brontë's *Jane Eyre*, with its search for home and family, is rewritten by the mother to give an alternative ending to the usual familial 'happy ever after'. *Oranges Are Not the Only Fruit* shows a society where families and having children is 'literally and figuratively disrupted'[39] – no other families with children are represented, and the mother constructs a family by non-biological means in aspiring to mirror the Virgin Mary. Moreover, within the extended family of the church, generational differences and hierarchical differences are non-existent. The very oddness of the church family and her mother illustrate to Jeanette the possibilities of subversion and, through the use of Victorian literature, discursive reading strategies for both rebellion and creation. It is therefore the mother and the extended family's use of the Bible and of other literature that allows the novel to refashion 'domestic spaces that incorporate and welcome "unnatural passions"'.[40] For Brinks and Talley, the mother's use of the Bible is thus much more creative and subversive, and the novel's intertextuality argues for Winterson's reve-latory use of language to fashion an alternative, lesbian-encompassing family structure.

In 1998, two further essays usefully considered the intertextual references of *Oranges Are Not the Only Fruit*, one focused on the popular genres, fairy tale and fantasy element, the other on the more literary allusions to *Le Morte d'Arthur* (1469–70) by Sir Thomas Malory (*c*.1470), to *Jane Eyre* and (once again) to the Bible. Tess Cosslett's 'Intertexuality in *Oranges Are Not the Only Fruit*: The Bible, Malory and *Jane Eyre*'[41] examines how the three texts create a dialogue within the novel, as she questions how such canonical texts could be appropriated as part of a feminist strategy. Cosslett calls the intertextual appropriation a form of 'pirating',[42] and sees it as a fundamental strategy of the novel, citing Deuteronomy's instruction to make one's own sandwiches from the past. Just as the protagonist's relativism challenges the mother's reli-gious strictures, so Malory challenges the Bible and argues for a different way of seeing the world. *Jane Eyre* offers two further alternative reali-ties, in the original and the mother's rewritten versions. The three all function as liberatory prototypes for the text and the narrator. Other intertextual references, such as the Bible chapter headings, are both iconoclastic comedy and serious referencing. Yet for Cosslett the precise congruence between the Bible's and *Oranges Are Not the Only Fruit*'s chapters is difficult to find, 'just vague general labels, indicating a mood and a few aspects of a story'.[43] Biblical references do not remain within their specified sections; Cosslett finds quotes from Genesis in Winterson's 'Numbers', describing the young girl's lovemaking, for example. Her reading of the 'Ruth' chapter acknowledges feminist biblical scholars' attempts to appropriate the Bible's Book of Ruth as written by a woman and giving the women characters agency, and since Ruth 'cleaves' to Naomi, a word usually used of married couples, as carrying lesbian undertones. Cosslett, however, while accepting the resonances these readings can have with Winterson's lesbian narrative, points out that by the 'Ruth' chapter, Jeanette has been abandoned by Melanie and betrayed by her mother, and there is no companion for her to cleave to. The main focus of the chapter, she argues, is rather loneliness and exile, themes found in the Perceval intertext, rather than the Ruth story. Nevertheless references to Ruth's relationship with Naomi, and Naomi's injunction to return to her mother's house after her husband's death, do stress a separation from a mother and a return to/with a mother, for all that they are two different mothers in the Bible and one, with two aspects, in *Oranges Are Not the Only Fruit*. Winterson uses different parts of the Book of Ruth to make 'a sandwich of her own'[44] rather than a faithful copy, and so has appropriated the parts of the text useful for her own narrative of lesbian exile, autonomy and loneliness, rather than effecting a slavish pastiche. Like Bollinger, Cosslett notes the discrepancy between the way the Bible's Book of Ruth ends on the heterosexual closure of marriage and a son, while Winterson's chapter ends with an open-ended absence of closure. Her freedom to ignore and to rewrite is seen as a feminist strategy, as the narrator recounts the malleable nature of story-telling itself.

Winterson's use of Malory's Perceval story is just as selective a rewriting, though here it is more than just allusion; the Perceval story is interleaved with the autobiography in four discrete sections, in the chapters 'Ruth' and 'Judges'. The Perceval sections focus on his relationship with Arthur, which parallels Jeanette's relationship with her mother. At times a direct correspondence, at others the chiming relationships within the narrative suggest opposing resolutions, ideal scenarios alongside what does happen. In 'Judges', the Perceval story appears with firstly a focus on the sadness of Arthur at their parting, and then, in the second of the sections, the young knight's sadness at having parted from the court and his lack of surety about succeeding in his quest for the Holy Grail of his dreams. Cosslett points out the analogy with the autobiographical sections of the church, with Jeanette's mother a leading member, attempting a last futile exorcism to expel Jeanette's lesbianism. The Evangelical church stands for the round table, with the mother as Arthur, while the Grail is clearly a successful lesbian romance. Winterson uses the Grail stories as 'relief' from the harsh story of the persecution, but more than this they provide an alternative narrative of the events. 'The Perceval story here moves forward to a point beyond the present upheavals and agonies, accepting Jeanette's leaving as already accomplished; it suggests (or wishes for?) a deep emotional bond between her and her mother.'[45] The two sections in 'Ruth' also focus on the relationship between Arthur and Perceval, developing the motif of the thread around the button as an enduring bond between the two. Where Jeanette's thread brings her back to visit her mother, Perceval's thread in contrast can be broken, as his dream of the Holy Grail brings him hope and peace, despite being in an alien environment where none can appreciate his quest.

Cosslett details how Winterson surpasses Malory's desultory use of the Perceval story, to develop other versions of the 'Parzifal' story, constructing the knight as a young fool or holy innocent. The focus on his youth and on his previous position as the favourite of the court allows her to develop the direct parallel between a paternal ruler and surrogate son and the mother–daughter relationships, in a way that stresses the loneliness of Jeanette's quest and Arthur's sense of loss at his going. The intense emotions of the two men, Cosslett suggests, raises a further issue of suppressed homosexuality that could refer to the lesbian theme, but the key aspect of the parallel stories, as well as of the Winnet Stonejar episodes, is the transferability of gender: the women from the autobiographical narrative, Jeanette, her mother, and Melanie, become male. 'Gender boundaries are crossed and blurred, though not abolished.'[46] Winterson's use of the Perceval story also omits the strong heterosexual element, Lancelot's adultery with Guinevere and the encompassing sense of sin within the Arthurian legend, as she did with the Bible story. Instead, Winterson privileges the innocence of the quester and the process of questing, linked to a lonely remembrance of the past warmth and companionship of Arthur's court. Again, the lack of closure to the narrative is stressed. Where Bollinger, using only the Ruth references, sees the close of Winterson's novel as a feminine return, Cosslett, using both the Ruth and the Perceval intertexts, argues that it is more ambiguous, 'both a return, and the middle of an unfulfilled quest'.[47]

Cosslett's final intertextual analysis focuses briefly on *Jane Eyre*. The use of this text is different from the earlier two considered, because it is referred to directly within the autobiographical sections, rather than forming an alternative narrative or an allusive meaning. Cosslett sees it as providing a strong reference through the similarity of its narrative, since both Jane and Jeanette are mistreated by someone in the maternal position who is not their mother, both are unhappy at school and fight a dogmatic zealous religion, both have a 'demonic alter-ego',[48] and both are separated from the one they love. Interestingly, where the narrative of *Oranges Are Not the Only Fruit* suppresses the heterosexual endings of Ruth and of Perceval, it is the mother who suppresses the heterosexual marriage in *Jane Eyre*. Both mother and narrator therefore rewrite stories, 'The only difference is that Winterson's narrator recognises what she is doing, admits to her sandwich making, while her mother claims to be in possession of the truth.'[49] All three intertexts come together in the final chapters to create a 'composite heroine ... Jeanette/Winnet/Ruth/Perceval/Jane'.[50] Where the intertexts unite in their stress on exile and questing, they also offer differing versions and a variety of outcomes. This relates in particular to the representation of the mother, who can be seen as both persecutor and desired object, and the representation of the quest's progress which involves both an escape from her and a return to her. Winterson's lesbian rereadings, through a detailed and revisionary intertextuality, ideologically challenge the canonical originals and subvert their power by claiming that no one version can be authoritative. Winterson's use of intertextuality is therefore seen as liberatory for women.

Isabel C. Anievas Gamallo's 'Subversive Storytelling: The Construction of Lesbian Girlhood through Fantasy and Fairy Tale in Jeanette Winterson's *Oranges Are Not the Only Fruit*',[51] in a book devoted to analysing representations of the girl, looks in particular at the use of the discourses of fairy tale and fantasy within the novel. These fabulations, she argues, subvert the realist depiction of formation and growth in the *Bildungsroman*, thereby 'emphasising the role of storytelling in our personal and collective arrangement of experience'.[52] Using French feminist theories, she suggests that this disruption by the magical allows a space for a specifically feminine voice that can 'challenge and relocate woman's position in the patriarchal realm of language'. Where psychoanalytic theorists like Jacques Lacan (1901–81)[53] argue that women within a patriarchal culture have no access to the symbolic order, to cultural signification or to language, Gamallo sees *Oranges Are Not the Only Fruit* attempting to renegotiate this and to reformulate the young lesbian girl's socialisation process, through the use of the magical and the fabulous:

■ Following his insights, French feminists such as Luce Irigaray have persistently denounced the fact that women have no access to language except through and within 'masculine' systems of representation. Winterson's novel, however, exemplifies the ongoing process of female appropriation of the symbolic realm that we are witnessing in contemporary women's literature. In her literary construction of lesbian girlhood, Winterson's storytelling engages in a literary project of self-creation and self-explanation that boldly rewrites the position of the female heroine in the patriarchal realm of language. She explores the bounds of traditional genres and crisscrosses the frontiers between autobiography, Bildungsroman, fantasy, romance and fairytale. Her risqué experiment convinces us that a young girl's access to language and representation does not have to be necessarily self-limiting and self-annihilating.[54] □

Where the masculine *Bildungsroman* often depicts a young man's conflict with a dominant father figure, Winterson's novel turns the gender constructions so as to have a young girl in conflict with a dominant mother. The very title of the book demonstrates the importance of this rebellion, as it challenges the mother's dominant belief that oranges are the only fruit, and defiantly asserts the contrary. 'Her mother has taught her that there is only one right "reading" and interpretation of the world, but Jeanette's answer is to contest it by writing and rewriting as many as she can.'[55] The multiple discourses, therefore, become a way of challenging the blinkered, oppressive view of the parent who negotiates her initiation into the world. Gamallo outlines the classic definition of the *Bildungsroman*, as a rites-of-passage narrative. Typically it depicts a young child of artistic sensibilities, brought up in the country or in the provinces. The family, particularly the father, constrains his imagination and school also proves inadequate to nurture his gifts. Two love affairs are shown, one debased and purely physical, the other exalted. The hero realises his artistic potential by escaping the provincialism of his environment and journeying to the city. The closure comes with the hero, confident in his artistic maturity, returning to visit the family. Though written by a young author, and close to the realities of that author's life, the *Bildungsroman* is presented as fiction rather than autobiography. Winterson's novel aligns itself with this traditional genre and, by including *Jane Eyre* within the narrative, points to other feminine versions of the form, but *Oranges Are Not the Only Fruit* carries a further disruption than just that of gender. It also combines with the 'Coming Out' novel, where the gifted but inexperienced heroine discovers her lesbian desire and is punished for her first affair by the community, with the lover often betraying her or reverting to heterosexuality. The 'coming out' format therefore subverts the genre even further, and takes over as the more contemporary and relevant form of the discourse. Where many critics have pointed to a universalist reading of the novel, Gamallo contends, as I have argued in chapter one, that the lesbianism is central to an understanding of the ideology of the novel, and that this is evident from a reading of the novel as an example of the *Bildungsroman*:

> ■ Winterson's construction of girlhood through fantasy, myth and fairytale challenges expectations about the conventional novel of growth and development while defying and unsettling any final interpretation of her own text. ... And it is this effort to free the reader 'for a time from gravity' that accounts for her use of fable and fairytales as a potentially subversive, and deeply destabilising, autobiographical device. By her interweaving of fabulous narratives, Winterson manages to build up a parallel and alternative plot that replicates and complements, while simultaneously problematizing, the realistic coming-of-age story. These fantastic tales comment on, explain, displace, condense, and/or allegorise some of the crucial elements displayed in the linear progression of

realistic events, subverting the possibility of a single, authoritative reading of her fiction.[56] ☐

Using *The Uses of Enchantment: The Meaning and Importance of Fairy Tales* (1978) by Bruno Bettelheim (1903–90) to argue that traditional fairy tales illustrate the psychological formation of the self, personifying inner conflicts and suggesting potential solutions, Gamallo amalgamates Bettelheim with the feminist criticism of fairy tales, as patriarchal attempts to socialise femininity, to theorise that Winterson's inclusion of mythical and 'folklike' stories allows her to switch between autobiography and myth in order to interrogate the formation of the female self and to argue for a different and alternative 'particular understanding of the world'.[57]

■ While discarding a single, autonomous, unitarian model of subjectivity, Winterson also conveys a clear awareness that experience – even auto-biographical experience – cannot be explained or legitimised by a single overarching narrative and that there is no one single established and accepted path through experience. Consequently, in Winterson's text we can find no reliable or unique pattern, historical, linguistic, or otherwise, but are forced to remain painfully aware of the instability and lack of finality of any narrative we construct. Since the act of storytelling itself is the most basic of all techniques for establishing an identity, the self becomes a constantly shifting entity, a product of language and narra-tives, and ultimately, a narrative in itself.[58] ☐

The self is narrated through the shifting boundaries of fairy tale and realism, illustrating and pointing to the self thereby always being in process. Multiple narratives thus lead to the assertion of that favourite postmodern thesis, the fluidity of subjectivity, alongside the refusal to see truth as singular that is made overt in the chapter 'Deuteronomy'.

In the final section, Gamallo argues that the destabilising, subversive potential of the fairy tales needs questioning from a feminist standpoint, since many feminist critics have established the patriarchal inscription within the tales, inscribing femininity as passive and functioning within the beauty myth through its 'source of negative and limiting stereo-types'.[59] However, fairy tales are not indelibly patriarchal, for all that they have carried that message during the eighteenth, nineteenth and early twentieth centuries, and Gamallo sees *Oranges Are Not the Only Fruit*, along with Angela Carter's *The Bloody Chamber* (1979), as part of the feminist rewriting of the fairy tale.

■ Contemporary feminist authors like Winterson are, however, currently engaged in utterly re-inventing the process. As we have seen, in many of the stories of *Oranges* gender roles are reversed, patriarchal values are questioned and problematized, and images of girlhood and femininity are challenged, subverted, or interrogated. Rejecting conventional gender hierarchies and challenging the cultural construction of heterosexuality, Winterson's storytelling becomes a source of alternative models of female identity. *Oranges*'s fairytales are inhabited by wise, resourceful, and brave heroines who make assertive choices instead of enduringly and self-sacrifingly staying at home, sweeping hearths and awaiting a charming prince. Winterson is undertaking the bold enterprise of rewriting the traditional tale in order to reinvent the position of women as gendered subjects in the patriarchal discourse of myth, romance, and fairy tale.[60] □

Gamallo considers how fairy tales can become 'countercultural' in the Marxist sense, and concludes that Winterson is also countercultural in her use of fairy tales. 'Loaded with a clear countercultural intention, Winterson's oblique and creative use of the folk- and fairy-tale tradition, her display of gender ambiguity, her disruption of the seductive happy endings of heterosexual romantic plots, and her offering of alternative models of female identity provide good evidence that storytelling is becoming an instrument of political subversion in contemporary feminist fiction.'[61] For Gamallo, the postmodern practices of intertextuality and plural narratives grant a fluidity of subjectivity that allows the young girl a feminist lack of structure.

Jan Rosemergy considers how the novel depicts the mother–daughter conflict, through the various discursive tropes of fairy tales and the metaphor of walls, for example, as part of a larger exegesis of motherhood in relation to the child's search for self-identity in Winterson's first four novels. 'Navigating the Interior Journey: The Fiction of Jeanette Winterson'[62] (2000) cites Elsie's illustration to the young Jeanette that she must negotiate both the external and the internal worlds, by banging first the wall and then her own chest, as seminal for this theme of the emerging self. Walls and pollution are metaphorically associated with the external, cultural world, the cultural expectations and gender stereotypes of both family and society as a whole. The mother is the child's defining experience of culture, one the child often needs to challenge, though mothers can be either oppressive or liberatory. The mother in *Oranges Are Not the Only Fruit* is the former, as the intertextual references cast her as first Abraham, dedicating the child to God, and then Zeus, creating his daughter through thought alone; though Rosemergy does not develop this masculine, authoritative analogy, it clearly links to Griffin's contention that the mother is a 'gatekeeper' for patriarchy. The search for the self is elaborated by creating one's own variant narratives via fairy tales, Arthurian myth and the fantasy orange demon. The fairy tale of the prince's search for an ideal woman, in 'Leviticus', dramatises Jeanette's own crisis in being unable to live up to her Evangelical community's expectations and the need to find her own answer to the balance between external and internal, within her own hands. The orange demon, Rosemergy suggests, is Jeanette's acknowledgement of the devil the church tries to exorcise from within her and stands for her unique and different creativity, the potential which will enable her to escape. Since walls enclose for both safety and imprisonment, Jeanette must learn to travel free of the laws of convention as she makes her own path in the world. Her choice of being herself, in exile from cultural values, is played out in the story of Winnet and the sorcerer. The magic powers the sorcerer teaches Winnet, an allegory for the imagination and the autonomy that the mother has fostered in Jeanette, will help her to create the magic chalk circle to surround herself with, a willed self-protection. Rosemergy focuses on how the Sir Perceval intertextual references centre on his hands, surprisingly unbalanced, with one sure of itself and the other discomforted, and suggests that the myth teaches that personal harmony is to be found in the hands of the quester's own self, but that this self is not a perfect one, far from it; Perceval demonstrates that it is the vulnerable, open self that will find the answer.

In 'Jeanette Winterson's Evolving Subject: Difficulty into Dream' (2003),[63] an essay arguing that Winterson's narrative mode develops from an intertextual variety of narratives, through the grotesque in *The Passion* and *Sexing the Cherry*, to the nomadic mode in *Gut Symmetries*, Kim Middleton Meyer begins by analysing *Oranges Are Not the Only Fruit*. Noting the similarities between Winterson's own life and the protagonist's in the novel, Meyer believes that this *Bildungsroman* blurs the boundaries of the literary genre; 'a thematic principle that allows the writer's life to spill over into her work is key to Winterson's literary practice. Rather than creating a *cordon sanitaire* [literally "a sanitary line", a measure designed to prevent communication or the spread of undesirable influences] between the two, however, *Oranges* aggressively works to trouble the boundary between fictional and "real" accounts of the author's experience.'[64] The main narrative adopts the realist mode and, linked to Jeanette's early Pentecostal experiences, the novel's chapters follow the first eight books of the Bible. Such intertextuality initially implies, Meyer suggests, an agreement with the Bible's strictures, but this is an assumption which the narrative contradicts. The diverse and intertextual narratives, rather than working for an authoritative view of the world, disrupt and dislocate the linear progress into a patchwork of meanings. The Sir Perceval stories, Meyer suggests, explore the Holy Grail of Jeanette's remaining within the church community as a lesbian, while Winnet shows Jeanette's escape from the power of the church and her oppressive mother. 'As these stories intersect with – and at points supersede – the guiding principle of each biblical chapter, Winterson calls into question any hierarchy of texts that might provide for the occlusion of others.'[65] Although narratives are important for how we understand the world, as discursive practices that help shape our subjectivity, no one text can ever be definitive. For Meyer, *Oranges Are Not the Only Fruit* argues for an aesthetics of plurality and uncertainty and paradoxically the 'multiple heterogenous stories' intersect 'to empower a young woman to shape her own identity'.

Where the criticism of *Oranges Are Not the Only Fruit* as a lesbian text came in waves, the critical discussion of the novel as a postmodern, plural-discoursed narrative had a more consistent pattern, averaging around one consideration per year from 1993 through to 2003 (that is, nine in the ten years). The critics largely agree on the reasons for the postmodern strategy of a fluid *mélange* or juxtaposition of stories crossing genre boundaries and subverting master narratives such as the Bible, in that the novel challenges the concept of a singular, bigoted, linearity of truth or meaning, and argues instead for a fluid, relative plurality of meanings. Bollinger, Cosslett and Meyer conclude that this is a specifically liberating strategy for women against a phallocentric culture. Doan, Onega, Brinks and Talley, and Gamallo see it as liberating for a lesbian within a culture of compulsory heterosexualism. Onega is the only one to raise the problem of feminist utopianism being at odds with postmodern deconstruction, as Duncker also discussed in chapter 1, explaining that postmodernism's deconstruction of the grand truths of history, via the New Historicists and Lyotard, the collapsing of the distinctions between story and history, results in history being seen as biased and subjective, a collection of relative truths only, but this proves a problem for feminists trying to establish a voice with which to demand change, and a stance of 'truth' from which to argue against oppression. Feminism's desire for a political presence finds it harder to embrace the postmodern 'death of the self'. For Onega, Winterson's answer, in asserting the juxtaposition of realism and fantasy, story and history, is to create a space of uncertainty and plurality that can accommodate the life writings of women, as a part of the myriad competing voices, a strategy of solipsism that she sees as equally modernist as postmodern. Cosslett sees Winterson as appropriating the intertexts and genres as a form of pirating, to form her own *mélange* or 'sandwich' that suggests a whole variety of different versions and outcomes to the plot, since no one version can be authoritative. Gamallo sees the crossing of masculinist genre boundaries as a countercultural strategy, claiming a feminine access to language, the Lacanian symbolic culturally denied to women, that refuses to be self-limiting.

Palmer, Bollinger and Gamallo all consider in detail the use of the genre of the fairy tale. Palmer sees the inclusion as partially a deliberate literary subversion, giving a feminist reading of fairy tales that regards them as phallocentric propaganda for young girls, asserting the active, heroic role for masculinity and the passive, victim role for femininity. Winterson's fluid transference of the gender roles, with both the mother and Jeanette taking on male personas at different times, suggests the transferability of gender (and hence a challenge to patriarchal notions of sex traits as given and fixed), while underscoring the phallocentric aspects of the original tales and appropriating the genre to a feminist rewriting with active, heroic female characters. Bollinger takes the same feminist reading of the traditional tales, but argues that the form, the genre, is too fixed and phallocentric to be available for appropriation by women writers. Gamallo, in contrast, agrees with Palmer and goes further, arguing that the genre is inherently transformative, because of its use of magic, where a frog can become a prince or Cinderella a princess. Using French feminism, Irigaray in particular, she states that the magic allows the feminine voice to be spoken and that, like Angela Carter, Winterson reinvents the genre through an appropriation that rebelliously challenges the patriarchal inscriptions.

Bollinger and Gamallo also consider the novel's use of the genre of the *Bildungsroman*. Gamallo gives a useful, detailed exegesis of the genre's traditional format. Bollinger argues that the canonical format is masculinist, because its structure reflects a male trajectory of an Oedipal discarding of the maternal home and a move outwards to the wider world; feminine trajectories involve a return and a reassessment of the maternal. The *Bildungsroman* genre is therefore yet another poor paradigm for women writers. Gamallo again disagrees, and analyses exactly how she sees Winterson as having radically feminised the form by amalgamating its format with a lesbian 'Coming Out' narrative. Alongside the consideration of how *Oranges Are Not the Only Fruit* subverts whole literary genres, the criticism also looks in detail at the intertextual use of three specific works: the Bible; Thomas Malory's *Le Morte d'Arthur* – although the version of the legend in *The Idylls of the King* (1849–72), by the Victorian poet Alfred Lord Tennyson (1809–92) is as useful an intertext of the Perceval story; and Charlotte Brontë's *Jane Eyre*. Of these three, the Bible has had by far the largest analysis, as befits a cultural 'master narrative' that is challenged by postmodern relativism. Palmer sees the intertextual choices from the religious text as deliberately incongruous in their use, as a form of mocking parody. Bollinger, having rejected the genres of *Bildungsroman* and fairy tale, finds in the Bible a feminised narrative in the Book of Ruth that gives an appropriate feminine voice for the mother–daughter relationship, stressing female solidarity and love. It also gives an appropriate narrative structure for the feminine trajectory of returning to the maternal and reassessing it, as she sees Jeanette doing at the end of *Oranges Are Not the*

Only Fruit. Brinks and Talley's reading of the Bible is surprisingly transformative; they see the mother's use of it as not prescriptive so much as subversive in her deconstruction of a patriarchal linearity and singularity, with the one chosen tribe and the one chosen leader, Abraham, for a self-willed matriarchy and a *mélange* of stories. They lay stress on Winterson's use of the biblical notion of the word as revelation, the generative power in the language that allows for the lesbian transformation of the familial domestic space. Cosslett, interestingly, agrees on the transformative power of reading practices, for all that she does not attribute this to the use of the Bible, but to the two literary intertexts. Her reading of the Bible sees it as purely prescriptive and judgemental and, in contrast to Bollinger, she contends that the Book of Ruth is not used to elaborate a women-centred loyalty, but rather loneliness and exile, since Winterson's pirating of the narrative deliberately omits the marital happy ending. Cosslett and Onega both argue that Jeanette does not return to the mother at the close of the novel, as Bollinger asserts, partially because they use a variety of intertexts and not just the Bible.

Cosslett also looks in detail at the Malory story of Sir Perceval searching for the Holy Grail and notes how Winterson suppresses the heterosexual element of Lancelot's affair with Guinevere in this intertextual usage too. She points out how Winterson focuses on the element of exile from Arthur and the Round Table, and delineates how Winterson has borrowed from other, earlier Arthurian legends to stress Perceval's youth and his innocence, his identity as a form of holy fool. Cosslett reads the grail that Jeanette is questing for, as a successful lesbian romance, while Meyer sees it as her desire to stay within the church and be accepted. For Cosslett, Winterson's appropriation of *Jane Eyre* has a different status within the novel, because it is overtly referenced, when the mother reads it to Jeanette, and the mother's rewriting of it is textually acknowledged. Winterson's reading practice, in appropriating and rewriting the earlier texts to her own ends, is seen as a liberatory strategy that challenges heterosexual marital closures and suggests more open and plural outcomes. Brinks and Talley agree that *Jane Eyre* along with Christina Rosetti's *Goblin Market* is used, through the mother's reading strategy, to challenge heterosexual happy families and to create an inclusive domestic space for the lesbian.

Finally, a number of the critics read the postmodern multiple narrative as not simply about postmodern intertextuality, but also as having a more psychological resonance that illustrates how subjectivity itself is constructed through the stories we tell ourselves. For Palmer, *Oranges Are Not the Only Fruit* demonstrates the multiplicity of selves within the postmodern fragmented identity, through Jeanette's imaginative fantasy identifications with various fairytale protagonists, illustrating both the fluidity of identity and of gender positions. Gamallo agrees in seeing the young girl's fabulation as linked to her personal formation of the self, a self-creation of a feminine voice that, through its variety and its crossing of genre boundaries, refuses to limit its potential. The self, via the differing narratives, is always shifting and always in process. Rosemergy reads the fairy tales as creative, psychic stories that the young Jeanette tells herself to navigate her construction of her own identity, but where she agrees with Palmer and Gamallo in seeing it as a self-creation, she also depicts it as singular, a psychoanalytic conception of the self, rather than a postmodern one. Meyer disagrees, seeing the novel as positing that narratives help to shape our subjectivity, but that no one narrative can ever be sufficient or definitive. In her reading, it is the very plurality and uncertainty of the narrative *mélange* that allows space for a feminine empowerment.

The critics' excitement with narrativity, the postmodern deconstruction of the divisions between history and fiction, and the fluidity of gender boundaries alongside the magical or fabulous in *Oranges Are Not the Only Fruit*, are all themes that are returned to in the critical discussion of Winterson's next two novels, the often overlooked comic novel, *Boating for Beginners* and the much more influential *The Passion*.

CHAPTER THREE

Boating for Beginners (1985) and *The Passion* (1987)

The critical construction of Winterson's oeuvre tends to omit *Boating for Beginners*, 'a comic book with pictures' as Winterson's website describes it, and thereby sidelines it from her other novels.[1] Not many critics have commented upon it, even in passing. When it first appeared, Emma Fisher in the *Times Literary Supplement*[2] was one of the few to review it in detail, opening of course with a reference to *Oranges Are Not the Only Fruit*, and explaining that this book questions what we do with issues such as reality, poetry and fiction when the Bible is no longer accepted as the revealed truth. Winterson in *Boating for Beginners* is playing a number of different games with the story of Noah's Ark, but she also mocks a number of other more contemporary aspects alongside fundamentalism – fashion, publishing and the food business, the romance genre, literature and literary criticism. Fisher gives a flavour of the book's comic narrative by looking at the characterisation of Noah, prior to the Flood. Noah runs a pleasure boat and is publicising religion by writing 'Genesis or How I Did It', which he is now turning into a film and in the process accidentally creates God out of Black Forest gateau and ice-cream. The comedic element does not prevent the book self-reflexively playing with its own narrative, carrying on from the 'Deuteronomy' chapter in *Oranges Are Not the Only Fruit*. 'This is self-consciously a writer's book', Fisher argues, pointing to the jokes about modern writers and how to write fiction and use fantasy. David Lodge (born 1935), considering Winterson's previous work before reviewing *The Passion*, claims *Boating for Beginners* is more radically postmodern in its narrative, and for this reason prefers it to both *Oranges Are Not the Only Fruit* and *The Passion*, even though it has not won the same accolades as them – 'it gave me more simple pleasure than the other two'.[3] Lodge sees it as a comic satire on the biblical 'Book of Genesis', where Noah exists in a contemporary, commercialised and media-saturated era. But then Lodge himself, both as academic and as novelist, had embraced the playfulness of the postmodern. He concludes that the novel is based on a detailed and even fond knowledge of the Bible, for all that it may be read as blasphemous.

Mark Wormald, eleven years later, considers this when he examines Winterson and Salman Rushdie's treatment of fundamentalism in their fiction.[4] Postmodernism, he points out, claims an end of ideology, but this only holds true for the postmodernists and not for the fundamentalists across the world, who embrace a very different set of beliefs. Their religious convictions are juxtaposed to Western liberalism and socialism. The

> ■ sheer frivolity of the linguistic detail of the writing emerges from a summary of the plot. Gloria Munde and her mother Mrs Munde take part in a Cecile B. De Millennarian remake of Genesis and the Flood, in which Noah is the director and God's omnipotence an accident that happens when Noah plays at being Frankenstein. Winterson's writing is more than usually anarchic, mining headlines and slogans from the literary culture of Shelley and since with an apparently random vigour, and applying the paraphernalia of late twentieth century consumerism to a decadent Nineveh with gay abandon.[5] □

Wormald relates how the hero, Gloria, finds the criticism of Northrop Frye (1912–91) in a railway station bookshop, and taking it for a romance adopts Frye's schema of development of language from metaphoric to didactic to prosaic as literally true. Gloria sees herself in the second stage, didacticism, but her mother remains fervently in the metaphoric, and this allows Wormald to analyse Winterson's voicing of the fundamentalist beliefs, 'Thus God's dayglow cloud, a neon display, descends proclaiming "GOD IS LOVE, DON'T MESS WITH ME" ',[6] even while he argues for her comic appropriation and subversion of them. The subversion, he shows, is yet another metaphor come to life; the orange demon from *Oranges Are Not the Only Fruit*, present because Noah's film of Eden has an orange tree rather than the traditional apple, illustrates the postmodern subversion of both narrative and fundamentalism, through its advocacy of plurality. 'It is then, ultimately the palimpsest[7] of patterns undercut, undermined, fluencies and fluidities interrupted by other fruits, from within a local literary history and from its outer reaches, which Winterson's own fiction becomes. The single, unitary, originary source of knowledge, and its old symbol, the fruit, the biblical apple, or the orange Jeanette's adoptive mother prefers, opens onto a plurality as fluent as its own segments.'[8] For Wormald, like Lodge, *Boating for Beginners* is 'more startlingly arresting' than the better-known previous work. Its comedy allows it to be something much more serious than merely a funny book; in its more schematic way, it is an equally challenging questioning of fundamentalist claims within a postmodern world. What, for Wormald, makes Winterson and Rushdie stand out from their contemporaries is the level of their knowledge of and inclusion of the texts they challenge, the Bible and the Qur'ān.

A year later, in 2000, Jan Rosemergy briefly considers *Boating for Beginners* in her examination of youth's quest for self-determination. The novel is a retelling of 'the biblical story of the Flood as a contemporary event, satirizing popular culture from religion to romance. Yet threading through the narrative is the story of Gloria, dominated by her mother, who is swimming to the surface of her life, coming to awareness.'[9] As her name suggests, Mrs Munde, the dominating, powerful mother, stands for the world attempting to define Gloria's identity. Gloria, so fearful of her power, must learn to create her own identity outside of the walls of her mother's vision. This is conveyed by the story of Gloria having to swim up from the deep pool to encounter the world of her mother; Rosemergy suggests that the water symbolises a birth or rebirth. Despite the mother's domination, she does tell the significant story of the young man looking for a secret knowledge. Of each of three women he asks for help, the old and young women do not help, but the third, the middle-aged woman, explains that he is destined to circle the world endlessly unless he looks inside himself. The three women, she suggests, could stand for the Great Goddess, and while the old and young represent the crone and virgin, the middle-aged woman could be read as the maternal aspect of the Goddess, and it is the mother who answers the riddle. 'This tale conveys a central premise about the quest for self which Winterson's fiction so consistently dramatises: although the quest involves an outward search leading to worldly knowledge, the quest ultimately requires an interior journey.'[10] Although Mrs Munde clings to religious precepts, despite her unhappiness with marriage, family or career, and tries to force them on Gloria, the church allows women a power unavailable elsewhere in society (again, like *Oranges Are Not the Only Fruit*) and Mrs Munde is celebrated as having a great heart. 'Because of societal walls of gender roles, the creativity of these women has been misdirected, yet still the "heart" deserves respect.'[11]

The most surprising aspect of the criticism of *Boating for Beginners* is its sparsity, perhaps related to what Wormald describes as Winterson's downplaying of its presence in her oeuvre. All the critics who do consider it, focus on its trope of comedy, some seeing it as frivolous and all as subversive. They discuss its postmodern self-reflexive narrative, and Lodge and Wormald also look at the blasphemy apparent in its rewriting of the Bible, which they agree is the result of a profound knowledge of the religious text. Wormald develops the clashing world views of religious fundamentalism and postmodernism in the novel and examines its attack on how advertising and the tabloid press have debased language. Rosemergy focuses on the mother–daughter relationship between Mrs Munde and Gloria, which she *sees* as echoing the relationship between Mother and Jeanette in *Oranges Are Not the Only Fruit*, and regards the novel as critiquing the church's prevention of women gaining more power within it. Lodge and Wormald prefer *Boating for Beginners* to the much more widely discussed *The Passion*, which they view as deprived of Winterson's anarchic humour, at least in any overt commentary.

Although later reviews construct *The Passion* in retrospect as brilliant,[12] the reviews at the time were, with some exceptions, less impressed by it. The *Guardian*[13] and the *Observer*[14] included it amongst a whole batch of new novels (six for the *Guardian*, three for the *Observer*) and so gave it a few column inches. Ann Duchêne in the *Times Literary Supplement*, despite some reservations about the 'cloudy' prose on passion, called it 'a book of great imaginative audacity and assurance',[15] while David Lodge in the *New York Review of Books* accords Winterson the space she would later command, with a two-page review and a line drawing of the author.[16] Lodge focuses on the inventiveness and the assurance of the novel, pointing out that whether Napoleon actually had a passion for chicken is immaterial – Winterson's authoritative poise persuades the reader to accept the historical details as if they were facts. Lodge concludes with a telling comment, perhaps from the voice of a comic novelist as much as a literary critic, when he outlines Romanticism as creating new myths but open to bathos in contrast to the more ironic self-consciousness of the modernists. Pointing to Winterson's first two novels which demonstrate her wonderfully absurd comic humour, he hopes she will not forget them in striving for a more serious tone, as she does in *The Passion*.

In a chapter of *Reading Dialogics* (1994) focused on *Sexing the Cherry*, Lynne Pearce made a swingeing comment that exercised later lesbian critics for the rest of the century. Pearce saw Winterson's portrayal of lesbian desire as a 'universalising' strategy that posited all love as being basically the same whatever the age, gender, race or orientation of the lovers. Such a strategy has often been criticised by queer theorists arguing for the difference of lesbian and gay desire, and it is along these lines that Pearce categorically dismisses *The Passion* as not being politically lesbian. 'Similarly in *The Passion*, Villanelle's love affair with another woman is made a part of the same romantic continuum as Henri's unrequited love for her, his hero-worship of Napoleon, or Patrick's fantasies about the mermaids. Despite her protestations that her desire for another woman was "not the usual thing", Villanelle's love affair cannot be said to be lesbian in any real political sense.'[17] That final sentence has proved contentious for critics of *The Passion*.

The more detailed critical analysis of the novel begins with three considerations of her oeuvre published in the mid-1990s: Laura Doan's 'Jeanette Winterson's Sexing the Postmodern' (1994), Cath Stowers', 'Journeying with Jeanette: Transgressive Travels in Winterson's

Fiction' (1995)[18] and Lisa Moore's 'Teledildonics: Virtual Lesbians in the Fiction of Jeanette Winterson' (1995).[19] Doan's discussion hinges on Villanelle's cross-dressing, which she reads, using Judith Butler's *Gender Trouble*, as a subversion of gender identities and gender boundaries. Cross-dressing thus becomes 'a cultural performance that illustrates how perceptions of external "appearance" and internal "essence" interrelate in a problematic state of flux'.[20] It is not so much that Villanelle hides one sex behind another's gender accoutrements, but that drag/cross-dressing questions the whole fixity of binary inner/outer, truth/disguise, and Villanelle comes to question who her 'self' is. Villanelle's body does this even more than her performance of genders, for her body traverses both sexes. 'Villanelle enters the male domain because of a genetic inheritance. The oddity of webbed feet can remain hidden for years beneath boots, but there is no mistaking the implications: the search for clear-cut distinctions where gender is concerned, is futile.'[21] Considering only Villanelle, and seeing her as figuring a postmodern trope, Doan concludes that 'What the reader discovers in the natural upset Winterson inscribes on Villanelle's female body (marking the masculine by the slightest tissue of skin strategically situated between the toes) or in Villanelle's probing interrogation of the "self" and the "real" is not a quest for a unified and coherent essentialized self but a consistent willingness to explore multiple and fragmented fictions of identity, that is, to engage in endless speculation.'[22] For her, Villanelle's fluidity, her ability to disrupt and deconstruct the binaries between male and female, raise questions about gender that allow an interesting space for the lesbian subject.

Lisa Moore's discussion of Winterson's remapping of sexual bodies, sexual boundaries and sexual identities, through the historical settings of eighteenth-century France and Venice, is one of the first analyses to focus on the theme of Romanticism in her oeuvre (identified by Lodge in his review) and to attempt to reconcile it with her postmodernism, by recourse to a lesbian aesthetic:

■ For all the obvious ways in which we can line up these novels with either of the slippery terms 'postmodern' and 'lesbian', Winterson's fiction also significantly refuses or complicates each of them. Readers of cyberpunk or David Lodge, for example, will find in Winterson's novels a perhaps disturbing faith in the transforming powers of romantic love, a Romantic investment in self-knowledge and sexual obsession, that accords ill with postmodern conventions of irony and isolation. These features of the novels, however, will be familiar to readers of lesbian fiction, in which 'all for love' is a recurrent theme and romantic obsession a structuring form; such themes and forms have characterized the important interventions lesbian novelists have made into the hegemony of the heterosexual love story, in the process creating their own canons and conventions. But Winterson's take on love is both romantic and Romantic, a fusion that produces interesting results. Her Byronic invest-ment in love-as-philosophy takes the form of a critique of the Cartesian subject [the individual unified by his ability to rationalise] that admirably furthers the goals of some postmodern theories. Perhaps surprisingly, the novels that most successfully challenge the modern regime of the subject-supposed-to-know are those set in its originary era, the European seventeenth and eighteenth centuries.[23] □

Moore develops this reading of lesbian obsession as challenging hetero-sexual depictions and thus creating plural love stories in relation to *The Passion*, one of the works set in the era of Enlightenment. Even though the novel's initial protagonist is a young man in the French army, he soon introduces the existence of lesbian women. Describing Villanelle accurately as bisexual, rather than lesbian, even though her significant love affair is with a woman, Moore also examines the minor characters whose lesbianism, significantly, is depicted as unremarkable, such as the prostitutes turning from the soldiers' brutality to the tenderness of each other's arms:

■ Henri's respect for lesbian relationships (including Villanelle's passion for the Venetian woman), the way in which they seem to dwarf his own, suggests a lesbian perspective made possible (paradoxically) by Winterson's use of a male narrator. For Henri, lesbian relationships exemplify the kind of passion for which he is searching. Thus lesbianism in *The Passion* is exemplary and definitive, rather than marginal and to-be-defined.

The novel's most sustained representation of lesbian cultural objects and conventions occurs in the 'Queen of Spades' section, when the novel is narrated from the point of view of Villanelle, a Venetian boatman's daughter. Villanelle is a girl born with a boy's body parts – the webbed feet characteristic of the males in her father's family fall to her. Birth attendants want to 'cut off the offending parts straight away' but the fans of flesh between her toes resist the knife, and Villanelle's hermaph-roditism remains intact.[24] □

Figuring Villanelle as the main lesbian protagonist, Moore suggests that her passion for the Venetian merchant's wife is defined in 'decidedly non-phallic' terms, particularly in its scene of the extended kissing where their bodies do not touch; this scene recalls, for Moore, the French feminist Luce Irigaray's construction of a lesbian eroticism focused on the mouth and vagina, in her theoretical essay, 'When Our Lips Speak Together' (1977).[25] Winterson is not only creating a lesbian presence in love stories, but also a decidedly lesbian erotica that negates traditional representations of erotic passion, and this links her to French feminist concerns with challenging a phallocentric view of female sexuality. However, while Moore sees Winterson as engaging in a lesbian aesthetic in her representation of Villanelle, she also views her as refusing to grapple with cultural homophobia:

■ It is this decisive distance from contemporary sexual politics that most clearly distinguishes Winterson's fiction and determines the way in which it will approach questions of history, identity and community. Such issues for Winterson are transcendent; her characters are engaged in the production of histories, identities and communities in ways that do not vary predictably along the lines of gender, sexual practice or historical period. This Romantic investment in the transhistorical qualities of human nature means that unlike other postmodern lesbian novelists such as Sarah Schulman [born 1958, author of *After Dolores* (1988)], Winterson is not intervening in or attempting to correct homophobic misrepresentations of or assumptions about lesbian relationships. Conflict in this fictional world is always romantic conflict. ... Thus, Winterson's novels may be read politically, but they themselves make no explicit political argument.[26] □

Moore's thesis of the 'virtual lesbian' in Winterson's novels argues that, rather than overtly depicting a particular lesbian existence and practice within the contemporary, Winterson's texts create a lesbian narrative strategy in relation to history. Her books argue for a fragmentation and relativity of sexuality and identity without necessarily embracing postmodernism's utopian deconstruction of difference which would leave the subject self-less. Winterson thus solves the hoary problem of how to develop a sexual politics while rejecting old-style humanist 'identity politics' within a postmodern era, through issues of form and aesthetics which, in *The Passion*, means the novel engages in issues of lesbian representation within the present of its publication, in 1987, even though it does not overtly represent contemporary lesbian characters. Instead, Moore argues, *The Passion* offers a negotiation of a romanticism of the body where the subject can be both 'fragmented yet still obsessed'. The subject position within the novel is therefore lesbian despite the rejection of an originary subject position. Moore's conclusion is that Winterson's narrative deployment of both postmodern and romantic practices allows for a decentred 'virtual' lesbian negotiation of narrative space.

Cath Stowers, in contrast, focuses on the travel narratives within *The Passion* in relation to actual historical documents. For her, it is the link to originary travel narratives that points to a feminine, and hence lesbian, voice. Stowers uses, as a model, the work of Sara Mills[27] and Mary Louise Pratt[28] on women travellers during the eighteenth and nineteenth centuries who, unlike their male counterparts, are significantly unconcerned with the discourse of conquest, mastery or exploitation in describing their travel experiences. These female voyagers give a different, more exploratory narrative of their travel experiences because of their gendered, marginal, subject positions within European culture. Stowers sees *The Passion's* traversing of the boundaries of separate countries as similarly unconcerned with discourses of mastery. Instead, she argues that, like the female travellers' narratives, it is a 'counter narrative' and as such, a form of *l'écriture féminine*, a specifically feminist discourse.[29] 'Can her repeated emphasis on cartography be read as symptomatic of a concern to reclaim woman and femininity, to write both onto the patriarchal map? Is fluidity of travel somehow connected with an attempted dissolution of gender binaries?'[30] She examines the narration of the various travels within the text as putting forward the two kinds of travel discourse, the masculine and the feminine:

■ Travel is figured in two differing paradigms. On the one hand, there are Henri's infantry expeditions and questing after Napoleon; on the other, the alternative model of Villanelle's shape-shifting, fluid Venice. Napoleon personifies the masculine linear force of history-making, rationality and war, where the feminine, woman's history, becomes charted out of sight, considered to have no place on patriarchy's official map of world events. Yet these tropes of travel are gradually re-worked in *The Passion* to disclose how history is not as indisputable as patriarchy would have us believe.

Set against the uniformity of Napoleon's military whereby 'straight roads follow, buildings are rationalised, street signs ... are always clearly marked' is the alternative non-uniform, multi-form model of Venice, which 'Not even Bonaparte can rationalise' ... Immediately a rebellious voyaging to new realms is made explicit, the focus on Henri's disobedient and contravening travels away from the masculine paradigm of Napoleon towards the fantastic – and decidedly female – Venice.[31] □

In unpacking history as itself a narrative, rather than fact or truth, Winterson challenges the dominant masculine discourses within culture and uses Venice as her place of difference, of femininity:

■ Already it should be clear that the innovative mercurial paradigm to which Henri turns has parameters which are not rigid or immoveable, and that this new female model spirals back and forth across time. Throughout *The Passion*, Winterson unsettles the taken-for-granted distinctions between past, present and future, in this place freed from linear temporality. Journeys, moreover, turn to a form of travel which is no longer based on the coherent, conquering self, being transposed instead to that mercurial interior exploration into a feminine multiplicity, a 'travel along the blood vessels' to 'the cities of the interior', 'another place whose geography is uncertain'.[32] □

Not only does *The Passion* feminise history and travel discourses, but it also challenges the construction of gender, in attempting to rewrite not only femininity but also masculinity. Winterson's fascination with feminising men, Stowers claims, is unusual as a lesbian strategy, the more usual form of which she sees as being either to demonise the male characters or to ignore them altogether (a strategy that *Oranges Are Not the Only Fruit* does develop).

■ Winterson goes further, however, than simply writing women into history. In keeping with feminist arguments, that we need to be aware of how much that very model of history owes to the patriarchal model which excluded women in the first place, Winterson has made clear the highly differing nature of women's history, in terms which figure a tracing of a female palimpsest: 'Women's history is not an easily traceable straight line. ... Following us is to watch for the hidden signs, to look in the gaps and be prepared for strange zig-zags' (Winterson, ['Introduction', *Oranges*] 1990, p. xxi). Henri offers just such an alternative anti-linear paradigm, countering the notion that history is composed of exceptional individuals and the public sphere of predominantly male activities. He veins the novel with his traces and memories of the home, the feminine, which has been lost: 'I was homesick from the start. I missed my mother.' Executing a re-positioning of history, a remapping of a palimpsestic herstory, he sets the 'stories' of his notebook against that history where 'old men blurred and lied'. Rejecting any claims to truth, stressing the subjective, story-telling nature of his accounts, Henri becomes reminiscent of what Mills and Pratt have identified as a rejection of any authoritative narrative voice by *female* travellers.[33] □

Henri's feminine representation challenges the binary oppositions of traditional gender roles just as effectively as Villanelle's masculine one. For Stowers, *The Passion* is not only a feminine text but also a lesbian text that works through its narrative of displacement to challenge the unitary, universal voice used by both realism and history. Stowers views Winterson's theme of a boy journeying away from the feminine and then returning to it, a recurring one which she also finds in *Sexing the Cherry*, as helping to unsettle and rewrite gender in a feminine, and ultimately lesbian, discourse.

Like Moore, writing in the same year, Stowers challenges early lesbian critics of *The Passion* and *Sexing the Cherry* as having turned their backs on lesbian politics, and looks instead to the discursive strategies of the novels for her thesis of a lesbian aesthetic. Both of them are written, in part, as responses to Lynne Pearce's brief dismissal of *The Passion*'s lesbian credentials because, in her view, it normalises same-sex desire out of existence. Both Moore and Stowers, looking at the narrative strategies in more detail, conclude that Winterson deploys a complex lesbian narrative aesthetic that proves to be a profound critique of heterosexualism.

The year 1997 saw two articles focused solely on *The Passion* as the text gained in critical status, one on the trope of gambling particular to Villanelle, the other on her city, Venice, in relation to Romanticism. Venice was also the focus in a further critical essay. Bényei Tamás's 'Risking the Text: Stories of Love in Jeanette Winterson's *The Passion*'[34] is particularly useful in its analysis of the gambling motif in its relation both to risk and to passion, through its use of *Visions of Excess* by Georges Bataille (1897–1962).[35] Gambling, Tamás explains, is one of Bataille's significant metaphors for how to live, 'to describe obliquely what he calls sovereign existence, a mode of life that characterises the world of passion. The Sovereign person is ruled by a will to be, subordinated to nothing, and refuses to conduct his or her life according to projects and plans; like the gambler, like the true Venetian, he or she forgets in order to live every moment as a moment of chance, risk and danger.'[36] Tamás unpacks Bataille's use of gambling as a metaphor for life and love, through the concept of passion, a conjunction that is shared by both Bataille and *The Passion*:

■ Gambling and passion are closely interrelated for Bataille; even though he admits that the former is an inferior manifestation of what he imagines as the supreme mode of human existence which seeks opportunitites of self-annihilation that are also opportunities for transgressing the discontinuous self. In religious and sexual passion, the self attempts to transgress its boundaries (lose itself) in a tangible, physical manner; in gambling, the desire to lose is much more abstract. Nevertheless, he sees in both the

> Life that measures itself against death. ... Acts undertaken in pursuit of seductive images of chance are the only ones that respond to the need to live like a flame. For it is human to burn and consume oneself to the point of suicide at the baccarat table; even if the cards reflect a degraded form of good and bad fortune, their meaning, which wins or loses money, also possesses the virtue of signifying destiny (the queen of spades sometimes signifies death).
>
> [Georges Bataille, *Visions of Excess*, p. 231]

As Villanelle, a gambling addict herself, puts it: 'Gambling is not a vice, it is an expression of our humanness.'[37] □

For Bataille, as for many analysers of gambling, the ultimate desire is to lose, rather than to win; but for Bataille this means a loss of the self rather than just money, which Tamás links to Villanelle's macabre story of the gambler who wagers his life:

> ■ According to Bataille, the gambler risks life, and his or her ultimate, secret desire is to lose: to lose the self, to be wrenched from ordinary, discontinuous existence. The protagonist of Villanelle's parable gets what he deserves and also exactly what he desires. Automutilation – that is, dismemberment at his own hands – is the consummation of the limitless desire to lose: 'the necessity of throwing oneself or something of oneself out of oneself remains the psychological or physiological mechanism that in certain cases has no other end than death' [*Visions*, p. 67]. The impulse behind gambling (and behind passion) is the desire to lose: 'Pleasure on the edge of danger is sweet. It's the gambler's sense of losing that makes the winning an act of love' □   [*Passion*, p. 137][38]

Villanelle, as the gambler who loses her heart to the Queen of Spades, demonstrates a life lived to excess and a self lived for the moment, and for the transcendent experience of passion. Winterson, Tamás argues, has come close to delineating the 'Sovereign' existence and has done this through the metaphor of gambling which goes further and affects the very narrative itself: 'The logic of gambling is provided by the tension between repetition, forgetting, and chance. Its temporality is based not on a causal, successive contiguity but on the rupture between the individual games, a rupture that erases the memory of the previous games. Its time is not a narrative time, or a time amenable to narrative – which might prove a key to the ambiguities of story-telling in *The Passion*. One of the refrains of the text that contributes to its repetitive, ruptured texture is this: "I'm telling you stories. Trust me." '[39] Georges Bataille has proved a rich and useful model for Tamás, in his reading of Villanelle's code of how to live, in contrast to the code that imprisons Henri in his madhouse. And through enacting its excess, he argues, the novel gets close to verbalising passion itself, the experience which transcends words, the 'unsayable'.

Judith Seaboyer takes up the theme of Romanticism in 'Second Death in Venice: Romanticism and the Compulsion to Repeat in Jeanette Winterson's *The Passion*',[40] focusing on the representation of Venice as a central topos of 'beauty and decay'. She gives a psychoanalytic interpretation that argues the book figures both the French and the Venetians as examples of Freud's 'death drive'. Her reading of Venice is of a city complicated by its many representations; 'the *idea* of Venice has come to serve a wider purpose than it did for the Romantics. For Winterson, Venice is a site within which the neat binary opposition of

true/false, pious/sinful, mind/body, masculine/feminine, Thanatos/
Eros [Death/Sex] collapse into a mixture that is at once confusing and
stimulating.'[41] Seaboyer divides Venice into two representations: the
first, the initial view of it as a floating world, offers an '[i]maginary
wholeness defined and contained by the surrounding moat of the
Adriatic',[42] the second view is of a labyrinth, which links it to the psychic journey of the self, surrounded by metaphors of abjection and
decay. This second representation, linked to the drive for death, she sees
as the predominant one of the novel. Through the similar descriptions
of being duplicitous and ambivalent, this Venetian urban space is linked
to representations of the female body. The two protagonists, Henri and
Villanelle, crossing from Napoleon's death camps to Venice's maze of
streets, negotiate 'a doubled labyrinth that is a site of birth, rebirth, and
reunion and a wasteland of exile, fragmentation, and death'.[43] While
Venice restores Villanelle, it drives Henri to madness and despair, coming as he does from a repressed, passionless people. France, through
repressing passion, allows the drive to pleasure to be channelled into
patriotism and hence ostensibly into the death drive, whereas Venice
is able to acknowledge pleasure as vital, and so resists the calls to
patriotism:

■ Armed conflict is exposed as a form of erotic displacement. The
unconscious desire for death masquerades as love, as the psychic drive,
which has no pregiven object, is all too easily redirected from the pursuit
of sexual love, children and community onto nationalism and *patria*,
Napoleon and empire: 'He was in love with himself and France joined in.
It was a romance. Perhaps all romance is like that; not a contract
between equal parties but an explosion of dreams and desires that can
find no outlet in everyday life.' The characterizing of the French as a
passionless people is of course an oversimplification. Winterson's
Venetians, with just as little basis in historical reality, seem not to be
susceptible to ideas of nationalism because they are not afraid to feel,
and so passion is not displaced. Venice's defeat by Napoleon brought to
an end a thousand years of independence, and while it is clear that the
French are scorned, they are ignored rather than hated; there is no suggestion of resistance, no suggestion that blood must be spilled in order
to restore lost national virtue. Instead of joining in the destruction that
is the conspicuous effect of French nationalism, Venetians have simply
'abandoned [themselves] to pleasure', and Venice has become 'an
enchanted island for the mad, the rich, the bored, the perverted'.[44] □

Seaboyer argues, using the later psychoanalyst, Lacan, that Freud
misread the death drive as a desire for stasis, for the stillness of unbeing
or the wholeness of being within the mother's body, but that it is this

drive for death-in-life that Henri elects for on San Servolo:

■ In a text whose trajectory takes it through eight years of war, and which ends in mutilation and murder, these layers of repetition uncannily inscribe on its surface and in its deeper structure what Freud posited is the subject's inarticulable longing for death. The text – or at least that portion of it related in Henri's voice – is on one level hystericized, the poetically encoded symptom that Henri constructs to maintain a fiction of coherence in the face of disintegration. 'Hysterics', as Joseph Breuer famously said,[45] 'suffer mainly from reminiscences', and reminiscence is embedded and re-embedded in Henri's narrative, which is a mixture of elegiac memoir and melancholic spiritual autobiography, a remembrance of things past.[46] □

While Henri follows the death drive, Villanelle chooses the more fluid and healthy route of pleasure and life, and this pleasurable route is signalled by her name: a form of poetry. Seaboyer's analysis of the musical form of the structure is particularly erudite:

■ Winterson's interest in musical form is more overt in *Art and Lies*, also set in part in Venice ... but *The Passion* is much influenced by T. S. Eliot, including *Four Quartets* [1943], and, like that poem, the novel recalls a musical structure. Its four sections could suggest a composition for two voices in imitative counterpoint – a fugue, perhaps. The voices are very different, but each turns upon the theme of passion, love, and loss. The opening theme is presented in a first movement by Henri. It is taken up and repeated in a different key, in a second movement, by Villanelle. In the third movement and in the closing coda, the voices interweave. Themes, phrases, and leitmotifs introduced and repeated in one movement by another voice are taken up and modulated in another movement by the other. It is a kind of dialogue, but it also suggests the way in which the repressed returns – and is returned to – again and again, in an *unheimlich* [Freud's term for the uncanny][47] recapitulation.

To stay with formal repetition, the lyrics of this 'fugue' recall the highly stylised, highly repetitive poetic form of the villanelle for which Winterson names her Venetian hero.[48] □

Manfred Pfister's '*The Passion* from Winterson to Coryate'[49] gives a more sustained analysis of the text's construction of Venice, with an illuminating historical contextualisation. Venice, he claims, 'is one of the most frequently and "thickly" represented places on this earth'. And he goes on, 'Everything in Venice is a palimpsest – down to its cats and down to the minor islands in the lagoon. Even San Servolo ... is not her literary discovery.'[50] San Servolo, initially a monastery before being turned into a hospital for the mentally ill, was used by the Romantic poet Percy Bysshe Shelley (1792–1822) in the poem 'Julian and Maddalo' (1819). A footnote observes that Winterson probably discovered San Servolo and the Shelley poem in Jan Morris's popular guide to Venice,[51] since, Pfister claims, all her information on Venice can be found in this travel guide. Pfister argues that Winterson's construction of Venice as a place of passion, both in the religious sense of suffering and in the secular erotic sense, has been used by English and American novelists and dramatists from the early modern Thomas Nashe (1567–1601) and William Shakespeare (1564–1616) through to the contemporary late twentieth-century Ian McEwan (born 1948) and John Berger (born 1926). 'Such stories construct Venice as a place of ardent and illicit, or transgressive passion, of *eros* and *thanatos*, of love and madness, of sensuality, licentiousness, prostitution and sexual perversion – as an Other that exceeds and endangers the symbolic order of the Self. And, indeed, these are not stories that the Venetians tell about themselves and to themselves, but stories written about them by foreigners and, more often than not, also crucially involving foreigners.'[52] For all the outrageous strangeness of Winterson's construction, it is also very familiar to those who have studied the literary representations of Venice. From the concept of it as labyrinthine, a maze, through to its shifting fluidity, a city of chance and madness, these descriptions can be found in English literature from the Renaissance and the Grand Tour through to the Romantic poets. Like other critics before him, Pfister looks at Venice as a place of difficulty for mapping, 'the fixitive art', and pushes his analysis further to examine the way Venice is characterised.

He unpicks how Winterson's text, like many before it, orientalises Venice, particularly through the Queen of Spades and her husband's travel curios, a Venice seen as liminal, as crossing the boundaries between Europe and the Orient because of its trade routes. It is also traditionally a place of performance and gender trouble due to the famous Venetian carnival, the time when everyone wears masked fancy-dress and transgressions can be performed incognito. The carnival, through the work of the critic Mikhail Bakhtin (1895–1975), particularly in *Rabelais and His World* (1968), has been seen as the popular site of transgression and misrule. Pfister contrasts Henri with Villanelle in his discussion of subjects of performativity:

■ Winterson's Henri, the timid Frenchman, obviously is no Lord Byron [Romantic poet, and contemporary of Shelley, 1788–1824]. This is why he dreams of returning to his unspectacular native village and refuses to return from the island of real madmen to the staged derangements of reason and the senses in carnivalesque Venice. He remains the undisguised in this 'city of disguises', which is Villanelle's city. Her Venice is not unlike the *città spettacolo* [city as spectacle] of the traditional fictions and fantasies: she works at the Casino, a place of subtle make-believe and deception; she participates in the celebrations of Bonaparte's birthday and New Year's Eve, that turn night into day, in the fabulously histrionic funerals and the fairs with their acrobats and their women 'who are not all of them ... women', she 'basks' in the theatricality of staged religion. Most importantly, her gambling and thieving involve staging her body in ever changing masquerades, particularly in cross-dressing, which makes her sex or heightens its ambiguous allure: 'It was part of the game, trying to decide which sex was hidden behind tight breeches and extravagant face-paste.'[53] □

In his final section on gender trouble, Pfister argues Venice has always been known for its courtesans. 'Venice and Venus were actually seen as etymologically related, and many a text punned upon the phonetic closeness of the two names.' But where Venice has been seen as the Scarlet Woman, this has historically been overwritten with the masculinisation of the city as potent symbol of the Doge, or of Neptune. Venice, then, has for centuries clearly always been figured as a place of gender issues and gender trouble, and Winterson's novel uses these stereotypes and conventions for her

■ fantasies of a sexually transgressive and metamorphic Venice. Here, too, erotic desire cannot be contained within the social code and symbolic order of binary gender divisions; it is as fluid, unstable, labyrinthine and amphibious as the city itself. Neither is Henri, smallish, passive, shy, and introvert, a paradigm of potent and self-asserting masculinity, nor is Villanelle unambiguously a woman. Her magically webbed feet mark her as a man rather than a woman and so does her, for a Venetian woman, unusual tallness and the smallness of her breasts. She seems to quite naturally take to cross-dressed masquerades, in which her androgynous charm makes her attractive as a lover and as a prostitute to both male and female suitors, and she in turn is attracted to both and has 'taken [her] pleasure with both men and women' – particularly with men who, like Henry are not imposingly male, and women, who, like the Queen of Spades, are bi-sexual like herself. Villanelle's lesbian desire for her, whose ominous name suggests the conjunction of male and female, *eros* and *thanatos*, is, however, the overruling passion of her polymorphous romance; ...

There is a religious intensity to her passion, and one of the leitmotifs actually situates religion and passion between 'fear and sex'. This blurs the borderlines between religious and sexual intensity, between religion and sex, in a way that is not unprecedented in the narratives and fictions of the travellers of Venice.[54] □

Winterson, Pfister therefore suggests, in choosing Venice as her place of liminality, transgressive perfomance, excess and passion, continues and reinforces the stereotypes used by English writers since the sixteenth century. Hers is an all too familiar depiction of the city. However, where she does differ from earlier narratives of Venice, and so break with former traditions, is in her positive promotion of the irresolution and indeterminacy. Where earlier writers saw it as a place of negated morality, Winterson sees it in much more positive terms as a place open to difference and plurality:

■ The crucial difference resides rather in a different conception of the self. Where the older confusion of the religious and the erotic could always be disentangled in terms of a religious hypocrisy that masks a real sexual licentiousness, with Winterson's Villanelle the passionate self is unentwinably sexual and religious at one and the same time. Where, in the traditional representations, Venice was male primarily in political contexts and female as the *città galante* [city of gallantry], Winterson's tropes define it as irresolvably androgynous. Where the transvestite masquerades observed, or engaged in, by the Grand Tourist were seen as a deviancy from the true self and its true gender identity, with Villanelle the distinction between self and mask does no longer apply. 'And what [is] myself?' she asks, and the answer the novel suggests is that it is neither her 'breeches and boots self' nor her 'garters'. One is as much a masquerade as the other, and her gender identity is as indeterminate as the masquerade in which she constantly re-defines it. In other words – not her own, but Judith Butler's: her self and her gender identity enact and define themselves in her performances: they are not stable essences but essentially and passionately performative. And so is Winterson's text which, in its interweaving of Henri's and Villanelle's voices and narrations, performs a subjectivity beyond binary divisions. And so is, finally, her Venice: all staged performances that, together, act out and explore the indeterminacies of in-betweenness – in between.[55] □

Pfister's erudite analysis of the representation of Venice in *The Passion* manages not only to show how similar it is to other, vastly different novels, poems and plays, but also to push through to showing equally how different it is in its postmodern deconstruction of fixed notions of gender, sexuality and self. For Pfister, unlike Moore, sees postmodern's deconstruction in purely positive and liberatory terms.

In the *Postmodern Studies* collection edited by Grice and Woods (1998) two essays discuss *The Passion*: Scott Wilson's 'Passion at the End of History'[56] and '*The Passion*: Storytelling, Fantasy, Desire' by Paulina Palmer.[57] Wilson provides a playfully fictional analysis of the novel through the voices of two 'future' characters. Henri's pregnant landlady discusses Henri's 'end of history' narrative where everyone has a say about the past, since everyone is different, in contrast to Hegel's originary concept of the discourse. Hegel's concept of history, Wilson asserts, fails because it leaves out the issue of desire:

> ■ For Hegel there is the master, the slave, and then there is Napoleon. But Napoleon is mastered in turn by his desire for chickens. The trouble with dialecticians, Winterson seems to suggest, is their inability to count up to four. Everything comes in threes: thesis, antithesis, synthesis. ... In his theory of history, Hegel did not consider a fourth term: something that could allow for chance, the unpredictable, the contingent, some event or happenstance, some predilection that exceeds the grasp of Spirit's all-consuming knowledge. Spirit, in Hegel's upwardly spiralling history, never seemed to fall in love. Spirit never fell on its knees in the glorious abjection of a grand passion. Dialectical history does not record these moments, they are left unremarked and forgotten.[58] □

Henri's postmodern narrative insists on taking passion and experience into account. In the second half of the essay, Ludwig, the grandchild of Henri and Villanelle, discusses Villanelle and passion in relation to Bataille, and then lists all the aspects feminist critics have seen Villanelle as figuring, 'chance, ecstasy, passion, synchrony, difference, to which I could add poetry, laughter, cruelty'[59] and the ways in which her sexually indeterminate lesbian desire has been discussed, while interposing the fact that she has also been a mother and as such stands as a trope for maternal difference. Ludwig mocks such earnest academic speculation with his comment, 'How like a woman to be expected to do so much *work*.'[60] Wilson's narrator concludes that the dismembered hands stand as the final moral of the text: that beyond the Hegelian desire for recognition and passion's desire for the love object, lies chance and the willingness to risk whatever one values most.

Paulina Palmer's more traditional critique argues that *The Passion* fits Linda Hutcheon's term 'historiographic metafiction'[61] for postmodern texts that parody and rewrite history for present concerns, and that for Winterson these concerns are significantly lesbian. Calling Henri a radical depiction, Palmer argues that it is he who introduces the lesbian discussion. Henri is feminised, taking on the traditionally feminine role of cook during the Napoleonic campaigns; he 'bridges the gap' between masculine and feminine worlds. Henri's inability to kill anything, even a rabbit, and his heightened sensitivity are at odds with the rest of the army, and his feminised character is portrayed as being due to his closeness to his mother. It is Henri who reveals her oppression, in being forced into marriage, and he also comments on the military camp's dehumanising of women. When the cook mistreats the woman in the brothel, Henri portrays the novel's first lesbian relationship. 'In addition to alerting the reader to women's oppressed plight, Henri also introduces the topics of compulsory heterosexuality and lesbian relations, both of which are integral to the novel.'[62] Palmer is thus setting up her argument that the text is focused on sexual politics in a specificially political sense, in order to challenge Lisa Moore's reading of Villanelle, in 'Teledildonics'. Henri's feminisation sets the scene for Villanelle who 'acts as a signifier for lesbianism throughout the text'[63] as she equally reverses traditional gender constructions as the masculine woman. Although Villanelle cross-dresses and loses her heart to the Queen of Spades, Palmer again points to the text's development of compulsory heterosexuality when circumstances force Villanelle into marrying the fat man, later revealed to be the abusive cook, and then into prostitution. Palmer argues that all Villanelle's affairs with men result from necessity, rather than from desire, and in this she mirrors Henri's own mother and the camp prostitutes. The only real passion that we witness is the nine-day lesbian affair with the Queen of Spades. Palmer has thus set up her reading to counter Lisa Moore's thesis that Villanelle's representation of lesbianism lacks political resonance in neither engaging with homophobia nor constructing lesbian love as problematic within conventional norms – a thesis which Moore is developing in relation to Pearce, remember, and arguing for a lesbian aesthetic if not a lesbian representation. Palmer, however, claims that the text is precisely lesbian in its representation because it does discuss the problems: Villanelle's affair ends abruptly when the husband returns and the text reinforces the 'outsider' nature of lesbianism within the oppressive sexual politics of compulsory heterosexuality:

■ A particularly moving incident, one which depicts the position of the lesbian in hetero-patriarchy as 'problematic' in the extreme, is the episode in which Villanelle, positioned in the marginal role of outsider and voyeur, to which throughout history the lesbian has generally been relegated, gazes through the window of the Queen of Spades' villa and watches her conversing with her husband in the social and financial security of the family home. He plants a kiss on his wife's forehead, affirming his ownership of her and signalling the control which he exerts on her life. This episode illustrates the constraints which a phallocentric economy imposes on women's lives, separating and inhibiting relations between them by curtailing their sexual and social freedom.[64] □

Villanelle, in refusing to marry Henri, and in getting him to rescue her heart for her, challenges the script of normalcy; 'instead of allowing him to co-opt her into becoming an actor in his drama, she induces him to perform a part in hers'.[65] Moreover, Villanelle wrests the narrative from him, to become the main narrator in his stead.

Having thereby argued for *The Passion* as a lesbian narrative, and as a specifically political lesbian narrative that highlights lesbianism's problematic and marginal status, Palmer turns to consider what exactly the term means in 1990, and how it has changed from the early years of lesbian criticism in the 1970s, when, linked to identity politics, a lesbian narrative simply meant a text written by a lesbian, for a lesbian audience, with identifiable lesbian characters and situations. More recent criticism has shifted to examining the more formal elements of the text, given the contemporary debates about defining the lesbian identity and about the 'death of the author' (Roland Barthes [1915–80], in an essay 'The Death of the Author' [1977], declared that the writer has no authority over the meaning of the text, the meaning is down to what the reader *finds* within it). Palmer demonstrates two formal elements in *The Passion* which have been identified in recent criticism as present within lesbian narratives: firstly, a disruption of 'heterosexual narrative structures and scripts, resulting in the reformulation of relations between the sexes and the refiguration of female desire,'[66] secondly, a triangular sexual relationship between two women and one man, in contrast to the usual triangle of two men and one woman. Villanelle's appropriation of both the story and the narrative from Henri, and hence her shift into agent within the novel, illustrates the first trope, Palmer argues, while Henri's love for Villanelle who loves the Queen of Spades, produces the second. Within the parameters of contemporary lesbian criticism, *The Passion* still successfully fits as a lesbian narrative. Moreover, the characterisation of Villanelle displays the contemporary queer strategy of foregrounding lesbian difference from other women, rather than a feminist focus on similarities. Her webbed feet are a sign of her grotesque bodily difference from traditional notions of femininity. Like Moore before her, Palmer links Villanelle's excess to Irigaray's lesbian aesthetic and focus on the mouth and, through the text's metaphor of the acrobats kissing, allies the performance of lesbian sexuality to stylisation, artifice and the precarious. Like Pfister, Palmer applies Butlerian notions of the cultural perfomativity of the self and gender to Villanelle's cross-dressing, so that the character highlights both the arbitrary nature of gender and sexuality and also the excess of femininity which, critical theory has argued, is appropriate to the characterisation of the lesbian performance. She ends with a consideration of the novel's narrative strategies. 'In keeping with a poststructuralist approach to textuality and the formation of the psyche, we have the impression that, rather than the text reflecting the individual self, the subject is a relational identity constructed through discourse and textuality.'[67] Passion takes over the self or subject, at times, dominating its reactions, whether it is desire for a woman, a chicken or a territory. The text erupts into magic realism at moments of heightened intensity as if to show how passion transmutes the ordinary into the fantastic. Alongside this, we get the complication of real historical events, personages and military campaigns. This jumbled focus on the narrative's artificiality leads to a self-reflexive treatment of story-telling, whether Henri's exaggerated *account* of his military adventures to the gullible villagers, or his 'factual' descriptions to us of Patrick's magical eye and Villanelle's webbed feet. His and Villanelle's repeated exhortation, 'I'm telling you stories. Trust me', simultaneously reassures the reader as to their veracity, while reminding us that it is a piece of fiction they are telling. The narrative thus challenges traditional founding distinctions such as fact/fiction or history/literature by playfully blurring the oppositions. Palmer concludes with a brief examination of how *The Passion* is an intertextual rewriting of the Venice in the postmodern *Invisible Cities* (1979) by Italo Calvino (1923–85, Italian novelist), exchanging his masculinist eroticised view of the city for a lesbian fantasy. Palmer therefore gives a full reading of the novel as both postmodern narrative and lesbian text.

A year later she returns to *The Passion*, looking at how it fits into the Gothic genre,[68] in her book *Lesbian Gothic: Transgressive Fiction* (1999).[69] In a study which argues that lesbian writers have used the gothic genre and thereby transformed it, she places *The Passion* in a chapter that deals with 'Spectral Doubles':

■ A feature of the conventional ghost story that writers of lesbian fiction frequently exploit is the portrayal of the spectral visitor as reflecting aspects of the heroine's identity and circumstances and representing, in this respect, her ghostly double. Winterson makes effective use of this device in *The Passion*, utilizing it very differently ... Instead of centring her text on the protagonist's encounter with a spectral visitor, she introduces the motif intermittently throughout, employing it to underpin the themes of love and war that the novel treats and to accentuate their emotional resonance.[70] □

As well as the motif of the double, Palmer finds other lesbian gothic tropes in *The Passion*, such as the use of the abject, and images of the grotesque. A novel that employs a male narrator to focus on war for the first half, and yet portrays an intense lesbian desire in the episode with the Queen of Spades, is an inventive and contradictory anomaly. It is also ambiguous in its political strategies, utilising lesbian feminist denunciation of compulsory heterosexualism and its oppression of lesbian agency, and a more queer political strategy in its merging of the heterosexual and homosexual dichotomies and in its suggestions for subversively different family groupings. Even the novel's overall tone is anomalous. 'The exuberant atmosphere of carnivalesque festivity and misrule that pervades many of the episodes is undercut in others by references to the spectral and the emphasis on the abject realms of death and *déréliction* which Winterson utilizes it to evoke.'[71] Palmer calls Winterson's treatment of Henri 'radical' in the way she links the masculinist and the lesbian, and she reiterates the argument of the previous year, in having Henri introduce the elements of compulsory heterosexual oppression on his own mother, and his experience of lesbian tenderness among the camp prostitutes. But her agenda is different now, for she is constructing a reading of Henri that allies him to queer theory. 'Winterson's portrayal of Henri, in deconstructing conventions of sexual difference, bridges the gap between these two different worlds. Henri displays traits conventionally regarded as feminine, such as sensitivity and a distaste for killing.'[72] His love for Villanelle and her refusal of his love are now seen as celebrating lesbian agency in rejecting heterosexualism.

> ■ By portraying herself not as the object of Henri's passion but as the lover of the Queen of Spades, she successfully positions herself in the text in the role of active agent. Role reversal and the deconstruction of conventions of sexual difference, as the active part she plays in the narrative illustrates, are as important a feature of Villanelle's portrayal as they are of Henri's. Whereas Henri exemplifies attributes conventionally regarded as feminine, Villanelle displays qualities typecast as masculine, such as daring and initiative.[73] □

Palmer sees the link between the two main characters as developing an ever more complex and challenging construction of relationship and gender:

> ■ Winterson depicts the two characters forming a bond which, in its emphasis on role reversal and its subtle blend of the 'brotherly' (on Villanelle's part) and the erotic (on Henri's), challenges the orthodox division between homosexual/heterosexual dimensions of experience and, in conflicting with conventional familial formations, emerges as distinctly queer. In transgressing the limits of their respective gender roles, both characters are stigmatised by society as freakish and odd. Henri's lack of aggression and his expressions of disgust at the brutal way in which the army treats women elicit derisive comments from his comrades, while Villanelle's independent attitude arouses puzzlement and indignation in many of the men she meets.[74] □

Palmer argues that *The Passion*, like the other lesbian gothic novels to which she compares it, does not try to fit lesbian characters into conventional frameworks, but rather strives to accentuate the difference from ordinary women and the rejection of the roles of wife, mistress and mother, as Teresa de Laurentis advocates in her essay 'Sexual Indifference and Lesbian Representation' (1993).[75] For de Laurentis, the best way to do this is to portray lesbian sexuality as 'otherwise' from heterosexual images, and to promote the lesbian difference through the motifs of the monstrous or the grotesque. Palmer links Villanelle's webbed feet to this element of the grotesque, indicating how it not only identifies her difference but also carries with it overtones of the animalistic, which homophobia often utilises as an expression of its disgust. Using Bakhtin's analysis of the grotesque in *Rabelais and His World* in relation to the carnival, with its ramifications of misrule and transgression, she points out that Bakhtin argues that the grotesque body is not fixed but in process, always becoming:

■ It thus comes as no surprise to the reader to find that, in portraying Villanelle, Winterson associates the morphology of the lesbian body, both literally and symbolically, with movement – frequently of a vertiginous kind. In addition to depicting Villanelle admiring the dexterity of the trapeze artists who visit the city of Venice during the Carnival festivities and climbing the railings to catch a glimpse of the Queen of Spades, she also represents her defying the laws of gravity. Emulating Wittig, who in *The Lesbian Body* (1973), represents the beloved gliding and hovering above the sea, she portrays her performing the miraculous feat of walking on the water of the canal.[76] □

Such an analogy of circus performer also places lesbians as outcasts from conventional society and evokes the 'image of vitality and transgressive jouissance [a psychoanaltytic term for extreme, surplus pleasure]'[77] in their performance upon the high wire that repels connotations of women as passive objects of the male gaze. Instead, 'the lesbian or woman-identified woman parodies the role of spectacle and entertainer that phallocentric culture assigns to her, exploiting it for her own particular ends'.[78] Finally, the richly expressive analogy with the acrobats and the trapeze artists also conveys the precarious dangers of being lesbian within a heterosexualist culture.

The dangers that Palmer delineates are both physical, in the abuse homophobia can launch against overt lesbians, and also symbolic in the danger lesbians run of being turned into a male sexual fantasy and thus placed back within the male specular economy of desire. Villanelle herself must walk a tightrope to escape heterosexualism: 'In order to survive the homophobic climate in which she lives and avoid falling into the abyss of shame, she has to strive to keep her balance and maintain a sure footing on the high wire.'[79] Taking this metaphor of the lesbian as acrobat into the depiction of Villanelle and the Queen of Spades having sex, focused on the mouth rather than the genitals, Palmer concludes that 'Winterson, in a typically poststructuralist/queer manner, associates lesbianism with artifice and stylisation.'[80]

Having explored the concept of the grotesque in depth in her reading of Villanelle's character, Palmer finally turns to the issue of the spectral double, highlighted by the title of the section she places Winterson's novel in. Where the carnivalesque acrobatics signal the positive transgressions of the lesbian representation, the novel also contains more disturbing elements such as the spectral and the abject, linked to death and a fascination with darkness, which both Villanelle and Henri share. Henri is 'haunted' by the horrors of war that he witnessed during Napoleon's campaign which, through his memory of corpses, can be read as an example of the conception of the abject developed by Julia Kristeva (born 1941) in *Powers of Horror* (1991).[81] 'The spectral corpses that invade Henri's fantasies, as well as being a device to impress the horror of war upon the reader, give us an insight into his psyche; they evoke both his feelings of guilt at participating in the bloodshed and his fear of death.'[82] For Kristeva, the corpse is both a carrier of pollution and in a liminal state between life and death, a shockingly destabilising image. When Henri is imprisoned on San Servolo and goes mad, he sees the ghosts of his past life, including Napoleon, but refuses to accept that they are his projections and insists that he converses with the dead. Henri's encounters with the spectral link to his experiences of war, while Villanelle's are linked to Venice and to love. Venice is the place of carnivalesque excess, but also the place of death, with funeral cortèges of gondolas ferrying the dead to the island cemetery of San Michele. Villanelle in Venice

> ■ encounters, as is usual with the entry of the heroine into the realm of gothic fantasy, a mirror image of herself. Catching sight of her reflection in the water of the canal, she sees 'in the distortions of my face what I might become'. She also encounters a more disturbing *doppelgänger* [double]. This is the unnamed woman with 'ghoulish green hair' ornamented with a crown of rats' tails who has made her home in a nook in the wall of one of the canals. Despite the derelict circumstances to which she is reduced, she boasts a set of ornate goblets, interpreted by Villanelle as a relic of her former aristocratic lifestyle, and entertains a group of invisible guests to supper with strips of rancid meat. She has an uncanny habit of materialising at crisis points in Villanelle's life and uttering warnings couched in riddlingly sibylline phrases. As a result, Villanelle regards her as a spectral messenger with access to occult powers.[83] ☐

Palmer reads the woman in two ways, firstly as the obverse, darker side of carnival, who stands as an omen for Villanelle at the end of the novel, alone, without either Henri or the Queen of Spades, as she rows a boat on the water. Secondly, she sees her as figuring the lesbian; her 'grotesque appearance and weird behaviour representing the monstrous image that patriarchal society assigns to woman/lesbian. She haunts the city of Venice in a manner similar to that in which ... the presence of the lesbian haunts hetero-patriarchal culture.'[84] Her character evokes a sense of the uncanny, entirely appropriate for a gothic atmosphere, and helps to turn what might be a solely celebratory novel into something much darker and more emotionally complex.

Jan Rosemergy traces the formative self's search for its own freedom and expression in *The Passion* as well as *Boating for Beginners*, as she examines the theme in Winterson's first four novels. She claims that the only real gender roles in *The Passion* are those of soldier or woman and the masculine role is one of aggression, both for the enemy and the prostitutes who serve Napoleon's army. Gender roles, Rosemergy argues, are a form of disguise but one that the text does not present as changeable. The soldiers are keen to feel adventurous passion and glory, but since they cannot, experience rage instead. 'As Napoleon brutalizes his soldiers, so the soldiers brutalize women, trapped in their gender roles of "meat" for men.'[85] When Villanelle suggests that Henri go with her to the city of disguises, Venice, Henri points out that his uniform is already a disguise, since Henri's 'true identity' is neither aggressive nor brutalised. This of course also accords with Villanelle's cross-dressing, since wearing a dress is no more real for her than wearing breeches. Her mix of sexes, demonstrated by her webbed feet, is hidden from the world and the feminine gender restricts her ability to be a gondolier. The fact that the two narrators sound so similar shows, for Rosemergy, 'that gender masks the essential self'.[86] The city of Venice, with its maze of streets and canals, is a journey that must be deciphered, in the exploration of selfhood:

> ■ The interior city symbolizes the interior self. When Henri, lost in Venice for five days, asks Villanelle for a map she replies that it would be useless, that the city is alive and changing, that the 'cities of the interior' are uncharted. This journey of the self, like Venice's canals, leads one in unpredictable ways; one must freely explore multiple paths. Henri recalls his boyhood face refracted into multiple images in his father's shaving mirror where he recognized the many possibilities for his future identity. Similarly, Villanelle saw her girlhood image refracted in the water of a Venetian canal. Ultimately, then, unconfined by a single identity, the self has many possibilities.[87] □

Rosemergy seems strangely unsure of how to figure identity in her exegesis of *The Passion*, seeing Villanelle as having an essential 'true' core and a variety of sliding possibilities, but her tracing of the concept of the performativity of gender through clothes and mirroring is a useful reading.

Where in the other texts she looks at youth's quest for self or selves, in this novel she sees the quest as being for passion instead, 'yet the two are inextricably bound together. Why does one seek passion? ... To escape ourselves ... but tragically in objects not worthy of our obsessions.'[88] Henri's passion is for Napoleon, but war is not an adequate release, indeed it is too destructive of our future. Neither does he find passion in the cold cathedral where he attends the Christmas mass, recognising that soldiers freeze emotion so as not to feel the pain of loss and death. 'Winterson transforms the cliché of losing one's heart from the figurative to the literal, first in Henri's story and then in Villanelle's', Rosemergy argues, concluding that the moral of these loss-of-heart stories might be 'that one must gamble, take risks, in order to discover what one values'.[89] Together, the narratives of Henri and Villanelle, man and woman, intertwining history and fiction, prove the most trustworthy way of seeing the world, because truth is not singular but multiple and relative.

In her essay, 'Jeanette Winterson's Evolving Subject' (2003), Kim Middleton Meyer's consideration of Winterson's narrative representation of subjectivity moves from *Oranges Are Not the Only Fruit* to *The Passion*. As with the earlier text, it is the multiple and heterogeneous narratives that Meyer focuses on, in relation both to the dual narrative of Henri and Villanelle, and to the mix of fantasy and history. Napoleon's history carries the same structuring authority in this novel as the Bible did in *Oranges Are Not the Only Fruit*, but here this structuring discourse is not undermined by the other stories. 'Neither superseding nor rejecting history outright, *The Passion* uses fictional narrative to expand and infuse objective historical fact with the specificity of human responses. ... Here, two forms often considered oppositional work together to imagine the ways that traditionally neglected historical voices could add depth and texture to flat factual accounts.'[90] However, Meyer sees *The Passion* as making a major shift from the first novel's use of fantasy to using instead the trope of the grotesque in its doubling. Where in *Oranges Are Not the Only Fruit* fantasy and realism cancel each other out in a warring of discourses, in this novel the dual narratives posit a dialogism that incorporates both within the one text. '*The Passion* exhibits the double in the single, a union of the two giving birth to a new "grotesque" form.'[91] It is in this novel that Meyer sees Winterson, in adopting this grotesque narrative mode, beginning to write postmodern historiographic metafiction. The two narratives, initially so dissimilar, converge in the second half of the novel, with Henri telling the story of Villanelle in Napoleon's army camp during the zero winter, and Villanelle telling the story of Henri's incarceration. Fantasy still plays a part, with Villanelle's retrieved heart and her webbed feet, but it undermines the power of the grotesque. 'Critics argue that even the most transgressive work of the grotesque is only an outgrowth of the real itself, which then uses fantasy to channel the revolutionary energy of the people solely into the realm of the imaginary.'[92] Henri's closure parallels this discourse, as he retreats into fantasy or madness in his island prison, but Villanelle holds out more hope as she rejects the 'disguises' of cross-dressing to accept her real nature. 'History and fiction, horror and fantasy – the grotesque formations that *The Passion* enacts allow for improbable narrative unions that hold out the promise of multiple interiorities to be explored, but at the same time reassert their inability to impact a world governed by realist notions.'[93]

In the same year, also in a chapter examining Winterson's oeuvre, this time in relation to the body, Jago Morrison begins by identifying the paradox of placing Venice, a 'counter-historical space',[94] at the centre of an avowedly historical novel, set during Napoleon's attempts to invade Britain and then Russia. Like others before him, Morrison focuses on Venice as a liminal space: 'Emerging from the water of the lagoon and intimately penetrated by it, it exists in a liminal relation between land and sea. It is a city of bridges that divide and connect rival territories, thresholds of neutrality where duels and deals are concluded, and canals whose labyrinthine contours interconnect with secret waterways and sewers that are not marked on the map.'[95] Winterson extends this spatial liminality into the representation of time as well, thus linking it to Bakhtin's term for the textual representation of time and space, the 'chronotope' (see chapter one). Just as Venice is spatially unmappable, so 'on a temporal level, the city is over-saturated with the power of memories and desires',[96] a place where all time exists in the present. While the two protagonists lead empty and meaningless lives during the Napoleonic campaign in Russia, simply performing the duties expected of them, the 'chronotope of Venice is precisely the opposite to this – a model of intimacy, uncertainty and possibility'.[97] This uncertainty relates specifically to how gender and sexuality are represented within the city. 'Established conventions lose power in a city where the past and future are shifting and subject to reinvention. It is a place where one can get lost, elude the past or be recaptured by it, a place where the permeable boundaries of classes, genders and sexualities erotically interpenetrate in a carnivalesque masquerade.'[98] Morrison elaborates how both Villanelle and Henri are constructed as indeterminate, between gender expectations, and often wear disguise or masquerade. In the camp Villanelle is forced to perform the subordinate role of femininity; only in Venice is she allowed the power of webbed feet. 'Only in the city does the mark of hermaphroditism take on meaning, opening up multiple, undefined possibilities for adventure and escape.' However, Morrison sees the central episode of Villanelle and the Queen of Spades as too 'cartoon-like' to be anything other than a parody.

'The image of the woman reunited with her heart is, in itself, a joke about the traditional idea of biology-is-destiny. When Villanelle tasks the enamoured Henri with stealing her heart from her lover's villa, the novel twists up various heterosexual romance narratives.'[99] Henri hopes, by rescuing her, to gain her love as his reward, but the novel refutes such a romantic happy-ending. Attempting to repeat his adventurous role, he next hands her the heart of her brutal husband as an antithesis to the traditional ending. Such an ending to the novel, with Henri entrapped in his tower, refusing rescue, rejects traditional narrative closure and ends on an opening up of a range of possible futures.

Winterson's *The Passion* has received a good range of critical analysis, since the mid-1990s, being taken quite rightly as a major and significant novel in her oeuvre. The range within the criticism has been less broad; most critics have focused on the lesbian representation and particularly lesbian narrative tropes or aesthetics, and on the city of Venice. The discussion of the lesbian representation began with Lynne Pearce's dismissal of Winterson's politics in 1994. A year later, Lisa Moore argues that though she may not be overtly polemical, and hence political, by developing a lesbian aesthetic of an 'all for love' desire and eroticism within an historical past, she is creating a 'virtual lesbian' narrative that is all the more effective for being less on the surface. Paulina Palmer then takes up Moore's argument in 1998, to challenge the view that *The Passion* is not political, since she claims it does present the cultural homophobia that lesbians have to contend with. It is also lesbian aesthetically in its tropes of the lesbian wresting the narrative from the male, and in presenting a love triangle where women dominate. Both Palmer and Moore discuss the issue of what constitutes a lesbian narrative within a postmodern critique, where the self of author or character is not fixed by sexual preference. Cath Stowers's assertion that it is a lesbian text ignores this debate, and focuses on the idea that it is a feminine, 'counter' narrative, in relation to its treatment of history and geography. Moore, Palmer (1998) and Stowers argue for its openness to French feminist analysis; Stowers, implicitly, to Hélène Cixous's thesis of an *écriture féminine* (a specifically feminine form of writing), Moore and Palmer (1998) to Luce Irigaray's lesbian feminist eroticism, and Palmer (1999) to Monique Wittig, who will become such an important reference for *Written on the Body*.

Geography becomes the next largest area of debate, in relation to Winterson's treatment of Venice. Stowers's feminist reading views Venice as the site of femininity and difference, in being opposed to Napoleon's linearity and fixitive map-making. Seaboyer's psychoanalytic analysis sees its labyrinthine maze as linked to pleasure and eroticism. Where eroticism is repressed, Venice leads to a desire for death and destruction, while if it is openly acknowledged it leads to health and to children. Rosemergy assents that Venice is represented as an internalised topos, and cites both Villanelle and Henri encountering refracted images of their childhoods, while Palmer (1999) agrees on the darker elements of the city, referring to the funeral cortèges of gondolas and the weird woman with the crown of rat's tails, as linking Venice to decay and the grotesque. For Pfister, with his careful tracing of the European orientalising of the Italian city, Venice stands for the libidinal and the fluid, a site of instability, performance and gender trouble. Morrison agrees that it is a liminal space, but allies time to the fluidity of the spatial, to argue it is a 'chronotope' of uncertainty and possibility. As in the past, Venice has proved a rich and complex metaphor.

Stowers initially links geography to history, to note the novel's confusion of linearity, an aspect that Seaboyer also picks up on. But it is left to Wilson to focus on the novel's postmodern challenge to history and historiography, in his playful fictionalised critique of Hegel's nineteenth-century view of what History should be, and of how *The Passion* problematises this grand claim for a master narrative and, with Henri, breaks it down into a series of mini or micro narratives, whose very plurality refutes Hegel's conception.

Where Wilson and Seaboyer construct Henri as the important protagonist to exemplify the novel's presentation of history as a discourse, or the negative drive to nationalism and the myth of wholeness, and Moore and Palmer see him as important in questioning gender stereotypes by his feminine characteristics, Tamás and Wilson, alongside the lesbian critics, see Villanelle as the major character because of her lesbian desire for the Queen of Spades and because of her embracing of a gambling, reckless way of life that they link to the ideas of Georges Bataille. Villanelle has been the focus of a number of critical discussions, both as a lesbian character and as a model of how to live within a fluid world. All agree that Villanelle deconstructs gender binaries, through her 'masculine attributes' of agency and independence, in contrast to Henri's more 'feminine' attributes of sensitivity and distaste of killing, and most highlight her webbed feet as problematising the cultural inscriptions of gender on the body and the body's own potential liminality. Morrison reads her as a hermaphrodite. For Palmer (1998 and 1999), the webbed feet signal a queer strategy of emphasising lesbian difference from other femininities. Her cross-dressing and disguise are seen as illustrative of gender as a performance, and of the fluidity of gender as an inscription.

Finally, Romanticism is an interesting categorisation in some of the discussions. Lisa Moore presents it as a founding aesthetic in the novel, which marries with Winterson's postmodern deconstruction of fixed assumptions to allow for a lesbian assertion of the importance of their sexual preferences, love as the highest value that transcends history. Seaboyer opens with the Romantic poets' presentation of Venice as site of beautiful decay and death, and Pfister develops this in detail in relation to Shelley and Byron's love of Venice, and to Shelley's poem 'Julian and Maddalo'. Palmer (1999) and Meyer go further back than Romanticism, to argue for a darker, gothic influence. For Palmer, the ghosts, spectral visitors, decaying corpses and Henri's abjection and madness, as well as the grotesque elements of the weird woman and Villanelle's feet, counter the exuberant carnivalesque subversion of the novel, with a grimness that creates a more complex emotional tone. Meyer sees the way fantasy undermines the discourse of history and the grotesque 'doubling' as part of a gothic horror trope. Seaboyer agrees with the motifs of abjection and decay but links it to a psychoanalytic reading of the death drive.

The Passion has been given a wealth of analysis, much of which discusses its postmodern deconstruction of the discourses of history and imperialism and of gender construction, while taking for granted the delineations of a postmodern narrative – an assumption that is unlike the discussions on *Oranges Are Not the Only Fruit*, but which points to the critics' growing comfortableness with Winterson's juxtaposition of history and fantasy, with the grotesque, the dual, relative narrators and a self-reflexive narrativity. This kind of postmodern mélange, or mixture, is pushed to its height in her next novel, the acclaimed *Sexing the Cherry*.

CHAPTER FOUR

Sexing the Cherry (1989)

In an interview given at the time of *Written on the Body*'s publication,[1] Winterson explained that the inspiration for *Sexing the Cherry* was a painting, by some unknown Dutch artist, of Charles II being given the first pineapple in England. She suggested that one could divide artists into priests and prophets – the priests offer solace and comfort whereas the prophet offers material that is much more challenging. Casting herself in the role of a prophet, *Sexing the Cherry* is duly challenging, more a poem than what one expects from a novel, with commentaries on time, truth and history developed from Winterson's interest in post-Einstein physics, which argues that reality is simply 'a trick of the light'. And, though accepting the label of lesbian feminist for herself, she claims the writing is not lesbian feminist, with all that entails.

The reviews of *Sexing the Cherry* have much more prominence than those of the previous novel, *The Passion*, demonstrating Winterson's continuing rise in status as a serious literary novelist. Shena MacKay in the *Times Literary Supplement* opens her review by linking the novel's themes to Winterson's previous work.[2] Identifying time, matter and reality as the central focus of *Sexing the Cherry*, as the novel time-shifts between the seventeenth and the twentieth centuries, she sees Winterson as engaged in the rewriting of history, as is recent New Historicist criticism, and argues that it is a continuation of the same theme from *Boating for Beginners* and *The Passion*. *Sexing the Cherry*, with its historical character of John Tradescant the Younger (1608–62), botanical explorer and gardener to the king, 'is a sort of *Boating for Beginners* meets Swift, Defoe, Hans Andersen and Mary Poppins, the New Physics and Green Politics'. Despite the glorious plethora of inferred influences, Mackay is ambivalent about the book as a whole. Praising, as all ambivalent reviewers usually do, the beautiful writing, she none the less feels that the *mélange* of fact, fantasy and exhortation never quite melds together and the central metaphor – of the grafting of a Polstead black cherry on to a Morello cherry stock, the resulting hybrid being a female – is one whose significance escapes her. She concludes that she is unable to decide whether the book is profound or just pretentious. MacKay's confusion over the significance of the grafted cherry is perhaps understandable, given the speed with which reviewers have to turn their copy around, but the significance of the grafting has been amply interpreted and developed by later lesbian literary critics, who often see its symbolism as one of the main strengths of the text. Another reviewer as uncertain as MacKay at the time, was David Holloway in the *Sunday Telegraph*. Although *Sexing the Cherry* was given the accolade of being chosen as the 'Novel of the Week', Holloway's review signals his uncertainty about its quality;[3] the relevant word for his review is 'maybe'. There are aspects that he sees as pretentious and silly, much that is difficult and exasperating, and some material that is deeply disturbing (the perversions in the brothel and the beheading are cited as examples). The rendering of seventeenth-century London, however, is completely riveting. Interestingly, Holloway locates his own disconcerted ambivalence about the novel in the realm of gender difference, suggesting that what we are being shown is truly a feminine fantasy and thus is unsettling to male readers, whose fantasies and dreams are very different.

Not all reviewers were unsure about the novel, though. Lorna Sage (1943–2001), a feminist academic, proved comfortable with issues of gender and complex narrativity in the *Observer*. She opens with a playful re-examination of light fiction, arguing that in contemporary literature 'light' no longer stands for superficial or easy reading but, in a blurring of the boundaries between popular and serious, means, rather, inventiveness that is eminently important without needing to be earnest in order to signal its importance. The review continues by claiming that Winterson has defied gravity in producing a novel that is a 'comprehensive celebration of weightlessness'.[4] The extremely favourable review concludes this theme with the comment that the novel is the very best of light reading available. Sage's more formal examination is of the multiple narration, which she links to the postmodern notion of multiple selves within the subject. She links the structure of the text to the appropriate seventeenth- and eighteenth-century picaresque mode of writing fiction. This mode, where the narrative simply follows the protagonist from place to place, country to country, is one that refuses a teleological form (a form which focuses its meaning by the closure) and hence is useful for postmodern texts. It was one that Sage's friend, the novelist Angela Carter, had used in *Nights at the Circus* (1984). But it would be wrong to imply that the reviewers were split along gender lines. In contrast to Holloway, Kenneth McLeish's review in the *Sunday Times* was positively gushing,[5] as he argued that Winterson's name is in itself a guarantee of readability. Where Holloway finds the subversion in the novel specifically feminist and therefore alienating, McLeish sees it as culturally more wide-ranging, envisioning Winterson as a literary skinhead of the carnivalesque. He singles out the character of the Dog Woman, arguing that she is an attractively Rabelaisian giant, wreaking havoc on the Puritan hypocrites. Jeanette Winterson is presented as a kind of skinhead raging against society, but doing so within a rarely used generic form of the 'Gothic farce'. In the USA, Michiko Kakutani, in the *New York Times*,[6] welcomed the wonderful inventiveness of the novel, explaining that its strength lies in its juxtaposition of the mythic alongside the commonplace, the wonderful and the terrifying. He dislikes, however, the interpolated digressions into love, time and identity, which he sees as marring the text by their cod philosophising, and he finds the addition of the two contemporary alter egos of the characters in the latter half of the novel similarly unconvincing. Nevertheless, his final assessment is largely positive: in *Sexing the Cherry*, Winterson is as inventive as a latter-day Scheherazade, the story-teller of the Arabian Nights, combining the keen parodic wit of Jonathan Swift (1667–1745) with the gossamer fantasy of a García Márquez (born 1928).

Two days later, in the prestigious *New York Times Book Review*, Michael Gorra[7] opens with a list of the fruits that had been used by Winterson up to this point, including oranges, cherries, pineapples and bananas, arguing that fruit has always stood as a metaphor for sexuality, and the new description via the pineapple is of an exoticism unknown to the commonplace. Enjoying the narrative mix of history and fairy tale, he is more exercised by the gender bias of the book. He sees the men as the butt of the text's antagonism, suggesting that the only ones to escape denigration are those who indulge in a bit of cross-dressing. However, having called it to our attention, he then confesses that the gender bias did not spoil his enjoyment of the novel and asks: if Kingsley Amis can use the novel as a form for his dislike of women, why can't Winterson repay the compliment? The lack of integration in the structure is more of a problem, since for Gorra the themes of gender are never related to the themes of time and both are close to being literary clichés of postmodernism by the 1990s. What saves the novel, for Gorra, is the 'emotional intensity' of the writing, and he ends on a favourable and almost lyrical commendation, explaining that what makes Winterson unique as a postmodern writer is her fascination with exuberant gender performance and gender ambiguity alongside a more melancholic focus on abandoned children, which sounds a note of emotional pain that gives depth and meaning to the text's playfulness.

All the reviewers focuses on the complex narrative, the postmodern juxtaposition of fact, fantasy, history and fairy tale, half feeling unsure about its effectiveness (MacKay, Holloway, Kakutani), while the other half embrace it with enthusiasm (Sage, McLeish and Gorra). Both Gorra and Holloway felt disconcerted by what they saw as the feminist agenda, Gorra discomforted by the attack on men, Holloway disturbed by the unpleasant brothel scenes. MacKay felt the novel was overly didactic, while Kakutani and Holloway found it pretentious. Sage and McLeish, on the other hand, welcomed it as bringing a whole new sense of lightness or farce to the serious novel. MacKay saw its focus as a rewriting of history, Gorra as cross-dressing and sexual ambiguities. Whether the reviewers were thrown by *Sexing the Cherry*'s complex narrative or whether they embraced it with delight, all the reviews on both sides of the Atlantic accorded Winterson a prominent position within the book sections of the newspapers.

Paulina Palmer, in her 1993 discussion of how the representation of subjectivity in Winterson's early novels relates to the narrativity of the texts, argues that *Sexing the Cherry* is more complex than *Oranges Are Not the Only Fruit* because it has two narrators.[8] To add a further complication, these two narrators illustrate how identity crosses history as well, in the guise of their two twentieth-century alter egos: 'identities and psychological attributes are envisaged as transcending the boundaries of time and space. Jordan and the Dog Woman are seventeenth-century figures, and each has a twentieth-century double or counterpart who displays analogous qualities and attitudes.'[9] The Dog Woman's alter ego is the twentieth-century ecologist whose fight against the pollution of a river with mercury by big business corporations mirrors the Dog Woman's angry attack on the Puritans who kill King Charles, and try to force England into their bigoted and narrow morality. 'Both women are ridiculed as "monsters" – the Dog Woman on account of her exceptional size and strength, which are regarded as unfeminine, and the present-day figure on account of her radical views and commitment to a politics of direct action.'[10] Jordan, the other protagonist, develops the theme of subjectivity, both in his philosophical enquiries and his quests across the world, suggesting that identity is multiple, a conglomeration of selves for each character. This extends into the fluid interaction between seventeenth-century subject and twentieth-century alter ego, in his case Nicholas Jordan. The fluidity between selves and characters is highlighted in Jordan's quest for Fortunata, the dancing princess whom he devotes so much time to searching for while yet questioning whether he is searching for the living woman, rather than what she stands for in himself, the projection of his own dancing self. This fictionality of the characters is developed by the self-reflexivity of the novel. 'The ambiguous relationship which some of the characters bear to reality – are they "real" or imaginary, we are prompted to ask? – highlights one of the novel's key themes. As Winterson playfully reminds us, by drawing attention to the fictionality of the text and the acts of representation which its construction involves, the question is ultimately meaningless since all the characters portrayed in it are fictions.'[11] In its self-conscious playing with the fictionality of the narrative to highlight how the individual subject is also a fictional self-construction, *Sexing the Cherry* continues the postmodern practices of *Oranges Are Not the Only Fruit*.

Palmer also considers whether the novel can be called a lesbian text, given that all of its protagonists are heterosexual, and concludes that it can be said to deal with the subject in an 'indirect' fashion. The only overt reference to lesbianism comes in the episode of the Twelve Dancing Princesses, where Winterson rewrites the fairy tale to connote lesbianism as a political choice, as the women reject patriarchal expectations and abuse, to choose in its place relationships with other women. 'Winterson portrays the princesses as liberating themselves, in some cases by violent means, from their husbands' control. Instead of living happily ever after in marital bliss, as convention dictates, they set up home together in a female community. The various narratives assigned to them highlight the social and economic power which men wield and the brutal punishments which they inflict on women if they dare to transgress the conventional role of object of exchange by forming sexual relationships with one another.'[12]

Palmer also sees the Dog Woman as a character that can be read as quasi-lesbian since her size serves to defamiliarise traditional relationships within a phallocentric culture and, in particular, to subvert the power relations in heterosexual coupling. Since the Dog Woman is so large, her male partner's penis is too insignificant to have any effect, a ridiculing of phallic power in relation to the feminine. The Dog Woman performs a number of amazing acts, like tossing elephants or scooping up handfuls of Puritans. 'Though recognizing that her height, flat nose and heavy eyebrows conflict with conventional concepts of beauty, she none the less prides herself on being "built to proportion". A writer with a phallocentric viewpoint would no doubt treat her as a target of ridicule but Winterson, writing in the tradition of the lesbian/feminist re-evaluation of the image of woman as monster, treats her in a celebratory manner. She focuses attention on her heroic qualities and describes her as representing the rebellious, transgressive aspect of femininity which patriarchy attempts to suppress.'[13] Palmer thus argues that *Sexing the Cherry* functions effectively as both a lesbian and a feminist text.

Lynne Pearce's chapter in *Reading Dialogics*, entitled 'Dialogism and Gender: Gendering the Chronotope',[14] looks at the use of fantasy in both *Sexing the Cherry* and *Beloved* (1987), by Toni Morrison (born 1931). Pearce's negative view of Winterson's oeuvre sees it as universalising lesbianism and so a disappointment for lesbian readers looking for specificity and difference to be accorded to women's same-sex desire. It is a thesis that perhaps articulates the confusion of Shena MacKay within a lesbian context:

■ Lesbian readers, in particular, have experienced this 'sliding' of gendered and sexual identity – this refusal to 'name' – as a serious political betrayal. What texts like *The Passion* and *Written on the Body* would seem to say is that love is love: that gender, age, class and ethnicity, nationality and social orientation are all accommodated within the great universals; that desire is an emotion that transcends all specificities, and which we all recognize and experience as 'the same thing'. In *Sexing the Cherry* ... as in *The Passion*, this universalism is ensured by the inclusion of a broad spectrum of characters of different gender and sexual preference. The stories of the Twelve Dancing Princesses in *Sexing the Cherry*, for example, place accounts of heterosexual and homosexual desire side by side, hence 'normalizing' the latter and giving the impression that one's sexual preference is a matter of chance not choice.[15] □

For Pearce, the strategy of using fantasy and magic, which other critics tie to French feminist or postmodern strategies of voicing 'otherwise', is seen as detrimental to a serious political agenda. 'It could be argued that it is by removing her characters to the realms of fantasy and history that Winterson has left behind the question of what it is to be a woman and/or a lesbian in any more material sense. Although *Oranges* is no more "realist" than the other novels in textual terms, its protagonists have to bear the historical and political consequences of their generation, gender and sexual preferences. In *The Passion, Sexing the Cherry* and *Written on the Body*, these constraints are apparently discarded as the characters free themselves from the shackles of "the single life".'[16] Concentrating on analysing the characters of the Dog Woman and Jordan, Pearce argues for the complexity of the Dog Woman's characterisation while rejecting the idea that she can be seen as a feminist despite her powerfulness. While she is ' "thick" with the materiality of the bodily present',[17] the Dog Woman is not some revolutionary carnivalesque figure because she is so concerned to preserve the status quo. 'Dog Woman's body may be seen to represent a deeply conservative force. The procreative and destructive powers of her body are unleashed not as a catalyst for change but for the preservation of the kingdom. While she avenges herself on *some* men, moreover, it is with the purpose of protecting others.'[18] Pearce argues that she cannot be seen as either protofeminist in her phallic power or unproblematically feminine in her material body, since she serves to uphold the existing patriarchal institutions such as the monarchy, the Church and the State and parallels are drawn between this preservation and the traditional female potential for procreation. The Dog Woman character prefers situations where gender relations are static rather than overturned and that is why,

Pearce argues, Jordan has to search elsewhere for the answers to his dilemmas.

The character of Jordan is, like many of Winterson's characters, not satisfied with narrow binary stereotypes of masculinity and femininity, and Pearce reads his quest for Fortunata, as a search for his own feminine side. His quest for a new masculinity will be defined by the heroism of the young woman chemist, campaigning for the ecology in the twentieth century. Linking Jordan in the sixteenth century with Nicholas Jordan in the twentieth century, Pearce argues that they both have to 'voyage out' on a male-dominated ship, aware of masculinity's limitations as they dream of an alternative feminine supplementarity to their characters – Jordan by dreaming of the city of Dancing Princesses. The ships thus become 'a spatio-temporal rite of passage that the two heroes have to pass through before they can renegotiate their gendered identities'.[19] But the places of enchantment might be viewed not as alternative possibilities but rather as the 'empty time and space of romantic love';[20] like the Dog Woman, they could be read less radically than the text implies. Comparing Jordan's narrative movement through time and change of genders (his female disguise) to Virginia Woolf's main character in *Orlando* (1928) as he evolves into the 'new man', Pearce queries, 'is it really that simple?'[21] She questions the liberatory ease with which the characters time-travel and puts the simplicity of *Sexing the Cherry* down to its being a fairy story that elides the material oppressions of history in relation to class, ethnicity and gender. Neither the Dog Woman nor Jordan ever manage to transcend their genders, Pearce concludes, because they never escape their sex.

Alison Lee[22] in the same year looks at the time and space-time elements of the narrative in two feminist writers, Jeanette Winterson and Angela Carter. In contrast to Pearce, she approves of the parodic playing with time and history of *Sexing the Cherry*, which she sees as a successfully postmodern text. Arguing that the date of King Charles I's beheading significantly ushers in an unknowable, uncertain future, she explores the concept of a continuing present in the time frame of the novel. '*Sexing the Cherry* is set in the years leading up to and following 1649, the year in which King Charles was beheaded and Cromwell and the Puritans assumed power. ... Both these dates are very specific transitions, moments in which time seems to stand still because, although the past has led to these moments, nothing can explain how they are going to lead into the uncertain future.'[23] In exploring how a continuing present in a sense stops time, the novel limits the uncertainty of the future since it never properly arrives. But the novel is doing much more than just negating time. Through cross-cultural comparison, it is arguing for time as a Western construct. Citing the epigraph that explains how the North American Hopi have no tenses to distinguish past from present or future, Lee argues that *Sexing the Cherry* explores 'the notion of time as a culturally or imaginatively constructed field in which past, present or future can exist simultaneously',[24] giving as an example the distinction between experiential and philosophical aspects of time. Jordan experiences time as an arrow moving in a straight line (a Newtonian[25] sense of time), but thinks about it as a simultaneity of space and time (an Einsteinian[26] sense of time).

■ It is not, therefore, surprising; when the novel moves to the twentieth century – because time, after all, cannot be stopped – where the characters bear marked resemblance to those from 1649. A modern sailor called Nicholas Jordan shares Jordan's enthusiasm for boats and sailing, and joins the Navy to pursue his adventures. He finds himself searching for a woman whose heroism in protesting the high mercury levels in a river has captured his imagination. This unnamed woman believes she has a huge, powerful alter ego, 'whose only morality was her own and whose loyalties were fierce and few'. Her fantasies, her behaviour and her sense of self recall the Dog Woman. As the Dog Woman fought the hypocrisy of the Puritans, with occasionally grotesque results such as the dismembering of two of them in their habitual brothel, so the twentieth-century woman sees herself as fighting modern Puritans, businessmen and politicians for ecological reasons. She fantasizes about her alter ego visiting the Pentagon and the World Bank, dropping its members into huge sacks and forcing all the men to 'line up for compulsory training in feminism and ecology'. She 'remembers' (or seems to remember) a past which looks like 1649, and although she does not understand it, she has memories and feelings which cause her to wonder.[27] ☐

Having illustrated the simultaneity of time in both Winterson and Carter, Lee develops her analysis of this representation, linking it outwards to encompass the reader's own experience of this time frame:

■ The concern with time in both these novels, and the possibility that they both suggest of a field in which all space-time can exist simultaneously, obviously contradicts our phenomenological experience of time as well as the Second Law of Thermodynamics. In true metafiction fashion, we as readers are faced with the paradox of reading forward in accordance with the arrow of time while simultaneously looking back to the past. We recognise too that our reading is what makes the novel always present to us as we read. In a sense, through reading we can defy physical laws as Jordan suggests.[28] ☐

This postmodern questioning of time as a Western construct also has a political dimension in Lee's interpretation, linked to the unnamed female ecologist.

■ However, *Sexing the Cherry* in particular, with its suggestion of history's repetition-with-difference seems to be implying a way of connecting time past to time present in order to do something about the future. The observer, as we know from Einstein, Bohr[29] and Heisenberg,[30] changes what is observed because the act of observation adds energy to the system. Like Jorge Luis Borges' famous remark that every writer changes our reading of all writers who have gone before, historiographic metafiction suggests that looking back to the past and mapping the 'other journeys' can change our perceptions of the past as well as our relationship to it.[31] □

The novel's questioning of Newtonian physics and apparently universal truths, is not simply postmodern deconstruction for its own sake, but to suggest an alternative practice. And it is this that makes it a political text and gives postmodernism a 'social conscience':

■ Postmodernism can, as *Sexing the Cherry* in particular proposes, have a social conscience without resorting to the totalising truths it so abhors. Rather than thinking about the future as a beast waiting in a lair, we could think of it as one of many journeys needing to be remapped. Reading *Sexing the Cherry* in the light of chaos theory leads to the observation that even the smallest cause, a woman sitting on the banks of a mercury-filled river, for example, can have large effects. This is necessary if the planet is not to go the way of tragic entropy [the shift of a stable system to disorder and chaos]. If there is a field in which time and space exist together, as Winterson suggests, then readers are as much a part of that as the fiction we are reading.[32] □

Laura Doan also considers the postmodern strategies of *Sexing the Cherry* in the same year in her 'Jeannette Winterson's Sexing the Postmodern'. 'Eschewing realism, Winterson constructs her narrative by exploiting the techniques of postmodern historiographic metafiction (such as intertextuality, parody, pastiche, self-reflexivity, fragmentation, the rewriting of history, and frame breaks) as well as its ideology (questioning "grand narratives", problematising closure, valorising instability, suspecting coherence, and so forth) in order to challenge and subvert patriarchal and heterosexist discourses and, ultimately, to facilitate a forceful and positive radical oppositional critique.'[33] Of the three texts Doan considers, *Oranges Are Not the Only Fruit*, *The Passion* and *Sexing the Cherry*, it is the last that proves the most successful as a lesbian postmodern text. And part of its success is in reintroducing the fruit metaphor in a more complex rendering. Doan sees it as Winterson's 'most successful incursion to overturn the "natural" and collapse such distinctions as nature/culture or inner/outer. ... The writer returns to the fruit metaphor by inserting a visual series of fruit icons at the head of individual sections to announce different narrators and by aligning each character with a fruit against conventional expectations.'[34] In a deliberate confusion of the expected Freudian symbolism, Jordan and Nicholas Jordan are identified with the pineapple, a traditionally female fruit, while the Dog Woman and the unnamed ecologist are identified with the phallic banana. Each character within the Restoration period is signalled by the whole fruit entire, while the twentieth-century characters have the fruit sliced or split in two. This reversal of expectations in the fruit imagery is important for Doan, because it shows Winterson continuing to use fruit as a way of challenging gender constructions through confusing the differences between masculine and feminine. The novel also questions gender constructions through the feminist fairy story of a princess and her female lover who exist within a private social space where oppositions are confused and ruptured, thus illustrating the arbitrary unnaturalness of normal gender relations. Finally, 'normal' society breaks into their haven and destroys the idyll, leading to the death of the lover. Such a conclusion suggests that Winterson's narrative warns against lesbians attempting a parody of heterosexual relationships. The same conclusion can come from an examination of blurring genders. Jordan's cross-dressing allows him an insight into women's private language and enables him temporarily to escape the burdens of living up to gender expectations. 'But Winterson also realizes that cross-dressing – cultural perversion as cultural subversion – is only a temporary strategy to facilitate a break from imposed restrictions; it cannot enact permanent authentic social change.'[35] The novel's much more serious attempt to problematise gender categories comes in the metaphor of the practice of grafting. Grafting predicates two gendered biological parents, or species of plant, which fuse together to create a third species, a new and different form of plant. The cherry developed in the novel is declared to be female, and where Shena MacKay had been perplexed by the meaning of this, Doan clearly sees it as a lesbian strategy, similar to Judith Butler's deconstruction of gender in *Gender Trouble*, that, in rendering the hybrid an excessive creation, challenges binaries as a valid category and suggests new options, both in plants and in gender identities and relationships. Jordan's choice of the cherry to experiment upon, whose name is a euphemism for virginity, implies for Doan that the solution to the fruit metaphor needs to be more deep-rooted than the 'superficial "peel" of cross-dressing'.[36] Grafting becomes an image of procreation beyond that of heterosexuality and though it cannot be seen as a complete strategy for the overthrow of compulsory heterosexualism, it is an effective way of calling its norms into question and undermining the conceptual basis for heterosexual prescriptions within cultural practice. 'Winterson's project then, encapsulated in the act of grafting the cherry, envisions the contours and logic of a lesbian postmodern that collapses binarisms and creates a space not just for lesbians but for productive, dynamic and fluid gender pluralities and sexual positionings.'[37] Winterson's fiction, Doan concludes, subverts gender and identity, striving to figure a more open and liberatory acceptance of cultural otherness, differences and 'monstrosities', allowing a feminist remapping of social and cultural order.

Lisa Moore's 'Teledildonics: Virtual Lesbians in the Fiction of Jeanette Winterson' (1995) focuses, alongside Lee and Doan, on the postmodern narratives of *Sexing the Cherry*, and the issues it raises in relation to identity and gender. Moore reads the novel as an attack on the Enlightenment project, a distinctly postmodern agenda:

■ This novel rewrites the origins of European modernity – colonial exploration, the rise of empirical science and Enlightenment notions of the unified self. Through the narration of Jordan, who accompanies one of the heroes of early modern exploration and scientific discovery as his apprentice, these technologies of modernity are called into question, their fantasmatic status and their limitations revealed. Thus modernity itself – the regime of the subject, of the bounded body, of fixed identity – is rewritten as only one of many possible ways of describing human experience, and postmodern understandings of fragmented bodies and multiple subjectivities are seen to have been there all along, produced by (and thus in some sense proper to) the impossible demands of Enlightenment modernity rather than challenging or rejecting them. Such an understanding deconstructs modernity's investments in fixed and knowable gender and sexual identities: the protagonists of this novel either move between and among gender and sexual identifications (Jordan), or simply exceed them (his foster mother, the Dog Woman). Once again, an understanding of the malleability of gender and sexual boundaries characteristic of the point of view of a marginalized sexuality is represented not as a minority position, but as the unproblematic possession of the novel's most admirable characters.[38] □

Rejecting the view of other critics that the novel's story is about John Tradescant, the historical botanist and plant collector, Moore cites Jordan's argument that the voyages of discovery are unimportant in themselves, that it is the journeys unmade, the alternatives to the choices experienced, that he wishes to uncover. Facts, history, documents, science and maps are all negligible; it is the mapping of the imaginary that Jordan is engaged on, the internal journey of discovery. These psychic journeys to the floating city, or the city of love, are treated in the same tone as the experience of real geographical places. Time, space and consciousness, the narrative argues, are all interpermeable, and in a state of flux. Science cannot fix or limit them to a series of explanations.

Time is a theme the novel has in its sights, particularly in how it intersects with consciousness to create a sense of identity. The 'novel is principally preoccupied with a challenge to Lockeian[39] notions of identity as the duration of consciousness through time'.[40] As the narrative voice attests, childhood memories are flawed; we all remember things that did not occur and forget ones that did. Our childhood thus becomes a fictional narrative we tell to explain ourselves to ourselves. Locke's notion of identity is shown to be just as flawed as all the other Enlightenment projects of science and geography. Having Jordan voice this lack, this inability to fix knowledge, either external or internal, thereby posits the troubling questions in the very time in which the modern world was being constructed. Postmodern questioning thus becomes not a progressive understanding of knowledge, a conception in itself modern, but an unpicking of questions suppressed during the time of the founding of Enlightenment. In this way, the novel manages the complex task of offering a critique of Enlightenment without falling into the trap of seeming to endorse a linear history of progress. The linking of Nick Jordan and the female ecologist with their seventeenth-century counterparts deconstructs linear time in a narrative of 'post-Einstein physics and post-Saussurean philosophy',[41] creating a dislocation of identity into a variety of fragmented selves.

The Dog Woman and Jordan demonstrate not only selves that are unfixed, but genders as well. Jordan cross-dresses and, when feminine, discovers the language of women and their love for each other. Neither lesbianism nor cross-dressing, Moore suggests, are depicted as unusual or remarkable. For her, the Dog Woman is a lesbian figure, given her imaginary genesis, released by a woman from a bottle, like a genie. Her unnatural birth is linked by Moore to the technique of grafting the cherry, the central metaphor of the novel, which the Church condemns as an unnatural practice since botanists are usurping God. The Dog Woman is similarly viewed as a freak of nature.

Despite the narrative links, the Dog Woman rejects the grafted cherry as monstrous and lacking any gender, and it is left to the cross-dressing Jordan to proclaim that it grows like any other tree and has a female gender, concluding with his own fantasy of being grafted to Tradescant in a homosexual joining. Moore ends with a consideration of the Dog Woman's subversive characterisation, linking female power, the material body and female sexuality in a way that refuses to idealise them, rather grounding it in a rank and monstrous depiction: 'Such exotic monstrosities inevitably suggested sexual aberration, providing lesbian readers with a way to read the Dog Woman's excess as success, her powerful monstrosity as virtually lesbian.'[42] Her representation reconfigures female hideousness as subversive power and, in her lack of an originary birth, links her to the subversive potential of the cyborgs of

Donna Haraway (born 1944),[43] whose focus is not on where they come from, but on how they survive. The Dog Woman, as virtual lesbian, seizes the power to survive, eschewing concerns of origin or naturalness, like the grafted cherry.

Maria Lozano also looks at the questioning of the historical discourse in the novel, in 1995, but considers how public history maps onto private discourses of intimacy. Her comparison of Julian Barnes's *The History of the World in 10 ½ Chapters* with *Sexing the Cherry* argues that the two novels, published in the same year (1989), both focus on history and love and, in her reading, are in a direct conversation with each other. The quotation in her title comes from Barnes, ' "How You Cuddle in the Dark Governs How You See the History of the World": A Note on Some Obsessions in Recent British Fiction'.[44] Like Moore, Lozano homes in on the metaphor of grafting as the central image of the text, but reads it more in relation to history, within the private and personal aspect of origins:

> ■ The central and most powerful image of the book is that of grafting/ sexing/engendering that we get in the title. ... To begin with birth/origin as a question of a willed artificial act of grafting is in itself a revolutionary act; it implies not the given, 'natural' and taken for granted mother giving birth or God creating a world, but a certain artificial and willed mastery of technique, which has certainly to be rooted in the specificity of the here and now. Not the 'once upon a time' of Adam and Eve, or of Noah and his Ark, but the precision of the time and place where the experiment has to be carried out. In the second place, grafting evades, so to speak, the traditional binary opposition and cannibalism of the sexes. In the third place, it highlights the terrifying non-originality of the 'without seed or parent'. And finally, the grafting-cum-reproduction is pointed out as a result of a traditional act of 'love' but as an action described as 'taking advantage of each other', so that 'this fruit is made resistant to disease'.[45] □

The novel's ability to subvert the cultural myths of origins, through its discussion of engendering and reproduction, is further developed through the Dog Woman's finding of Jordan, rewriting Western myths of motherhood and beatitude in a more scatological vaunting of the abjected and the ugly.

Issues of engendering develop further with Jordan's travels with Tradescant and their discovery of the strange fruit. Lozano argues that the fruit is 'marginal' and dual in nature, and teases out the duality and marginality in relation to a Britain historically moving into the 'modern' period after the beheading of the king and the discoveries of the British sailing ships 'that brought back to the island *marginal* tropical fruits such as the pineapple (pine and apple). When and by whom was the pineapple introduced into England? When and by whom the banana? ... The banana and pineapple enter physically into the order of the signifiers, taking on a visible presence in the double discourse, double voice.'[46] Like other critics before her, Lozano notes the subversion of traditional icons in giving the phallic banana to the female voice, the Dog Woman, and the pineapple to Jordan, but sees as even more interesting the fact that the Dog Woman also transgresses aspects of the feminine beauty myth in her size and her hideousness.

Lozano's final point is to link issues of engendering and origins, through dualism, to a concept of metamorphosis which she argues is relevant to her other topic, that of 'cuddling'. Grafting and tropical fruits thus come to rest on an image of protean potential. The structuring principle of the novel is metamorphosis, she suggests. When it comes to love, or cuddling, the ancient Roman poet Ovid's (43BC–AD17) *Metamorphoses*, his extended poem of mythical and legendary transformations with its descriptions of Orpheus or Actaeon changing form, is particularly relevant:

■ in love, Winterson reveals a word of transformation and metamorphosis, which nevertheless hides contradictions. In the passage we are referring to, beside the Ovidian metamorphoses of a woman into a lotus, or Actaeon into a stag, we have the historical one of Sappho, 'who rather than lose her lover to a man, flung herself from the windy cliffs and turned her body into a cliff'.

But the theme of metamorphosis is reproduced at different levels in the text, not only the central image of grafting posits origin and birth as a form of metamorphosis but the text itself and the voices suffer a process akin to this Protean strategy, as the voices adopt different forms in different journeys through different fabulated spaces of the imagination.[47] □

For Lozano, this argues for a multiplicity of different forms or journeys that subverts Western heterosexual norms of desire and subjectivity.

Marilyn R. Farwell's chapter 'The Postmodern Lesbian Text', in *Heterosexual Plots and Lesbian Narratives* (1996),[48] argues that women have a different relationship to the breakdown of Western metaphysics than men do, and moreover that gays and lesbians have an even more variant relationship to it, since the marginalised have always had a divergent, fractured identity in contrast to the dominant centre of society. Lesbian texts necessarily negate the possibilities of closure, 'that point in the narrative where the reader expects to have the subjects and identities settled',[49] because they reject the possibility of a fixed identity. Winterson, in *Sexing the Cherry* and *Written on the Body*, is a 'postmodern writer who tests the precepts of postmodernism'[50] and has more in common with lesbian feminist writers than male postmodernists.

Winterson's texts do not 'trade directly on lesbian images and themes. In fact, they seem to avoid making lesbianism a narrative concern'.[51] *Sexing the Cherry* has two main characters who are heterosexual, although the Dog Woman, because of her size, is only technically heterosexual since her attempted liaisons prove disastrous. Looking to other contemporary lesbian writers such as Kathy Acker (1945–97) and Monique Wittig (born 1935) as representing the textual lesbian subject 'in bodily terms that shock and disgust the reader',[52] Farwell argues that the Dog Woman is a metaphoric lesbian character through her giganticism; not only in her bodily size and hideousness to the heterosexual reader, but also in her narrative within the text:

■ The novel juxtaposes two primary narrators whose bodily representations function as challenges to the narrative categories of agent and narrator. ... But what is at stake in these wonderful flights of fancy is not psychology or philosophy in spite of the lengthy mid-novel philosophical discussion of time and space, but the narrative. The juxtaposition of alternative narratives underscores the artificiality of the narrative system, especially the male heroic story. Although, on the surface, Jordan is the proponent of traditional heroic values through his narrative trajectory and stated desires, both narrators explode that system. It is the Dog Woman as the lesbian body who engenders a firm alternative story and who eventually encompasses Jordan in her narrative rather than she by his.[53] □

This contestation of who is the narrator and who a part of the other's story is also fought out between Jordan and Fortunata. Jordan looks to her as the closure and happy-ever-after of his quest, but she refuses to be a part of his story, in refusing to accompany him. In the battle between the male's and the female's story, the women win. Fortunata's story of Orion and Artemis, which Jordan retells to the Dog Woman, encapsulates the battle of the two narratives; 'Orion claims his traditional narrative prerogative by raping Artemis, and she, in return, refuses her positioning in the story by killing Orion.'[54] Artemis challenges Orion's patriarchal assumption that the woman will form part of the man's heroic story, by eliminating him from the narrative altogether. Similarly, Jordan wants to be a hero and, in the traditional heroic narrative, find a beautiful wife for his traditional closure, but Fortunata refuses to provide such a closure and tells him to be self-sufficient. 'The parodic *coitus interruptus* of Jordan's journey signals postmodern issues.'[55] Jordan's questionings about time and space and matter are, for Farwell, profound postmodern issues, but the narrative in which he poses them, the quest for Fortunata and the pineapple, is commonplace, and the reader needs to take this into account in their reading. 'Jordan traverses vast spaces, asks philosophical questions, and cross-dresses, all suggesting his narrative as the center of questions about dichotomous difference. At the same time his narrative journey is structurally familiar. Because Jordan's journey is both traditional and disruptive, he learns to become a different narrative agent, eventually positioning himself as part of the Dog Woman's story rather than his own.'[56]

Jordan's cross-dressing adventures allow him to develop a new relationship to the women's narrative, accepting that they have repositioned themselves in relation to the male story, and focus instead in relation to each other in a clearly lesbian negotiation that has no use for the masculine. In his acceptance of this, rather than forcing them to become part of his story, Jordan figures as a new type of masculinity, that allows him to become subsumed into his mother's dominant narrative. (Henri, of course, does something similar in the previous novel, *The Passion*.) 'The Dog Woman as narrator and protagonist of her own story appears to offer a conservative and humorous resistance to Jordan's story; but the conservatism is a ruse for a bodily female subject that reorders the narrative gender positionings.'[57] Like Pearce, Farwell points out the conservative and reactionary aspect of her support of Charles I and her rejection of grafting as a process of reproduction, but unlike Pearce, Farwell does not see this as the whole picture. She agrees that, in a humorous mode, she can be seen as a traditional mother in resisting change and wanting the best for her son and his heroic endeavours, but her size militates against such a conservative characterisation being the whole story. Her 'size functions as the text's refusal to acquiesce to culture's attempt to control the woman's body. The grotesque female body positions Dog Woman as the narrator and agent of her own story, a story which gradually absorbs Jordan into it, repositioning him at the closure of her narrative. Her size, then, functions on a narrative level as a source of power and agency.'[58] Her textual violence castigates the hypocrisy of the Puritan's denouncement of the flesh, and stands instead as a transgressive and self-sufficient magnified body. As such, she stands symbolically for the lesbian figure and the lesbian discourse, not because she tries to have sex with women, nor because she develops a lesbian community, because she does neither, but because of her size, which subverts heterosexual norms and boundaries. 'She is the grotesque and exaggerated female body that conditions postmodernism's metaphoric construction of the lesbian body, and she functions primarily as a disrupter of textuality and its positioning of woman. Her sexual encounters ... imply the impossibility of hetero sexuality in a woman who creates her own narrative and claims her own agency.'[59] The Dog Woman is, first and foremost, the material female body, asserting the importance of sexual difference alongside

Jordan's deconstruction of gender constructions and expectations. As such, she asserts a space for the lesbian body that challenges the construction of femininity and refuses to be seen in relation to any masculine agenda; on the contrary, she wrests the narrative for her own ends. For Farwell, *Sexing the Cherry* is a successful lesbian narrative through the figure of the Dog woman and through the complex narrativity it encompasses.

Elizabeth Langland's 'Sexing the Text: Narrative Drag as Feminist Poetics and Politics in *Sexing the Cherry*' (1997),[60] uses Judith Butler to argue for a feminist poetics of narrativity in *Sexing the Cherry*. Langland reads the novel as a parodic rewriting of 'The Mower, Against Gardens' (1681) by Andrew Marvell (1621–78). She argues that the intertextual reperformance, imitating the earlier poem in order to subvert its message, destabilises the original conventions and the traditions of the earlier male text: 'it is precisely the performative, citational dimension of Winterson's postmodern novel that allows it to be read *as* a feminist text'.[61] Marvell's poem, written during the seventeenth century, reflects the same world as *Sexing the Cherry*, 'a time of religious/monarchical conflict, heroic travel, adventure, and discovery, and scientific experimentation, particularly in the realm of plant grafting. Both works are interested in exploring how these events and discoveries, particularly the grafting and sexing of the cherry, upset the order of nature and the so-called "natural" world.'[62] Marvell's mower denounces grafting as going against nature, a forbidden, unnatural practice, seeing it as procreation without sex. 'While the mower reads grafting as unlawful, Winterson's text and her character Jordan explore it as one central means to escape the tired binarisms of reproduction.'[63] Citing the intertextual references to 'My Last Duchess' (1842) by Robert Browning (1812–89) and to Byron by the second and third of the Twelve Dancing Princesses respectively, as indications of how Winterson rewrites poetic references that challenge the traditional by shifting the gender or the sexuality, Langland considers Winterson's use of Marvell in more depth:

■ In the case of Marvell and Winterson, the broad and arresting similarities in the philosophic orientation of the speakers and the subject addressed by the works motivate this consideration of what happens when the shape of the speaking body is changed, both person and text. Although Winterson's novel employs four narrators, two from the seventeenth century and two from the twentieth century, to generate a montage of responses, one character shares Marvell's mower's perspectives and expresses fairly standard and conventional opinions for her time: that is the seventeenth-century Dog Woman. Her responses to the arrival of the banana in England echoes what might have been the mower's opinion. ... And on the subject of grafting, she is as unequivocal as Marvell's mower.[64] □

Having introduced the Dog Woman as conservative and traditional in her views, the essay complicates her portrayal by examining her appearance; like Farwell, Langland sees this as radically subversive, and goes further in linking her appearance to Butler's concept of drag as unsettling gender categories. 'Although the most traditional character in her *expressions* and *reflections*, the Dog Woman is the most radically unconventional physical presence in the novel. The echo of traditional doctrine in the mouth of a mountainous woman, huge and imposing, heavier than an elephant, with a clitoris the size of an orange and nipples the size of walnuts, possessed of an almost superhuman strength, has a disturbing effect. Her every action, performed in the name of the "feminine" virtues of charity, graciousness, or maternality, cites those concepts in ways that transform them.'[65] The Dog Woman's performance of traditional feminine traits serves to destabilise them as 'natural' to women. For the Dog Woman is indisputably female by sex, but is not feminine by gender, since no man can impregnate her and her size confounds them. As far as the Dog Woman's character is concerned, the old adage 'anatomy is destiny' no longer holds true. The Dog Woman's size works in ways similar to Butler's concept of drag. 'The Dog Woman's performance of gendered traits of tenderness, charity, and the maternal reveals the extent to which those things seen as inherent to woman and to femininity are produced within a cultural context that scripts behavioural norms out of relative size, mass, and strength. Put another way, the anatomically huge physical body that readily cites gender norms of tenderness or charity or maternality while threatening or performing mayhem destabilizes the conventional meanings of those terms and exposes their cultural construction.'[66] Winterson's Dog Woman illustrates the way her 'ritualized repetition of gender norms, can have a destabilising effect'.[67]

In Langland's reading, Jordan not only champions grafting, but also seeks to reproduce it in himself, in grafting his limited body onto something better. Jordan feels unable to live up to the heroic ideals of masculinity, overshadowed by his mother who performs them so much more effectively. In the twentieth century too, while Nicholas Jordan has been brought up with the *Boys Book of Heroes*, it is the unnamed woman ecologist who performs the heroic acts in defence of the mercury-polluted river.

■ This tension between the women who stay at home, yet live dangerously, and the men who voyage, yet face no threat, comments obliquely on the obtuse intransigence of Marvell's speaker in 'The Mower, Against

Gardens'. That speaker posits pastoral against heroic ideals, domestic against imperial virtues, endorsing an idealized and static view of 'plain and pure' nature against the concept of cultivation and innovation as vice-ridden. Conclusively, for the mower, 'the gods themselves with us do dwell' (line 40). The poem, of course, which establishes this juxtaposition, represents but does not participate in the mower's simple resolution of these tensions – tensions that Winterson's novel elaborates; the heroic versus the pastoral, the imperial versus the domestic, masculine versus feminine. But these cannot resolve themselves into evil versus good; the corruption that the mower would forestall already exists, as old as human nature itself. And it is the women at home who must do battle with it. *Sexing the Cherry* picks up on the nostalgia for stability embodied in a pastoral paradise but recognizes that it has, in fact, never existed; life is flux, quest, and challenge.[68] □

The metaphor of grafting and the materiality of the Dog Woman's size upset traditional conceptions of gender identity and performance in ways which tie directly to issues of feminist gender politics and a feminist poetics. Langland hovers between arguing that whether Winterson deliberately cites the Marvell is immaterial, since the theory of intertextuality argues texts resonate earlier texts to a knowing reader, and asserting that 'her citation' of Marvell's world in the poem is deliberate. Though she cannot point to any intentional referencing and, given her postmodern focus, may well not wish to, the comparison of poem and novel proves a fruitful one.

Sarah Martin's 'The Power of Monstrous Women' (1999)[69] takes a much less admiring view of the Dog Woman's depiction. In a comparison of three monstrous women created by feminist writers – Winterson, Angela Carter and Fay Weldon – Martin situates their tameness in relation to male depictions of monstrous women. Comparing how the three women writers use a mix of fantasy and historical reality and irony for their larger-than-life characters, she questions whether they can be as triumphant a portrayal as the writers wish for. 'By creating grotesque female monsters they deny men the privilege of being the sole producers of monstrous portraits of women. Seemingly, contemporary women writers are not interested in considering how woman shares in the humiliation of contemporary man and prefer instead taking female monstrosity away from the hands of patriarchy. What is to be done with powerful female monstrosity now that women writers have it in their hands is not so clear, though.'[70] Martin finds the gender politics of the Dog Woman's characterisation more dubious than Langland or Farwell. In an overly literal reading of her portrayal (signalled by her over-identification as audience), she deciphers Winterson's message as being that all women have just such an abusive and monstrous alter ego buried inside of them, ready to burst out. 'But where is the triumph in all this? … seeing ourselves as triumphant monsters is a step forward in comparison to the humiliation of having men portray us as abject monsters. Hence the sense of triumph. Yet this seems to be a very limited solution, quite inadequate to make post-feminist women, if that is what we are, consider the dangers of not facing our weaknesses. What is more, it is still too bound to patriarchal man's view of woman as an eminently physical object.'[71] Where Langland sees the Dog Woman's materiality and size as a parody of femininity as a discourse and hence successful, Martin sees her as simply reinforcing patriarchal views of women as an object, while displacing male depictions of the feminine virago with another, whose main difference is that it is penned by a woman. Placing Winterson's Dog Woman in a direct comparison with the protagonist of *The Iron Woman* (1993), a children's story by Ted Hughes (1930–98), she takes little account of their different ideological contexts as she compares their textual detail. Both women, she suggests 'use radical, violent methods to teach patriarchal men to behave properly – that is to say, as women would like – but they cannot be taken as role models because they are as violent and narrow-minded as any patriarchal man. Both read as parodies – though it is not clear whether they are parodies of the excesses of feminism or patriarchy.'[72] Reading their gigantic size as indicative of the levels of disgust and rebellion hidden within the women, Martin is still indicating an unease about how to read the novels, or what each character's monstrosity signifies. Grappling on the surface of the texts, Martin signals how readers of both genders can be discomfited by the Dog Woman's violence, reading it as violence pure and simple, rather than the textual violence Farwell deciphers:

■ The Dog Woman does possess a formidable body capable of eliciting fear and disgust, a body that enables her to kill men as she pleases. However, it is doubtful whether the reader is supposed to sympathise with her androphobia [fear of men] or to condemn it as the dark side of contemporary feminism; it is also disputable whether the reader is supposed to feel amused by the Dog Woman's various sexual misadventures or horrified by them. What is to be made for instance, of the episode in which the Dog Woman bites off the penis of a man who has persuaded her to perform fellatio for him? She naively claims that she has hurt him because until then she believed that men's genitals could grow again if an accident happened. Later, when she is better informed, she comes to the conclusion that if this is not the case, 'this seems a great mistake on the part of nature, since men are so careless with their members and will put them anywhere without thinking' (p. 120). If this is simply provocative humour, the least that can be said about it is that Winterson does not quite dominate the register – the worst is that it is at the level of sexist dirty jokes at the expense of women.[73] □

Where Martin is clearly unable to come to terms with the Dog Woman's violence and, like Pearce, reads Winterson's depiction as conservatively retrograde and the Rabelaisian ribaldry as sexist dirty jokes (rather than the mocking materiality of the feminine within a seventeenth-century context), she has a stronger point to argue in relation to the twentieth-century female character:

■ The modern version of the giantess is a rather attractive woman who believes that she carries within herself a monster of enormous proportions that will burst out of her body when her tolerance of men's hypocrisy finally collapses. At a point in the novel she has a long fantasy in which she hallucinates how her own body becomes indeed that of her gigantic self. In her fantasy she becomes a virago ... trapping in a huge sack all the men who displease her ... and only chooses men in positions of power, who will become the targets of a peculiar kind of re-education. ... Feminism and ecology replace men's greed apparently because all the men are cowed into submission not with powerful arguments but with powerful magic. Why the 'compulsory training' dreamt by Winterson's heroine ... is better than patriarchal men's unfairness and misogyny is the question the text never answers ... the real issue at stake in the representation of monstrosity is power, or, alternatively, that women's dreams of power can only lead to creating monsters, no matter how effective they may be in redressing the wrongs of monstrous patriarchy.[74] □

Although the reading is overly literal, the issue of the woman's enforced training is one that is too easily configured within the discourse of twentieth-century heroism, and does demand a more careful deliberation. The real strength of this flawed article, though, comes in its argument that women's texts need to be seen in the context of their male contemporaries. 'Where indeed', she asks, 'is that power to offend that Winterson, Weldon and Carter are credited with?'[75] Ignoring, now, the fact that she herself has been offended by the textual violence, she posits that, since all three writers are popular, they cannot be subversive but only a kind of 'provocative conformist' and hence their monstrous women nothing but 'a sham'.[76] In contrast, the work of the Scottish renaissance writers, such as Alasdair Gray (born 1934) in *Poor Things* (1993) and Iain Banks (born 1954) in *The Wasp Factory* (1984) contains 'really disturbing, unsettling female monsters – in the sense of being really disruptive of essential ideas of femininity, and even about humanity'.[77] Her conclusion that women cannot write truly disturbing, subversive fiction about powerful women is problematic, but the idea implicit in this negative analysis, that feminist writers in the 1980s are in some very real sense part of a mainstream literary tradition, whereas the urban Scottish writers are more marginalised and hence edgier, is worth exploring. By the late 1980s, Carter and Winterson were being reviewed as serious novelists, but I would contend, as do the majority of the critical essays, that their popularity came because their subversion hit a necessary spot with many 1980s and 1990s readers.

Jan Rosemergy's study of the theme of self-discovery through a reaction against the mother's precepts, explored in *Oranges Are Not the Only Fruit* and *Boating for Beginners*, shifts its ground with *Sexing the Cherry*, since Rosemergy sees the Dog Woman as a much more liberatory mother than the mothers of the two earlier texts. While their oppressive domination of their daughters gets translated into her gigantic size, she herself respects Jordan's independence, since she too has it and can recognise its value in others. Not only does she name him after a river, water being a symbol of the individuating self in Rosemergy's reading, but she also shows him an explorer of the world at the age of three, which has significant influence on his later life. In this novel, like her first, Winterson uses fairy tales to challenge sexism and homophobia, particularly the stories of the Twelve Dancing Princesses. In his search to find Fortunata, Jordan's cross-dressing allows him to experience the oppression suffered by women and to question whether either sex can be whole while trying to live up to their stereotypes. In the *Red Fairy Book* (1890) by Andrew Lang (1844–1912) the twelve princesses are locked into a tower each night but each morning their father finds their shoes worn away. Any man who can decipher the riddle of the incarcerated women's worn shoes can choose one for his bride. Finally a lowly gardener discovers their secret and they are all married off to princes except his choice, the youngest. Rosemergy points out how the traditional tale constructs the women as having their autonomy taken away by men. In Winterson's retelling, the moral is very different. 'Winterson's transformation of this fairy tale explodes the myth that every woman is a princess rescued by marriage to a prince. In Winterson's tale each woman suffers in different ways but ultimately acts to rescue herself.'[78] Though they were all married off to princes, the princesses free themselves from their spouses to live happily with the lovers of their choice. They run away to be with a mermaid, Rapunzel, or murder their husbands for their infidelity, their destruction of the woman's property, their gluttony, their imprisonment of the woman, or, in the case of the eleventh princess, because he asks her to. One woman walks out on the marriage to be free while the only one to find love discovers that she has married a woman. These princesses confound the usual closure of fairy tales, which reinforces the marriage myth, and instead illustrate that, whether heterosexual or homosexual, love can incur pain and marriage can be an oppression. These are women who have rejected the role of property to take back their own independence. Fortunata, the twelfth and youngest princess, when Jordan finally discovers her, tells him that she has taught herself to dance alone. 'Thus this twelfth princess symbolizes freedom – freedom of movement (free even of gravity) and freedom of spirit, free to change identities, free to create the self. Jordan and Fortunata part, both continuing their individual quests to explore self and world. In the tale of the eleven princesses, attempts to own the beloved destroyed their relationships. By contrast, Jordan and Fortunata love one another enough to free the beloved to be his or her essential self.'[79]

Winterson's rewriting of the Ancient Greek myth of Artemis and Orion similarly asserts women's freedom from male dominance. In the original myth there are a number of variant stories about why Orion dies. He challenges Artemis to a discus-throwing competition, or he tries to rape one of her servants and she kills him, or he tries to rape Artemis herself and a giant scorpion kills him. In truncating these into Artemis killing him for his actual rape of her, Rosemergy sees the text asserting women's vengeful ability to transcend victimisation. Artemis, living a masculine life on her island, finds self-discovery without journeying the world when she realises that each potential persona, child, woman, hunter, queen, necessitates the loss of the others. Orion's entrance demands she listen dutifully to his braggart stories, but rather than be the dutiful audience, she insists on talking too, and is raped as a consequence. Her swift despatch of him changes her conception of herself and shows her that value is demonstrated through what one is willing to risk. The original myth has Artemis punished for usurping masculine ways, but Winterson allows her an effective retaliation against male domination. 'The lessons seem complex. First, no matter where one travels, ultimately the self must be confronted. Second, one must avoid choosing a single image of the self, since that limits one's freedom. Finally, one must accept the risks of freedom, for freedom is necessary not to explore the world but to explore the self.'[80] The Dog Woman's aggression against the Puritans continues the same theme, of women's rejection of phallocentric oppression, that is evident in the portrayal of the unnamed ecologist, the Dog Woman's alter ego. The ecologist dreams about forcing men to shift their conceptions of the world, by teaching them the tenets of feminism and ecology, whereby both sexes would live in harmonious co-operation. She, and the Dog Woman, have 'the strength to change self and world'.[81] Dog Woman burns London in the Great Fire, to purge it of corruption and the plague, while the ecologist burns the mercury factory with the help of Nicholas Jordan because she sees the way it pollutes the river. Man and woman work together to help better the world. The multiple discourses of history and fairytale, myth and fantasy, paired with narrators of both sexes in two different time periods, structure both pairing and counterparting into the narrative, as a way of conveying the truth. Even though modern, post-Einstein physics argues that the world is not solid, and the world is round, we experience it as solid matter and flat. 'In other words, our perception of reality is a fiction that we adopt.'[82]

Kim Middleton Meyer's consideration of Winterson's developing narrative discourse, in 'Jeanette Winterson's Evolving Subject', sees *Sexing the Cherry* as a more evolved form of the grotesque than *The Passion*. While the novel contains the multiple narratives and the grotesque of her previous novels, here she 'begins to aggressively test the limits of the grotesque figurations she has depended on previously. Here the characters consistently search for alternatives to their present circumstances, but they also push their exploration beyond traditional boundaries of time and space. ... Challenging two of the most firmly held beliefs of the nineteenth century – the ultimate rationality of time and space – Winterson delineates the territory she intends to re-survey. The experiences traversed by her dual narrators reflect a world that indeed takes neither conventional time nor solid matter for granted.'[83] While Jordan travels in the land of the fantastic, the Dog Woman's monstrous materiality apparently exists within a real historical period, that of Cromwell's protectorate (1653–9). The difference between the Dog Woman and Jordan recalls the difference between Henri and Villanelle in *The Passion*, and their initially separate narratives that intertwine. The central metaphor of the grafting of the cherry Meyer sees as the epitome of the grotesque trope. 'On the surface, this allegory evokes images of the grotesque: two strains are fused and produce a third, that in turn allows for new possibilities.'[84] However, the novel evolves beyond simply reproducing grotesque figures and the 'grafted' tropes of history and fantasy, when the contemporary characters of Nicholas Jordan and the female ecologist are introduced towards the end of the novel. Where other critics find their inclusion intrusive, Meyer sees them as central to Winterson's discursive purpose, for they begin to undermine the nature of the grotesque discourse. 'Its theory of union and synthesis cannot account for the relation between Jordan and Nicholas Jordan, between Dog Woman and the activist. In *Sexing the Cherry*, then, Winterson begins to map out a theory of multiplicity specific to subjectivity, one that simultaneously seeks to more fully integrate fantasy into the real, even while erasing the distinction between the two.'[85]

Neither of the two narratives, the historical, fantastic one of the Dog Woman and Jordan, or the contemporary one of the later two characters, can be declared the 'true' one, and this inability, this hesitancy, Meyer suggests, not only undercuts the division between fantasy and realism, between Jordan in the past and Nicholas in the present, but also begins to gesture towards a new form of fluid and disconnected subjectivity that accords with the concept of 'nomadic subjectivity' developed by

Rosi Braidotti (born 1954).[86] 'Nomadism, then, allows the character the necessary and useful facets of multiple homogeneous identities without being cornered by the bounded limits of a solitary one.'[87] The discourse of the nomad fits Nicholas Jordan and the activist more effectively than the grotesque, and allows them to carry out radical social acts as they destroy the factory that is damaging the environment. This political action argues for the further potential of a nomadic conception of subjectivity, powerful through its very multiplicity.

In the year after Meyer, 2003, Jago Morrison's consideration of Winterson's oeuvre also examined *Sexing the Cherry*, using Bakhtin's chronotope of literary space and time. The novel's epigraph about the Hopi Indians' lack of tenses in their language, since time is continuous for them, sets the focus on a different conception of time, while the use of the post-Einstein physics argues for a different conception of space and time. Morrison goes on to sketch out the relevance of the Relativity and Quantum theories. 'Within relativity theory, one of the characteristics of space-time, when compared with the fixity of the older Newtonian universe, is its capacity for curvature and deformation. *Sexing the Cherry* makes much of this possibility. Within the novel, moreover, it is also possible to see the influence of Quantum Theory. In this tradition, the principles of "complementarity" and "uncertainty" enshrine the idea that no object may be viewed in its entirety, but instead it presents different qualities to the observer in different circumstances.'[88] Jordan believes both that the world is round and that it is also flat, and the sense of time within the novel challenges traditional notions of linearity and of distinctions between past and present and future, to argue for a simultaneity of different presents so that Jordan and the Dog Woman exist in the seventeenth century and simultaneously in the twentieth. The Dog Woman's selves, the gargantuan grotesque, the goddess Artemis and the ecologist share two themes that link the various selves together: all are oppressed by phallocentric heterosexualism, and each signals her disapproval through fire, whether aiding the Great Fire of London, ringed with fire as she meditates on life, or stokes a furnace, respectively. Thus, how the novel explores the space-time continuum has ramifications for the depiction of identity. If identity is split, then clearly gender cannot be seen as fixed either, as is signalled by Jordan's masquerade, or drag. Jordan, disguised as a prostitute, learns the lack of fixed distinctions between the good and the bad, through the slippage of women between bawdy house and the adjacent nunnery. 'Instead, by cartoonish means, there is a constant movement and exchange of women between the two.'[89]

Like many other critics, Morrison also considers the narrative of the Twelve Dancing Princesses, and returns to the Brothers Grimm rendition to compare the patriarchal use of the princesses as exchange and property; he notes that their fate, apart from the eldest, is not elaborated in Grimm. In comparison, Winterson subverts cultural expectations of what the princesses should desire and makes them more women-centred, giving each of them a form of happy ending that does not rely on a husband. 'From a story about patriarchal control and the duplicity of women, Winterson turns the tale into a playful representation of the plural scenarios of sex and desire.'[90] Through Fortunata and the Dog Woman, Winterson allows the scope of femininity to stretch from the sublime to the grotesque, and thereby raises questions about the nature and naturalness of the feminine body that are tapped by the metaphor of the cherry's grafting. 'The conservative culture which locates "femaleness" in reproductive "body parts" of course encourages a whole set of cultural anxieties about the attainment of successful heterosexual femininity, and particularly about the "naturalness" or "unnaturalness" of particular kinds of pleasures, bodies and individuals.'[91] Taking the procedure used by gardeners to graft trees from warmer climates onto root stock used in colder climates, to enable them to grow tastier, deli-cate varieties that were able to survive the English winters, Winterson transforms grafting into a metaphor for creating new life that bypasses the heterosexual matrix and produces a progeny that is better than the original parts. Morrison uses Judith Butler's *Gender Trouble* for the thesis that both gender and sex are culturally determined, and that the inscriptions are constructed through time, adapted and bequeathed from generation to generation. Winterson's combination of the new physics and Butler's conception of how sexed bodies are historically engendered, results in an even more playful deconstruction of gendered identities. 'If the body is a tissue of times, and time itself is destabilised, what possibilities does this open up for the re-imagination of the body?'[92] If Quantum theory denies the existence of solid matter, posing instead energy fields, how can one talk about bounded, fixed bodies as stable and normative?

Like the reviewers before them, the critics see the postmodern narrative of *Sexing the Cherry*, with its juxtaposition of variant discourses and its self-reflexivity, as a major focus of interest. Moore, Palmer and Rosemergy discuss its narrativity, Doan sees it as having a political as well as a poetic postmodernism, and Lee agrees, seeing it as postmod-ernism with a social conscience. Farwell and Doan argue that it is specif-ically lesbian and feminist in focus. Moore believes the novel attacks the Enlightenment project, which itself began during the seventeenth century, while Lee and Lozano point to the historical period being the time of the overthrow of authority, with the beheading of King Charles I, and therefore a time of potentially more subversion and anarchy. Palmer, Langland and Farwell analyse the dual narrators as granting only relativist narratives, and argue for the twentieth-century characters as alter egos that cross time. Lee and Morrison claim more specifically that the four characters exist simultaneously within separate time zones, and Pearce, Lee and Morrison discuss the space-time representation and the non-linear simultaneity of time within *Sexing the Cherry*. Lee and Morrison, as well as Moore and Rosemergy, examine the use of the 'new physics', or post-Einstein views of space, time and matter, with Morrison elaborating in useful detail how Einstein's relativity and quantum physics, in making matter fluid and relative, necessarily deconstruct gender and sex identities as well.

The main focus of the challenge to gender expectations in this novel, though, is seen as being the Dog Woman and her encapsulation of the monstrous. Palmer introduces the reading, arguing that the grotesque figure stands as quasi-lesbian despite her heterosexuality, and Moore sees it as clearly lesbian because of her excessive and subversive power, while Farwell views it as a metaphor for how heterosexuality views lesbianism. Lozano claims it simply transgresses feminine beauty myths. Pearce, in contrast, positions the Dog Woman as a profoundly conservative character and Martin sees her as tame. The two argue for her ineffectiveness. Farwell partially accepts their view while also trying to redeem the characterisation by explaining that although the Dog Woman is superficially conservative in her views, the grotesqueness of her appearance argues for a much more subversive assertion of power and agency, and Langland agrees with this ambiguous split between the conservative views and the unconventional appearance that subverts her own ideas. Where Doan and Farwell see *Sexing the Cherry* as a successful lesbian text, Palmer argues it is only indirectly lesbian in its focus, and Pearce denounces the attempt to 'universalise' lesbians alongside heterosexuals as a way of trivialising the differences and a disappointing strategy for lesbian readers. While almost every critic analyses the character of the Dog Woman, less than half accord the same importance to Jordan as challenging gender norms. Doan, Farwell, Moore and Rosemergy pick out the fact that he cross-dresses and thereby discovers women's hidden language, Moore arguing that he is putting forward a new type of masculinity that does not try to oppress and dominate women. Doan and Lozano analyse the central metaphor of the novel, the act of grafting, in detail, and where Doan reads it as standing for a third generative space, which, in being an excessive image of procreation beyond the heterosexual formation, can be read as lesbian, Lozano points to it being artificial and willed, rather than a traditional myth of origins, and so likewise a lesbian figuration. Moore links the grafting, as a freak of nature, to the Dog Woman's unnatural birth to reinforce her as a lesbian figure. Of the various stories related within the book, two are singled out for discussion. The tale of the Twelve Dancing

Princesses is examined by Pearce, Doan, Rosemergy and Morrison, to analyse how they present the only overt lesbian narratives, or how they subvert masculine narratives of male agency and female passivity, and marital closure. Rosemergy compares Winterson's rewriting in relation to the British late nineteenth-century, Andrew Lang version, while Morrison has recourse to the German version earlier in the nineteenth-century, with the Brothers Grimm. Rosemergy, along with Farwell, also argues for the importance of the rewriting of the Orion and Artemis myth to deny women being the object of male narratives, and asserting a similar agency and rejection of heterosexual oppression to the fairy tale. Lozano argues that the sexuality of the novel is linked to a metamorphosis that argues for a multiplicity and changing forms of both sex and love. Apart from Pearce and Martin, the critics were extremely favourable, and while some questioned the efficacy of specific strategies – Doan sees cross-dressing as being of only temporary usefulness and Meyer sees the novel testing the limits of the grotesque as a literary trope – they did not feel that these invalidated the scope and engagement of the novel as a whole. The size of the critical debate and its largely positive readings point to *Sexing the Cherry* as being one of Winterson's most successful novels after *Oranges Are Not the Only Fruit*, an accolade that cannot be accorded to her next novel, *Written on the Body*, where the similarly 'indirect' lesbian focus, given the narrator's deliberately and ingeniously genderless status, raised much more of a furore and provoked more interrogative criticism.

CHAPTER FIVE

Written on the Body (1992)

After the broad sweep and magical mix of narratives of *Oranges Are Not the Only Fruit, Boating for Beginners, The Passion* and *Sexing the Cherry*, readers probably began to think they knew what to expect from a Winterson novel. If so, her next novel was to prove a surprise; *Written on the Body* was a close study focused on the relationships within a love triangle, a theme that was to become perennial in her later work.

Laura Cumming in the *Guardian*[1] discussed the beautiful writing and decided ambivalently that if the reader gets past the opinionated 'bravado' of the narrator, they uncover a more serious import in the idea that desire can best be measured by the grief experienced at the loss of the desired, rather than by the ardour felt in its presence. Once the loved one has disappeared, the narrator stops voicing a cod laddishness and begins to take on Winterson's characteristic narrative voice. The appropriation of religious tropes such as the sermon and the hymn, for the examination of Louise's anatomy invaded by cancer, gives rise to a poetic rendering of love that touches both the heights of fallible hope and the depths of Evangelical dogmatism. Valerie Miner in *The Women's Review of Books* was more dismissive, despite the obvious possibilities of a genderless narrator, who can raise crucial theoretical questions about the concept of essentialism and what constitutes gender identity; but Miner sadly feels that what might have proved to be a 'subversive portrayal of androgynous passion' never develops past being a 'gimmick' and remains 'disappointingly conventional'.[2] Nicoletta Jones, in the *Sunday Times*,[3] also found the book disappointing, because it did not live up to Winterson's earlier reputation for originality and verve which had made her the 'voice of her generation'. She also judges *Written on the Body* conventional and sees it as playing safe. Purporting to be a work that delves behind the clichés about love to find untrammelled metaphors for intense desire, Jones finds it simply regurgitates old conventions with an alienating smug self-satisfaction. The genderless narrator, striving to blur the distinctions between heterosexual and lesbian stereotypes, presents a self-indulgent, wallowing monologue little different from the conventional 'NW3[4] adultery novel'. Jones excuses the harshness of her criticism by explaining that the innovatory brilliance of Winterson's earlier novels means that her work is always judged against the highest of standards, and she acknowledges that there are still felicities of style and phrase in small pockets of the text.

In the USA, Jim Shepherd is similarly ambivalent, but with a more positive conclusion than Jones. Beginning with a strong representation of the novel as an ambitious mixture of love story and theoretical deliberation on the body as a material object, and also the manifestation of our sense of our own selves, 'our bodies as our embodiment',[5] he states conclusively that the novel is 'consistently revelatory' about that oldest of subjects, love. He suggests that the intensity of focus of Winterson's meditations on the loved one's body gives love a physicality and materiality within the text, but that this strength is hampered in particular by the genderless narrator. He finds this too staged, calling attention to itself as subversive in ways that prevent it truly being so. For Shepherd there are enough pointers for him to feel confident in asserting that the narrator is female. The misanthropy of the text's view of everyone but the loved one is suggestive, and while he finds the husband's 'black-hearted' manipulation of the situation contrived to construct the narrator's noble self-sacrifice in giving up Louise embarrassingly gratuitous, he also raises an important critique of the end of the novel. Since it had suggested throughout a relationship of shared openness and true intimacy between Louise and the narrator, the decision to end the relationship being unilaterally the narrator's paradoxically raises questions about the consensual relationship as a whole. It is a fair question that points to a serious elision in the plot, but despite his caveat, Shepherd was more favourable than other reviewers towards the novel, particularly in relation to its unique focused meditation on the phenomenon of love.

Where Cumming's review of *Written on the Body* was ambivalent, acknowledging the serious endeavour to write about love but disliking the tricksiness of the narrative voice's lack of gender specificity, Miner and Jones found it more disappointing, Miner because the subversive intent of the genderless narrator was not fully explored. Both Miner and Jones agree that what results is a conventional text, Jones seeing it as close to a Hampstead adultery novel from a writer such as Margaret Drabble (born 1939). Shepherd, in contrast, welcomed it as an ambitious and revelatory novel and though he agrees with the other reviewers that the genderless narrator does not work, he finds that the juxtaposition of the philosophic meditations on the body and the more realist narrative is successful.

The critical discussion for *Written on the Body* takes place mainly in two specific years, 1996 and 1998, the latter being the date of the *Postmodern*

Studies special issue on Winterson, edited by Grice and Woods, where the predominant interest was *Written on the Body*; four of the nine essays looked at it. However, Lisa Moore's consideration of 'virtual lesbians' in Winterson's texts examined *Written on the Body* as well as *The Passion* and *Sexing the Cherry* in 1995. Moore centres on the narrator, whose gender is deliberately withheld from the reader, as being an example of a virtual narrator, consciously constructed to confound the reader's expectations of how to read the representation of the highly charged erotic desire. With a knowledge of Winterson's past texts and a grasp of current lesbian sub-cultures, she argues, it would not be difficult to read the relationship between narrator and Louise as a lesbian one, listing the homophobia of the people in the street, the term 'pervert' inscribed on the hospital notes, and the discussion about lesbian-feminist politics. But this would be to miss the point, to try to fix the ambiguities and fluidities of both identity and sexual desire that are one of the main strengths of the novel. The narrator's terrorist attack on a men's urinal, with her previous girlfriend, Inge, gives rise to constructions of men as the Other. When they are caught in the act of urinating as the warning of the bomb is calmly announced, Moore argues that the text presents a specifically feminist reaction to men. The narrator is not androgynous, nor shifting from being a man to being a woman, Moore contends, but rather 'a figure constructed of disparate body parts, desire, identities and histories, put together in a postmodern pastiche that nonetheless allows for the grand romantic obsession of lesbian romance fiction in the best identitarian tradition of lesbian cultural politics'.[6] The narrator thus figures as a postmodern deconstruction of gender and sexual stereotypes that refuses to develop a construction of its own gender identity. Into this narrative practice are placed two discourses, one of religious mysticism, reminiscent of the language of *Oranges Are Not the Only Fruit*, and the other of the new physics of relativity and uncertainty, to represent a love without bounds or conditions. The understanding of physics and religion which develops positions the narrator's claim that the world can be reframed by choice, if we only have the creative arrogance to do it. The world is of necessity, therefore, a virtual experience, and it is we who alter history. Moore introduces *Neuromancer* (1984) by William Gibson (born 1948), the seminal cyberpunk science fiction novel, into the discussion, explaining that it contains a similar *mélange* of the 'informatic', digital technology, and the 'millenarian' [the seventeenth-century belief in the importance of the coming of the millennium] narrative discourses. Moore shows how *Written on the Body* also discusses revolutionary scientific developments such as biochemical molecular docking, the chronobiology of the narrator's circadian clock, and Elgin's study of gene therapy. She uses *Neuromancer* to compare the experimental uses of virtual reality in cyberspace and points out that where

Gibson's novel treats love and the body of his lover as false simulations, suggesting one cannot trust the senses, Winterson in contrast uses the religious lexicon to assert a revaluation of love and of sexual rapture for the physical body of the beloved. In so doing, rather than mirror the machismo rhetoric of cyberpunk, *Written on the Body* aligns itself rather with the lesbian romantic obsession of writers such as Sarah Schulman in *After Delores* and Renee Hansen in *Take Me to the Underground* (1990). The sections devoted to the re-examination of the anatomical discourses of the body recall Monique Wittig's *The Lesbian Body* (1975) for its similar catalogue of the various parts of the loved one's body opened to the gaze. Winterson is therefore seen as trying to amalgamate two contemporary genres – the narrative of postmodern cyberpunk and the plot and subject matter of lesbian fiction – to create a category of the postmodern lesbian.

In 1996, Christy L. Burns's 'Fantastic Language'[7] also focused on the language and narration of *Written on the Body*, suggesting that Winterson 'tries to reclaim both the flattened word and the desensitised body, and she effects this through an erotic revival'[8] that becomes a 'fantastic reconstruction of the body of the dead (or dying) lover whom the narrator has lost'.[9] While acknowledging the critical discussion surrounding the strategy of the 'genderless' narrator, Burns's main preoccupation is with the narrating of the loved one's body as an erotic invocation:

■ In *Written on the Body*, Winterson develops the relationship between the body and language most extensively, as a nameless narrator attempts to recover Louise, her/his lover, by calling up parts of her body in clinical form, suffusing them and reconfiguring them with erotic language and imaginings. The novel's biggest claim on audiences has been the mystery surrounding the narrator's sex. Nameless and carefully degendered, she/he tells the story of finding, loving, and then losing Louise. The story of the narrator's frantic attempts to find Louise is interrupted, midway through the novel, by a series of prose pieces that seem to be the narrator's attempt to reclaim Louise's body against the thought of its physical absence and inevitable decay. This mid-section is split into four parts: 'The Cells, Tissues, Systems and Cavities of the Body'; 'The Skin'; 'The Skeleton'; and 'The Special Senses'. Each part contains one or more passages that opens with a quotation from a medical text-book and is followed by the narrator's own resistance to the callousness of that language and her/his attempt to fantasize Louise's presence into being.[10] □

The narrator reconstructs the body of Louise through memory and desire, so that the erotic scrutiny itself becomes an alternative form of 'invasion' that replaces the invasions of the cancer. 'Just as she/he once engaged competitively with Louise's husband – a doctor who studies bodies through a scientific lens – the narrator now battles with the language of science in an attempt to reclaim the body, and language, for romance and memory.'[11] The evocation of skin in all its sensual detail and fantasies stands as a contrast to the medical discourse's poverty-stricken definition. But evoking the lover's body is a way, simultaneously, of acknowledging its absence as well as its presence. Words cannot capture the actuality, existing as they do within their own discourses. 'As Winterson presses on the limits of language, she hits upon its necessary mediation, the recognition that words call up visions distinctly different from those they actually present, letter-by-letter, on the page. From the ways in which words can be sensuous and metaphors pungent, eroticism develops. The body is not a literal, scientific object in the middle section; it is only real *through* imagination, as it is metaphorically recalled and erotically invoked.'[12] Burns also introduces Monique Wittig's novel *The Lesbian Body*, though he sees the comparison as relating to the narrator torn between desire for the lover as object of desire, and identification with her as subject, which has a direct resonance with the erotic attempt to merge body and language. But *Written on the Body*, in its Romantic attempt to transubstantiate the body through language, also comes up against the limits of language and of fantasy. The words may be inspired by desire, but are they able to satisfy that desire? The narrator, having lost Louise, fantasises her return, a return that perhaps is actually called up by the power of the imagination. 'It is as if Winterson pushes fantasy to the extreme implications of its use and here refuses to turn back from the madness it invokes, "madness" defined by Lacan as the total release of the Real. One is shocked to remember that fiction is no more than fantasy, however, be it historical or more radically imagined, and it functions only as a focal point of our desires, being perhaps useful but not ultimately able to call up the object of desire.'[13] Burns, then, sees language in *Written on the Body* as attempting the transubstantiation of the body and of desire, resulting in an innovatory novel that pushes language systems to their very limits.

Marilyn Farwell's consideration of the novel alongside *Sexing the Cherry*, in the same year, discussed both texts' refusal to fit into expected frameworks for a lesbian narrative, and so looked at the genderless narrator. *Written on the Body* 'entices the critic of lesbian fiction but remains problematically aloof. In *Written on the Body*, Winterson depicts a love relationship in which the beloved, Louise, is identifiably female, but the lover, the first person narrator, exhibits no corresponding gendered markings, and in fact displays an ambiguous variety of stereotypical markings.'[14] The problem of designating it a lesbian novel, Farwell notes, was one that exercised the judges of the Lambada Literary Awards for that year. *Lambada*, the gay and lesbian journal, annually awards prizes for the best gay and lesbian writing, but in 1993 a dispute developed between the judges. 'As reported in a local gay newspaper, the selection committee could not decide whether or not Winterson's novel was, in fact, lesbian fiction. One faction believed that it should be disqualified, and the other faction claimed that the book could only be understood as lesbian fiction.'[15] However, for Farwell, the literary hunt to locate the gender of the narrator is actually a red herring. The analysis of the novel as a lesbian text resides for her in the depiction of the lover, Louise, whose body has been reconfigured and repositioned as excessive in a different but analogous way to the Dog Woman's. The 'excessive female body is a challenge to the traditional Western textualization of the female body'.[16] How the text positions the two lovers in relation to each other, allows the romance story to be reclaimed for lesbians, since the narrator's position within the romance narrative shifts. Initially positioned as a traditional male lover, or a butch lesbian, with a past of unsatisfactory women lovers before the arrival of the beloved, the narrator is aware that s/he is speaking within a narrativising system that trivialises the feelings as trite and cliché-ridden. For Farwell, the important element is not the gender of the bisexual narrator but rather that s/he is aware of being 'trapped within a story which is fraught with clichés',[17] which s/he must try to escape from in order to speak the words afresh. The narrator's conception of love therefore comes to her/him through cultural traditions and initially Louise is configured as a heroine from some earlier textual tradition in the Gothic or Victorian novel. 'The question becomes how to love without being trite, without repeating the same story.'[18] The indeterminacy of the narrator's gender therefore becomes linked to his/her shifting position in relation to the reader. While *Written on the Body* often provides a breathless first-person narrative inviting identification, it shifts at other times to a more distanced rejection of engagement. The narrator invokes the artificiality and fictionality of the narrative, lacing it with other texts, crime fiction, opera and Russian novels to question his/her own veracity as a narrator. 'These shifts of narrative level and voice highlight the metafictional nature of this novel. It is a story about story, about the possibility of telling the same story in a different form but not in an unrecognisable form. The revised story must begin not with the refusal of trite phrases like "I love you" or melodramatic tragic endings nor with the narrator, but with Louise.'[19] Only once the lover's body has been retextualised in ways that manage to escape the traditional Western romance, can the narrator succeed in being repositioned within a differing, specifically lesbian story.

Louise's body becomes this site of the narrative renegotiation. The desired body is configured in traditional sixteenth-century images reminiscent of John Donne (1572–1631) and Shakespeare but this all changes with the introduction of the cancer. The narrator's distant attempts to share in the body's experience of cancer result in a poetic evocation of the narrator's love:

■ Winterson's narrator anatomizes the female body that is out to destroy itself, a body that duplicates itself outside of the rules. This excessive female body is imagined through a disease that reproduces itself wildly at a cellular level. In effect the disease remaps the body and changes the narrator to the bones of his/her own body. Like the romantic narrative which provides both the grid and the opposition for the narrator's story, Louise's diseased body represents both the traditionally negative and disruptively positive descriptions of the female body as excessive. Once restructured as excessive, the love relationship and the lovers become lesbian.[20] □

The central portion of the novel abandons the plot to focus on the description of various parts of the female body, using both medical and poetic discourse in a narrative that shifts from recounting events to cataloguing details. Narrative time is disrupted to reposition the female body as excessive and grotesque. 'Winterson takes a predictable, in this case medical, vocabulary, and refuses its terms: instead, she writes her own medical description of the body as a poetic amalgam of reversals, puns and metaphors.'[21] The narrator learns the body of the beloved in anatomical detail, and then, through the poetic rendition, both transforms the body and inhabits it, in a non-phallic penetration. 'It is this mutuality, this sameness rather than heterosexual romantic difference, which constitutes the narrator and Louise as the lesbian subject.'[22] The medical detailing, allowing as it does an intimate knowledge of the beloved, thereby repositions the two lovers in a relationship of sameness. Louise is granted narrative agency and becomes the desiring subject as well as the desired object, as the narrator also becomes her object of desire. The capital 'L' which has come to stand for both Louise and Love could as easily, for Farwell, stand for Lesbian. *Written on the Body* frees the female body from the male parameters of heterosexual and homosocial desire, and so therefore writes a lesbian desire, writes 'the lesbian subject into lesbian narrative space'.[23] At the close of the medical section, Winterson places the 'reinscribed bodies and the realigned positionalities of the lovers'[24] back into the linear plot, where Louise is only present through her absence. The novel's closure becomes effectively two possible closures, as either Louise returns or the narrator imagines she returns and Winterson reverts to citing the trite endings of traditional Western romance fiction, while at the same time questioning them as she gestures towards more multiple possibilities that continue rather than close off. In this, Winterson innovatively combines both the traditional form and the postmodern dissonance, 'by repositioning the categories of narrator, agent and object'.[25]

Where Farwell analyses the narrative of *Written on the Body*, Heather Nunn gives a psychoanalytic reading in 'An Anatomy of Horror, Melancholy and Love' (1996).[26] The very title of the novel, she argues, focuses attention on both textuality (written) and sexuality (body), and relates to the contemporary debates around whether the body can be seen as a fetishised site of the source of truths, the real that we can actually experience, or as something inscribed and constructed by cultural discourses, that we can only access through cultural expectations. For Nunn the latter holds true and identity and sexuality are unstable and unfixed processes. Nevertheless the lovers believe in the former, and search for an ideal dyadic[27] wholeness through their relationship with the other, and this inevitably leads to disappointment and loss alongside the partial satisfaction of desire. The narrative uses the body itself as the site on which to explore the psychological affects of love, betrayal, melancholy and the complex amalgam of attraction and repulsion that lovers experience. The cultural discourses that seek to map the body and to police it are further examined. Starting from a conventional representation of Louise's body, initially a closed, contained body, as the object of desire and site of identity, Nunn argues, like Farwell, that Winterson's text first explores Louise's body, then splits it asunder into its constituent parts, before finally reinventing it anew for a transgressive, specifically lesbian sexuality. Such a strategy is only possible because of the narrator's non-gender-specific identity, since it serves to highlight society's vulnerability in relation to patriarchal gender binary divisions, through his/her troubling, intriguing position; Nunn sees the narrator as 'unstably gendered' rather than genderless. As s/he discusses the clichés and intertextualities of trying to express love, the reader's own reception also proves unstable. Nunn looks in detail at the narrator's previous love affairs, when s/he positions her/himself in the role of a Lothario, and argues that this parallels Julia Kristeva's Don Juan figure, who is in love with phallic mastery for its own sake, a form of symbolic game. Winterson's narrator demonstrates a similar phallic mastery and so successfully usurps the traditionally male, heterosexual prerogative. Nunn suggests that the lesbian body is constructed as a 'third term' and this necessarily challenges the mutuality of the binary division of male and female. Within *Written on the Body*, the essay argues, this is portrayed as the abject, unstable body, by definition a non-heterosexual body where the genders meet and transmute into both the feminine *and* the masculine, the male *and* the female and so, in Lacanian terms, the 'being' *and* the 'having' the phallus.[28] Lesbian identity, through this third term of alterity, subverts the concept of any fixed gender identity, positing instead a more fluid series of traversable identificatory positions. Coming from a very different critical discourse, postmodern psychoanalysis, Nunn arrives at a very similar reading to Farwell's postmodern analysis of narrative.

In the fourth of the considerations in 1996, 'From He and She to You and Me',[29] Lisa Haines Wright and Tracy Lynn Kyle also agree on the fluidity of the narrator in *Written on the Body*, linking him/her to Virginia Woolf's fluidly gendered protagonist in *Orlando*, but insist that Winterson is attempting to create 'a new grounding of identity. ... Defined in relationship to others through time, "self-constancy" is the capacity for fidelity.'[30] Fidelity allows a sense of constancy for the fluid identity. They claim that Winterson is in a direct intertextual dialogue with *Orlando*, since it too defines identity as fluid and mutable but also, paradoxically, self-constant, and hence they see Winterson as the 'direct heir to Virginia Woolf'. *Written on the Body* seeks to ground identity on both the power to remember and the capacity for faithfulness, for fidelity, without thereby arguing for a fixed, immutable self. 'If fidelity enables identity, memory enables fidelity. Here, the body figures meaning: "written on the body ... [are] the accumulations of a lifetime". Meaning is defined between text and reader, so too [the narrator's] identity, between [the narrator's] self-text and Louise's "reading hands".'[31] Winterson's narrator creates a sense of self-identity through the way s/he relates to the loved one; the commitment and constancy of the feeling help to focus the shifting selves of the narrator. Finally, having allowed Woolf's text to clarify the theme of identity in *Written on the Body*, Wright and Kyle argue for a reciprocal relationship; given the dialogue with *Orlando*, Winterson's text allows us to read the earlier text with more clarity as well. 'At the end of *Written on the Body*, the narrator affirms a speaking identity by commitment to Louise. ... Louise answers that call. ... Words grounded in fidelity engage response; meaning is located where the two meet. That meeting figures another, which Winterson flags with her last words. ... Like Woolf, Winterson defers closure. Rewriting Orlando's closing, she helps open it to us.'[32]

In 1998, Helena Grice and Tim Woods edited the collection of essays on Winterson, *'I'm telling You Stories'* for *Postmodern Studies*. Lynne Pearce's essay, 'The Emotional Politics of Reading Winterson'[33] continues her investigation into what happens when we read, exploring the event and the context and the experience of reading (rather than how we interpret texts). Winterson, she suggests, is a writer who appeals to the readers' emotions, stunning and capturing them through their emotional responses, and initially she was no exception. 'It was that special sense of having your own thoughts and feelings written out for you.'[34] This identification with the writing developed into an identificatory relationship with the author, despite her acceptance of Barthes's poststructural criticism that 'the author is dead', and has no authority for the meaning of the text. Pearce's relationship therefore became one of a fan rather than a critic. 'By locating my "textual other" in an author-function rather than a specific text, my readerly-enchantment ... manifested itself as exemplary adolescent fandom (although I was no longer an adolescent).'[35] The event that changed this adulation and resulted in her double-consciousness of herself as both fan and literary critic was the publication of *Written on the Body*. The public acclaim for Winterson as the young genius shifted with this text, which she remembers as having a particularly negative reception. Whether this was due to the text itself, to Winterson's outrageously arrogant public persona, or because the reviewers were fed up with lauding so obviously young a writer, she cannot tell. Her main memory is of the 'quality' broadsheets 'stamping their reservations all over the book', disliking the politics of the gender-less narrator, its panegyric form which few recognised as actually a reference to courtly love poems, and its lack of closure. In the face of such a barrage of criticism and the question of whether Winterson had 'sold out' as a lesbian, Pearce the fan felt the need to defend the text against a hostile world, to the detriment of, she now feels, her honest, critical reactions. In retrospect, her essay notes that once a reader has made an emotional investment in a particular writer they are remark-ably reluctant to let it go. The investment has become part of the reader's own identity as a reader, they are defined as the sort of reader who likes Winterson. For a critic, this has further academic implications in relation to essays already published and the sense of one's own academic identity. Pearce's reaction, she explains, was to elide the autonomy of *Written on the Body* and discuss Winterson's oeuvre as a whole, but it was, for her, the beginning of the end of her fandom. However, Pearce, writing in 1998, argues that the fault lay not with the book so much as with her as a reader. Since she found it impossible to engage with the new and divergent sexuality the book promotes, she became frustrated and projected this, and the consequent lack of author-identification, onto the text, arguing that the failure lay there. This helps Pearce to understand that 'what presents itself as critical and political judgement and discrimination is often concealing a far more messy and desperate struggle between text and reader'.[36] Pearce, unable to engage emotionally with most of the novel's description of Louise's body, found the narrative personally alienating and reached for aes-thetic explanations for her dislike, the role as emotionally involved reader fuelling the role as critic. Examining in detail the way *Written on the Body* describes Louise's disease as seductively attractive was a problem for both personal and academic reasons. Having had personal experi-ence of watching cancer's depredations created the first difficulty and the text's similarity to the Pre-Raphaelite glamorisation of female suffering, a particular expertise of Pearce's academic life, compounded the difficulty. These two contexts created an anxiety and discomfort surrounding her reading of the passages. What she finds particularly difficult, pursuing her analysis further, is not so much the diseased body's representation as simply the representation of Louise's body in itself. Winterson's change in how she represents the female body is at the crux of Pearce's disenchantment as a reader, because for her the sexualising of it proves a detriment to its role as love object. At the time of *Written on the Body*'s publication, the publicity included a photo of Winterson posed naked in the *Guardian*, and Pearce read this as part of her commodification of her own female body and of the female body's representation in the novel. Pearce, as a reader, unable to come to terms with the loss of her own identity as a Winterson fan, still holds out hope that her identificatory position may return in the future, with some later text, just as the narrator of *Written on the Body* holds out hope that the lost Louise may someday return.

Ute Kauer's 'Narration and Gender',[37] examines the issues of gender and narrative, and begins by drawing on the narratology of Gérard Genette (born 1930).[38] The narrator, who she argues is not trying to merge male and female but rather to erase gender as of any relevance or importance within the text, is a 'homodiegetic narrator' since s/he is part of the action of the fictional world, relating the events to the reader, 'the narratee'; but the reader's position shifts and changes, as the relationship between the narrator and narratee shifts throughout. Kauer traces the different forms of 'you' used by the narrator, sometimes addressed to an absent Louise, sometimes to an implied reader whom s/he will enter into a dialogue with, through the response to the reader's implied reactions. 'So we have a situation of communication where the narrator changes the narratee, establishes a quasi-oral relationship to the implied reader and thus attaches the role of confidant and moral authority to the reader.'[39] However, the narrator also calls attention to him/herself as fictitious and potentially unreliable, thus problematising the quasi-oral relationship between reader and narrator even further. The narrator in fact develops an ironic deconstruction of the narrative itself through these complex narrative interactions. Like Winterson's previous fiction, *Written on the Body* raises metafictional questions about the sliding distinctions between fact and fiction and argues that what is important in any scene is not its veracity, its truth value, but the ability to convey the emotional value in developing the experience of being in love. Pedantic issues such as whether she fed Louise plums in August, when plums are unavailable in August, are irrelevant, since it is always going to be impossible to capture the real in words. 'The self creates his or her own biography by finding metaphors for experiences because those metaphors are a more precise expression of emotion than facts.'[40] The boundaries between fiction and reality are further breached when the narrator visibly lies to other characters in the novel, for example when s/he lies to Inge, at the beginning, about Renoir painting with his penis. Inge's assertion that she is lying, has the narrator respond with a tense that alerts the reader to his/her unreliability in relation to the narrating of the whole novel: not 'did I?' but 'am I?' For Kauer this illustrates the narrator's role in disturbing the distinctions between fiction and reality. The reader is shown, by the answer to Inge, that all we will be given is fictionality and an undermining of what to believe, as the narrator 'coquettes with his/her uncertainty' and 'chooses to withhold all information about the narrator-persona'.[41] Kauer lists the remarkable amount of information withheld from the reader about the narrator: name, gender, age, appearance, beliefs, or the narrator's historical and geographical context. It is as if the narrator were talking to her- or himself, a private discourse that would need no objective placement. But, questions Kauer, is the gender actually meant to be withheld, or is it simply a further ironic mask?

Traditionally, first-person narration brings with it certain limitations: the writer is locked into the narrator's mind and cannot show any information beyond what s/he can plausibly know, such as the thoughts of other characters, or the external appearance of the narrator; s/he cannot range over time or countries. *Written on the Body* deliberately plays with these restrictions to whet and challenge the reader's interest. References to clothes are inconclusive, as are references to lovers, since both sexes are mentioned. When the narrator looks into a mirror, it is only to examine the internal mental state, eschewing the external reflection. The novel seeks to unmask the clichés about love and gender by deliberately ignoring the importance of these cultural markers. Alongside gender, the text also seeks to deconstruct discussion of love and the body. Medical discourse and romance narratives are shown for their paucity, while poetic evocations of passion in the middle section of the novel attempt to write love anew. For Kauer, the lack of irony in these evocations, since this is the one section that does not strive to deconstruct discourses but to assert a rewritten one, proves unpalatable and its juxtaposition of excessive metaphor and poetry recalls the writing of passion of D. H. Lawrence. The text plays with the reader; in relation to gender, the reader is supposed to struggle with the stereotypes as the narrator lays a series of red herrings and gender stereotypes to confuse them. The narrator chooses both female and male identifications, carefully balanced to confound expectations, though on closer inspection it is the stereotypes about femininity that are challenged directly, while masculine attitudes and masks, such as hard-boiled insouciance, are more humorously invoked. Nowhere is there a comparable feminine mask. Kauer sees this as pointing to an attempt to deconstruct the myths of masculinity while broadening the culturally acceptable roles for femininity. Since the only masks are male, it follows she believes that the hidden identity behind the masks is feminine, and this accords with the feminist agenda of attacking the clichés applied to women. A further pointer is that when telling us of minor characters, the narrator identifies and empathises with the female characters rather than the male ones. However, for Kauer, her ability to analyse the narrator's status and name the gender does not invalidate the narrator's status as inconclusive, nor the deconstructive effect of the apparent displacement; it is after all the masks she hides behind that are the very things which are being parodied. But we do not get a gender-free narrative; it is a feminist one that problematises gender roles by employing a mask of gender-ambiguity. The readers' perceptions are, hopefully, changed through the book's feminist redirection of their gaze.

Patricia Duncker's 'Jeanette Winterson and the Aftermath of Feminism' draws a division between the 1970s and 1980s, when feminists believed they could change the world and embraced political slogans and certainties, very much like Jeanette's mother in *Oranges Are Not the Only Fruit*, and the 1990s sceptical, deconstructive 'post-feminism', less able to believe in the power of feminism to affect society. In the 1970s and 1980s, radical feminists argued that they could exceed the patriarchal construction 'woman', the second sex, and redefine it as an alternative and lesbian presence. Radical feminist women writers were 'a jubilant crew of man-haters and lesbians, bent on disrupting the settled order of men's power over meanings, language and texts'.[42] For Duncker, Winterson's texts aim to do much the same. Looking at lesbian poets of the 1980s, as they struggled to wrest language from heterosexual discourses on love, to express the 'peculiar, erotic mirroring of sameness and the tensions and difficulties of even the most minor struggles within intimacy',[43] she sees a similar rendition in *Written on the Body*. The internalised hypocrisies of heterosexual love are questioned by both Winterson and the 1980s lesbian feminists, but the latter were more straightforward in their provocation, Winterson more 'duplicitous'[44] in allowing a comfortable space for the heterosexual male reader of *Written on the Body*, who could distance himself from the negative character of Elgin and so not feel under attack. It can be seen as a text that questions heterosexuality none the less, because of its genderless narrator and the central discourse on the body. Like others before her, Duncker links this to Wittig's *The Lesbian Body* and explains how, though not so well known as other French feminist texts, it was cult reading for the lesbian audience. Wittig's text demonstrates the completely different libidinal economy in play within lesbian desire, and the different dynamics involved in sex between two same-sex bodies, where the 'I' and the 'you' are not different and no aspect of the bodies elicits disgust because unknown. Despite the genderless narrator's refusal to conform to an obviously lesbian narration, Winterson's discussion of the body links her to such experimental lesbian writers. *Written on the Body*'s representation of the body as a land to be scaled, mapped and invaded is, for

Duncker, the most effective part of the novel and an indication of the opportunities lost in not 'coming out' as a lesbian text. By not declaring a sex, the narrator is forced to conform to heterosexual clichés alongside the experimentation and so 'closes down'[45] the potentially subversive elements of the text. In reproducing the traditional eternal triangle, Duncker believes, we learn more about the narrator's relationship with the rival than with the loved object, who remains a fantasy rather than a realised character. These failings, all of which stem from choosing a genderless narrator, militate against the novel as an effective political text and show up, she suggests, what lesbians lose in embracing queer theory to the detriment of old-style feminist politics.

Cath Stowers's 'The Erupting Lesbian Body: Reading *Written on the Body* as a Lesbian Text'[46] is the last of the essays to consider the novel in '*I'm telling you stories*' and argues for a lesbian reading of the novel as one of the available readings, acknowledging that the narrator could be defined as bisexual as much as lesbian. In her opinion, Winterson has, through previous novels, developed a focus on female sexuality, attempting to reposition sexual pleasure from the feminine experience, rather than the masculine point of view. In all of Winterson's novels one can find that 'female characters frequently excavate the female body in a re-appropriation and parodying of the power of the phallus'.[47] *Written on the Body*, because of the genderless narrator, explores the female body in the opening chapters in metaphors that appear to reflect the masculine libidinal economy of penetration, and have led critics to argue that the novel has been unable to escape the discursive hegemony of heterosexualism (and colonialism) in its exploration of sexual desire. For Stowers, this is a poor reading of Winterson's continuing fascination with deconstructing both gender and the exclusionary projections of the 'other'. The focus on the anatomy of the female body rather develops a lesbian commitment to the erotic pleasures of the flesh, reclaiming the woman's body for women's desire: 'if the narrator is a woman, we have a lesbian celebratory reclamation of the female form; if a man, a rare male acknowledgement of no passive idealised body but one empowered'.[48] The focus on the lack of gender in the narrator, moreover, mixes and reverses the usual gender signifiers and as such, in rejecting any 'essentialist' sex position and arguing instead for a deconstructive 'subject position' in relation to sexuality and desire, s/he does fulfil lesbian aims, even though not identifiably lesbian. Stowers's interpretation is therefore the very opposite of Valerie Miner's negative review, which saw the critique of essentialism in relation to gender and sexuality thrown away. Stowers uses a different Monique Wittig text, *The Straight Mind* (1992), where Wittig argues lesbianism should not be aligned with either the masculine or the feminine 'but rather ... highlight the duplicity of division between the two'.[49] In mixing and revising the gender markers, Winterson could be argued to be doing exactly that, highlighting the duplicity of trying to make arbitrary divisions between the two sexes. For Wittig, the dividing up of gender means that femininity, as the other of masculinity, is objectified and denied a subject position and a voice within the higher cultural discourses such as philosophy or politics, which are reserved for the male. *Written on the Body*'s appropriation of the medical and the travel exploration discourses can also be read as following Wittig's dictum and the narrator can be positioned as a 'lesbian subject who trespasses the forbidden space of male-centred letters'.[50] In these terms, Winterson's narrator refuses to conform to heterosexual expectations and so refuses to be either male or female. Although able to inhabit the spheres designated as masculine, the narrator rejects them, refusing to value the mastery of the masculine, and opts instead for a more reciprocal engagement with the female loved one. The fact that the narrator rejects masculine paradigms implies for Stowers as well that she is female, and this is because Stowers sees the refusal to name the gender as implying simply that the dichotomies can be upset, not that they do not exist. The narrator, therefore adopts a performance of masculinity, in the Judith Butler sense, to show up the fact that all gender is a cultural production and not some essential real. The performance of gender calls into question not just gender but sexuality as well, and thereby challenges the idea that heterosexuality is the norm, or normative. In *Written on the Body* the discourse of medicine is added to the metaphor of travel, also employed in *The Passion* and *Sexing the Cherry*. The text situates medical attempts to define and create boundaries as masculine and contrasts it with the lesbian feminist move into poetic descriptions that contain metaphors of the maze and the labyrinth, which is reminiscent of the feminine Villanelle and Venice (in contrast to the French soldiers' masculinity) in *The Passion*. Winterson renegotiates the relationship between lovers from one of an unequal power relation, of dominance (male) and passivity (female), to one of a mutual and fluctuating exchange appropriate for lesbian desire where both partners as women are the same. Images of conquest, where travel and desire merge, are therefore no longer appropriate and are rejected for a more mutual reciprocity with each character becoming the seducer at some point. Desire therefore is portrayed as an activity of 're-mapping, transgressing, and merging'.[51] Stowers challenges the reviews that argued Winterson fell into masculine discourses of annexation and rage against the feminine and claims instead that the novel parodies these discourses in order to move beyond them into a specifically lesbian discourse of desire. In doing this, both gender and sexuality escape from their traditional expectations and the narrative 'exceeds'[52] conventional narrative logic. Since the lesbian is portrayed as the excess of femininity, the narrative becomes by definition a lesbian narrative. Using both Foucault's *The Order of Things* (1970) and Hélène Cixous and Catherine Clément's *The Newly Born Woman* (1986), Stowers argues that *Written on the Body* deconstructs the heterosexual norm and positions itself as a disruptive excess of the norm. Both narrative and the body the narrative is trying to encompass come to stress a mutual sameness and interiority that demands a rethinking of how we discuss and textualise desire. The narrator becomes both subject and object of desire, simultaneously. Winterson's questioning of the dichotomies set up within gender and desire, of the male/female, self/other, and of the compulsory nature of heterosexualism, allows the eruption of the lesbian body into the text in ways clearly too profound for many of the reviewers to recognise. The travel discourse shows up the paucity of masculine conquering in relation to a female body/land rich in unimagined potential. *Written on the Body* therefore demonstrates, for Stowers, a successful lesbian aesthetic.

In 2002, as part of a survey of Winterson's oeuvre, Kim Middleton Meyer briefly considers the narrative discourse of *Written on the Body*. 'Equally as concerned with multiplicity and formal innovation as her early works, *Written on the Body* constructs an argument within the philosophical domain of the Self/Other relationship dictated by love. What is desire ... without the objectification of the beloved?'[53] The narrator's unfixed gender is seen as disconcerting readerly expectations, since both genders are invoked at particular points in the novel: the narrator has had sex with both men and women, brawls with Louise's husband but also asserts a likeness to Lauren Bacall. For Meyer, this fluidity of gender, the refusal to be fixed by either, relates to the trope of nomadism that she has explored in *Sexing the Cherry*. 'In the process of deconstructing the multiple codes that have traditionally defined and confined gender expression, particularly in the ways that these codes map love between two people, Winterson again employs a version of nomadism'.[54] And it is this nomadism that finally allows the narrator to regain the beloved. Initially, the narrator views Louise as someone to be possessed, to be consumed, in a traditional invocation of love that objectifies the loved one, a form culturally encoded as masculine. This is clearly the way the narrator has loved in the past, and it has proved inadequate. Once Louise has disappeared, the obsessive study of anatomy is a continuation of the objectification. But summoning the remembrance of her body leads to an identification that allows Louise an autonomous agency, and a power to touch the narrator: 'having marked the reciprocal relation between Louise and him/her self, the narrator becomes able, through concentration, to conceive of Louise in her own right, materially attached and yet conceptually whole'.[55]

This new relationship to the loved one, a reciprocal rather than a purely possessive one, gestures towards a 'new system of desire between two subjects' where 'neither is Other'.[56] It is a system of desire between nomadic subjectivities, subjectivities that have escaped the fixed binaries of gender expectations, and allows for the return of Louise within the realms of the fantastic.

Similarly, Jago Morrison in the following year (2003) considers how the body is constructed within the space–time continuum of the 'chronotope' (the Bakhtinian concept discussed in Chapter 1). *Written on the Body* is seen as the most radical reconfiguration of the sexual body of the three previous novels, from *Oranges Are Not the Only Fruit* through *The Passion* to *Sexing the Cherry*. With each text, the representation gets more subversive and challenging, but the last of the four is by far the most extreme, in Morrison's view. As with *Sexing the Cherry*, the new physics is invoked to aid this, but here Morrison questions Winterson's effectiveness in understanding all of it. He singles out a quote about being on the edge of a black hole, able to watch history pass because of the event horizon, and challenges Winterson's use of the 'event horizon' to conjure a sense of omniscience, since such a concept does not exist within astrophysics: 'a black hole is a collapsed star whose gravitational pull is so great that not even light can escape. The "event horizon" is that orbit around it, beyond which everything is pulled to the centre. In Relativity Theory, time is not assumed to be a fixed and objective quality, and thus can only be thought of in terms of simultaneity or the gaps between the observable events. Beyond the event horizon, there are no observable events.'[57] Morrison teases out other misjudged uses of physics, and again argues that only from an omniscient, God-like position would her grasp of the theories make sense, and that therefore suggests that 'her texts try to map an over-arching ethical viewpoint on to the parameters of science'.[58] Morrison cites an interview where Winterson explains that her adopted status, without a past or known history, allows her to think of time from the point of view of how one should use the time that one has, an ethical viewpoint that he links to her Pentecostal upbringing. He sees Winterson as trying to fuse together the religious 'meaning-laden model of time' and Einsteinian relativity. 'In *Written on the Body* there is certainly a drive to make time meaningful, to reject the blankness of the secular universe.'[59] Morrison suggests that Winterson is also creating a body without a past, outside of history, and this is supported partly by the narrator's lack of gender definition. The text attempts to free the narrator from inherited gender norms, while also focusing 'closely on inherited language, and its colonisation of the flesh',[60] through the reproduction of phallocentric clichés about colonising or conquering the female body, or the trite metaphor of the sea for femininity, giving the tired clichés a knowing, erotically charged twist. Instead, Winterson's focus on the body of the beloved forms an attempt to reinscribe the body in ways that are even more fluid and destabilising than Judith Butler's attempts in *Gender Trouble*. 'In the many different segments of the text, the sexed body is constantly dismembered and re-membered, across multiple planes of past/present/future, memory, imagination and desire.'[61] The novel develops the paradoxical tensions between a narrator whose sex is withheld and a beloved whose body is obsessively overwritten, and the contrast between these two characters. But it is also always a renegotiation of the language of description and inscription. When Louise is discovered to have cancer, the narrator battles with the husband, who is acquainted with the discourses of disease and lymphocytosis. The narrator strives to acquaint her/himself with the medical jargon but, rather than strive for a similar mastery of the language, begins to subvert its discourse and its metaphors. In the anatomical section, Morrison reads Winterson as reappropriating the body in a deliberately anti-medical discourse, using cancer (rather than the poetic discourse cited by other critics) as a way of reinscribing it from a feminist stance; 'like Butler's "parodic" mis-representation of gender and sex, cancer represents precisely a self-generating mutation of the body, the text seems to suggest – a subtle malignancy that, indefinitely reproduced, threatens the very stability of the body itself.'[62] This takes the form, in the final section of the novel, of Louise being multiple, both dead and living, lost and present, in a manner reminiscent of 'molecular docking'. Louise exists, within the novel, in multiple existences, in memory and in actuality, in past and in possible futures in a fluid jigsaw. But there is no conventional romantic ending, for love is presented as the antithesis of ownership (reminiscent of Jordan and Fortunata setting each other free in *Sexing the Cherry*), as the sexed body is equated with the relativity of time and history.

The critical reception, when it does come, is largely positive and in some cases clearly written as a refutation of the poor reviews. All the analysis focuses on the textuality of the representation of gender and sexuality, with only Nunn attempting a psychoanalytic interpretation of the characters. Farwell and Kauer give a close textual reading of the words and discourses; the others concentrate more on the confounding of gender stereotypes and the erotics of the gaze, so their sights are firmly on cultural expectations and, at times, the reader. The majority of the critical analysis has the narrator's genderless state as its main interest, Moore, Burns, Nunn, Kauer, Haines-Wright and Kyle and Meyer all see it as of central importance in showing up society's vulnerability in relying on such dualistic cultural myths. Haines-Wright and Kyle point to Woolf's *Orlando* as a modernist intertextual reference for the fluidity of gender constructions. Some critics, despite acknowledging the importance of the narrator's refutation of gender identities, and the enormous potential of destabilising and deconstructing expectations, then go on to try to name the narrator's 'real' gender position behind the masks. Moore and Stowers read this as a lesbian narrative position, Kauer as female and feminist. Farwell, on the other hand, rejects the issue as unimportant and a critical red herring. Instead, Farwell concentrates on how the novel seeks to rewrite a discourse of romance and desire that is too clichéd to be effective, and strives to create a fresh discourse for love. Kauer and Morrison agree on the centrality of this theme, and Kauer relates it to the same agenda (and failings) in the work of D. H. Lawrence. Two critics focus on the rewriting of the discourse as a specific challenge to the masculinist discourses of science, which objectifies and 'others' the female body. Burns and Stowers examine the novel's transcending of the medical elaboration of the body, with a more poetic, emotional rendition that is seen as a feminine appropriation of discourse. Burns sees this as a consciously Romantic attempt to transubstantiate the word, which links him to Moore's thesis about Winterson's Romanticism, while Stowers includes the discourse of travel and imperialism – topics she also uses in her analysis of *The Passion* – alongside the medical. All the critics agree that what the book does is to posit a lesbian body as the site of desire, and see Louise's absent representation as worthy of critical discussion. Moore, Burns and Duncker cite Wittig's *The Lesbian Body* as having a similar lesbian agenda and textual anatomical representation, while Stowers chooses another Wittig text, *The Straight Mind*, to argue for the duplicity of cultural stereotypes that see feminine identity as a binary negative of the masculine and, in the binary construction, deny the feminine a voice within the intellectual scientific discourses: a position which she regards *Written on the Body* as refuting in its voicing of the medical discourse and then transcending through poetic lyricism. Stowers, along with Duncker, Farwell and Meyer discusses the lesbian representation as signified through a figure of sameness and mutuality, rather than binary opposition, and Farwell and Stowers further elaborate this as linked to the notion of the lesbian as excessive, a strategy that many of them relate back to Wittig's *The Lesbian Body*, and read in terms of queer theory as illustrating lesbian femininity's difference from heterosexual femininity. About half of them also consider the ending, and discuss whether Louise really does return at the end, linking this to a postmodern challenge to closure through giving various potential endings. Burns and Meyer say that she returns but in the realm of the fantastic, Burns seeing this as a sign of madness, while Haines-Wright and Kyle read it as Louise's actual return. Morrison argues for it representing Louise being lost and present simultaneously. While the reviewers were lukewarm in their praise, the critics can be more self-selecting, only choosing to write on texts which hold an interest and a fascination for them. The majority of the critics write in defence of the novel, or assume its importance and its success as a narrative without overt discussion. Kauer voices a feeling that the attempt to rewrite love anew does not work, because the rapturous depiction loses the parodic edge of the rest of the novel, which for her is important to its textual effectiveness; but she does see the challenge to readerly expectations of the narrator's lack of gender as a successful attempt to change readers' habits. Only Pearce and Duncker feel the text does not work, though for differing reasons from the reviewers. It is certainly true that the reception of the novel comes in waves, with the early critics positive in their analysis, and the re-evaluation and questioning of its strategy coming in the 1998 collection. But where *Written on the Body* created controversy and a high level of critical debate, the following novel, *Art and Lies*, seemed to create only a sense of confusion in the reviews and a silence in the critical analysis – apart, that is from Burns, who extends his discussion of *Written on the Body*'s use of language and discourses into his analysis of Winterson's next book.

CHAPTER SIX

Art and Lies (1994)

Lorna Sage, who had been so enthusiastic about *Sexing the Cherry*, was less certain of *Art and Lies* when she reviewed it for the *Times Literary Supplement*.[1] Not, she hastens to explain, because of the novel itself, despite its complexity, but because the reviewer has also to negotiate the minefield of publicity that surrounds the writer; in this case it proves heavy going since to try to criticise Winterson positions the reviewer as being against Art itself. But the novel is a mix of both good and bad, 'an arbitrary erection' consisting of three narrators – two women and a man who has no penis. The lack of connection between them or the topics they discuss means the book remains sketchy, and is only saved by a minor character, a bawdy seventeenth-century woman who is clearly a self-plagiarism of the marvellous Dog Woman from *Sexing the Cherry*. Sage enjoys Winterson's use of intertextual referencing, calling the plethora of quotes, from contemporary novelists such as Italo Calvino and Angela Carter, through earlier poets such as Robert Browning and W. B. Yeats (1865–1939), to the seventeenth- and eighteenth-century writers Shakespeare and Laurence Sterne (1713–68), an original form 'of finders keepers', and it is this idea that gives the title to her review. She praises the presentation of Picasso's family as predatory, vicious and abusive, seeing it as an effective critique of patriarchal family values. The 'ease with which she steps off into unreality is marvellous' but '[t]oo often she is marking time'. The main thesis, that art is timeless, is declared banal and Sage dislikes the pretentious attempts at proverbs, which she finds excruciating. The review's ambivalence is reflected in the summing up, which implies that the novel does not quite convince or bring off its intentions, and Sage concludes with the surprising decision that it is 'safely good', better than *Written on the Body* but nowhere near the success of *Sexing the Cherry*.

Similarly, the review by Michèle Roberts (born 1949) was taken up with the publicity and hype surrounding the writer as much as with the novel, pointing out that while Winterson might insist on critics sticking to the texts, she is marketed as an icon and so tries to have it both ways. *Art and Lies* is viewed as a typical Winterson mix of beautifully crafted writing and the censure of contemporary life that has cast her as the 'prophet of the late twentieth century'.[2] The review acknowledges the strengths of Winterson as a writer, and her ability to escape the usual typecasting of women writers – feminist or feminine or like a man – that prevents women being taken as seriously as male writers (the slight tone of envy along with admiration coming from Michèle Roberts herself being a woman writer who is often typecast in such ways). She positions Winterson as escaping being 'othered' as a lesbian writer and instead having a magic wand that allows women to fantasise a view of femininity that boldly escapes patriarchal strictures. She also acknowledges the scope of the intention of the novel, calling it her most ambitious to date, in encompassing the themes of time, space and history in a bravura repudiation of the poor reviews of her last novel, which implied she could not hack it. But ultimately Roberts is alienated by the intertextual references which, in contrast to Sage, she sees as the novel simply showing off its own erudition, and by its meandering, fruitless commentaries; she ends her review by questioning what, as a whole, it is trying to say, with barbed references to the Emperor's new clothes.[3]

While Michèle Roberts's review, although negative, strove to acknowledge the good things about Winterson's oeuvre, Philip Hensler's review in the *Guardian* was simply derisory.[4] Seeing her career as going downhill, with each novel worse than the last, he dismisses her latest as not even a novel. The attempts at tasteful prose do not excuse the empty posturing of its content and the lack of any overall structure. Seeing it as pompous, with swathes of it making little sense, he concludes that, despite some stylistic fireworks that remind one of Winterson's better days, she is now unfortunately trying to mimic the worst excesses of Virginia Woolf and so 'something has gone seriously wrong'.[5]

William Pritchard in the *New York Times*[6] sees the prose's attempts to be poetic as 'gaseous' and thinks the novel is gratuitously shocking. Winterson shows in all her work a contemptuous dismissal of the family, home and patriarchal values. In *Art and Lies*, the one major male character is unable to speak effectively for men since, lacking a penis, he is 'in no danger of speaking phallocentrically'.[7] The novel is 'either too clever or too perverse for words'.[8]

The worst of the reviews was a long discussion in the *Sunday Times* by Peter Kemp,[9] an unremittingly negative slating of the novel. Beginning with her own claim that she is one of the best and most exuberant writers of the time, Kemp clearly does not see *Art and Lies* as living up to this. Nevertheless, though put off by the hype surrounding the novel, he does demonstrate a good grasp of the text itself, and has not simply given up, like Hensler. The plot and realisation of the three protagonists on a train are called sketchy and lacking in conviction. Kemp explains that *Art and Lies* is set in the near future, when the monarchy has been removed and the church disestablished from the state, but that the centre of the novel is the three interior monologues by characters named as aesthetic genres – Handel for music, Picasso for painting and Sappho for poetry – and, despite their to some extent damaged state (the castrato, the incest victim and the lesbian), they stand testimony to the notion that art transcends time in a continuum of past and present, an idea that he suggests belonged to the modernist poet T. S. Eliot, in his essay 'Tradition and the Individual Talent'(1920). *Art and Lies* also copies its structure from Virginia Woolf, so given the modernist influence on the main theme and the structure, he is not surprised also to find the snobbish hauteur and prejudices of the high modernists; the dismissal of ordinary people and of scientists as opponents of the arts. (Kemp only seems to think of the high modernists, and not the more radical avant-garde writers of the early twentieth century such as Gertrude Stein [1874–1946] or Mina Loy [1882–1966].) Kemp argues that there is a paradox in Winterson's narrator denouncing ordinary people as stuck in a rut of the mundane, the habit that prevents them truly experiencing the world, when in voicing such clichéd modernist sentiments she is being just as hidebound. He finds the prose strives too hard in trying to convey an ardent fervour, in 'rarefied verbal curlicues',[10] which reaches its pinnacle in the paeans to lesbian desire, whose faintly scriptural tones he links back to the Pentecostal upbringing which Winterson mocked in *Oranges Are Not the Only Fruit*. He takes her to task for choosing to use arcane words that send the reader, mystified, to the dictionary, picking out 'fanon' (a veil worn by a Pope) and 'telesma' (something consecrated that averts the evil eye) as examples of this. He is also alienated by what he calls the 'graffiti of gender spite'[11] that caricatures the male characters as either incestuous predators, misogynistic murderers, or breast surgeons with an over-eager knife. Winterson's treatment of men is just as sexistly offensive as the abuse she depicts against women, the only man who escapes the diatribe being the castrated Handel, since he lacks the offending phallus. The 'messianic vehemence' of *Art and Lies* carries a strident certainty that her first book mocked, but which has now returned as the tone of the piece, and reveals a novelist too self-regarding to utilise her undoubted talents as a writer.

In contrast to the worst excesses of Peter Kemp, Philip Hensler and William Pritchard, Rachel Cusk's review in *The Times*[12] is both perceptive and favourable. Arguing that the shock of trying to read the difficult text is simply the shock of the new, the never-before-read, and that readers need to ditch their preconceptions of what a novel is like before they can fully appreciate this one, she explains that they will find it both infuriating and exciting. The infuriating element relates to Winterson's grandiose claims for it, while the exciting aspect is that, despite the apparent impossibility, as one reads on the grandiose claims are met, in an almost magical, alchemical novel, 'the marriage of invention and compassion'. Cusk suggests that *Art and Lies* is an attack on contemporary technology that sees it bankrupt of any true progress and champions instead a belief in beauty, love and language. She explains that the narrative consists of three dramatic monologues given by three travellers on a train, the spokespeople of contemporary culture moving towards a bleak future: Handel, the ex-priest and breast-surgeon, Picasso, the girl abused by her family, and Sappho the lesbian poet. Each reveals a past scarred with oppression. Each of the characters has been removed from the social fit, through violence for Picasso and Handel, and from sexual preference for Sappho. Cusk finds Handel the most interesting and the most touching, in his compassionate acknowledgement of the failings he has made in his life, both as priest and as doctor. The futuristic technological setting, where the city of London has been divided into three and the countryside nationalised as a gigantic park, is contrasted to the civilisation of ancient Greece, to illustrate how technology has lost sight of culture and of art, and show that all good art transcends time and period to coexist in its own continuum. While acknowledging that there are infelicities in the novel, Cusk's conclusion is favourable, seeing *Art and Lies* as 'optimistic' because of the overwhelming belief in love, in beauty and in the redemptive power of language itself. The attempt to encompass all three of the arts, music, painting and poetry, is, though shaky, breath-taking in its dexterity. But for Cusk, the thing that proves truly moving about the novel is the depth of Winterson's compassion, the depth of the book's feeling.

The initial reviews of *Art and Lies* run the whole gamut, from extremely positive, like Rusk, to extremely negative, like Hensler, with a number left in the middle, such as Sage and Roberts, confused and alienated by the public image projected at the time, though hopeful of the writer. The majority of the reviewers either argue that the book makes no sense at all, or omit to hazard a reading. Pritchard accurately diagnoses the critique of phallocentrism which, as a man, he finds alien-ating, and Kemp also dislikes what he terms Winterson's spitefulness towards men. He does, though, explain that the novel argues that art transcends time, which he links to modernism, and that the three narrators speak in some way for three aesthetic genres. The novel is a hymn to lesbian eroticism. It is left to Cusk's review to give a fuller understanding of the novel's agenda. She sees it as attacking the bank-ruptcy of the postmodern, technological culture while championing a belief in beauty, language and love. She agrees with Kemp that the three protagonists stand for music, painting and words, and finds Handel the most moving in his regret for his past life. Where the men see the novel as purely antagonistic, Cusk is moved by the depth of its compassion.

The critics on the whole have been few and far between. Christy L. Burns has written two general articles which both comment on the novel, and Patricia Duncker also included an examination of it alongside *Written on the Body*, but the absence of discussion for this text signals either dismay or dislike from the academics.

Christy L. Burns's 'Fantastic Language: Jeanette Winterson's Recovery of the Postmodern Word' (1996) argues that Winterson fuses her use of the fantastic into a whole language system in her later novels. 'In *Art and Lies*, Winterson adopts the voice of Sappho to articulate her concern for the flattened state of language. ... Winterson not only attempts to recover the words of the dead – the history of literature brought into the present – but more importantly she works to overcome the "death" of language. Fantasy is no longer a vision that fills up the imagination; it is the inspiration that arises in and through the sensuous and erotic aspects of language.'[13] One of the ways he identifies this as being done is in her use of repetitive refrains: 'repeated phrases work like musical motifs, associatively accruing different levels of meaning across the text'.[14] It is specifically through the emphasis on pleasure and eroticism that she attempts to revitalise language, to make the words live again, and Burns views this as a Romantic rather than a postmodern agenda. *Art and Lies*, he argues, is Winterson's attempt to revive 'the social imaginary, which has been disrupted by postmodern media and consumerism'.[15] Handel, the doctor, lives in a disconnected society,

> ■ [a] media-absorbed populace that, confronted as it is by a doubled and divided field of representation, ceases to respond thoughtfully and only scatters itself along a chain of unrelentingly trivial displacements. While advertising facilitates this fragmentation, the media in his world alternately assaults the public with images of suffering and deprivation, then offers up sitcom clichés as the only model of sentimental response. Leery of becoming automatic kitsch, Handel's contemporaries are caught between maudlin reaction and emotional withdrawal. Thus Handel falls into dispassionate disinterest and desensitised self-absorption'.[16] □

Burns uses the concept of the simulacrum developed by Jean Baudrillard (born 1930),[17] of the copy that has no original, to argue that language has little relevance to reality 'the real', in a postmodern world, but simply refers to other images and other signifiers, with a consequent dulling of feeling or affect in the audience. 'Art, and for Winterson especially literature, provides the link between both the real and the imaginary through its medium: the Word'.[18] Sappho, in contrast to Handel, embraces desire and sex as the real, sensate connection and links language to the physical experience, since language itself, when uttered, is part of the sensate world:

> ■ words are not simple windows into thoughts but are themselves embodied. ... These embodied effects have a subtle but powerful impact on the significations we give to words. Winterson comments explicitly on this aspect of textuality in *Art and Lies* whenever Sappho's voice takes over the story. For Sappho, the word and sex are one in their mutual linkage of imagination and embodiment. ... Language and sex are brought together through an eroticisation of speaking, synecdochically [a part standing in for the whole] focusing on the mouth of the speaker and playing on the sensate properties of language – the rhythm, sound and effect of mouthing such words linked together by overlapping consonants. Winterson uses that which exceeds rational meaning – sensation – as she also uses fantasy and the imagination to mediate the rupture between a given and often harsh reality. She presses towards an erotic use of language that moves her writing away from cold and rational sense, taking it toward sensate meanings that mix reference with desire and seduce readers towards change rather than commanding or instructing them.[19] □

Sappho thus becomes the agent of the novel's attempt to resuscitate language and resensitise the body to desire. Picasso, the third narrator in this disconnected narrative, rejects the sentimentalised narrative of her childhood that her mother peddles to obscure her daughter's sexual abuse by her son, Picasso's brother, and turns instead to Sappho's writings as a release from all the lies. Burns sees Winterson's main literary agenda in *Written on the Body* and *Art and Lies* as the re-embodiment of passion and desire, through a language renewed to signify their importance and their reality. Hence the importance of the meta-narrative elements of language and literature in her work. 'At the book's close, Sappho, Picasso, and Handel – as contemporary Londoners – are drawn together by an experience that both reaches back historically and connects them contemporaneously through the act of reading a small book'.[20] This small book , incorporating the remains of the Library of Alexandria, one of the wonders of the world before its conflagration, contains Greek philosophy, parts of the Bible, and erotic literature from both the original Sappho and the eighteenth century. Fantasy, in *Art and Lies*, is not escapist, but connected to real desires. 'Desire is what is real, in Winterson, more so than historical events or material objects.'[21] And it is through fantasy that Winterson allows the reader to reconnect with the real – an experience which, paradoxically, motivates readers rather than allowing them to escape reality, the traditional notion of fantasy. 'Fantasy, in Winterson's works, is not an experience that leaves a reader content, but one that fuels desire, denies catharsis [the purging of emotions], and propels readers back out into their contexts.'[22]

Two years later, Burns again considered *Art and Lies* in an essay entitled 'Powerful Differences: Critique and Eros in Jeanette Winterson and Virginia Woolf' (1998),[23] and further developed his analysis of her use of language and desire, but now incorporating a sense of social critique as well, of feminism. Winterson is compared to Woolf, a modernist writer whom Winterson herself extols, in her work as a feminist writer. Winterson, like Woolf before her, embraces fantasy and rejects realism as a narrative form. *Art and Lies* is seen as an 'art that functions simultaneously as both critical and erotic',[24] a dualism that Burns sees as forming a new aesthetic. Again, he regards Sappho as the central and crucial narrator of the three. 'She is, for Winterson, the speaking icon, the poet, and the philosopher of *eros*. With irony she introduces herself, commenting on the reductive treatment of her poetic invocations of desire.'[25] Despite the fact that her poems have been suppressed by the Church and largely forgotten even where they do partially exist in fragments, they are credited with a powerful and seductive resonance. 'Repeatedly, Sappho invokes the power of the word as transubstantiation; it even lifts up Sappho's body as she jumps off the cliff.'[26] Doll Sneerpiece, the eighteenth-century heroine in love with Ruggerio, reads Sappho's poetry, and these articulations are interleaved with Winterson's own lesbian poetry: 'if Doll's passages in *Art and Lies* parody eighteenth-century pornography, Sappho's is an erotic of ear and eye, mining both the sensual and sentimental side of romantic imagination. Winterson plies her medium as alternately threatening and seductive; rather than opposing language and comprehension, however, she weds them. Words fill one up with substance and give "the spirit" or imaginary back to the world.'[27] Now, though, Burns views the female erotic as also the space of a feminist critique, an unspoken feminine desire that challenges the status quo, and he compares Winterson's invocation of desire and rapture to Woolf's technique in *The Waves* (1931):

■ In Winterson's writing, eroticism is operating *associatively* with female pleasure and arousal, gleaning its force of seduced consciousness in a manner reminiscent of Woolf's recurrent collection of a string of associative suggestions. In fact, Winterson calls out to the senior author in the novel: 'Sappho to Mrs. Woolf – Mrs. Woolf to Sappho' – invoking female heritage and lesbian identification as well as a poetry of *eros*. She links herself to Woolf in just these terms, arguing that in *The Waves*, language is not realistic but poetic. ... This rhythmic approach to rapture, which draws together an ever-gathering strength of associations, is the aspect of Woolf that Winterson most often praises.[28] □

Going on to consider the feminist impact of the novel, which he positions as a radical feminist stance, he sketches a synopsis for the uninitiated. 'The novel poses the problem of how to live in the postmodern world of London in the year 2000. Winterson reveals a hollowing of language through the culture's proliferation of cliché and abusive sexual intimidation. The novel is written in three voices, and if Sappho is Sappho (Greek poet of c.600 BC), Handel and Picasso are not the historical figures but others who have taken on these names. All voices offer at least tongue-in-cheek critiques of society, with Doll and Sappho functioning as the more humorous and erotic figures, while Handel and Picasso enact serious and pressing social criticism.'[29] Handel, the doctor who has been a priest and who is finally revealed as a eunuch, symbolises, for Burns, the abject phallocentric world of men, frightened of experiencing desire. Handel's displacement of desire, part of his shame and his damnation, results in a living death of desensitised disengagement. Passive and an aesthete, he becomes Winterson's critique of 'both men and capitalism, revealing the insecurities behind the powerful and the hollowness of the postmodern, industrialized, media-saturated world'.[30] As a cancer specialist, he has performed countless unnecessary mastectomies, and this is seen as a critique of male medicine's lack of concern for the female body. Reflecting on his life, Handel can experience only despair at its worthlessness. For some, Burns acknowledges, this didactic attack on phallocentricism could prove alienating, Handel's extreme abjection too despairing and too directly critical of patriarchal society. Handel delivers Picasso, when she is born to the maid raped by Sir John. Abandoned on his doorstep, Picasso is taken in by her father and sexually abused by her half-brother. 'Picasso's repeated rape by her half-brother thus replays her father's rape of the maid, with the added dependence on familial as well as economic bonds ... beyond critiquing the inequities and the abuses of protection the family might otherwise provide, Winterson raises the stakes of social complicity with the abuse of women by turning it into an incest case. ... This is a crucial critique and, in many ways, the powerful center of the novel. It also functions as the negative "other" to eroticism as the enactment of lust forced upon a girl who resists.'[31] Picasso elaborates the dangers to women of a phallocentric society that denigrates women, views them as sexual objects, or refuses to believe their stories. Finally pushed off the roof of their house by the father to stop her revealing the incest, she is saved by Sappho. 'Picasso is thus repeatedly figured as a witness who is denied, suppressed, and silenced.'[32]

Her struggle to escape the prison-like family structure is much more violent than Handel's dislike of his life, and invokes a necessary feminine anger, but transformed into a work of art as she paints herself, her own body, as an act of rebellion and inspired by Sappho. 'Picasso paints herself and in the process paints the family, so that her father is purple, her brother envy-green, her younger brother blue. In this art, she externalises or makes literal the knowledge that mentally and emotionally she affects them, shakes them, as she answers back with her work. She walks away naked – but painted – in the snow, free from the social collusion that claimed her physically and emotionally, before and after her leap from the house.'[33] Handel's social criticism and Picasso's artistic resistance amalgamate with Sappho, whose erotic language, Burns argues, perhaps surprisingly given the usual private/public dichotomy, is the strongest of the voices for social change. Winterson, like Woolf, favours a 'feminist art that rolls back the supremacy of masculine perspective',[34] and like Woolf she uses the concept of androgyny (having both sexes, an androgyne). The term can apply to Handel, or Picasso on the train, but primarily for Burns it refers to the narrative voice. He sees Winterson's oeuvre as progressively developing the masculine voices and characters since the early *Oranges Are Not the Only Fruit*. So, following on from *The Passion* and *Sexing the Cherry*, Winterson gives a male character part of the narrative voice. Handel is another of Winterson's feminised men, a contrast to the rampant men in Picasso's family. But the concept of androgyny, so favoured in the 1970s, has had a poor reception since, as it appears to erase gender differences, rather than to counter and challenge them as constructs. Where Woolf might use androgyny, Burns suggests, Winterson's characters are crossing the genders more than denying them, exchanging traits with feminine men and masculine women. 'Thus, the differences between genders are neither crystallised nor ignored; Winterson's androgyny works to open up possible variations in personality and act'.[35] Through her mix of enraptured prose, fantasy and androgynous characters, Winterson focuses on difference in a way that argues for the social potential to change, and hence forms the political critique of her work. '*Art and Lies*'s split between critique and eros is an orchestrated interweaving of the two necessary elements of feminist vision. If Winterson utilizes anger to bring about social revision, she also cautions against art as pure rant. There is a fine line between rage and witness, and Winterson has chosen the very dangerous task of walking that line.'[36] For Burns, her work manages to escape the label of a rant, but is a form of excess, moving between the 'radical extremes, of righteous anger and ecstatic vision'.[37]

In the same year, Patricia Duncker's 'Jeanette Winterson and the Aftermath of Feminism' (1998)[38] considers *Art and Lies* as well as *Written on the Body.* Continuing her thesis that Winterson is a lesbian and feminist writer, because of her angry critique of phallocentric society and the normalcy of heterosexualism, she argues that where *Written on the Body* concealed its politics through the genderless narrator, *Art and Lies* 'has the courage of its convictions'.[39] She sees it as a 'queer' text, asserting a lesbian identity that is different from other, heterosexual women, in a number of different ways. Its narration and naming of the narrators is one way, since they have the names of famous historical artists, but they are not intended to be the characters of those person-ages, and this device immediately confounds the reader's expectations of how characters should conform to textual specifications. The musical score of *Der Rosenkavalier* (1909–10) by Richard Strauss (1864–1949) is another way, since it is not authorial indulgence but a meaningful part of the queer text, as opera is seen to epitomise queer art. Queer fiction primarily calls attention to the fact that the division between masculine and feminine is not a fixed divide, but a performance we enact to fit within expectations; it demonstrates that gender is more flexible and shifting than heterosexual society admits to. In disrupting the binary gender divisions and codes and in refusing to accommodate them, queer politics problematises the concept that power should be associated with the masculine. Queer politics is thus oppositional, challenging, and at its best, angry. Winterson's *Art and Lies* conforms to all these descriptions; it is 'a polemical book, an angry book. It is not delicate, playful or self-indulgently vain. There is something at stake.'[40] It is a queer text, but one informed by the aftermath of feminist theory in its social critique. The three protagonists are restless, dissatisfied and searching for something: Sappho for the women who flew the familial coop, Picasso for a life free from abuse, and Handel for an end to his dissatisfaction with his life to date. All three characters fit the notion of queer charac-ters, the two women as lesbians and Handel as a castrato, or eunuch, so in themselves they all problematise gender roles and expectations. Duncker explains how the castrato had become a figure of intense interest to queer theory during the 1990s, for the way in which it questions the importance of the phallus for masculinity or for female desire. Similarly, Sappho is seen as hermaphrodite rather than feminine, because this used to be a term used to describe lesbians. In the novel, the narrative asserts men's ingrained dislike of women, whether Handel, Picasso or Sappho is narrating, and this message, Duncker argues, is also informed by past feminist theory. *Art and Lies* uncompromisingly asserts the aggression heaped upon women, through three queer characters all at odds with conventional notions of gender division.

Two of the three articles discussed in this chapter focus on the importance of language to *Art and Lies*, since that is Burns's main interest in regard to the novel. In his first article (1996), he agrees with Rachel Cusk's review, in seeing *Art and Lies* as an attack on postmodern culture and the way that language has been flattened, deadened, and a collective social imaginary destroyed. Handel is the character who mainly expresses this through his desensitised self-absorption. Winterson, Burns argues, is trying to revive language and resurrect a whole social imaginary, with Sappho as the main focus of this attempt, creating a language that is both rich and sensate in its eroticism. As an example, all three characters are linked by their reading of the one small remnant of her poetry, rescued from the library of Alexandria. Burns argues that Winterson's attempt is a Romantic gesture and this links his article to Lisa Moore's 'Teledildonics' (1995), where she also delineates Winterson's strategy as a Romantic one. Two years later, Burns links Winterson's project to modernism, and specifically to Virginia Woolf, who also uses language in a poetic way, in order to construct language as a substantive entity in the world, as revelation in the biblical sense. In 1998, Burns also focuses on the critique of phallocentrism and Winterson's feminist politics. Handel's castrated character is now a symbol of abject, empty phallocentrism, and it is he who describes most of Picasso's family sexual abuse. The incest forced upon Picasso is the negative, darker side to Sappho's celebration of eroticism, while Picasso's painting of her family is an act of feminist rebellion. Duncker agrees with Burns on the political effectiveness of the anger against phallocentric oppression in the novel, but deems it a queer text in its characterisation, because of its disruption of the binary codes of gender stereotyping. All three characters are queer, in her reading, since two are lesbian and one a castrato, an important figure within the queer debates of the 1990s. Burns suggests that they are androgynous in the postmodern sense, since they cross gender constructs, and his reading of the characters' challenge to gender agrees very much with Duncker's, despite the different terminology. Indeed, Duncker's suggestion that Sappho is a hermaphrodite chimes closely with androgyny. She and Burns (1996) both agree on the importance of the music within the novel; Burns sees language used in musical terms while Duncker defends the inclusion of the opera score, since opera is a queer art form. *Art and Lies*, like the following novel, *Gut Symmetries*, appears to have confounded the critics but those who do tackle the books find them hugely rewarding and fascinating.

CHAPTER SEVEN

Gut Symmetries (1997) and *The PowerBook* (2000)

A s Winterson's more recent novels, *Gut Symmetries* and *The PowerBook* have naturally received the least critical discussion as yet in 2004. This situation may well soon be remedied, allowing them to have the critical interest of *Sexing the Cherry* and *Written on the Body*, if not the massive critical debate of *Oranges Are Not the Only Fruit*. *Gut Symmetries* is beginning to lay down a body of essays that suggests it will, in time, develop a critical presence, but the analysis of *The PowerBook* seems less secure.

The reviews for *Gut Symmetries* are as mixed as for the previous novel, *Art and Lies*. Adam Mars-Jones in the *Observer* signals his dislike in the title 'From Oranges to a Lemon'.[1] Mars-Jones opens by complaining that the new novel is really an amalgamation of past themes: habit's ability to deaden experience, from *Art and Lies*; a triangle of sexual partners, from *Written on the Body*; the city as phantasmagoria, from *The Passion*; religion as granting a serviceable symbolism, from *Oranges Are Not the Only Fruit*. As a difficult and 'writerly'[2] text, the novel is not aided by what he sees as her 'rhapsodic sermons or sermonising rhapsodies'. He finds little discrimination in what is held up for such vaunting significance, whether it is the enormity of a lover's betrayal or simply the pretty red leaves of a Canadian Fall. He suggests that the novel is in fact old-fashioned, harking back to the themes and styles of the 1980s, and so implies a lack of innovation. During the 1980s, he explains, novels sported with erudite philosophy and scientific discoveries and they also played with magical realism as a form. *Gut Symmetries*, he feels, simply does this once again and though miracles may well be uplifting as an experience, 'in novels they tend to lower the spirits'. The book begins in a promising manner, and seems to be building satisfactorily, but loses its way, and rambles plotless towards its conclusion. The characterisation does not find favour either; Mars-Jones claims the characters all sound the same and share the same poor grammar. The pre-scientific beliefs in the Tarot, the Kabbalah and alchemy are used, but fail to catch light from the prose which lacks endeavour because it appears that Winterson is 'hypnotised by her own performance, radioactive with self-belief'. Philip Hensler is less negative, but just as uninventive in his title, 'Too Many Lemons, Not Enough "Oranges" ',[3] in the *Mail on Sunday*. In a back-handed compliment, he argues that *Gut Symmetries* is the best of her past four books, and the only one not to be worse than its predecessor, despite what he sees as Winterson's typically didactic passages on issues in no way related to the plot or the overall subject of the novel, and her risible, serial romance comments on love. He feels that she does have a stronger grip on the prose and is strongest when writing about the past childhood experiences of the characters. When she simply goes back to a more realist engagement with the characters, he sees her as 'fresh, engaging and even witty'. When she concentrates on being a writer, rather than posing as a guru or a poet, the novel is forceful and reminds us of her powers as a novelist.

Hugo Barnacle in the *Sunday Times*[4] picks on her prose in some detail, having dismissed the science as pretentious. Discussing the image of a suitcase filled with hope, used by Alice, the English physicist who has the affair with first Jove and then his wife in a sexual triangle, he argues that it is as poor a metaphor in this novel as it is in Hitler's *Mein Kampf*. In the unlikely event that it is an intertextual reference, since Stella is Jewish, Barnacle calls it 'intellectual kitsch rather than meaningful allusion'. He also picks on the reference of Stella drifting afloat Jove's boat, like a 'diadrom' without a lifejacket, and having explained the two possible meanings for the word, either a fish or a leaf, questions why either would need a lifejacket. He excuses his pedantry with the claim that, in the absence of plot or characterisation, there is only the prose, overburdened with metaphor, to look at. Despite Winterson's undoubted abilities as a writer, the talent is, he suggests, crying out for a more self-critical editing and he finds the book both corny and cliché-ridden. Like Hensler, he holds up the narratives that deal with Alice's and Stella's childhoods, in Liverpool and New York respectively, as showing her real potential.

James Wood in the *Guardian*[5] has a stronger sense of her potential as an innovatory writer, and believes that she will still produce something major, though, the implication runs, this novel is not quite it. Where the others enjoyed themselves in trashing the novel, Wood seriously considers its themes and structure. Like Hensler, he sees Winterson as a composite of three things, but where for Hensler it was novelist, guru and poet, for Wood the trilogy is Writer, Modernist and Sentimentalist. He concurs with Mars-Jones's view that the Modernist aspect is concerned with its own status, but believes that it is nevertheless a high-minded effort, linked to Woolf and T. S. Eliot in striving for a complex, allusive and innovatory style. The novel's structure engages with the postmodern concept of perpetual flux and fluidity, fuelled by the 'new physics', but it is a physics the text deals with more aesthetically than scientifically. For Wood, the fact that contemporary novelists are enamoured of the new physics is a matter of lament, since they all get their ideas from the same few popular non-fiction texts and so all use the same clichéd references to Superstring Theory, Heisenberg's Uncertainty Principle and Stephen Hawking's conception of Time, 'and how we are all really stars'. Since the writers insist on interpreting these scientific theories aesthetically, they mess up the exciting power of the physics and, in Winterson's case, the three characters, two of whom are physicists, are implausibly eager to impart their knowledge at every possible opportunity. Winterson has, Wood notes, become enamoured of the aphoristic delivery, imparting knowledge with a tautness that can imply a dismissive hauteur. This leads to the paradoxical 'experience of being told we are in flux in tones of formal clarity'. Alongside this aspect, which he terms the earnest Modernist, we have, however, the Sentimentalist who softens everything with a magical realism that is bogusly sentimental in its sugaring of reality, and the use of the Kabbalah also smacks of sentiment. It is this tendency to hide behind a prettifying magic that Woods judges turns her into a conservative writer, keen to tie herself down to 'tart lessons and snappish maxims', while the reader wills her to be more ambitious in her scope. Winterson, he declares, has the ability to transform the language with her writing, once she decides to stop tying herself down to a preaching, patterned certitude, flavoured with opaque exoticism.

Katy Emck, in the *Times Literary Supplement*[6] was the most enthusiastic, calling it a New Age 'mad, beautiful, prophetic book', fiction that contains a contemporary 'Big Idea'. Emck notes how, in every Winterson novel, there is a rhapsodic point when a character sails off to a new world of visionary, mythic possibility. In *Gut Symmetries*, though, thanks to the new physics of the Grand Unified Theories (the GUT of the title), the voyage spans the high seas, the skies and the universe, mixing Euclid and Einstein, astrology and alchemy, to encompass the world within its pages. Focusing on the shared motif of ships in many of Winterson's novels, she discusses the rampant plethora of ships in this one, whether sailing the seas or the skies, linked by allegory or by dreams, their quests open-ended and inconclusive. The main model for the motif is a Ship of Fools that transmutes into an intergalactic spaceship. The novel begins on a boat too, where Jove, the American physicist interested in time travel, meets Alice, also an American physicist and working on the connections between the fifteenth-century Paracelsus and post-Einstein physics. The two have an affair, and then Alice falls for his wife, Stella. Emck finds this triangle of two women and one man in *The Passion* and *Written on the Body*, but here the difference is in the ambiguous lack of certainty she sees in the sexual permutations, an uncertainty that links it to the new physics. If particles can possess both simultaneity and contradiction, why not lovers choosing between partners? The ship motif continues with Alice, who we learn was born aboard a tugboat, the daughter of a shipping magnate. Her history, Emck feels, is Winterson at her best, with the magical and marvellous father of Alice a huge, self-made and self-invented monster of a man, who makes his wife wait for the consummation of the marriage until after he has made his fortune. Where *Gut Symmetries* differs from the earlier novels, Emck suggests, is in the fact that here the women identify firstly with their fathers and secondly with the masculine world of Jove, rejecting radical lesbianism for the position of new women instead. Stella's father, the link to the mysticism of the Kabbalah through his Jewish bookstore, also reads the new physics, and 1950s New York is rendered in vivid detail. Where Alice was born on a tugboat, Stella is born aboard a dog-sleigh hurtling through the winter snow, a miraculous birth for the new age. Like Woods and Mars-Jones, Emck too discovers three voices in the novel, three Wintersons: the magical narrator who enraptures the reader with wonder, creating stories that are vivid and unforgettable; the knowledgeable narrator who instructs the reader, eager to show off her learning, piling gloss after gloss onto tales that become overburdened with comments on post-Einstein physics and postmodernism; and finally the lover, invoking the lyricism of longing, alongside the sensual materiality of desire. For Emck, unlike the male reviewers, *Gut Symmetries* avoids the cloying sentimentality of Winterson's previous texts by the objectivity of its stance. Nevertheless, she acknowledges that structurally it shifts from story to physics to subjective pronouncements without any governing logic, while the reader struggles to keep up. For all the beauty of its writing and the marvels of its inventiveness, the book does not ultimately cohere, for the narrative is less interested in the dramatic love triangle played out between the humans, and more concerned to pontificate. Despite this major flaw, Emck concludes, perhaps even because of its presumption, the novel succeeds in the range and the power of its scope, a stirring and mystical mix of a book.

Michèle Roberts, in the *Independent on Sunday*[7] salutes the novel on gender grounds, for refusing to stay safely within the ghetto of tame women's novels, in blowing a raspberry at literary expectations. Commenting on the other, predominantly male reviewers, Roberts points out that Winterson has breached the golden rule to be self-deprecating, in her claims to be a great writer and the heir to Virginia Woolf, and that reviewers are harsher to women who embrace hubris, than to men. While welcoming the ambitious scope of the novel, Roberts is alienated by the science. She acknowledges that it is a genuine attempt to 'wrestle with the need for' appropriate fictional modes to encompass 'a world trying to understand advances in scientific knowledge', but feels daunted as Winterson piles on to the modish new conceptions of time, space, quantum physics and chaos theory, the Kabbalah, the Tarot and alchemy as well. The resultant baroque, sumptuous mixture is too undigested to fit the rest of the text, though she acknowledges the novel's exciting suggestiveness. She too, like Emck, identifies a phallocentric leaning in the two female characters, which, she suggests, Lacanians would read as the overvaluation of the phallus by lesbians reacting against it. However, Roberts says, the novel is not really about love or sex, since Jove's seductions are never properly realised and nor are the two women's encounters. The flesh and the materiality of the sexual encounters is entirely absent, as the author focuses instead on life, death and the meaning of the universe. Alice's character, indeed, mirrors the lesbian refusal of gender stereotypes, as she escapes sexual identity by her very lack of materiality, though overly eager to demonstrate her knowledge of the sciences, which Roberts constructs as masculine knowledge. Despite its flaws, such as the characters' similarity of voice, the disdain for ordinary people, and the undigested science, Roberts concludes that it is an engaging and subversively 'stroppy' book.

In the United States, Bruce Bawer argued that Winterson had 'struck gold' with *Gut Symmetries*.[8] For Bawer, Winterson's trilogy of narrative positions is as preacher, as researcher and as lover, and he believes the experimental text has breathed new life into the literary novel. Opening with the plot of Alice meeting Jove on an ocean liner, and having an affair with him, and then meeting his wife Stella, Bawer explains that the plot is, in a sense, immaterial; it is not what happens to them that is important, but how they see the world, how they voice experience and explain it to themselves in order to make sense of the world. Above all they, along with the narrator, argue for the dictum of the Romantic poet John Keats (1795–1821) in his 'Ode on a Grecian Urn' (1820), that beauty is truth, truth beauty. Given the fallibility of reason, as illustrated by quantum physics, with its demand for a trust unproven by fact, beauty certainly seems a safer bedrock. Modern physics, Bawer suggests, looks not unlike ancient myth or a religion, and the novel gestures towards its own Grand Unified Theory that unites scientific knowledge, religious rapture and individual subjectivity. This short novel, he concludes, is outside of the usual run of the mill and, for all its concentration on an interior space, the insight is astonishing.

Mars-Jones and Emck focus on the repetition of previous themes, an issue that becomes much more prevalent among the critics in the following work, *The PowerBook*, where it becomes a main concern. Hensler, Wood, Emck and Bawer all suggest that *Gut Symmetries* demonstrates three types of discourse or 'voices' of Winterson, though what the three are varies slightly, but they all signal the disjunction in the juxtaposition. Mars-Jones, Hensler, Barnacle, Emck and Bawer develop this into a discussion of the lack of plot; those broadly in favour of the novel see the plot as immaterial, the more derogatory reviews term it a plotless ramble. It is certainly true that those who grapple with the significance of the new physics within the book are the most enthusiastic about the novel as a whole, while those who do not, like it least. Roberts, in the middle, openly admits she finds the material daunting, but others quietly elide it or mock its inclusion without trying to understand why it is there. One could argue that if the critics have not tried to engage with the central metaphoric and structural way in which the novel uses post-Einstein physics, then they have not bothered to engage with the novel at all and in some way have derogated their job as reviewers, in taking the easier way out. This is obviously not an issue with the few critics that have chosen to write about the novel because the critics, in a very real sense, have self-selected into those who wish to engage with the new physics, a luxury of choice which few reviewers have.

Helena Grice and Tim Woods, the joint editors of the 1998 *Postmodern Studies* special issue on Winterson, reserved their own chapter for *Gut Symmetries*. In Grand (Dis)Unified Theories? Dislocated Discourses in *Gut Symmetries*',[9] they examine both the new physics as it is represented in the novel, and the representation of heterosexual and lesbian relations in the love triangle. Opening with the thesis that structuralism sought to construct a unified theory of narrative, but that postmodernism's deconstruction of certainties has challenged and fractured the attempt to fix the meanings of the literary text, they go on to analyse the similar attempts to find a grand unified theory within science, looking at the explanations that try to fix theoretical physics, as started by Einstein and still being attempted in Superstring Theory – the idea that matter does not consist of minute particles or atoms, but of one type of elongated string, which creates the seemingly different effects by its various different vibrations. Like the structuralism/poststructuralism analogy, they argue, *Gut Symmetries* simultaneously raises the possibility of a unified, stable universe where everything connects, and the rebuttal of fixity in a random universe. The 'Prologue' opens with the fifteenth-century alchemist and astrologer, Paracelsus, who looked for a unified pattern in the heavens that corresponded to the pattern of the human body, and the novel goes on to connect the medieval search for the 'Correspondence' with contemporary theories of hyperspace. Newton's theory of matter, twentieth-century cosmology, astrology and the Tarot are all in their ways attempts to find a single all-embracing concept to explain the world, what in the twentieth century has been termed 'Grand Unified Theory'. This is one version of the GUT in the title of *Gut Symmetries*. The other, they argue, links to the more intuitive and emotional reactions described in the term 'gut feelings'. The book sets up a number of patterns and parallels between these two 'guts' – the metaphysical and the material, the theoretical and the emotional – but ultimately loses its way in its own complexity, rather than managing to bring the whole thing together.

Jove is a physicist at Princeton, with an expertise in Superstring Theory and Grand Unified Theory, which is being complicated by the fact that gravity does not fit the theory as it stands. Stella, his wife, argues that if GUT and gravity could find a similar overarching thesis, it would be like hearing a lute and a harp playing together, different and yet in tune, like Pythagoras' perfect harmony of the spheres, and would posit a perfect cosmology. The stringed instruments of course recall the theory of the superstrings, each vibrating to create sound or matter. But Winterson includes other, more destabilising theories of physics in the novel, alongside the attempts at unification, including Einstein's Theory of Relativity, Quantum Physics and the Indeterminacy Principle. These challenge any attempt to construct a thesis of absolute stability in our understanding of the world, let alone our notion of our own selves. *Gut Symmetries'* three protagonists reflect on the fluidity of identity, caught as we are within the mirror of expectation. Heisenberg argued that since the minute particles of matter are too small to observe, our examinations of the electron, photon or quark are predicated on theoretical knowledge and so the discourse we use to measure them will reinscribe the qualities we expect to find. We can never see beyond the discourse. The truth of physics becomes problematic. This highly theoretical and fluid concept of the physical world is allied to postmodern concepts of knowledge and narrative, not always effectively. Grice and Woods question whether 'gin' and 'tonic' are truly binary opposites as implied in the narrative, for example.

The text invokes both rational, empirical ways of explaining the world and the more irrational, metaphysical explanations in a shifting barrage of references. Einstein's love of numbers links him to mystic numerologists, and the tarot cards that name the chapters and indicate the protagonists' characters are linked to the Jewish Kabbalah that Stella's father studies. Like James Wood, Grice and Woods read the representation of Jewish mysticism as bogus and overly sentimental. Stella, the poet who embraces fluidity, is constructed as being more in tune with the currents that connect life with life, than Jove the scientist who is keen to fit everything into separate disciplinary boxes, but this opposition of poet and physicist crumbles when it is revealed that Stella's father, the religious mystic, had, before the war, been in correspondence with Austrian quantum physicists, including Heisenberg, and that the two had in fact inspired each other. The novel constantly opposes poet to scientist, the mystic to the material, the empirical to the magical, the linear to the non-linear in binary oppositions. Where Newton envisaged time as a linear arrow, and Einstein saw it as a river, Alice argues that time is figuratively more like a whirlpool. The 'gut feeling' that life is chaos and entropy is reinforced by the exponents of chaos theory; Grice and Woods cite Feigenbaum, Lorenz and Mandelbrot. Using Michel Serres's essay 'Lucretius: Science and Religion',[10] they argue that the novel positions the fixed, epistemological, rational sciences as masculine (Mars) and the fluid, irrational, chaotic knowledges as feminine (Venus). Where the masculine strives to compartmentalise and control matter in a linear master narrative, the feminine embraces duality, instability and relativity. Despite Winterson's claim to deconstruct binary opposites, Grice and Woods argue, this stereotyped gender division does not really challenge traditional positions but reinforces them, reinvoking the masculine as intellectual and concerned with fact, and the feminine as emotional, intuitive and concerned with feeling. She does try to complicate the dualism of male and female, husband and wife, by including a third figure and constructing a triangular relationship for the binary, but unfortunately the tarot card used to introduce the image of the sexual triangle positions the man in the position of power over two women, and so the image undermines the more subversive potential of the relationship.

Winterson's characters challenge the binary heterosexual relationships by positing an equally strong competing lesbian one, between Alice and Stella, which the critics see as a Radicalesbian commitment to other women over men. (Radicalesbians, such as Anne Koedt, Ellen Levine and Anita Rapone, argue that lesbians' primary reference is to other women, where heterosexual women's primary reference is to men. Men therefore become irrelevant to lesbians.) While Jove's affair with Alice is sketched in only cursorily, the relationship between Alice and Stella is afforded much more weight and detail. Jove's relationships are marginalised to the beginning and the end of the novel while the women's move centre stage. A description of their childhoods, Alice in Liverpool, the daughter of a self-made shipping magnate, Stella in New York, the daughter of a Jewish bookseller and Kabbalist, develops their characters and demonstrates the similarities of their early years despite the material and geographical differences. The heterosexual encounters of both women are portrayed as focused on Jove's pleasure, on his patriarchal satisfaction, with little consideration for the women's, despite their roles as narrators. Grice and Woods point out that having it told through their perspective means the male eroticised gaze is completely absent from the novel. Alice also recounts the lesbian love-making, that positions both women as equally desiring agents and objects of desire. The focus on sameness, familiar in Winterson's lesbian aesthetic, shows a female desire as the primary referent. Grice and Woods suggest that the text positions this sameness as a narcissistic mirroring, which refutes the novel's triangular structure, and echoes Virginia Woolf's *Night and Day* (1919). The Euclid triangle, invoked at the beginning of the novel, is superseded and the 'impossible' meeting of the parallel lines takes over the 'geometry' of relationships. Even when Jove, becalmed at sea, eats Stella's flesh in a desperate attempt to reinstate the patriarchal possession of his wife, the lesbian relationship triumphs. Evoking Hélène Cixous's rejection of the binary, and Luce Irigaray's affirmation of female narcissistic eroticism, Grice and Wood place *Gut Symmetries* within a French feminist agenda in challenging patriarchal and heterosexual conventions. This feminist agenda, they suggest, sits awkwardly alongside the conventional gender stereotyping used in portraying the binaries of science and art, the rational and the intuitive.

Kim Middleton Meyer's examination of Winterson's narrative evolution from intertextuality to the grotesque and finally to the nomadic conception of subjectivity, concludes with a brief examination of *Gut Symmetries*. Where science, in the guise of the medical discourse of anatomy, was rejected as a mode of conceiving of the world in *Written on the Body*, here in contrast it is accepted as a viable discourse to encapsulate and describe love. The love triangle of Jove, Stella and Alice, she suggests, refuses to remain within the two-dimensional, as the lesbian relationship grows and comes to dominate. 'As post-Newtonian physics works to engender their connection, so too it marshals to save it from destruction.'[11] When Jove sails away with Stella, reasserting his possession as husband, the boat's engine fails and the two are stranded without food or water. Jove's literal consumption of Stella clearly seems to lead to her death, but this is foreclosed by Alice's miraculous rescue of them and Stella's full recovery. The narrator flaunts these 'miracles', one of cosmology and the other of love, and argues for their existence within science in the fluidity of the space-time continuum and the impact of quantum physics. The new physics' conceptions 'of space and time lend a scientific basis to Winterson's nomadism, previously demarcated by the fantastic. In *Gut Symmetries*, the material that earlier was considered fantastic is now characterised as more real than common perception allows.'[12] While the characters constructed as embracing a nomadic subjectivity in *Sexing the Cherry* and *Written on the Body* at times wondered if they were mad, the characters in this novel see as mad those who do not embrace the nomadic concept of the fluid multiplicity of the self. Winterson's utilisation 'of contemporary scientific thought ... provides them with a set of discourses that work to explain the mechanics behind what previously appeared to be fantasy.'[13] The new physics serves to incorporate the apparently inimical discourses of the real, the historical and the scientific alongside the fantastic, the fairy tale and love.

The two critical essays considered so far engage with different issues, though both discuss the themes of the new physics. Grice and Woods develop the juxtaposition of the scientific attempt to find one explanation that can embrace the whole of scientific matter, the grand unified theory, and its historical counterparts, with other scientific arguments that deconstruct this attempt as yet another mythic endeavour in the face of chaos theory, entropy and the random fluidity of time. The fact that the two theoretical positions are at odds with each other, dislocated as discourses, reinforces the postmodern flux. And Grice and Woods invoke Serres to link the attempt at a grand fixity to the masculine, and the enjoyment of relativity and fluidity to the feminine, while arguing that such a construction in itself falls into old-fashioned gender stereotypes, rather than critiquing them. They agree with the majority of the reviewers in seeing the interrelation of themes getting lost in its own complexity and finding the novel unable to resolve them all at the end; in this, they perhaps do not pick up on the structural importance of the thematic disjunction of discourses. If the novel were to have a conclusive resolution as its closure, then in a sense its form would militate against the theme of dislocation and flux of meaning and argue structurally for a potential unification, at least within narrative. They do analyse the problematising of neat theories and binaries in relation to the poet/scientist binary initially set up by the contrasting perspectives of Stella and Jove, but then complicated by Stella's father's mystical influence on the earlier twentieth-century scientist, Heisenberg.

Both Grice and Woods, and Meyer, focus on the lesbian readings as superseding the heterosexual, in the love triangle, and both read Jove's eating of Stella as his attempt to reassert heterosexual ownership. Meyer also develops the theme of nomadic subjectivity, fuelled by the fluidity of life within the new physics, and this is a theme that would mesh well with Emck's identification of the extended metaphor of ships and voyaging.

The reviews of *The PowerBook* have been less kind. Phil Baker's 'A dotcom. enterprise gone dotty',[14] was the first to employ the dotcom. metaphor, and links the novel, through a whole stock market analogy, to the failure of the trendy internet companies which the financial pages dubbed the 'dotcom bubble'. The trendy internet book, he argues, is equally unrewarding from its inception. Aware that Winterson's 'own stock' as a writer has had a bad mauling by the critics in recent years, he concludes that this novel is not going to change her falling reputation.

The novel lacks any central narrative as the main character, either Ali or Alix, composes interactive stories over the internet for those who commission her. Ali smuggling tulips into seventeenth-century Holland down her trousers, while she is dressed as a boy, and pleasuring a princess with the stalk and bulb as a pretend phallus, Baker finds ridiculous. Other stories around love, Lancelot and Guinevere, or Mallory lying dead on the peak of Mount Everest with his beloved wife's letter as his treasured possession, form other bits of the oddly assorted stories. Winterson's reusing these well-known stories, he finds tired, while the contemporary narrative of Alix and her married lover travelling between Paris and Capri, he finds distasteful in its elitism. The characters' misanthropic asides about ordinary people on package holidays alienate the reader. There *is* an important point to be made about the notion of us all inhabiting the world as tourists, in a postmodern era, Baker suggests, unknowingly gesturing towards Meyer's thesis of nomadic subjectivity, but Winterson does not make it in this novel, satisfied simply to poke scorn in patronising clichés that never develop past truisms, despite her belief in their originality. The prose he sees as banal, though reaching for profundity, and all in all Winterson 'has lost her way'.

Kasia Boddy in her *Times Literary Supplement* review, 'Love, Again'[15] suggests that Jeanette Winterson is simply repeating herself once more in the new novel about being in love with a married woman. At the kindliest construction of the repetitiveness, she argues that, like the American modernist Gertrude Stein, Winterson is repeating things in order to explore the potential for different variations within the similar. Stein called her process 'insistence'. Not only does each of the novels about an affair with a married woman, *Written on the Body, Gut Symmetries* and *The PowerBook*, give a variant closure to the story but the final one gives two differing possibilities of closure, the only two available, Boddy suggests. Love has thus become Winterson's sole focus, and she is well known for her interest in the new physics and relativity, in the idea of the alternative potentials and paths existing at any point. In this novel, the title and chapter headings point to the use of computers as a narrative trope, but for Boddy, this metaphor does not develop in any depth, and many of the comments about the new technology are unsurprising: that e-mail allows one to play with identities or that the interactive narrative (the powerbook of the title) dislodges the linear narratives of the printed text, for example. This insistence on the provisional and the fluid is at odds with the pure evangelism of the belief in love and of art, of the thesis that art needs to strive beyond the normal and to reach beyond the attainable, to change the way the world sees and feels. This is the central crux of the novel, not character or plot, but the narrator's meditations on love, which at times dissolve into the cloying statements of the infamous greeting cards, 'Love is …'. But for Boddy, this failure to delineate the features of love is in itself 'touching' since, by its very nature, love is impossible to grasp.

Elaine Showalter, in her *Guardian* review 'Eternal Triangles',[16] also concentrates on the repetition of love triangles. Despite its interesting use of the metaphor of e-mail to explore sexual licence and power, she sees the novel as exhibiting an emptiness. Winterson, she decides, is becoming 'a mannered novelist', and despite its erudition and the aestheticism, *The PowerBook* is little different from all the other romance novels filling the bookshop shelves. It is not in the repetitive story of adulterous bisexual love triangle, nor in its style and structure with the rejection of plot and realism, that Showalter really locates her sense of disappointment; it is primarily because she finds the novel reductive and stultifying.

E. Jane Dickon also used internet terminology for her review in the *Independent on Sunday*, 'Dot.com Dominatrix',[17] where she called *The PowerBook* 'a heaving millennial effort of a novel'. The emphasis is on the heaving and straining after a millenarian importance, which she feels the text fails to achieve. The language and imagery of computers allows for some entertaining insight, as when we 'download' time or choose a 'window' of opportunity. The protagonist, dubbed the Orlando of cyberspace because of her shifting of genders, from Ali to Alix (the protagonist of Virginia Woolf's novel, *Orlando*, changes sex and travels through four centuries) becomes through the internet stories either a Lancelot saving Guinevere or a Francesca da Rimini dying with the beloved Paolo, but mostly remains as herself, boringly demanding that the married woman listen to her harangues about what love constitutes. The acknowledged bravery in inventing a protagonist who exists beyond time, Dixon feels, needs to be matched with a profundity in the text's statements about love, and it is unable to deliver this. The strength of the novel is in the more realist, grounded delineation of life on the streets in Paris, London and Capri, but this is marred by the striving to be significant in the twenty-first century.

Kate Kellaway in *The Observer* does not agree, as the title of her review suggests, 'She's Got the Power: Jeanette Winterson's New Novel is a Virtuoso Trip into Virtual Reality'.[18] The book's layout and titles remind her of a computer manual but, thankfully, she soon realises that the novel does not employ computer terminology as more than a literary conceit to explore its theme of our ability to transmute our lives through our dreams, with a style that eschews the jargon of technology for something much lighter and more bewitching, as Alix and her 'punter' experience love in a complex variety of countries and historical times, communicating through virtual reality. Winterson has never shifted from her fascination with the theme of love, and Kellaway dubs her 'gallant' for her continued attempt to uncover the unsayable about love, particularly since her attempt is linked to a political agenda in her lesbian focus on the theme. The controlled grandeur of the novel leaves her breathless and totally in awe of its assured juxtaposition of philosophy, humour and the real with an 'elegance' that sustains the complex mix, even, for Kellaway, the outrageous pleasuring of the princess with the tulip. Where it falters briefly is in the idea that the text has two interactive narrators, which she finds too modishly 'tricksy'. But overall the shifting, unreliable narrative reminds her of Thomas Hardy (1840–1928) in *Return of the Native* (1878) and John Fowles (born 1926) in *The French Lieutenant's Woman* (1969), both of whom also provided alternate endings to their books for the reader to choose from. Kellaway casts Winterson as the 'ancient mariner' of Samuel Taylor Coleridge's poem, 'The Rhyme of the Ancient Mariner' 1798), who holds the listener spellbound by his marvellous and exquisite narrative. For her, the novel is a huge, ambitious success that reinforces the power of Jeanette Winterson as a writer.

The reviews of *The PowerBook* mainly argue that the computer analogies are simply a conceit, a literary metaphor, rather than anything more deep-seated, and are unanimously grateful for this. Boddy, Showalter and Kellaway remark on the repetitive element in this novel's themes, and Boddy links this to a feminine modernist practice of 'insistence', used by Stein at the beginning of the century. Baker ridicules the episode of the tulip as a sex toy, while Kellaway disagrees and feels it works effectively. But overall the reviews are not that enthusiastic and, as yet, there has not been any critical engagement to lift and challenge this reception with a more considered and mature understanding. It is to be hoped that, this will come with time. However, it is noticeable that the critical debates on Winterson's novels emerge, on the whole, a surprisingly long time after the text's publication. While critical analysis of the later ones, *Sexing the Cherry* or *Written on the Body*, took around four years to begin, *The Passion* or *Oranges Are Not the Only Fruit* took eight years to get going. Perhaps these dates stand testimony to Winterson's novels being ahead of their times, and certainly they would explain why, in 2004, the critical reception of *Gut Symmetries* has just started and we may need to wait another year or so for some considered discussion of *The PowerBook*.

Conclusion

An initial, erroneous reading of the critical debate reflected in this book would be that Winterson's early novels met with huge popular and critical success, but that it has been downhill all the way since then. Certainly that is a narrative constructed by some of the reviewers, particularly by Maya Jaggi in her profile of Winterson in 2004, when she quotes approvingly Michèle Roberts's claim that during the novelist's 'middle period' the texts became self-indulgently 'about art for art's sake, language for language's sake',[1] and lost all sense of telling a story. Winterson herself, in this interview, seems to concur with her confession that the 1990s was a 'dark decade' both personally and professionally. However, this narrative of the reception ignores two facts: that the reviewers' reception does not always echo the academic assessment; and that Winterson criticism appears to have a longer gestation period than that for many other writers. It is noticeable that essays only begin to appear some time after each text's publication, usually ranging from four to eight years. Perhaps these dates stand testimony to Winterson's novels being ahead of their times and academic critics only realising this much later. What is unquestionable is that to critics surveying contemporary British literature in the twenty-first century, such as Rod Mengham in *Introduction to Contemporary Fiction* (1999), Richard Lane et al. (eds) in *Contemporary British Fictions* (2003) and Jago Morrison in *Contemporary Fiction* (2003), Winterson has a status that demands not merely her inclusion, but a whole chapter to herself.

Once the critical debate begins, it also has a long shelf-life; *Oranges Are Not the Only Fruit*, for example, is still being discussed almost 30 years after its publication. The reviews of Winterson have almost all been ambivalent, with some highly critical of and others hugely enthusiastic about the same book. Again, this stands testimony to the strength and power of the writing, along with its difficulty and its 'writerliness' which makes large demands upon the readership. Review reception is no pointer to how the critical debate will go, since academic literary critics have the luxury of a more considered and thoughtful analysis.

At the moment, it seems that the novels using a playful intertextual reference to fairy tales and other mythic material like the Bible or King Arthur and the Round Table, such as *Oranges Are Not the Only Fruit* and

Sexing the Cherry, have been highly popular for their exuberant and satiric critiques, while the texts using the new physics, such as *Art and Lies* and *Gut Symmetries*, have proved less so, but this may also be due to the accessibility of the material used; more people are conversant with aspects of fairy tales and the Bible than with the theory of relativity and chaos theory. The structure of the 'quest' in the first four books has been received differently from the eternal triangle with a twist of the later three. Winterson herself ignores these differences in her argument that, with *The PowerBook* (2000), she has completed a cycle of narrative fiction that began with *Oranges Are Not the Only Fruit* (1985), suggesting that *The PowerBook* culminates a 'single emotional journey'.[2]

Winterson's latest novel, *Lighthousekeeping* (2004), has just been published to high acclaim and the usual media circus surrounding a major novelist's new work: ITV's prestigious arts programme, *The South Bank Show*, gave a profile of Winterson while the BBC, not to be outdone, made her the subject of their political programme, *This Week*, with Andrew Neill. Winterson engaged in the inevitable readings and talks that form part of the publicity machine, culminating in the prestigious annual Hay-on-Wye Literary Festival. Most of the reviews and interviews describe *Lighthousekeeping* as her eighth novel, probably following the publicity blurb supplied with the novel, thereby once again sidelining *Boating for Beginners*. While Winterson places *Lighthousekeeping* as the first of a new cycle of her fiction, the consensus of the reviewers tends to be that she has refound her earlier voice, or returned to an earlier success, thus positioning it as part of the same cycle.

The newspaper reviews exhibit the same range as for her earlier novels, from rapturous acclaim, through ambivalent acceptance, to dislike. But the balance of approval has shifted, with more liking it and fewer slating it, than in previous years. Charlie Lee Potter, in the *Independent on Sunday*,[3] called *Lighthousekeeping* 'an entrancing, gleaming crystal' of a novel. For Potter, the narrative is on an 'endless loop' with neither beginning nor end, although Silver, the young girl adopted by blind Pew the lighthouse keeper, is at the centre of the loop. She concludes with the assessment that the latest novel is a 'virtuoso display' and 'close to her best'. Viv Groskop, in the *Express*,[4] agreed that it was 'a gem', a 'lyrical fairytale' and 'brilliantly accomplished'. For her, it was Pew's story-telling that proved of most interest, as Silver is reared on his stories rather than attending a school. She praises the unique 'winning combination' of 'slow, languid, descriptive prose' and the paced, 'suspense-filled plot'. Justine Picardie, in the *Evening Standard*,[5] was also entranced by Pew's teaching that stories light up the darkness and provide the moments of illumination that belie our lives as something continuous and meaningful, and while she acknowledges that such a description of the novel might sound daunting, explains that Winterson's 'prodigious talent' brings it to life. Christina Patterson, in the *Independent*,[6] also raves over its 'luminous, lyrical intensity', entranced by the 'sheer beauty of the language'. Suggesting that love is the main theme of the novel, she positions Winterson as a romantic writer, a form of 'Romantic modernist'.

Amanda Craig, in *The Times*,[7] while welcoming *Lighthousekeeping* as a 'return to form' and praising its 'hypnotic, pared down allusive style' as 'witty, heartbreaking and charming', qualifies her praise with the reminder that, as a postmodern novel, it remains difficult and writerly and only readers who enjoy that type of writing will be pleased by it. Anita Sethi, in the *Observer*,[8] under a title that signals ambivalence, 'To the lighthouse, by the self-appointed heir to Virginia Woolf', writes a review that is completely positive. Suggesting that the settings of the novel, such as the lighthouse, are places 'where solidity meets restless motion' symbolic of the human desire for stability within a shifting, postmodern world, Sethi admits that while the thesis is not original, the form in which it is given to us, the exquisite use of language, makes it special. Joanna Briscoe, in the *Guardian*,[9] gives the most ambivalent of the reviews in her detailed consideration of the book. *Lighthousekeeping* is a 'flawed return to form' because she does not enjoy the middle section set in Capri, where Silver steals the bird that speaks her name. The beginning, with Silver's childhood, the death of her mother and her adoption by Pew, she calls classic Winterson, '[u]tterly skew whiff, deeply and gloriously odd'. The lighthouse works well as a setting because, despite the 'weightless, magical realism', the novelist is at her 'best with ballast'. Briscoe details the dual structure of the narrative, the story of Silver being intercut with Pew's story of Babel Dark, the nineteenth-century clergyman with a Jekyll and Hyde[10] personality. She decides that the novel is stunning when centred on the character of Pew and the theme of love. But not everyone is so ecstatic. Christopher Taylor in the *Sunday Telegraph*[11] was irritated by the 'self-consciously intricate borrowings' which he saw as aimed at impressing the 'laboratories of English literature'. Robert Hanks, in the *Daily Telegraph*,[12] both admired and found himself irritated by the novel, suggesting that the attempts at 'beautiful simplicity' succeed only in collapsing 'into faux-naiveté'. Suggesting that while this Winterson novel should have been easier for having only two sub-plots, Silver and Dark, it is too 'cut off from the outside world' to work and in one instance a 'glaring inconsistency' indicates that Winterson has even lost her own plot – a comment that the *Guardian*'s 'Critical Eye' mischievously misreports as saying that Winterson has lost the plot. Alex Clark, in the *Sunday Times*,[13] finds Pew too intrusive and, since he is a major narrator of the stories in the novel, this is a serious flaw. His review ends negatively with the hope that in a future novel she might succeed in 'expressing her prodigious talent'.

Overall, though, *Lighthousekeeping* has had a relatively auspicious reception. Unfortunately, we may well have to wait a good few years for the literary academic community to add its voice to the criticism, if her earlier novels are anything to go by.

Notes

INTRODUCTION

1 For example see: Rod Mengham, ed., *An Introduction to Contemporary Fiction* (Cambridge: Polity Press, 1999); Abby Werlock, ed., *British Women Writing Fiction* (Tuscaloosa: University of Alabama Press, 2000); Jago Morrison, *Contemporary Fiction* (London: Routledge, 2003); and Richard Lane, Rod Mengham and Philip Tew, eds, *Contemporary British Fictions* (Oxford: Polity, 2002).

2 Lynne Pearce, ' "Written on Tablets of Stone"? Jeanette Winterson, Roland Barthes and the Discourse of Romantic Love', in *Volcanoes and Pearl Divers: Essays in Lesbian Feminist Studies*, ed. Susan Raitt (London: Onlywomen Press, 1994), pp. 147–68.

3 Pearce (1994), p. 148.

4 Gabrielle Griffin, 'Acts of Defiance: Celebrating Lesbians', in *It's My Party*, ed. Gina Wisker (London: Pluto, 1994), pp. 80–103.

5 Laura Doan, 'Jeanette Winterson's Sexing the Postmodern', in *The Lesbian Postmodern*, ed. Laura Doan (New York: Columbia University Press, 1994), pp. 137–55.

6 Lisa Moore, 'Teledildonics: Virtual Lesbians in the Fiction of Jeanette Winterson', in *Sexy Bodies: The Strange Carnalities of Feminism*, ed. Elisabeth Grosz and Elsbeth Probyn (London: Routledge, 1995), pp. 104–27.

7 Paulina Palmer, *Lesbian Gothic* (London: Cassell, 1999).

8 Kim Middleton Meyer, 'Jeanette Winterson's Evolving Subject: Difficulty into Dream', in *Contemporary British Fictions*, ed. Richard Lane et al. (Oxford: Polity, 2003), pp. 210–26.

9 Susana Onega, ' "I'm telling You Stories, Trust Me": History/Story-telling in Jeanette Winterson's *Oranges Are Not the Only Fruit*', in *Telling Histories*, ed. Susana Onega (Amsterdam: Atlanta 1995), pp. 135–47.

10 Lisa Haines-Wright and Tracy Lynn Kyle, 'From He and She to You and Me', in *Virginia Woolf: Texts and Contexts*, ed. Beth Daugherty and Eileen Barrett (New York: Pace University Press, 1996), pp. 177–82. Jago Morrison, *Contemporary Fiction*, pp. 95–114.

11 Ute Kauer, 'Narration and Gender: The Role of the First-Person Narrator in Jeanette Winterson's *Written on the Body*', in *'I'm Telling You Stories': Jeanette Winterson and the Politics of Reading*, ed. Helena Grice and Tim Woods (Amsterdam: Rodopi, 1998), pp. 41–52.

12 Kasia Boddy, 'Love, Again', *Times Literary Supplement* (1 September 2000), p. 9.

13 See Jeanette Winterson, *Art Objects: Essays on Ecstasy and Effrontery* (London: Cape, 1995), and she has since edited Virginia Woolf's work with Margaret Reynolds, her partner at that time, for Vintage in 2000.

14 Lyn Pykett, 'A New Way with Words? Jeanette Winterson's Post-Modernism', in *'I'm Telling You Stories'*, ed. Grice and Woods (1998), pp. 53–60.

15 Winterson (1995), p. 53.

CHAPTER ONE

1 Katherine Simpson, *Oranges Are Not the Only Fruit: Jeanette Winterson* (Harlow: York Notes, 2001).

2 Roz Kaveney, 'With Lord Wigan', *Times Literary Supplement* (22 March 1985), p. 326.

3 Ursual Hegi, 'In Short', *New York Times Book Review* (8 November 1987), p. 26.

4 Gabrielle Griffin, 'Acts of Defiance: Celebrating Lesbians', in *It's My Party*, ed. Gina Wisker (London: Pluto, 1994), p. 81.

5 Griffin (1994), p. 83.
6 Adrienne Rich, 'Compulsory Heterosexuality and Lesbian Existence', *Signs*, 5 (4) (Summer) 1980 pp. 631–60, reprinted in *Blood, Bread and Poetry* (London: Virago, 1987).
7 Griffin (1994), pp. 96–7.
8 Griffin (1994), p. 86.
9 Griffin (1994), p. 87.
10 Griffin (1994), p. 88.
11 Griffin (1994), p. 89.
12 Griffin (1994), p. 96.
13 Lynne Pearce, *Reading Dialogics* (London: Edward Arnold, 1994), p. 173.
14 Laura Doan, ed., *The Lesbian Postmodern* (New York: Columbia University Press, 1994), p. 142.
15 Doan (1994), p. 144.
16 Doan (1994), p. 145.
17 Doan (1994), p. 147.
18 Doan (1994), pp. 147–8. For further discussion of this passage, see chapter 2.
19 Isabella C. Anievas Gamallo, 'Subversive Storytelling: The Construction of Lesbian Girlhood through Fantasy and Fairy Tale in Jeanette Winterson's *Oranges Are Not the Only Fruit*' in *The Girl: Construction of the Girl in Contemporary Fiction by Women*, ed. Ruth O. Saxton (New York: St Martin's, 1998), pp. 119–34. A more detailed discussion of its rewriting the *Bildungsroman* can be found in chapter 2.
20 A plot where the protagonist grows from childhood to a sense of their mature, artistic self. See next chapter for more discussion of this format.
21 The term for a homosexual or lesbian declaring their sexual preferences publically, rather than hiding it from society.
22 Gamallo (1998) p. 124.
23 Gamallo (1998), p. 124.
24 Gamallo (1998), pp. 124–5.
25 Gamallo (1998), p. 125.
26 Gamallo (1998), pp. 125–6.
27 Patricia Duncker, 'Jeanette Winterson and the Aftermath of Feminism', '*I'm Telling You Stories*', ed. Grice and Woods, *Postmodern Studies*, 25 (1998), pp. 77–89.
28 Duncker (1998), p. 83.
29 Lauren Rusk, *The Life Writing of Otherness: Woolf, Baldwin, Kingston, and Winterson* (New York: Routledge, 2002), chapter 5, 'The Refusal of Otherness: Winterson's *Oranges Are Not the Only Fruit*', pp. 105–32.
30 Rusk (2002), pp. 109–10.
31 Rusk (2002), p. 110.
32 Rusk (2002), p. 107.
33 Rusk (2002), p. 107.
34 Rusk (2002), p. 108.
35 Rusk (2002), p. 115.
36 Rusk (2002), pp. 118–19.
37 Rusk (2002), p. 111.
38 Rusk (2002), p. 112.
39 Rusk (2002), p. 121.
40 Rusk (2002), p. 121.
41 Rusk (2002), p. 105.
42 Jago Morrison, *Contemporary Fiction* (London: Routledge, 2003), pp. 95–114.
43 In *Gender Trouble* (1990) Butler argues that all gender and sex are self-created fluid fragments of identity; we perform to create our own sense of an identity; and that drag can deconstruct the apparent fixity of gender constructions.

44 Luce Irigaray was one of the three major French feminists who in the 1980s challenged cultural constructions of femininity. See *This Sex which is Not One* (1985). The others were Hélène Cixous and Julia Kristeva.

45 Morrison (2003), p. 97.

46 Morrison (2003), p. 97.

47 Morrison (2003), p. 100.

48 See Mikhail Bakhtin's *The Dialogic Imagination* (1934–41). Lynne Pearce also uses the chronotope in her discussion of *Sexing the Cherry.* See chapter 4.

49 Directed by Beeban Kidron and produced by Phillipa Giles, the adaptation ran over three episodes. The protagonist's name was changed to Jess. The screenplay was written by Winterson, see *Oranges Are Not the Only Fruit: The Screenplay* (London: Pandora, 1990). The adaptation won a BAFTA award for best drama series.

50 Cited in Hallam and Marshment, see below. Brooks, however, cites viewing figures for the first transmissions as being nearer three to four-and-a-half million for each episode.

51 Rebecca O'Rourke, 'Fingers in the Fruit Basket: a Feminist Reading of Jeanette Winterson's *Oranges Are Not the Only Fruit*', in *Feminist Criticism: Theory and Practice*, ed. Susan Sellers (Hemel Hempstead: Harvester, 1991), pp. 57–70.

52 O'Rourke (1991), p. 63.

53 Workers Educational Association, which provides classes for people who want a general discussion of a subject without studying for an award.

54 O'Rourke (1991), p. 66.

55 O'Rourke (1991), p. 66.

56 O'Rourke (1991), p. 67.

57 Hilary Hinds, '*Oranges Are Not the Only Fruit*: Reaching Audiences Other Lesbian Texts Cannot Reach', in *New Lesbian Criticism*, ed. Sally Munt (Hemel Hempstead: Harvester, 1992), pp. 153–72.

58 Hinds (1992), pp. 153–4.

59 Hinds (1992), p. 155.

60 Hinds (1992), p. 156.

61 Cited as in *Ms* (October, 1985).

62 Hinds (1992), p. 157.

63 Hinds (1992), p. 158.

64 Hinds (1992), p. 159.

65 The Islamic cleric who issued the *fatwah* against Rushdie.

66 Hinds (1992), p.164.

67 Hinds (1992), p. 162.

68 Hinds (1992), p. 163.

69 Hinds (1992), p. 165.

70 Hinds (1992), p. 167.

71 Hinds (1992), p. 168.

72 Hinds (1992), p. 169.

73 Hinds (1992), p. 170.

74 Marilyn Brooks, 'From Vases to Tea-sets: Screening Women's Writing', in Wisker (1994), pp. 129–44.

75 Brooks (1994), p. 129.

76 Brooks (1994), p. 130.

77 Brooks (1994), p. 133.

78 Julia Hallam and Margaret Marshment, 'Framing Experience: Case Studies in the Reception of *Oranges Are Not the Only Fruit*', *Screen*, 36 (1) Spring 1995, 1–15.

79 Hallam and Marshment (1995), p. 2.

80 Hallam and Marshment (1995), p. 5.

81 Hallam and Marshment (1995), p. 14.

CHAPTER TWO

1 Paulina Palmer, *Contemporary Lesbian Writing: Dreams, Desire, Difference* (Buckingham: Open University Press, 1993).
2 Palmer (1993), p. 101.
3 Palmer (1993), p. 101. In invoking the French feminist Hélène Cixous (born 1937), Palmer is clearly linking the created self as a feminine self. The Cixous quote comes from her essay 'Sorties', in *New French Feminisms*, ed. Elaine Marks and Isabelle de Courtivron (Hemel Hempstead: Harvester, 1981), p. 97.
4 Palmer (1993), p. 101.
5 Palmer (1993), p. 102.
6 Palmer (1993), p. 102.
7 Palmer (1993), p. 103.
8 Palmer (1993), p. 103.
9 Laura Doan, 'Jeanette Winterson's Sexing the Postmodern', in *The Lesbian Postmodern*, ed. Laura Doan (New York: Columbia University Press, 1994) pp. 147–8.
10 Laurel Bollinger, 'Models of Female Loyalty: The Biblical Ruth in Jeanette Winterson's *Oranges Are Not the Only Fruit*', in *Tulsa Studies in Women's Literature*, 13 (1994), pp. 363–80.
11 Carol Gilligan was the author of *In a Different Voice: Psychological Theory and Women's Development* (Cambridge, MA: Harvard University Press, 1982), and editor, with others, of *Mapping the Moral Domain: A Contribution of Women's Thinking to Psychological Theory and Education* (Cambridge, MA: Harvard University Press, 1988).
12 Bollinger (1994), p. 363.
13 Bollinger (1994), p. 365.
14 Bollinger (1994), p. 366.
15 Bollinger (1994), p. 367.
16 Bollinger (1994), p. 368.
17 The Bible (King James version), Ruth, 1: 16–17.
18 Bollinger (1994), p. 370.
19 Bollinger (1994), p. 375.
20 Bollinger (1994), pp. 376–7.
21 Bollinger (1994), p. 377.
22 Susan Onega, in *Telling Histories: Narrativizing History, Historicizing Literature*, ed. Susan Onega (Amsterdam: Rodopi, 1995), p. 137.
23 Lyotard was one of the founder thinkers of the postmodern, in texts such as *The Postmodern Condition: A Report on Knowledge* (1984).
24 Onega (1995), p. 138.
25 Onega (1995), p. 139.
26 Onega (1995), p. 140.
27 Onega (1995), p.141.
28 Onega (1995), p. 141.
29 Onega (1995), p. 142; Rosemary Jackson, *Fantasy: The Literature of Subversion* (London: Methuen, 1981).
30 Onega (1995), p. 143.
31 Onega (1995), p. 143.
32 Onega (1995), p. 146.
33 Onega (1995), p. 146.
34 Onega (1995), p. 146.
35 Ellen Brinks and Lee Talley, 'Unfamiliar Ties: Lesbian Constructions of Home and Family in Jeanette Winterson's *Oranges Are Not the Only Fruit* and Jewel Gomez's *The Gilda Stories*', in *Homemaking: Women Writers and the Politics and Poetics of Home*, ed. Catherine Wiley and Fiona R. Barnes (New York: Garland, 1996), pp. 145–74.
36 Brinks and Talley (1996), p. 148.

37 Brinks and Talley (1996), p. 149.
38 Brinks and Talley (1996), p. 151.
39 Brinks and Talley (1996), p. 154.
40 Brinks and Talley (1996), p. 159.
41 Tess Cosslett, 'Intertextuality in *Oranges Are Not the Only Fruit*: The Bible, Malory and *Jane Eyre*', in *'I'm Telling You Stories'*, ed. Helena Grice and Tim Woods (Amsterdam: Rodopi, 1998), pp. 15–28.
42 Cosslett (1998), p. 16.
43 Cosslett (1998), p. 16.
44 Cosslett (1998), p. 17.
45 Cosslett (1998), p. 20.
46 Cosslett (1998), p. 21.
47 Cosslett (1998), p. 21.
48 Cosslett (1998), p. 24.
49 Cosslett (1998), p. 24.
50 Cosslett (1998), p. 24.
51 In *The Girl: Construction of the Girl in Contemporary Fiction by Women*, ed. Ruth O. Saxton (New York: St Martin's, 1998), pp. 119–34.
52 Gamallo (1998), pp. 119–20.
53 The poststructuralist psychoanalyst who rereads Freud's concepts.
54 Gamallo (1998), p. 120.
55 Gamallo (1998), p. 121.
56 Gamallo (1998), p. 126.
57 Gamallo (1998), p. 127.
58 Gamallo (1998), p. 127.
59 Gamallo (1998), p. 133.
60 Gamallo (1998), pp. 131–2.
61 Gamallo (1998), p. 132–3.
62 Jan Rosemergy, 'Navigating the Interior Journey: the Fiction of Jeanette Winterson', in *British Women Writing Fiction*, ed. Abby H. P. Werlock (Tuscaloosa: University of Alabama Press, 2000), pp. 248–69.
63 In *Contemporary British Fiction*, ed. Richard Lane, Rod Mengham and Philip Tew (Oxford: Polity, 2002), pp. 210–26.
64 Meyer (2002), p. 211.
65 Meyer (2002), p. 212.

CHAPTER THREE

1 http://www.jeanettewinterson.com/biography.
2 Emma Fisher, 'Boating for Beginners', *Times Literary Supplement* (1 November 1985), p. 1228.
3 David Lodge, 'Outrageous Things', *New York Review* (29 September 1988), pp. 25–6.
4 Mark Wormald, 'The Uses of Impurity: Fiction and Fundamentalism in Salman Rushdie and Jeanette Winterson', *An Introduction to Contemporary Fiction*, ed. Rod Mengham (Cambridge: Polity, 1999), pp. 182–202.
5 Wormald (1999), pp. 189–90.
6 Wormald (1999), p. 193.
7 A palimpsest is a piece of writing that has later writing inscribed upon it, so that one can decipher layers of script beneath the surface one.
8 Wormald (1999), p. 194.
9 Jan Rosemergy, 'Navigating the Interior Journey: the Fiction of Jeanette Winterson', in *British Women Writing Fiction*, ed. Abby H. P. Werlock (Tuscaloosa: University of Alabama Press, 2000), p. 249.

10 Rosemergy (2000), p. 252.

11 Rosemergy (2000), p. 253.

12 Shena Mackay reviewing *Sexing the Cherry* in 1989 called it a 'bravura' novel; Katy Emck, reviewing *Gut Symmetries*, in the *Times Literary Supplement* in 1997, saw it as a brilliantly magical and poetical book.

13 Hilary Bailey, 'Women of the World', *Guardian* (12 June 1987), p. 15.

14 Nicholas Shrimpton, 'Emperors and Mermaids', *Observer* (14 June 1987), p. 23.

15 Ann Duchêne, 'After Marengo', *Times Literary Supplement* (26 June 1987), p. 697.

16 David Lodge (1988), *New York Review*, pp. 25–6.

17 Pearce (1994), p. 174.

18 Cath Stowers, 'Journeying with Jeanette: Transgressive Travels in Winterson's Fiction', in *(Hetero)Sexual Politics*, ed. Mary Maynard and June Purvis (London: Taylor and Francis, 1995), pp. 139–58.

19 Lisa Moore, 'Teledildonics: Virtual Lesbians in the Fiction of Jeanette Winterson', in *Sexy Bodies: The Strange Carnalities of Feminism*, ed. Elisabeth Grosz and Elsbeth Probyn (London: Routledge, 1995), pp. 104–27.

20 Laura Doan, *The Lesbian Postmodern* (New York: Colombia University Press, 1994), p. 148.

21 Doan (1994), p. 149.

22 Doan (1994), p. 149.

23 Moore (1995), pp. 105–6.

24 Moore (1995), pp. 105–6.

25 Luce Irigaray, 'When Our Lips Speak Together' (1977), in *This Sex Which is Not One*, trans. Catherine Porter (Ithaca, NY: Cornell University Press, 1985).

26 Moore (1995), p. 113.

27 Sara Mills, *Discourses of Difference: An Analysis of Women's Travel Writing and Colonialism* (London: Routledge, 1991).

28 Mary Louise Pratt, *Imperial Eyes: Travel Writing and Transculturation* (London: Routledge, 1992).

29 Hélène Cixous famously advocated an *écriture féminine* in 'the Laugh of the Medusa' (1976).

30 Stowers (1995), p. 94.

31 Stowers (1995), pp. 142–3.

32 Stowers (1995), p. 143.

33 Stowers (1995), p. 144.

34 Bényei Tamás, 'Risking the Text: Stories of Love in Jeanette Winterson', in *Hungarian Journal of English and American Studies*, 3:2 (1977), pp. 199–209.

35 Georges Bataille, *Visions of Excess*, trans. Allan Stoekl (Minneapolis: University of Minnesota Press, 1985).

36 Tamás (1977), p. 201.

37 Tamás (1977), pp. 201–2.

38 Tamás (1977), p. 202.

39 Tamás (1977), p. 202.

40 Judith Seaboyer, 'Second Death in Venice: Romanticism and the Compulsion to Repeat in Jeanette Winterson's *The Passion*', in *Contemporary Literature*, 38:3 (1997), pp. 483–509.

41 Seaboyer (1997), p. 484.

42 Seaboyer (1997), p. 484.

43 Seaboyer (1997), p. 485.

44 Seaboyer (1997), p. 487.

45 Joseph Breuer (1842–1925) was a psychoanalyst who worked with Freud on *Studies in Hysteria* (1895).

46 Seaboyer (1997), p. 489.

47 Sigmund Freud's (1856–1939) essay on 'The Uncanny' (1919) develops an analysis of the feeling of horror and disturbance experienced for everyday things.

48 Seaboyer (1997), p. 493.

49 Manfred Pfister, '*The Passion* from Winterson to Coryate', in *Venetian Views, Venetian Blinds: English Fantasies of Venice*, ed. Manfred Pfister and Barbara Schaff (Amsterdam: Rodopi, 1999), pp. 15–29.

50 Pfister (1999), p. 15.

51 Jan Morris, *Venice*, new edn (London: Faber, 2005).

52 Pfister (1999), p. 16.

53 Pfister (1999), p. 20.

54 Pfister (1999), p. 24.

55 Pfister (1999), p. 25.

56 Scott Wilson, 'Passion at the End of History', in Grice and Woods (1998), pp. 61–74.

57 Paulina Palmer, '*The Passion*: Storytelling, Fantasy, Desire', in Grice and Woods (1998), pp. 103–16.

58 Wilson (1998), pp. 62–3.

59 Wilson (1998), p. 69.

60 Wilson (1998), p. 69.

61 See Linda Hutcheon, *A Poetics of Postmodernism* (London: Routledge, 1988).

62 Palmer (1998), p. 104.

63 Palmer (1998), p. 104.

64 Palmer (1998), pp. 104–5.

65 Palmer (1998), p. 105.

66 Palmer (1998), p. 105.

67 Palmer (1998), p. 106.

68 An offshoot of the horror narrative, widespread in the eighteenth and nineteenth centuries, where passive female narrators are terrorised by spectres or mouldering corpses or madness, imprisoned in gaunt castles or caves etc., for example *The Castle of Otranto* (1764) by Horace Walpole (1717–97).

69 Paulina Palmer, *Lesbian Gothic: Transgressive Fictions* (London: Cassell, 1999).

70 Palmer (1999), p. 78.

71 Palmer (1999), p. 79.

72 Palmer (1999), p. 79.

73 Palmer (1999), p. 79.

74 Palmer (1999), p. 80.

75 Teresa de Laurentis, 'Sexual Indifference and Lesbian Representation', in *Lesbian and Gay Studies Reader*, ed. Henry Abelove et al. (London: Routledge, 1993), pp. 141–58.

76 Palmer (1999), p. 81. Monique Wittig, the lesbian French feminist theorist and novelist, will be cited extensively in chapter five, where critics compare her *The Lesbian Body* to Winterson's *Written on the Body*.

77 Palmer (1999), p. 81.

78 Palmer (1999), p. 81.

79 Palmer (1999), p. 82.

80 Palmer (1999), p. 82.

81 See Julia Kristeva, *Powers of Horror: An Essay on Abjection*, trans. Leo S. Roudiez (Hemel Hempstead: Harvester, 1991).

82 Palmer (1999), p. 83.

83 Palmer (1999), p. 84.

84 Palmer (1999), pp. 84–5.

85 Rosemergy (2000), p. 253.

86 Rosemergy (2000), p. 255.

87 Rosemergy (2000), pp. 254–5.

88 Rosemergy (2000), p. 259.

89 Rosemergy (2000), p. 262.
90 Kim Middleton Meyer, 'Jeanette Winterson's Evolving Subject: Difficulty into Dream', in *Contemporary British Fictions*, ed. Lane et al. (2002), p. 213.
91 Meyer (2002), p. 213.
92 Meyer (2002), p. 214.
93 Meyer (2002), p. 214.
94 Jago Morrison, 'Jeanette Winterson: Re-membring the Body', in *Contemporary Fiction* (London: Routledge, 2003), p. 101.
95 Morrison (2003), p. 101.
96 Morrison (2003), p. 102.
97 Morrison (2003), p. 102.
98 Morrison (2003), p. 103.
99 Morrison (2003), p. 104.

CHAPTER FOUR

1 Jennifer Selway, 'Tasting the Sweet Fruits of Success', *Observer* (3 September 1992), p. 45.
2 Shena MacKay, 'The Exotic Fruits of Time', *Times Literary Supplement* (15–21 September 1989), p. 1006.
3 David Holloway, 'Disconcerting Dreams, Maybe', *Sunday Telegraph* (3 September 1989), p. 38.
4 Lorna Sage, 'Weightlessness and a Banana', *Observer* (10 September 1989), p. 51.
5 Kenneth McLeish, 'Larger than Life', *Sunday Times* (10 September 1989), p. G7.
6 Michiko Kakutani, 'A Journey through Time, Space and Imagination', *New York Times* (27 April 1999), p. C33.
7 Michael Gorra, 'Gender Games in Restoration London', *New York Times Book Review* (29 April 1990), p. 24.
8 Paulina Palmer, *Contemporary Lesbian Writing: Dreams, Desire, Difference* (Buckingham: Open University Press, 1993).
9 Palmer (1993), p. 103.
10 Palmer (1993), p. 103.
11 Palmer (1993), p. 104.
12 Palmer (1993), pp. 104–5.
13 Palmer (1993), p. 105.
14 Lynne Pearce, 'Dialogism and Gender: Gendering the Chronotope', in *Reading Dialogics* (London: Edward Arnold, 1994), pp. 173–96.
15 Pearce (1994), pp. 173–4.
16 Pearce (1994), p. 174.
17 Pearce (1994), p. 178.
18 Pearce (1994), p. 179.
19 Pearce (1994), p. 182.
20 Pearce (1994), p. 182.
21 Pearce (1994), p. 184.
22 Alison Lee, 'Bending the Arrow of Time: the Continuing Postmodern Present', in *Historicité et Metafiction dans le Roman Contemporain des Îles Britanniques*, ed. Max Duperray (Provence: Université de Provence, 1994), pp. 217–30.
23 Lee (1994), p. 220.
24 Lee (1994), p. 222.
25 Isaac Newton (1642–1727) described time as an arrow.
26 Albert Einstein (1879–1955), a physicist who developed a more relative conception of time and developed the General Theory of Relativity (1915–17).
27 Lee (1994), p. 223.

28 Lee (1994), pp. 223–4.
29 Neils Bohr (1885–1962), Danish physicist; his theory underpins Quantum Theory.
30 Werner Heisenberg (1901–76), German physicist, known for his Uncertainty Principle, a consequence of Quantum Theory.
31 Lee (1994), p. 225.
32 Lee (1994), pp. 227–8.
33 Laura Doan, 'Jeanette Winterson's Sexing the Postmodern', in *The Lesbian Postmodern*, ed. Laura Doan (New York: Columbia University Press, 1994), p. 138.
34 Doan (1994), p. 150.
35 Doan (1994), p. 151.
36 Doan (1994), p. 153.
37 Doan (1994), p. 153.
38 Lisa Moore, 'Teledildonics: Virtual Lesbians in the Fiction of Jeanette Winterson', in Grosz and Probyn (1995), p. 116.
39 John Locke (1632–1704) wrote *Essay Concerning Human Understanding* (1690), which examines philosophically how we come to understand knowledge, including knowledge of ourselves.
40 Moore (1995), p. 117.
41 Moore (1995), p. 118.
42 Moore (1995), p. 121.
43 See Donna Haraway's *Simians, Cyborgs and Women* (London: Free Association Books, 1991), where she argues that monkeys and cyborgs allow a discourse that challenges and transcends the concept of the human, from which women have always been marginalised.
44 Maria Lozano, ' "How You Cuddle in the Dark Governs How You See the History of the World" ', in *Telling Histories*, ed. Susana Onega (Amsterdam: Rodopi, 1995), pp. 117–34.
45 Lozano (1995), pp. 129–30.
46 Lozano (1995), p. 131.
47 Lozano (1995), pp. 133–4.
48 Marilyn R. Farwell, 'The Postmodern Lesbian Text', in *Heterosexual Plots and Lesbian Narratives* (New York: New York University, 1996), pp. 168–94.
49 Farwell (1996), p. 177.
50 Farwell (1996), p. 177.
51 Farwell (1996), p. 177.
52 Farwell (1996), p. 169.
53 Farwell (1996), pp. 179–80.
54 Farwell (1996), p. 180.
55 Farwell (1996), p. 180.
56 Farwell (1996), p. 181.
57 Farwell (1996), p. 183.
58 Farwell (1996), p. 184.
59 Farwell (1996), p. 185.
60 Elizabeth Langland, 'Sexing the Text: Narrative Drag as Feminist Poetics and Politics in *Sexing the Cherry*', in *Narrative*, 5 (January, 1997) pp. 99–107.
61 Langland (1997), p. 100.
62 Langland (1997), p. 100.
63 Langland (1997), p. 100.
64 Langland (1997), p. 101.
65 Langland (1997), pp. 101–2.
66 Langland (1997), p. 102.
67 Langland (1997), pp. 102–3.
68 Langland (1997), p. 104.

69 Sarah Martin, 'The Power of Monstrous Women: Fay Weldon's *The Life and Loves of a She-Devil* (1983), Angela Carter's *Nights at the Circus* (1984) and Jeanette Winterson's *Sexing the Cherry* (1989)', *Journal of Gender Studies*, 8:2 (July 1999), pp. 193–210.

70 Martin (1999), p. 195.

71 Martin (1999), p. 195.

72 Martin (1999), p. 201.

73 Martin (1999), p. 202.

74 Martin (1999), pp. 202–3.

75 Martin (1999), p. 204.

76 Martin (1999), p. 204.

77 Martin (1999), p. 205.

78 Jan Rosemergy, 'Navigating the Interior Journey: the Fiction of Jeanette Winterson', in Werlock (2000), pp. 256–7.

79 Rosemergy (2000), p. 257.

80 Rosemergy (2000), p. 258.

81 Rosemergy (2000), p. 258.

82 Rosemergy (2000), p. 264.

83 Kim Middleton Meyer, 'Jeanette Winterson's Evolving Subject: Difficulty into Dream', in Lane et al. (2002), p. 215.

84 Meyer (2002), p. 216.

85 Meyer (2002), pp. 216–17.

86 Rosi Braidotti, *Nomadic Subjects: Embodiment and Sexual Difference in Contemporary Feminist Theory* (New York: Alfred A. Knopf, 1993).

87 Meyer (2002), p. 217.

88 Jago Morrison, *Contemporary Fiction* (London: Routledge, 2003), p. 105.

89 Morrison (2003), p. 106.

90 Morrison (2003), p. 107.

91 Morrison (2003), p. 108.

92 Morrison (2003), p. 109.

CHAPTER FIVE

1 Laura Cumming, 'Romantic Quips and Quiddities', *Guardian* (3 September 1992), p. 22.

2 Valerie Miner, 'At Her Wits End', *Women's Review of Books* (April 1993), p. 14.

3 Nicoletta Jones, 'Secondhand Emotion', *Sunday Times* (13 September 1992), Books section, p. 11.

4 The postcode for Hampstead, the expensively artistic and bohemian suburb of North London.

5 Jim Shepherd, 'Loss is the Measure of Love', *New York Times Book Review* (14 February 1993), p. 10.

6 Lisa Moore, 'Teledildonics: Virtual Lesbians in the Fiction of Jeanette Winterson', in Grosz and Probyn (1995), p. 110.

7 Christy L. Burns, 'Fantastic Language: Jeanette Winterson's Recovery of the Postmodern Word', in *Contemporary Literature*, 37 (1996), pp. 274–306.

8 Burns (1996), p. 294.

9 Burns (1996), p. 295.

10 Burns (1996), p. 295.

11 Burns (1996), p. 296.

12 Burns (1996), p. 297.

13 Burns (1996), p. 301.

14 Marilyn R. Farwell, *Heterosexual Plots and Lesbian Narratives* (New York: New York University Press, 1996), p. 178.

15 Farwell (1996), p. 179.

16 Farwell (1996), p. 187.
17 Farwell (1996), p. 188.
18 Farwell (1996), p. 188.
19 Farwell (1996), p. 189.
20 Farwell (1996), p. 190.
21 Farwell (1996), p. 191.
22 Farwell (1996), p. 191.
23 Farwell (1996), p. 193.
24 Farwell (1996), p. 193.
25 Farwell (1996), p. 194.
26 Heather Nunn, 'Written on the Body: an Anatomy of Horror, Melancholy and Love', in *Women: A Cultural Review*, 7:1 (Spring 1996), pp. 16–27.
27 Dyadic refers to the original close bond between mother and baby, which allows for no other distractions.
28 Jacques Lacan argues that psychoanalytically, men 'have' the penis which stands in for the phallus but that women, striving to be what the mother/men desire, try to 'be' the phallus.
29 Lisa Haines-Wright and Tracy Lynn Kyle, 'From He and She to You and Me: Grounding Fluidity, Woolf's *Orlando* to Winterson's *Written on the Body*', in *Virginia Woolf: Texts and Contexts*, ed. Beth Rigel Daugherty and Eileen Barrett (New York: Pace University, 1996), pp. 177–82.
30 Haines-Wright and Kyle (1996), p. 177.
31 Haines-Wright and Kyle (1996), p. 180.
32 Haines-Wright and Kyle (1996), p. 181.
33 Lynne Pearce, 'The Emotional Politics of Reading Winterson', in Grice and Woods (1998), pp. 29–39.
34 Pearce (1998), p. 30.
35 Pearce (1998), p. 31.
36 Pearce (1998), p. 33.
37 Ute Kauer, 'Narration and Gender: the Role of the First-Person Narrator in Jeanette Winterson's *Written on the Body*', in Grice and Woods (1998), pp. 41–51.
38 Gérard Genette, *Narrative Discourse* (1980).
39 Kauer (1998), p. 42.
40 Kauer (1998), p. 43.
41 Kauer (1998), p. 44.
42 Patrick Duncker, 'Jeanette Winterson and the Aftermath of Feminism', in Grice and Woods (1998), p. 82.
43 Duncker (1998), p. 81.
44 Duncker (1998), p. 81.
45 Duncker (1998), p. 85.
46 Cath Stowers, 'The Erupting Lesbian Body: Reading *Written on the Body* as a Lesbian Text', in Grice and Woods (1998), pp. 89–102.
47 Stowers (1998), p. 90.
48 Stowers (1998), p. 91.
49 Stowers (1998), p. 91.
50 Stowers (1998), p. 91.
51 Stowers (1998), p. 93.
52 Stowers (1998), p. 95.
53 Kim Middleton Meyer, 'Jeanette Winterson's Evolving Subject: Difficulty into Dream', in Lane et al. (2002), p. 218.
54 Meyer (2002), p. 219.
55 Meyer (2002), p. 219.
56 Meyer (2002), pp. 219–20.

57 Jago Morrison, *Contemporary Fiction* (London: Routledge, 2003), p. 110.
58 Morrison (2003), p. 110.
59 Morrison (2003), p. 111.
60 Morrison (2003), p. 112.
61 Morrison (2003), p. 113.
62 Morrison (2003), p. 114.

CHAPTER SIX

1 Lorna Sage, 'Finders Keepers', *Times Literary Supplement* (17 June 1994), p. 22.
2 Michèle Roberts, 'Words Are Not the Only Art', *Independent on Sunday* (19 June 1994).
3 The fairy tale goes that everyone admires the Emperor's new clothes except the child who, uninfluenced by the need to seem fashionable, states truthfully that the Emperor is not wearing any clothes.
4 Philip Hensler, 'Sappho's Mate', *Guardian* (5 July 1994), p. 13.
5 Hensler (1994), p. 13.
6 William Pritchard, ' "Say my name and you say sex": A Trip into Prose-Poetry, with a General Contempt for Family – and for Men', *New York Times* (26 March 1995), pp. 14–15.
7 Pritchard (1994), p. 14.
8 Pritchard (1994), p. 15.
9 Peter Kemp, 'Writing for a Fall', *Sunday Times* (26 June 1994), Books section, pp. 1–2.
10 Kemp (1994), p. 1.
11 Kemp (1994), p. 1.
12 Rachel Cusk, 'A Wretchedness New to History', *The Times* (20 June 1994), p. 39.
13 Christy L. Burns, 'Fantastic Language: Jeanette Winterson's Recovery of the Postmodern Word', *Contemporary Literature*, 37 (1996), p. 278.
14 Burns (1996), p. 279.
15 Burns (1996), p. 281.
16 Burns (1996), p. 282.
17 See Jean Baudrillard, *Simulations* (1983) and *The Evil Demon of Images* (1987). Simulacra are imitations of the real thing, rather than the real itself, which Baudrillard argues is now unavailable in a media-saturated society.
18 Burns (1996), p. 293.
19 Burns (1996), pp. 293–4.
20 Burns (1996), p. 302.
21 Burns (1996), p. 302.
22 Burns (1996), p. 302.
23 Christy L. Burns, 'Powerful Differences: Critique and Eros in Jeanette Winterson and Virginia Woolf', *Modern Fiction Studies*, 44:2 (Summer 1998), pp. 364–92.
24 Burns (1998), p. 369.
25 Burns (1998), p. 371.
26 Burns (1998), p. 371.
27 Burns (1998), pp. 371–2.
28 Burns (1998), p. 372.
29 Burns (1998), p. 376.
30 Burns (1998), p. 377.
31 Burns (1998), p. 379.
32 Burns (1998), p. 380.
33 Burns (1998), p. 383.
34 Burns (1998), p. 385.
35 Burns (1998), p. 387.
36 Burns (1998), p. 388.

37 Burns (1998), p. 388.
38 Patricia Duncker, 'Jeanette Winterson and the Aftermath of Feminism', in Grice and Woods (1998), pp. 77–88.
39 Duncker (1998), p. 85.
40 Duncker (1998), p. 85.

CHAPTER SEVEN

1 Adam Mars-Jones, 'From Oranges to a Lemon', Observer (5 January 1997), p. 15.
2 Roland Barthes's term for texts with narrative difficulty, like modernist prose, where the reader has to work to decipher the meaning.
3 Philip Hensler, 'Too Many Lemons, Not Enough "Oranges" ', Mail on Sunday (5 January 1997), Books section, p. 30.
4 Hugo Barnacle, 'No, no Jeanette', Sunday Times (5 January 1997), Books section, p. 7.
5 James Wood, 'The Three Jeanettes', Guardian, (2 January 1997), Books section, p. 11.
6 Katy Emck, 'On the High Seas of Romance', Times Literary Supplement (3 January 1997), p. 21.
7 Michèle Roberts, 'Girls Will Be Girls', Independent on Sunday (5 January 1997), p. 31.
8 Bruce Bawer, 'Sexing the Cosmos', New York Times Book Review (11 May 1997), p. 17.
9 Helena Grice and Tim Woods, 'Grand (Dis)Unified Theories? Dislocated Discourses in Gut Symmetries' in Grice and Woods (1998), pp. 117–26.
10 Michel Serres, 'Lucretius: Science and Religion', in Hermes: Literature, Science, Philosophy, ed. Josué Harari and David Bell (Baltimore: Johns Hopkins University Press, 1982).
11 Kim Middleton Meyer, 'Jeanette Winterson's Evolving Subject: Difficulty into Dream', in Lane et al. (2002), p. 221.
12 Meyer (2002), p. 221.
13 Meyer (2002), p. 221.
14 Phil Baker, 'A Dot com.Enterprise Gone Dotty', Sunday Times (27 August 2000), Books section, p. 43.
15 Kasia Boddy, 'Love, Again', Times Literary Supplement (1 September 2000), p. 9.
16 Elaine Showalter, 'Eternal Triangles', Guardian (2 September 2000), Book section, p. 9.
17 E. Jane Dickson, 'Dot.com Dominatrik', Independent on Sunday (2 September 2000), p. 32.
18 Kate Kellaway, 'She's Got the Power', Observer (27 August 2000), Review section, p. 11.

CONCLUSION

1 Maya Jaggi, 'Jeanette Winterson: Redemption Songs', Guardian (29 May 2004), pp. 20–3.
2 Jaggi (2004), p. 21.
3 Charlie Lee Potter, 'Winterson's Brilliant Beam', Independent on Sunday (9 May 2004).
4 Viv Groskop, 'A Beacon of Delight', Express (21 May 2004).
5 Justine Picardie, 'Casting Light on Darkness', Evening Standard (4 May 2004).
6 Christina Patterson, 'Of Love and Other Demons', Independent (7 May 2004), Review.
7 Amanda Craig, 'Shine on Brightly', The Times (24 April 2004), p. 15.
8 Anita Sethi, 'To the Lighthouse, by the Self-appointed Heir to Virginia Woolf', Observer (2 May 2004).
9 Joanna Briscoe, 'Full Beam Ahead', Guardian (8 May 2004), Review, p. 26.
10 The Strange Case of Dr Jekyll and Mr Hyde (1886), a story by Robert Louis Stevenson (1850–94) of a man with two opposing personalities, one civilised and gentle, the other monstrous.
11 Cited in 'Critical Eye', Guardian (8 May 2004), Review.
12 Robert Hanks, 'Stories Give Way to Stories', Daily Telegraph(1 May 2004), p. 9.
13 Alex Clark, 'Telling Tales', Sunday Times (2 May 2004), p. 56.

Bibliography

WORKS BY JEANETTE WINTERSON
NOVELS
Oranges Are Not the Only Fruit (London: Pandora, 1985).
Boating for Beginners (London: Methuen, 1985).
The Passion (London: Bloomsbury, 1987).
Sexing the Cherry (London: Bloomsbury, 1989).
Written on the Body (London: Jonathan Cape, 1992).
Art and Lies: A Piece for Three Voices and a Bawd (London: Jonathan Cape, 1994).
Gut Symmetries (London: Granta, 1997).
The PowerBook (London: Jonathan Cape, 2000).
Lighthousekeeping (London: Fourth Estate, 2004).

SHORT STORIES
'The Architect of Unrest', in *Granta*, 28 (Autumn 1989), pp. 179–85.
The World and Other Places (London: Jonathan Cape, 1998).

OTHER BOOKS
Fit for the Future: The Guide for Women Who Want to Live Well (London: Pandora, 1986).
Oranges Are Not the Only Fruit: The Script (London: Pandora, 1990).
Great Moments in Aviation (Script) (London: Vintage, 1994).
Art Objects: Essays on Ecstasy and Effrontery (London: Jonathan Cape, 1995).
The King of Capri, a children's story, illustrated by Jane Ray (London: Bloomsbury, 2003).

AS EDITOR
Passion Fruit: Romantic Fiction with a Twist (London: Pandora, 1986).
Virginia Woolf's Novels: The Vintage Series (London: Vintage, 2000), with Margaret Reynolds.
  Winterson also introduced *The Waves* with Gillian Beer.

WEBSITE
www.jeanettewinterson.com, the official Winterson website.
http://w1.181.telia.com/~u18114424/main.htm, the Jeanette Winterson Reader's Site.

CRITICISM
TWO OR MORE NOVELS
Bengtson, Helene, Borch, Marianne and Maagaard, Cindie, eds, *Sponsored by Demons*: *The Art of Jeanette Winterson* (Agedrup, Denmark: Scholar's Press, 1999).
Burns, Christy L., 'Fantastic Language: Jeanette Winterson's Recovery of the Postmodern Word', *Contemporary Literature*, 37 (1996), pp. 278–306.
Doan, Laura, 'Jeanette Winterson's Sexing the Postmodern', in *The Lesbian Postmodern*, ed. Laura Doan (New York: Columbia University Press, 1994), pp. 137–55.
Duncker, Patricia, 'Jeanette Winterson and the Aftermath of Feminism', in *'I'm telling you stories'*, ed. Helena Grice and Tim Woods, pp. 77–88.

Farwell, Marilyn R., 'Chapter 6: The Postmodern Lesbian Text: Jeanette Winterson's *Sexing the Cherry* and *Written on the Body*', in *Heterosexual Plots and Lesbian Narratives* (New York: New York University Press, 1996), pp. 168–94.

Grice, Helena and Woods, Tim, eds, *'I'm telling you stories': Jeanette Winterson and the Politics of Reading* (Amsterdam: Rodopi, 1998).

Lodge, David, 'Outrageous Things', *New York Review* (29 September 1988), pp. 25–6.

Meyer, Kim Middleton, 'Jeanette Winterson's Evolving Subject: Difficulty into Dream', in *Contemporary British Fictions*, ed. Richard Lane, Rod Mengham and Philip Tew (Oxford: Polity, 2002), pp. 210–26.

Moore, Lisa, 'Teledildonics: Virtual Lesbians in the Fiction of Jeanette Winterson', in *Sexy Bodies: The Strange Carnalities of Feminism*, ed. Elizabeth Grosz and Elspeth Probyn (London: Routledge, 1995), pp. 104–27.

Morrison, Jago, 'Jeanette Winterson: Re-membering the Body', in *Contemporary Fiction* (London: Routledge, 2003), pp. 95–114.

Palmer, Paulina, *Contemporary Lesbian Writing: Dreams, Desire, Difference* (Buckingham: Open University Press, 1993).

—— *Lesbian Gothic: Transgressive Fictions* (London: Cassell, 1999).

Pearce, Lynne, ' "Written on Tablets of Stone"? Jeanette Winterson, Roland Barthes and the Discourse of Romantic Love', in *Volcanoes and Pearl Divers: Essays in Lesbian Feminist Studies*, ed. Suzanne Raitt (London: Only women Press, 1994), pp. 147–68.

—— 'The Emotional Politics of Reading Winterson', in *'I'm telling you stories'*, ed. Helena Grice and Tim Woods, pp. 29–40.

Pressler, Christopher, *So Far So Linear: Responses to the Work of Jeanette Winterson* (Nottingham: Pauper's Press, 1997).

Pykett, Lyn, 'A New Way with Words? Jeanette Winterson's Post-Modernism', in *'I'm telling you stories*, ed. Helena Grice and Tim Woods, pp. 53–60.

ORANGES ARE NOT THE ONLY FRUIT

Bollinger, Laurel, 'Models of Female Loyalty: the Biblical Ruth in Jeanette Winterson's *Oranges Are Not the Only Fruit*', *Tulsa Studies in Women's Literature*, 13 (1994), pp. 363–80.

Brinks, Ellen and Talley, Lee, 'Unfamiliar Ties: Lesbian Constructions of Home and Family in Jeanette Winterson's *Oranges Are Not the Only Fruit* and Jewell Gomez's *The Gilda Stories*', in *Homemaking: Women Writers and the Politics and Poetics of Home*, ed. Catherine Wiley and Fiona Barnes (New York: Garland, 1996), pp. 145–74.

Cosslett, Tess, 'Intertextuality in *Oranges Are Not the Only Fruit*: the Bible, Mallory, and *Jane Eyre*', in *'I'm telling you stories'*, ed. Helena Grice and Tim Woods, pp. 15–28.

Gamallo, Isabel C. Anievas, 'Subversive Storytelling: the Construction of Lesbian Girlhood through Fantasy and Fairy Tale in Jeanette Winterson's *Oranges Are Not the Only Fruit*', in *The Girl: Construction of the Girl in Contemporary Fiction by Women*, ed. Ruth Saxton (New York: St Martin's, 1998), pp. 119–34.

Griffin, Gabrielle, 'Acts of Defiance: Celebrating Lesbians', in *It's My Party: Reading Twentieth-Century Women's Writing*, ed. Gina Wisker (London: Pluto, 1994), pp. 80–103.

Hallam, Julia and Marshment, Margaret, 'Framing Experience: Case Studies in the Reception of *Oranges Are Not the Only Fruit*', *Screen*, 36 (Spring, 1995), pp. 1–15.

Hinds, Hilary, '*Oranges Are Not the Only Fruit*: Reaching Audiences Other Lesbian Texts Cannot Reach', in *New Lesbian Criticism*, ed. Sally Munt (Hemel Hempstead: Harvester, 1992), pp. 153–72.

Kaveney, Roz, 'With Lord Wigan', *Times Literary Supplement* (22 March 1985), p. 326.

Onega, Susana, ' "I'm telling you stories. Trust me": History/Storytelling in *Oranges Are Not the Only Fruit*', in *Telling Histories*, ed. Susana Onega (Amsterdam: Rodopi, 1995), pp. 135–47.

Rusk, Lauren, *The Life Writing of Otherness: Woolf, Baldwin, Kingston and Winterson* (New York: Routledge, 2002).

Simpson, Kathryn, *York Notes: Oranges Are Not the Only Fruit: Jeanette Winterson* (Harlow: York Notes, 2001).

BOATING FOR BEGINNERS
Fisher, Emma, 'Boating for Beginners', *Times Literary Supplement* (1 November 1985), p. 1228.
Wormald, Mark, 'The Uses of Impurity: Fiction and Fundamentalism in Salman Rushdie and Jeanette Winterson', in *An Introduction to Contemporary Fiction*, ed. Rod Mengham (Cambridge: Polity, 1999).

THE PASSION
Duchêne, Ann, 'After Marengo', *Times Literary Supplement* (26 June 1987), p. 697.
Palmer, Paulina, 'The Passion': Storytelling, Fantasy, Desire', in *'I'm telling you stories'*, ed. Helena Grice and Tim Woods, pp. 103–16.
Pfister, Manfred, 'The Passion from Winterson to Coryate', in *Venetian Views, Venetian Blinds: English Fantasies of Venice*, ed. Manfred Pfister and Barbara Schaff (Amsterdam: Rodopi, 1999), pp. 15–28.
Pickering, Paul, 'Passionate about Life', *Sunday Times* (7 June 1987), p. 52.
Seaboyer, Judith, 'Second Death in Venice: Romanticism and the Compulsion to Repeat in Jeanette Winterson's *The Passion*', *Contemporary Literature*, 38 (1997), pp. 483–509.
Stowers, Cath, 'Journeying with Jeanette: Transgressive Travels in Winterson's Fiction', in *(Hetero)sexual Politics*, ed. Mary Maynard and June Purvis (London: Taylor and Francis, 1995), pp. 139–58.
Tamás, Bényei, 'Risking the Text: Stories of Love in Jeanette Winterson's *The Passion*', *Hungarian Journal of English and American Studies*, 3: 2 (1997), pp. 199–209.
Wilson, Scott, 'Passion at the End of History', in *'I'm telling you stories'*, ed. Helena Grice and Tim Woods, pp. 61–74.

SEXING THE CHERRY
Gorra, Michael, 'Gender Games in Restoration London', *New York Times Book Review*, (19 April 1990), p. 24.
Holloway, David, 'Disconcerting Dreams, Maybe', *Sunday Telegraph* (3 September 1989), p. 38.
Kakutani, Michiko, 'A Journey through Time, Space and Imagination', *New York Times*, (27 April 1999), p. C33.
Langland, Elizabeth, 'Sexing the Text: Narrative Drag as Feminist Poetics and Politics in Jeanette Winterson's *Sexing the Cherry*', *Narrative* (5 January 1997), pp. 99–107.
Lee, Alison, 'Bending the Arrow of Time: the Continuing Postmodern Present', in *Historicité et Metafiction dans le Roman Contemporain des Îles Britanniques*, ed. Max Duperray (Provence: Université de Provence, 1994), pp. 217–30.
Lozano, Maria, ' "How You Cuddle in the Dark Governs How You See the History of the World": a Note on Some Obsessions in Recent British Fiction', in *Telling Histories*, ed. Susana Onega (Amsterdam: Rodopi, 1995), pp. 117–34.
MacKay, Shena, 'The Exotic Fruits of Time', *Times Literary Supplement* (15–21 September 1989), p. 1006.
Martin, Sarah, 'The Power of Monstrous Women: Fay Weldon's *The Life and Loves of a She Devil* (1983), Angela Carter's *Nights at the Circus* (1984) and Jeanette Winterson's *Sexing the Cherry* (1989)', *Journal of Gender Studies*, 8:(July 1999), pp. 193–210.
McLeish, Kenneth, 'Larger than Life', *Sunday Times* (10 September 1989), p. G7.
Pearce, Lynne, *Reading Dialogics* (London: Edward Arnold, 1994).
Sage, Lorna, 'Weightlessness and a Banana', *Observer* (10 September 1989), p. 51.
Selway, Jennifer, 'Tasting the Sweet Fruits of Success', *Observer* (3 September 1992), p. 45.

WRITTEN ON THE BODY
Cumming, Laura, 'Romantic Quips and Quiddities', *Guardian* (3 September 1992), p. 22.
Haines-Wright, Lisa and Kyle, Tracy Lynn, 'From He and She to You and Me: Grounding Fluidity, Woolf's *Orlando* to Winterson's *Written on the Body*', in *Virginia Woolf: Texts and*

Contexts, ed. Beth Rigel Daugherty and Eileen Barrett (New York: Pace University, 1996), pp. 177–82.

Jones, Nicoletta, 'Secondhand Emotion', *Sunday Times* (13 September 1992), Books section, p. 11.

Kauer, Ute, 'Narration and Gender: the Role of the First-Person Narrator in *Written on the Body*', in *'I'm telling you stories'*, ed. Helena Grice and Tim Woods, pp. 41–52.

Nunn, Heather, 'Written on the Body: an Anatomy of Horror, Melancholy and Love', *Women: A Cultural Review*, 7 (Spring 1996), pp. 16–27.

Shepherd, Jim, 'Loss is the Measure of Love', *New York Times Book Review* (14 February 1993), p. 10.

Stowers, Cath, 'The Erupting Lesbian Body: Reading *Written on the Body* as a Lesbian Text', in *'I'm telling you stories'*, ed. Helena Grice and Tim Woods, pp. 89–102.

ART AND LIES

Burns, Christy L., 'Powerful Differences: Critique and Eros in Jeanette Winterson and Virginia Woolf', *Modern Fiction Studies*, 44 (1998), pp. 364–92.

Cusk, Rachel, 'A Wretchedness New to History', *The Times* (20 June 1994), p. 39.

Hensler, Philip, 'Sappho's Mate', *Guardian* (5 July 1994), p. 13.

Kemp, Peter, 'Writing for a Fall', *Sunday Times* (26 June 1994), Books section, pp. 1–2.

Sage, Lorna, 'Finders Keepers', *Times Literary Supplement* (17 June 1994), p. 22.

GUT SYMMETRIES

Emck, Katy, 'On the High Seas of Romance', *Times Literary Supplement* (3 January 1997), p. 21.

Grice, Helena and Tim Woods, 'Grand (Dis)Unified Theories? Dislocating Discourses in *Gut Symmetries*', in *'I'm telling you stories'*, ed. Helena Grice and Tim Woods, pp. 117–26.

Hensler, Philip, 'Too Many Lemons, Not Enough "Oranges" ', *Mail on Sunday* (5 January 1997), Books section, p. 30.

Mars-Jones, Adam, 'From Oranges to a Lemon', *Observer* (5 January 1997), p. 15.

Roberts, Michèle, 'Girls Will Be Girls', *Independent on Sunday* (5 January 1997), p. 31.

Wood, James, 'The Three Jeanettes', *Guardian* (2 January 1997), Books section, p. 11.

THE POWERBOOK

Boddy, Kasia, 'Love, Again', *Times Literary Supplement* (1 September 2000), p. 9.

Dickson, E. Jane, 'Dot.com dominatrix', *Independent on Sunday* (2 September 2000), p. 32.

Kellaway, Kate, 'She's Got the Power: Jeanette Winterson's New Novel is a Virtuoso Trip into Virtual Reality', *Observer* (27 August 2000), p. 11.

Showalter, Elaine, 'Eternal Triangles', *Guardian* (2 September 2000), Books section, p. 9.

LIGHTHOUSEKEEPING

Briscoe, Joanna, 'Full Beam Ahead', *Guardian* (8 May 2004), p. 26.

Clark, Alex, 'Telling Tales', *Sunday Times* (2 May 2004), p. 56.

Craig, Amanda, 'Shine on Brightly', *The Times* (24 April 2004), p. 15.

Groskop, Viv, ' A Beacon of Delight', *Express* (21 May 2004).

Hanks, Robert, 'Stories Give Way to Stories', *Daily Telegraph* (1 May 2004), p. 9.

Jaggi, Maya, 'Jeanette Winterson: Redemption Songs', *Guardian* (29 May 2004), pp. 20–3.

Lee-Potter, Charlie, 'Winterson's Brilliant Beam', *Independent on Sunday* (9 May 2004).

Patterson, Christina, Of Love and Other Demons', *Independent* (7 May 2004), Review.

Picardie, Justine, 'Casting Light on Darkness', *Evening Standard* (4 May 2004).

Sethi, Anita, 'To the Lighthouse, By the Self-appointed Heir to Virginia Woolf', *Observer* (2 May 2004).

INDEX